continued . . .

WAKE OF THE
PERDIDO STAR

Gene Hackman
&
Daniel Lenihan

A SIGNET BOOK

SIGNET
Published by New American Library, a division of
Penguin Putnam Inc., 375 Hudson Street,
New York, New York 10014, U.S.A.
Penguin Books Ltd, 27 Wrights Lane, London W8 5TZ, England
Penguin Books Australia Ltd, Ringwood, Victoria, Australia
Penguin Books Canada Ltd, 10 Alcorn Avenue,
Toronto, Ontario, Canada M4V 3B2
Penguin Books (N.Z.) Ltd, 182–190 Wairau Road,
Auckland 10, New Zealand

Penguin Books Ltd, Registered Offices:
Harmondsworth, Middlesex, England

Published by Signet, an imprint of New American Library,
a division of Penguin Putnam Inc. This is an authorized reprint of
the original hardcover edition, published by Newmarket Press,
18 East 48th Street, New York, NY 10017.

First Signet Printing, September 2000
10 9 8 7 6 5 4 3 2 1

Copyright © Gene Hackman and Daniel Lenihan, 1999
All rights reserved

 REGISTERED TRADEMARK—MARCA REGISTRADA

Printed in the United States of America

PUBLISHER'S NOTE
This is a work of fiction. Names, characters, places, and incidents are either the
products of the author's imagination or are used fictitiously, and any
resemblance to actual persons, living or dead, business establishments, events, or
locales is entirely coincidental.

CONTENTS

BOOK ONE

1. New England   3
2. Cape Hatteras   33
3. Paul   50
4. Habana   60
5. The Road to Matanzas   85
6. Return to the *Star*   98

BOOK TWO

7. Latitude 52   107
8. O'taheiti   128
9. Storm   132
10. Wrecked on a South Sea Isle   147
11. They Meet the Natives   162
12. Settling in on Belaur   171
13. Sizing up the Salvage Problem   178
14. Salvage   189
15. Problems   197
16. Success and Tragedy   203
17. An Eye for an Eye   212

18. Resolution Made, Unexpected Ally Found   220
19. Plans Born, Preparations Made   232
20. Showdown   244
21. Reclamation   269

BOOK THREE

22. East 121° South 8°   305
23. Manila   311
24. Orchid   316
25. Fiery Departure   325
26. Caribbean Bound   344
27. Ninety Miles from Cuba   347
28. Compensation   357

Epilogue   404

Acknowledgments   409

About the Authors   411

*A man who studieth revenge keeps his wounds green,
which otherwise would heal and do well.*

—SIR FRANCIS BACON

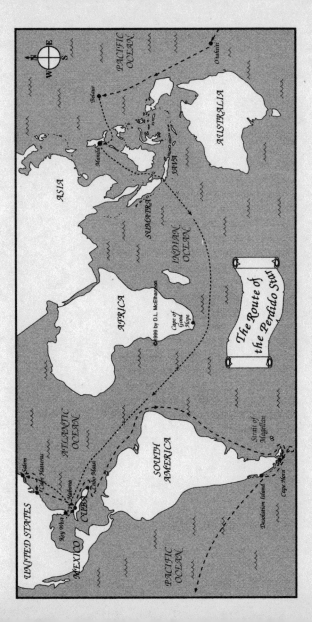

BOOK ONE

Book One

NEW ENGLAND

HAMDEN, CONNECTICUT. 1805. Jack O'Reilly, son of Ethan, gunsmith, walked a step behind his father as they approached First Episcopal Church. A cold wind drove at them, stirring leaves in the twilight, swaying the lantern in the church rector's hand. Ethan turned to his son as they approached the massive archway.

"You are not to speak at this meeting. Since you insisted on coming, you'll sit in the choir loft. Quietly. Understood?"

Jack felt a familiar knot take shape in his stomach. "Why can't I sit with—"

"You'll sit where I say or not come in at all." There it was, the tightness in his voice. He had come to this meeting primed for trouble.

Ethan O'Reilly turned and brushed past three men conversing in the doorway. Jack watched them stare at his father's back, whispering, then made his way inside.

He climbed the steps to the choir loft, a tug on his breeches alerting him to the presence of other fathers' sons. He turned and they smiled back. They were waiting for the outbursts that characterized these gatherings; knowing his father's mood, Jack couldn't share their eager anticipation.

Dreading what he knew would come, Jack sank against the hardwood bench. The other boys were at the far side of the loft, perched as if to watch a schoolyard brawl. Jack looked up; as usual, the warmth of the rough oaken beams seemed to mock the meeting's impersonal chill. He let his eyes fall to the mob below.

The most important politicians and leaders of business had gathered. Jack could see the prim schoolmaster wedged between two fat men who conversed back and forth as if he wasn't there. His father's landlord, wealthy property owner Peter Slocum, sat rigid as a stump beside them, next to his married son. The young O'Reilly stirred. He wished they'd get on with it.

Finally, Mr. Slocum stood and the crowd quieted. He raised his voice in his usual self-righteous protest: "The invasion of foreign heathens, who have taken jobs from the hardworking, God-fearing citizens of this land must be stopped. I, for one, won't hire any of this pack nor continue to step aside for them as they weave their drunken way down our cherished streets. If we're to become a strong nation, we can't be a dumping ground for dark-skinned mongrels and hordes of papists." He paused, enjoying the applause lauded upon him by his compatriots, although some shifted uncomfortably in their seats. Slocum's eyes settled on Ethan, and he spoke in more deliberate tones, directed at the gunsmith. "There's a privilege here that's being ignored, a privilege granted to us by the pastor of this church to worship and enjoy the sanctity of these hallowed walls. But that *privilege*"—his voice took on a new volume—"can readily be exempted from certain members if they're found to be continually disruptive and combative—"

"How dare you speak of foreigners invading this land!"

The crowd gasped. Jack felt his face turn hot; it was his father's voice. As the only Catholics in Hamden, the O'Reillys sat quietly in the back when they attended the Episcopal ceremonies, not participating in the Eucharist; a fact, Jack felt, not overlooked by the "good people" of the community.

Ethan O'Reilly thrust his arm at the landowner. "You, sir, are once removed from a foreign land yourself, as are a score of others in this room."

Several townsmen rose, shouting back.

Jack could feel the eyes of the other boys on him and didn't know whether to be embarrassed or proud. Most of the seventy-five or so men in the room were livid, but Ethan's voice, full of loathing, rose above them.

"You aim to rile me because of my family's foreign heritage. But let me make this clear: never, and I repeat never, will I be driven from this city because of bigotry and intolerance."

Jack's ears rang as if they'd been slapped, but he drove all expression from his face.

The mayor, a gaunt man of considerable intelligence, rose from the back of the church. In a black high-collared suit, with starched white shirt and florid kerchief, he was the very picture of a successful politician. "You, sir, are out of order."

A hush enveloped the room.

"The remarks, sir," the mayor continued, "were not directed at you or your family, but rather at the riffraff and flotsam that have recently invaded from coastal cities. Stealing, cheating, littering these streets with their unsavory behavior. I also suggest to you, sir—"

"I need no suggestion from you," Ethan interrupted in only slightly more measured tones. "Nor can I ignore the implication."

Jack could see his father's face had turned crimson; he leaned over the rail, scanned the room, and saw a pair of eyes looking up, frozen on him. They belonged to Slocum.

"This nation's independence," Ethan went on, "so recent even you could not be unaware of it, was built upon the dictum that all men are created equal, and being so, are welcomed into our great country. This land is populated with foreigners." Ethan paused to catch his breath. Jack knew his father had gone too far, and being the man he was, would plunge ahead. "The 'riffraff,' as you call them, were oppressed in other lands, and have as much right to be here as you gentlemen sitting here smug and comfortable. You seem to have forgotten how this nation was formed."

Several men began stirring and prepared to leave the assembly. Jack could feel his father's frustration.

"This nation was not founded to propagate the notion of an empire, but to free the oppressed, allow freedom of speech, and grant the right to pursue one's God-given talents." Silence ensued.

Suddenly laughter erupted from various parts of the room. This metalworker had overstepped his bounds. Perhaps realizing this, Ethan stopped, and made his way between the pews of the old church toward the entrance. When he reached the door, he paused, his back to the congregation, and in one swift move he flung it open and slammed it behind him.

Jack felt numb; his friends shifted nervously. He knew his father's words were true, but voicing them so stridently gave them a life of their own, a vision of the villagers' behavior that would be hard for them to accept. The townspeople were nosy and narrow-minded but Jack sensed that they probably weren't much different than people in most places. It was just that his idealist father brought out the worst in them. Over the years, in three different towns, Jack had fought schoolyard battles with bullies who made fun of his mother's accent or ridiculed his father's wild-eyed fervor for justice and "rightful authority based on the rule of law, not entitlement."

Jack rose, staring back at the boys until they averted their eyes. He descended the steep stairs and followed his father out into the night.

By nature, Jack was a loner. Generally liked and respected by his peers, he had still made no close friends in his years at Hamden. Most hours in the day, if not spent beside his father's forge, were spent reluctantly with books. Not a natural student, he pursued his studies at an age when most young men in Hamden had turned from schooling to more practical matters.

Hunched against the cold, his feet crackling through dead leaves, Jack mulled over the meeting with a heavy heart. He felt events in his life were building toward some change. His father had really angered people tonight. Deep down he knew that his mother would be readily accepted by most of the townsfolk if it weren't for his dad. Despite her Cuban heritage, his mother's features—brown eyes, full lips, and light-olive skin—were attractive, and she radiated a warmth that disarmed people, accent or no. But Ethan's manner made many uncomfortable. Jack recalled an incident several years earlier in which his father railed against slavery in a public meeting. Although many in the crowd were like-minded, his father's tone had been accusing and unconvincing. After the meeting, a young hooligan, perhaps sensing the gunsmith was unpopular, lobbed a piece of dried horse dung at the O'Reilly carriage as the family was riding home. It hit his mother in the back of her head. Not quite thirteen at the time, Jack quietly wiped her soiled hair with a kerchief while his father launched into a red-faced tirade, threatening mayhem against the retreating schoolboy. Onlookers shook their heads. Two days later, the ruffian who had offended his mother was spotted extricating himself from a manure pile at Harmon's Stables with a black eye and bloody nose. He was afraid to name his attacker but no one doubted it was Jack O'Reilly. Short-lived satisfaction, brooded Jack.

Nor was the family's financial status improving. As talented an artisan as his father was, the diminishing opportunities for fine gun makers was not helped by his outbursts; it seemed life was becoming harder all the time.

A chilled breeze promised an early snow as Jack rounded the next corner. He felt resentment take hold as various signs indicated he was near home: Slocum Dry Goods, Slocum Chandlery, Slocum Livery. He picked up his pace, kicking at rocks and dirt clods in his path. The family lived in two small rooms behind his father's workshop, which they rented from Slocum. Most craftsmen would have owned their homes and shops after working so many years, but the O'Reillys seemed never to settle more than five years in any one place. Jack tried to shake away the gloom. He broke into a trot to catch up to his father, and they arrived home almost simultaneously.

⋙ ✹ ⋘

The O'Reilly family sat huddled in hard-backed chairs around a dying fire after their sparse meal of boiled potatoes and turnips which they had scarcely touched. Ethan stared intently into the weakening flames. Jack's mother, Pilar, hummed softly.

"Ethan, mi hito, there is no need to despair. Things, they will improve." Pilar's dark features wrinkled in concern. "They show only their ignorances by keeping us from their church."

"They haven't actually said we can't attend, Mother," Jack offered. "But you're right, their purpose is clear." Jack wanted to help in some way. "Father, maybe if we traveled to New Haven on a Sunday there would be a Catholic church to attend and—"

"Jackson, don't speak of things you know nothing of."

Jack fell silent, feeling as he often did that his father was treating him like a child.

"We must not let this trouble split our family . . . we must not." Pilar's voice was breaking, but filled with resolve.

The group sat engulfed in thought when Ethan rose and slammed his chair on the wood floor. "Damn them!" He stopped as a light from outside refracted across the ceiling. Someone was approaching. Ethan peered out the window.

Pilar jumped to her feet. "Ethan, let Jackson answer the door. You're not of a condition to let the neighbors see." His father nodded to his son and reached above the fireplace for his rifle; overreacting, Jack thought. A shout came from the street.

"Jack O'Reilly! Come out here!"

Jack knew the voice. It was Billy Slocum, the middle son of their landlord. The young O'Reilly threw open the door; he saw two figures in the street, their breaths forming clouds in the cool night air. Billy waved the lantern.

"Pa sent David and me down here to give you this note." He tossed a small crumpled envelope at Jack's feet and giggled. Unamused, Jack eyed the bit of parchment.

The smaller of the two taunted, "I could tell you what was in the letter but that would spoil the fun of your big-mouthed pa's look when he reads it to you and your funny-looking ma."

Jack thought about charging into the pair with his fists but decided it would only make things worse.

"Why didn't your father come himself, Billy? Was he too busy in the barn, diddling the sheep?" Jack stooped and retrieved the note, slowly straightening the crinkled edges. The Slocum boys continued to shout, but Jack just stood his ground, smiling at them.

Billy backpedaled down the road. "Read the note. You may be living in some other town!" David grabbed a rock from the street; his aim at Jack was on target but Jack stepped easily to one side.

"Who was that?" Ethan emerged at the end of the exchange.

"The Slocum boys." Jack handed his father the note. Ethan snatched it and walked inside.

The elder O'Reilly stood by the dim light of the fire, reading aloud:

> Mr. Ethan O'Reilly, I regret to inform you of the urgent need I have of your rental property number 38 Hamden Town Road. As you are on a month to month arrangement, by all rights I could ask you to leave by October first, but as this is only two weeks away, I shall generously grant you until the first day of November, 1805, to abandon said property. Regards, Peter Slocum.

Ethan spun to face Jack. "What in the hell have you done now? You've gotten us evicted by bullying those boys. Now their father is taking it out on your mother and me. What do you have to say for yourself?"

Jack stood in the middle of the room, stunned. "Pa, I—"

"Don't you 'Pa' me, damn you." Ethan stepped threateningly closer. "I want an answer."

Pilar came between them, facing her husband. "You must look to yourself on this." She placed her hand firmly on her husband's arm. "This is not Jackson's doing. My love, you often say 'the truth will set you free,' but you forget, most people fear the truth and crucify its prophets." Her tone was pleading and intense. At times such as these, his mother's strength and intelligence took him off guard, as it did her husband.

Jack watched his father's anger thaw under her gaze. "I . . . I'm sorry, Jackson. I'm very sorry."

Jack watched his father slump into a chair and cradle his head in his hands. When he finally sat up, he said, "It would appear now that we are without funds, prospects . . . without a home, again."

Although Ethan was the finest gunsmith for miles, his skill was not appreciated, was not even in demand; instead, he found himself relegated to fabricating barn door hinges and wagon hardware, and repairing common muskets far inferior to the custom firearms for which he was known. A perfectionist, he found it increasingly difficult to compete with the influx of Eli Whitney's mass-produced weapons that satisfied military demand for shoulder arms. Ethan specialized in the Kentucky rifle, valuable only on the frontier; other smiths, from Pennsylvania, were closer to the wilderness and took most of that business.

But Jack knew his father's feeling of dejection came from more than that. He saw the land of the free and equal fast building its own class system.

"There is always the land in Cuba," Jack's mother offered in a quiet voice. Ethan turned away, grimacing; but Pilar approached him, her voice full of hope and pride. "It is waiting for us, Ethan. It is not America, and it also has its problems, but we would be, how is it they say? ... gentry. I love that land ... and Jackson would grow to love it, too; after all, it is his birthright. The count assured us in his letter many months ago that in another few years the sugar cane will grow well and provide an income. And remember that in the last Easter greeting from my childhood friend, Dolores, she told me how well the surrounding farms in Matanzas had been doing."

Pilar then said with a determination Jack had not heard before, "Our son has learned his Spanish well. We will be accepted in Cuba. I want to see the finca again."

It was always a mystery to Jack why his mother had been taken away from her homeland. She never talked about what happened between her parents, saying only that "God forgives all." But she had adored her father, who never wanted her to go to England with her mother. Pilar's eyes would shine at his memory, and she would often say, "Jackson, in your grandfather, kindness met strength." Though Jack never met him, he had become proud of this man of strength and kindness whom his mother cherished, and who had ensured that the finca would become her inheritance, even though he himself had failed as a farmer, landowner, and husband. The land was officially hers upon his death five years earlier, but it was still in no condition to provide a living for his daughter and her family. Pilar allowed her father's friend and neighbor, Count de Silva, to recultivate the barren fields for a share of the profits, but Jack knew his mother never gave up hope that one day they would manage the land themselves.

Jack thought more about the land called Cuba. His mother had told him stories of her happy childhood there, sometimes in English, more often in her native tongue—of hot days filled with endless play in the fields, running from morning until dusk with friends from the other farms.

Jack watched his father pace the floor in the small sitting room, half-listening to his mother, obviously buried deep in thought. "I know nothing of farming, and I'm of an age where I'm too old to learn," he finally said, although he spoke without conviction. The prospect of owning land, being for once part of the "privileged" rather than the "struggling" class, must have a powerful appeal for him, Jack thought. A proud man, Ethan had once been a young firebrand in Ireland and, with great hopes for the new American republic, had fought as a soldier in the Continental Army. But he was tired now; his disappointments and setbacks in the new land had confused him. He wanted it so badly to be what Paine and Jefferson promised, but he seemed to realize, when he was calm, that he wished for too much.

Jack watched his father intently; his faraway look of resignation eventually seemed to be replaced with what might be hope. Land. Land could mean everything to a man who had none. Ethan was a fine gunsmith, but Jack questioned for the first time that perhaps his father's spirit was too strong for his flesh. A radical change to a new land would be difficult for him, but maybe not as hard as continuing life in America.

After a long hard look around the meager room at their few possessions, a look that seemed to last an eternity, Ethan said in a voice so faint even Jack could barely hear, "All right. We'll gather our wares and travel to this so-called paradise so sweetly rich in sugar."

≈ ❋ ≈

Jack felt as if he had been dipped in tar. He was lethargic, unable to help his parents in any meaningful way. The farewell words to his schoolmates had seemed false. He found himself staring at the ground, pawing at the dirt; part of him resented his father for deciding to go and part of him was strangely attracted to it.

Yet here they were, three humble souls with their earthly belongings piled high on a creaking wagon, slipping thieflike into the night.

"Jackson, did you say good-bye to your friends?"

Jack, sitting on the tailgate, was silent as he watched the disappearing lamps from the town while his father drove the team along a rutted track.

"Jackson? I know you hear me."

His mother sat resolute on the hard wagon seat.

"Your son has suddenly developed ear problems," Ethan said.

"Please, Ethan. Leave him be," she answered quickly. "He's feeling bad. And please don't speak of him as my son. He is our son, mi hito."

Jack eased himself quietly off the wagon and stood staring at the few lights still visible in the distance. His father's voice ruffled the evening air. He knew he could slip into the night and return to the familiarity of Hamden, or stay and become part of something new, foreboding, and in some odd way, exciting. He stood alone on the road. A nighthawk swooped past, heading east toward the rising moon.

"Jackson, please come now."

Without taking his eyes from the bird of prey, Jack smiled to himself and said quietly, "Yes, mother. I'm ready. I'm coming."

⊰ ❄ ⊱

The road from Hamden to Providence was ruined from the recent fall rains. It was lined with leaves, gold turning brown, stacked against the rock fences bordering the highway. On either side, fields crackled with the rustling of dry corn, the air thick with the scent of ripe fruit and Indian summer.

They were chasing down a ship bound for Cuba. It was nearly ten days since they had left home, and the mysterious Providence was still nowhere in sight. The sound of wheels grinding against the road became sickening to Jack; the flat clop of the mares' hooves, the working of the timber that held the wagon together— after the first day it was a constant irritation. Jack leaned over the wagon bed and tried to count the revolutions, the sun burning the back of his neck.

They arrived in East Haven, then took the coast road toward New London, where "there be ships a-plenty heading for southern climes out of Providence town," according to one passerby.

Jack's hip was raw from the constant movement of the wagon, and he shifted back and forth, alternately sitting on clothes, bedding, and boxes. Nothing helped. He stared at the backs of his parents' heads, his father's hat and mother's bonnet keeping time with the swaying wagon. They were talking, really more of a mumble, and Jack made no effort to overhear.

He told his father he would walk for a while.

Hours later, Jack moved between the tired horses,

coaxing them gently with the reins in each of his hands. Ahead, there was the beginning of a hill that seemed to rise gradually for several miles.

"Providence is probably just beyond the crest," his father said. "Let's push on before nightfall."

⊷ �֍ ⊶

In Providence they missed the boat to Cuba not by hours but by days. They were told by the harbor master that because it was so late in the fall, there might not be another ship going south until spring. Then he told them of a boat sailing for Habana and points beyond in just five days, out of Salem harbor: the *Perdido Star*.

The strain of being on the road left the O'Reillys exhausted and concerned for their diminishing resources; but they pressed on. Ethan decided to skirt the city of Boston, as they could no longer afford the proper inns and now took to camping out on the way to Salem. He and Pilar slept in the open wagon bed, Jack bundling in a thin blanket, always by a dwindling fire. He awoke each morning bone-chilled, made worse when a wet snow caught them unprepared.

It was three weeks since their start in Hamden when one morning they saw a group of towering masts jutting above a smoky city: Salem.

When they arrived in the city, Jack was fascinated by the energy. Children ran and shouted on the dirt streets; drivers in wagons transported lumber, hides, and barrels of whale oil, shouting pleasantries at one another.

"Maybe we should ask directions to the wharf, Pa," Jack said.

"All in good time, Jackson. All in good time." Ethan seemed oblivious to the exotic sights and sounds. He pushed the wagon forward, a man obsessed.

Pilar looked at her husband, smiling. "Mi hito, please

ask directions so we can make our travel arrangements and become settled."

Ethan pulled the horses to a stop and stepped down to the street. He mumbled, "Wait here," and disappeared into a dry goods store.

After a few minutes, Jack could tell that his mother was growing impatient at his absence. She called to a teenage girl passing by. "Excuse me, miss. Could you please to give us directions to the India Wharf?"

She turned, and to Jack, she was beauty itself. He felt his face contort in a stupid grin.

"Well now, it would be Derby Street that you would be wanting," she answered, in a thick Irish accent and a smile to match the sun. She had a warm laugh, her eyes bespeaking an inner brightness.

"It's a bit of a trick from here. But if you mind, you'll find it. Stay this road to North Street, then you'll be wantin' to make your right. Keep the course to Summer Street. It's here on your left hand you'll be seeing Norman. The street, that is. Continue straight and it becomes Front. You'll cross Market and look for Fish. That would be Fish Street on your right side. Fish swims around to the left and becomes Wharf."

The girl paused and Jack reddened when he realized his mother had caught his expression. The corners of her mouth curved upward.

"You'll pass Norris Wharf and Hodges and a few others and then it becomes Derby," the girl continued. "All the way toward the end, when you feel you've gone too far, you'll see Becket's shipyard—and that would be India."

Ethan had come out of the shop and heard most of the directions. Even he, despite his weariness, was taken with her. "Thank you, miss. Much obliged." He hoisted himself onto the wagon and urged the horses on.

Jack moved to the back of the wagon. He waved to the girl and mouthed silently, "I'm Jack," pointing to himself. She stopped and seemed to see him for the first time. Her wide-open eyes knitted her fair brow. At just over six feet and exceptionally strong for seventeen, Jack's features were impressive. His dark hair hung past his jaw, and his large hazel eyes were offset by a tan complexion. A breeze brushed her burnished hair across emerald eyes. Her hand came up and tossed the hair away. A word popped from her mouth: "Colleen."

Jack sat frozen, overwhelmed. She didn't move as they pulled away. They lost sight of one another briefly when a wagon, then a pedestrian, came between them. Finally, as the wagon turned on North Street, Jack could no longer see her. He leapt from the wagon and ran to the corner. She was gone.

Suddenly, the enticement of faraway lands seemed less overpowering to Jack; there were obviously things of great interest here in Salem.

They made their way along Derby Street, passing countless wharves brimming with sailing vessels. Shouts from the many dockworkers and sailors heralded ships being built or unloaded. The streets were filled with bustling people, the smell of cinnamon and coffee strong in the air. Merchants weighed goods and traded openly. Lumber, fresh off a ship, was stocked along the road. The air was heavy with odors of the sea making Jack's imagination soar. He was mesmerized. These were scents of a world he did not know. Sailors strutted the pier with gaits that convinced him the seas were running beneath their feet. Even the sorriest and densest of these seamen knew firsthand of lands that only brushed the edge of his wildest fancy. It was an amazing place, this Salem.

The sense of superiority the seamen carried—even in the presence of gentry—intrigued Jack most. They tipped their hats and did the expected around their betters, but clearly they were playing a part. They seemed quietly smug, as if they had a hidden knowledge that could not be found in a gentleman's reading room.

They gazed upon the town women with a palpable hunger. Months at sea seemed to make their eyes burn through the women's stern New England clothing. The ladies frowned and hurried by, but Jack wondered if they deliberately took this route.

Jack preferred to walk beside the wagon. Some of the jostling he felt was from pickpockets, he reckoned, but he paid them no heed; they would have to be magicians to find anything of value on his person.

"Excuse me, sir," Jack inquired of a sailor. "Could you direct us to the *Perdido Star*?"

"The *Star*? Well now, you'd just be following your nose, lad. When you get to the end of the wharf and the stench be the highest, thar she lie." The sailor, reeking of gin, broke into hysterical laughter, revealing a row of small, broken teeth.

The O'Reillys glanced at one another but said nothing. Ethan urged the horses on, passing several ships in the process of loading. At the end of the wharf they found the *Perdido Star*.

Jack was transfixed by the black-hulled ship. Even with her peeling paint and worn decks, there was an air of importance about this tattered machine of the sea. He strolled along the wharf to its stern and began pacing off the distance.

"She be a hunnert 'n twelve feet if she be an inch, lad." A gap-toothed sailor cackled and leaned over the rail. "A brigantine by name. And a merchantman of fame. I'll be Hansumbob, I am."

"Hello, I'm Jack," he called back.

"Glad to meet ya, lad," he waved, then descended belowdecks.

Jack returned to his father, who stopped a seaman amidst the activity, asking for the captain. An arm pointed to the quarterdeck was the sailor's reply, and

Jack followed it to see a stout, gray-haired man with flowing beard standing beside the rail. He seemed to be carving in the teak with a buck knife, an activity Jack thought peculiar, but he was issuing orders over his shoulder and was obviously in charge. And not a little bit drunk. Jack followed his father over to him.

"Captain Deploy?"

"Who the hell would be asking?" The captain glared at Ethan while furtively trying to cover a portion of the rail with a piece of sailcloth.

"I've come from Providence and beyond and I've been told that you would be leaving soon for the island of Cuba. More specifically, Habana." Ethan lost the timbre in his voice.

"Aye, that I am. But I'm full to the gunwales with cargo if that's what you'd be wanting." The captain looked the blacksmith up and down.

"I'd like to book passage for myself, my wife, and son. A small amount of personal wares as well." Ethan took his stance with more determination.

The captain glanced at their wagon on the dock, piled with the blacksmith's forge. "It'll cost you eighty-five dollars apiece plus fifty for the freight. It's not negotiable. We leave tomorrow night on the evening tide."

Jack could tell his father was thinking quickly of the money he had remaining.

"You set a hard bargain, sir. I had been told it would be just half that amount!"

"I'll have two hundred seventy-five dollars for the whole lot then. And not another word on it." Captain Deploy tossed his head and strolled to the far rail. His back was to Ethan so he wouldn't have to look him in the eye. "You can come aboard now, stow your freight and your personals, and save yourself a night's lodging." He turned. "That's the best I can do. And if you decide to go, you're to keep your travel arrangements to yourself. Not a word. Understand?"

Jack knew then that the owner of the ship would never see any of the passage money. But he could tell by his father's grin that he did not care.

"First mate, see to these good people." The captain took Ethan's money as the mate, a large, swarthy man who looked of mixed blood, led the three landsmen to their quarters.

"Mother, let me carry those bags, please," Jack said.

"They're as if nothing, Jack. They're as feathers, for I'm so happy to be off that wagon." Pilar turned and the three weary souls made their way slowly down the companionway ladder.

Reaching their quarters, the first mate turned to the family and announced, "My name be Quince, people, and this be your berths." The bunks were arranged in a semicircle, sad-looking straw mattresses, stained from years of use, sitting like lumps on the oak slats. "If you need something on the trip and if I can help, I will."

"Thank you," Ethan answered. Quince returned a goodhearted grin and departed, the deck creaking under the weight of the burly giant. Jack was amazed at how easily he moved. There was a strength and confidence about him that reassured the whole family.

After storing their belongings belowdecks and seeing that his tools were safe in the hold, Ethan spoke briefly to his wife then left the ship; Jack followed to the edge of the deck. Turning the wagon around on the wharf, he called to Jack, "Keep your mother company. I'll be back soon."

Pilar emerged from below.

"Is Father going to sell the team and wagon?" Jack asked.

"Yes." She dropped her eyes. "Your father needs to do this."

The horses, Jen and Mary, had been Jack's domain, feeding and tending them for years. A mist of anger floated just behind his eyes; he was disturbed to think his father would not have allowed him to run his hands down their soft manes one last time.

"I'd like to go with him, Mother."

"Yes. Go and give to Jen and Mary my good-byes."

Jack raced off the boat and down the wharf to where his father had just turned the corner. He caught him within a block and scrambled onto the back of the empty wagon. Jack's father glanced at him without expression.

"Ma said it was all right for me to come along."

For a few moments Ethan said nothing. "You seem to be getting very independent, young man. Nothing I say to you seems to have any effect. But I want you to listen to me very closely."

His father leaned close.

"I'll say this once. Don't interfere in this matter of the sale of the horses and wagon. Do you understand?"

"Yes, Father."

Ethan seemed to know where he was going, for he glanced from time to time at a small handwritten map he evidently had been given on the ship. They pulled up to a livery stable at the edge of town. A well-muscled man was shoeing a mare next to an anvil and forge.

"Good afternoon, sir," Jack's father called out. "The name is O'Reilly. I am also of the trade."

The man ignored him completely, continuing his work.

"I had my own business in Hamden, Connecticut. Did mostly rifles and such."

"As you can see, I'm busy," the blacksmith said. He looked at the horses and wagon, his eyes stopping on Jack. "If it's shoeing you need, can't get to it before Thursday."

"No, brother. It's not shoeing I need," Ethan said gently, "but a home for this fine team and wagon. My family and I are bound for the southern islands and need to sell our team."

The smith dropped the horse's hoof and walked slowly around the wagon, shaking his head.

"I couldn't do you any good, mister. But my brother Cyrus maybe could. Tell you what—there's a tavern back toward town. You might have passed it. Peele's with a double 'e.' If you like, we could maybe go talk to my brother. He owns the place. By the way, when would you be leaving town?"

"Tomorrow afternoon, late. We sail on the *Perdido Star*."

Jack didn't like the man. Rude and slippery, he thought. He hoped his father recognized the man's slyness.

The smithy quickly took his horse inside the barn and came back buttoning a shirt around his ample waist. "My brother bought the tavern about a year ago. Does pretty well with it, all in all."

Jack hoisted himself on the back of the wagon while the two men climbed up front. He watched the man, who introduced himself as Jonah Peele, speak to his father. Ethan nodded politely and clucked at the horses, deaf to the man's rattling. When they got to the tavern, Peele quickly went inside while Ethan tied up the horses.

"The man is full of himself," he told Jack. "But he seems an honest sort."

"Pa, I don't like this fellow. I think—"

"You mind what I told you before, Jackson."

Jack felt a quick flush come to his face, but remained silent. He wondered if this was yet another one of his father's business dealings that would go astray. Ethan was an honest man who assumed others would act accordingly, and Jack had seen him defeated a number of times in the simplest of transactions.

The interior of the tavern was dark, with a sour smell of ale and urine. Crowded with some very rough types, Jack thought: sailors, dockworkers, laborers. The blacksmith had already begun whispering to his brother, who tended bar. Jack and his father stood awkwardly in the middle of the room.

The bartender, a large man with a red beefy face, finally looked over his brother's shoulder at the two. He signaled them over.

"What will it be, lads? First one's on me."

"No, nothing, thank you," Ethan said.

The man's quick grin faded. "If we're to do business, you'll first have a drink."

"My son will have a sarsaparilla," Ethan said, shrugging. "I'll have an ale, thank you."

The other patrons sensed something was going on and drifted closer. Jack felt trapped. After allowing father and son a few polite sips, the bartender eased his bare arms down to the wet bar top.

"What do you need to get for your team and wagon? My brother Jonah says they're fine animals and the wagon's in good repair."

Ethan took a sip of the foamy ale. "I would need fifty dollars apiece for the horses and another fifty for the wagon."

The men at the bar were listening intently. The bartender dropped his head down to his thick hairy arms; he seemed to be thinking. Jack didn't like any of this; it felt like an act. Then with a ball-fisted bang on the bar, he yelled, "Done!"

Startled, Jack flinched. He caught the two brothers glance at each other.

"I'll have your money for you tomorrow at one o'clock sharp. Be here with the team and wagon."

Pleased, Ethan reached across the bar to shake hands, but Cyrus Peele had already turned to his waiting customers. With a nod to the brother, Jack and his father left the suddenly hushed establishment.

"They're a different breed of people here," Ethan said expansively. "You can't really compare them to the small-town folk we're used to." He seemed in good spirits. "They're loud and boisterous, but I think if you look through all that, you'd see an honest lot."

Jack didn't agree. The brothers had a foxlike quality, and he felt the deal was consummated too quickly. The bartender never even went outside to see the team; but his father had told him to stay out of his business, so he said nothing.

Still, he did not share in his father's satisfaction as Ethan related the story of the trade to his wife back at the ship. It disturbed Jack to have his excitement over the coming trip interrupted by this gnawing uncertainty about the horses. Finally, though, he allowed his thoughts to drift to the high seas, to billowing sails, and a million stars guiding them south to Cuba.

On deck, Jack marveled at the complexity of ropes and cables stretching to the tops of the masts. Walking down the gangplank to get a better look, he spotted two young women staring at the ship from the end of the dock. There was something familiar about the tall one with the red hair. As Jack moved toward them, they turned quickly and started down Derby Street, giggling. He followed, and caught them at Hodge's Wharf.

"Please don't think me rude. I just wanted to thank you for the fine directions you gave. Colleen, wasn't it?"

The girls looked at each other and laughed.

"Yes, it's Colleen. And this would be my friend, Prudence." The brilliant green eyes teased as Colleen spoke. "And what would be your name?" Jack was stunned that she pretended not to remember.

"It's Jackson, but everyone calls me Jack—except my parents, at times."

"Jacksooon." She elongated his name as if making fun of it. "I'll be off. Have yourself a day of sun and health." She grabbed Prudence by the arm and started down Derby.

"Would you join me in a cup o' tea at the inn yonder?" Jack asked.

Colleen turned. "Tomorrow, Jacksooon, maybe tomorrow."

His hands were shaking as he watched her walk away. What if they had accepted my offer of tea? he wondered. I have not a penny to my name.

⤙ ❈ ⤚

The next day at one o'clock, Jack and his father returned to Peele's tavern with the horses. What looked to Jack like the exact same group of people filled the pub. Cyrus Peele started speaking almost before they were through the door, his brother standing quietly at the far side of the room.

"Mr. O'Reilly, good to see you again, sir. I have a bit of bad news, I'm afraid. You see, the bank is after me, and a few of my suppliers came this morning unexpectedly. And, well, the upshot is, I don't have the money for the team. I know this puts you in a bind, what with your boat leaving in just a few hours and not having time to go looking for another buyer." The bartender glanced around, making sure he had his audience. "But I'll do this: I'll give you thirty-five dollars for the lot, and I'd be stretching things to do that."

Ethan's color faded after the man's first words. The patrons began to stare. He knows he's been duped, Jack thought; Peele obviously waited until the last minute so they would have no other choice.

Jack's misgivings about the Peeles were accurate. That sense of cold calmness he knew so well rose up his spine. He looked across the room at the younger brother, who put on an innocent face but seemed to grow nervous under Jack's steely gaze. Jack contemplated smashing the whiskey bottle on the bar into the face of the bartender and then getting the fat one across the room before he reached the door. His thoughts stopped, though, when he noticed his father's head drop slightly, nodding in recognition of what had happened. A wave of caring poured through Jack.

"I don't believe, sir," Ethan began in a weak voice, "that you are dealing in good faith."

The bartender's eyes went cold. "You can take it or leave it, bumpkin."

Ethan's humiliation caused outright laughter. The whole bar seemed in on the joke. Jack felt his face burning, and he did everything he could to control himself.

"I'll take your money, sir," Ethan said, "on one condition."

The bartender spread his arms on the bar and looked around, thoroughly enjoying the moment. "Name it."

"You've bested me in this deal," he said. "That I can live with. But you, as a man, will give me your promise that you'll treat the animals well. Do I have your word?"

"You have my word as a Peele, sir," the bartender said. Jack wondered what that was worth. There was loud clapping from customers and the show was over. The two out-of-towners had been taken down a notch or two, and all seemed to have had a good time at their expense.

They walked back to the ship in silence. Jack's father seemed to have aged over the last two hours, his gait halting, eyes unfocused. Jack wanted to comfort him, say something to relieve his pain. But when they reached the ship without a word, Ethan slipped quietly to the bowels of the boat, and the comfort of his wife.

Jack stayed above deck. Quince, the huge sailor who had shown the family to their quarters, stood off marking goods as sailors carried provisions belowdecks. He glanced at Jack.

"Are you looking forward to shipping out, lad?"

"Yes," Jack answered, having taken an immediate liking to this man. "But maybe a little scared, too."

"Well, that be natural, boy. We're all a little frightened at first. You'll get use to her and once you got yer legs under ya, there be nothing like it."

Jack thought a moment. He wanted desperately to confide in this man, to ask his advice on something that had been running through his mind for the last hour. "Excuse me. But your name is Quince, right?"

"Quince it be. Oliver Quince, but all the lads call me Big Q or Quince, whatever pleases ya."

"I've a problem that needs solving," Jack raced on, trusting his instinct about the fellow. "If you've been wronged by a knave of a man and have limited time to make things right but feel it must be done, what would you do?"

"You got but one life to live. If you want your peace of mind, you need to set to rights what's bothering ya."

This relieved Jack. "Exactly what time do we leave?"

Hansumbob passed by just then and shouted, "Six bells on the noggin, and if you're not on board, you're sure to get a floggin'." Ole Bob grinned wide, as ugly a face as Jack had ever seen, but with a warmth that was irrepressible. Jack crossed the deck and made his way down the gangplank.

Hansumbob walked along the deck parallel to Jack. "What be your name, lad?"

Jack shouted his name as he picked up his pace away from the ship.

"Be proud of yer name, Jackson, we got plenty a strange ones on board: Coop, Red Dog, Cookietwo. One day, Bosun Ben Mentor asked Cookietwo how he arrived at that name and he near threw 'im in the bay, did Cookietwo, so now Mentor checks his soup real careful." Hansumbob had reached the stern of the ship but was still talking. "The captain won't wait and it's a long swim to Cuba."

The old sailor stood watching as Jack waved and walked toward town. With a quick look back at the boat, Jack broke into a full run. He had four hours to do what he must.

—◄ ❋ ►—

The blacksmith hummed tunelessly as he worked in front of the barn. Jack knew the pounding on the anvil would drown out the noise, and he slipped the latch on the back door of the barn. Jen snickered as Jack slipped the halter over her neck. He was exhausted from the run back to the smith's, but a fire inside him suffocated the pain. Mary slobbered over his neck as he haltered her and led the two out back. Jack quietly latched the doors, then led the mares down the street, expecting to hear a shout from the smith at any moment. He mounted Jen, and with the rope lead to Mary, picked up his pace.

After several blocks, the houses thinned out to farmland. Jack didn't know how far he would have to go but he was determined the brothers Peele would never see these animals again. He kept the team at a gallop for the better part of an hour until he saw what he was looking for: a small farm off to his left, horses and cows in a large meadow.

Jack pulled up next to a sprawling oak and dismounted. Heading the animals toward the distant pasture, Jack said his good-byes as his mother had requested. With a shout from Jack, Jen and Mary trotted toward their own kind.

Jack ran back down the road at a killing pace. Elated, he had just one more job to do.

—◄ ❋ ►—

The rear door to Peele's tavern was unlocked, since it led to the privy out back for the patrons. Jack slipped through, unnoticed in the noise and darkness of the bar, and crept into the storeroom he had spotted during his previous visit. Kegs of beer were stacked five high. Seizing a wooden mallet, Jack proceeded to smash the bungholes on the barrels, each blow filling him with a wild joy. The beer began to pour out in torrents. He had smashed all but two when Cyrus Peele came through the door.

"What the hell—"

Jack turned and with one mighty move cracked the man on the kneecap with the mallet. Peele went down like a load of dung; he clutched his damaged leg and screamed, "You bastard. I'll break your neck."

Jack took the mallet and smashed the bartender's fingers.

"Oh God! I'll kill you and your father! You shit you!" The man was clearly in a great deal of pain, but still dangerous.

The door swung open. One of the dockworkers rushed in.

"What's all the ruckus?" He saw Peele writhing in the frothing suds. "What happened, Cyrus? Did you slip?" He smirked until he looked up and saw Jack with the mallet.

"Get your red nose out of this business, sir, or I'll whack you like I did your friend," Jack yelled, feeling invincible. The man quickly vanished behind the door.

Jack straddled the sprawled bartender. "You humiliated my father. You cheated us out of our team and wagon. I want an apology." His voice was cool. He knew he couldn't get more money from Peele, but he would make him pay in other ways.

"Get off me, you weasel. We had a deal. It's not my fault if your old man's an ass!" Jack's left hand was around the man's throat. His right became a fist and he drove it into Peele's fat face. He waited.

"I won't apologize for—" He never got out the full sentence; Jack broke his nose with a hammering blow and then picked up the mallet. Someone pounded on the door.

"I have all night, Peele, and the first man through that door gets a broken leg."

"All right, damn you. What would you have me say?" Jack just stared and waited.

Peele murmured, "I think it was a misunderstanding . . ." Jack slapped Peele across the face. Blood from the broken nose mixed with the beer on the storeroom floor, the liquid running pink. Jack pressed his left hand harder into Peele's neck.

"I'm sorry," he sputtered.

"For what?"

"What you asked me for." The bartender was confused. "All right. I'm sorry for cheating you and your father." He could barely get the words out through his broken teeth.

"And will it happen again, sir?"

"No, never."

"Good." Jack slipped off the man. "I'm leaving now with your mallet. Call out to your friends that I'm not to be harmed. Otherwise, I'll come back and finish you." He opened the door.

"Let the good lad go!" Peele shouted, terrified. "We've settled our differences."

Jack, at the door, looked back. "You're a quick learner, bumpkin," he said.

Jack raced back to India Wharf, grinning all the way. He made it just in time, the crew readying the ship for departure. His parents rushed to greet him at the head of the gangplank.

"Jackson, we were worried sick," said Pilar.

"Where in God's name have you been?" Ethan barked.

"I'm sorry. I guess I just got caught up in town." Jack realized he still had Peele's mallet in his hand. He forced the handle up his sleeve and palmed the striker. Backing to the rail, he dropped the offending tool over the side.

Pilar looked him over. "Mi hijo, your blouse is soaking wet. What have you been up to?"

"Nothing, mother—" Jack stopped. He hated lying to her. "May I tell you later?"

Pilar consented. Ethan angrily turned away.

There were shouts from quarterdeck to dockside to let go the spring lines. Jack loved the race of activity as the ship creaked and groaned. A burning sensation in the back of his neck caused him to turn to the wharf side.

A number of people crowded the dock, speaking to the departing sailors. There stood Colleen. Seeing her, Jack realized that his choice to seek revenge prevented him from perhaps spending time with this lovely creature. Now he just stared, his heart yearning. She brought her right hand to her lips and turned up her thumb and forefinger held together in a gesture of drinking tea; then she cocked her head to one side and with fists planted firmly on her hips, stuck her tongue out at him. Jack brought his hands up, requesting forgiveness.

Suddenly, an entourage of angry men stalked down the wharf, the brothers Peele leading the pack, the bartender limping. But they were too late. Jack bid goodbye to them as the *Perdido Star,* fifty yards out, made its way slowly south.

As the *Star* sailed out of Salem harbor, Jack tried to rekindle the excitement he had felt about the upcoming trip. Sailors scampered up to the yards; shouts and orders drifted across the darkening bay. Jack grabbed a ratline and heaved himself onto the rail, looking south.

Slowly, though, his eyes were drawn back to the dock. She was still there, alone. He waved but she turned away. Jack promised himself he would return. And he would be able to offer a thousand days of tea.

2

CAPE HATTERAS

"MIND THE SPRAY, LAD! It's chilly, you'll catch your death."

Ole Hansumbob sounded the friendly warning. Jack didn't know how long he had been standing on the bow. The spray, as the sailor had said, was cold, but to Jack it felt blessed: the water on his face refreshed him. He breathed deeply of the salted mist and was flooded with a great sense of anticipation. He wanted to shout.

The ship plunged headlong into a giant roller. Jack folded his arms around the rail, meeting the wave as a friend. The sea fulfilled him like nothing else, providing the sense of adventure he had always longed for. He could not get over the feeling of being safe, yet part of the vast roaring expanse of sky and water.

But he dreaded going below; the light was poor and a stench of sickness gripped the air. The companionway hatch, ajar from heavy seas, banged against its stop. Taking one last clean breath, Jack started down the narrow steps.

The smell overpowered the berth area. With no individual cabins, his family's belongings and bedding lay scattered over the three bunks assigned to them.

His father's face was drenched with sweat, skin waxen, his breathing shallow. "How are you feeling, Pa?"

"It was a mistake coming on this ship, Jack." Ethan's eyes were moist, his jaw slack. "We should have waited until spring; we would have missed this weather."

His mother sat on Ethan's bunk, her hand in his.

Jack was disappointed his father had given in to the sea. Ethan had been ill for the seven days they'd been on the ship. Jack watched his mother patiently sponge his forehead with a cloth. Looking alternately green and white, Ethan tried to put on a brave face.

"You will be better soon, sweetheart," Pilar said. "Try to eat something. Some biscuits or soup."

Jack hung back and watched the scene with a sad heart. He felt bad about his father; he was almost fifty and still strong, but his life had been difficult. The decision to give up life in America had been hard on him. Even his mother, at thirty-six, seemed to have aged.

Pilar moved to Jack's berth and held his hand. "Jackson, please to listen to me." She spoke softly so her husband would not hear. "Your father, my great and only love in my life, is muy difícil. I adore him but he has put us in a terrible condition. Because it is impossible for him to judge with a good eye the qualities of men, he judges them always as honest until they prove otherwise. It has always been so.

"When I was a young woman in school in England, my mother told me that she had decided never to return to Cuba and not to remain my father's wife, but to go back to Spain to be with the man she loved. She said she was leaving me in England until I completed school, then I could choose whom to live with. I spent many days praying that the news was not so . . . that somehow there had been a mistake. . . ."

In a whisper, she continued: "Soon after my mother left, an Irish man I knew only casually sat beside me in church and, much to my chaperone's horror, this man took my hand and said simply, 'I believe you to be a most beautiful woman. You are unhappy and I want you to come away with me.' "

The ship suddenly lunged forward several times before settling down again. Pilar straightened her back, as if struck by a memory. She looked at Jack. "Your father and I lived together on the ship coming from England to America, for six long weeks, huddled as if man and wife. Your father was even sicker on that trip. Please be understanding of him; he is ill now but he is physically strong. In this regard you are his equal." Pilar looked at Jack with such love, he was forced to smile. But he also saw a troubling uncertainty.

"What is it, Mother?"

"You have in you a strength that is beyond—" Pilar again hesitated. "It is a thing in your blood we Spanish call machismo. Do you know this word, mi hijo?"

"I have seen this word written, but I have not heard it spoken." Jack didn't understand what she was trying to say.

"It is to say only that your love of your father must not be tempered by his failings. You have too much of a dangerous thing, my love."

"What is that, Mother?"

"You are far too strong and big as a boy without the knowledge and sense of a man."

"I don't know what you speak of," Jack said, suddenly irritated, her words making him uncomfortable.

"As we left the port of Salem and you asked me, 'Can we speak of this later,' I knew then that you had taken some sort of revenge on the men that cheated your father out of our horses."

Jack started to speak.

"Momento, por favor. Not only was your blouse soaking wet, but, I could see it in your eyes. They glistened. Your body was swollen in victory. I did not miss the angry crowd of men at the wharf or the deadly look in their eyes. Whatever you did, I pray it was only just. Remember most men are not as gifted as you, mi hijo." She kissed his forehead. "Your father is a wonderful man. But I will need your strength—and most of all your intelligence—these next few months. It will be wonderful on the island. You'll see the finca; beautiful with rolling hills, looking out to the ocean. All will be well, I believe, and yet—I feel that things may not be so easy. I'll need your help."

"I'll be everything you want me to be, mamacita," Jack said, his anger vanishing. "And if you wish me to tell you of that day's events in Salem, I will."

"No, please." She held up her palm. "But tell me why the girl of good direction happened to be at the wharf, dressed as if to go to church?"

Jack smirked. Trying not to disturb Ethan, they laughed and Pilar embraced her son warmly.

⊷ ✸ ⊷

The *Star*'s rudder began to bind, steadily getting worse over the next two days. The helm took two able-bodied seamen to correct her path; each tack grew more arduous. In the open ocean this may not have been a problem, as a ship could be on one tack for days. But maneuvering in the close proximity of Diamond Shoals off the outer banks of North Carolina was extremely dangerous.

Jack heard from Hansumbob that the captain was going to take the ship into shore to fix the rudder. He stood in his usual place of observation as far forward as he could get, propped between the bowsprit and port handrails. The seas were thrashing, whitecaps casting an unearthly glow on the water. In the distance, Jack spied a long spit of land. The sky—gray lead—was streaked with purple clouds, lit by a red sun. Thin shafts of light spread across the horizon. But behind to the east rolled dark clouds, racing them to the protection of the inlet.

The wind behind the ship drove them quickly toward shore. It seemed there were two bodies of water vying for the same ocean; a different color and temperament sea, equally violent, reared from the opposite direction. The temperature dropped and the wind picked up.

Jack could hear crisp orders to shorten sail. They came from Cheatum, the second mate, a large over-bearing sailor with a mole on the port side of his nose. Three sailors bolted past Jack, scampering to a line stretched under the bowsprit. Jack felt an urge to climb the foremast and lend a hand to another group of men trying to gather the flapping sails sixty feet above the swaying deck.

Quince stood by the starboard rail, a large coil of rope in his left hand. With a mighty heave he tossed the weighted line over the rail, letting the rope trail through his hands until it went slack. Bending out over the rail, he shouted, "Starboard side, seven fathoms and deep water!"

From the port side of the ship came a similar call, but only "six fathoms." The inlet still lay south by several miles.

"We'll head for Drum Inlet, mister." The captain had come on deck. "Take five points off your starboard helm."

Jack inched closer so he could hear over the raging wind.

Cheatum diplomatically suggested they steer the ship further north. "The wind is backing around, Captain. We're in the lee off the Hatteras Cape. We may have to settle for Ocracoke, sir."

Jack strained to hear the exchange. The choices made by the seamen were endlessly exciting to him.

"Have your way, then," the captain said. "Just don't run us aground till we get into the bay."

Cheatum seemed to eye the captain with a sense of discomfort. The captain, an unsteady hand on the sec-ond mate's shoulder, whispered, "You know the *Star* can't be seen in Portsmouth harbor, don't you?"

"Aye, aye, Capt'n."

The captain turned, then suddenly whirled back. "I detect a manner of insubordination from you, Mr. Cheatum. You did understand my orders?"

"Aye, aye, Capt'n."

"Repeat them verbatim."

"I believe you said that the *Star* could not be seen in Portsmouth harbor, sir."

"Indeed, and why is that?"

"I have no idea, sir."

The captain began to pace between the binnacle and the port rail.

"No idea? Not a glimmer of a thought?"

He stopped to look out at the sea. Jack saw him suddenly raise his hand as if to wave at someone in the water, then just as quickly change his mind, making an unsteady departure for his cabin. The few crew members who witnessed the interchange passed knowing looks and continued the ship's work. Jack heard one of them whisper that the captain was off to the comfort of his rum.

Disheartened, Jack pondered the exchange. The captain made the men uneasy; they didn't seem as much afraid as they were wary of him. As if something was wrong.

They pitched toward land, the ship rising and falling in great surges. Quince, passing by, told Jack they were going into North Carolina, headed for Pamlico Sound. Jack could see the barrier reef and two inlets. The ship was inexorably rushing to the north. The call from the sounding lines warned that they were rapidly approaching shallow water. Cheatum stood calmly next to the helm, issuing orders for small changes in the ship's direction. Jack marveled at his demeanor—to be so calm, when it seemed a mistake of fifty feet in either direction would lead to disaster. With a shout from the port side, Cheatum yelled, "Hard a starboard," then after a moment, "now, center your helm."

In the week he had been on board, Jack constantly was amazed at how well the men managed the ship. The crew seemed rough and surly—and yet they obeyed without question. Easy to see, Jack thought, how any abuse of power would lead to trouble.

Ensconced in his spot, Jack could make out the approaching sand dunes on either side of the passage. The opening was narrow, the dunes coming right down to the water. He could smell the sweet native grasses as they bent in the wind. The ship raced into the sound, speeding between the two bodies of land. The wind continued to drive them forward, but the water became suddenly calm as the dark clouds caught up with them. Jack could see lights from a village tucked behind the south side of an island.

Quince continued taking soundings as they proceeded south. After half an hour, they headed directly for a long, thin island about fifty yards from shore. Dense shrub thickets sat on the dunes and a salt marsh lined the beach. Suddenly the island became nothing more than a black mass as the storm blocked out the sun. The rain started and the crew scurried to batten down.

Cheatum guided the boat straight onto the beach. The direct manner in which the ship was driven ashore fascinated Jack. As a landlubber, he thought they would tear the bottom out of their craft. The second mate shouted at the bosun, Mentor, "Form a shore party! I want lines port and starboard, fore and aft, as far ashore as possible. Look lively now!"

The salt marshes slowed the boat as she cleaved her way onto the sand. A groan, and the one-hundred-ninety-ton ship stopped abruptly. Jack felt his stomach go queasy as the boat stopped pitching beneath his feet. The world seemed to spin as he made his way belowdecks.

"Mi caro," said his mother as soon as he walked in. "I hear a loud bump."

"We've purposely run aground on a small islet. We're in a bay off North Carolina and we need to make repairs." Jack caressed her hands. "You and father should try to come on deck, to get some air."

His father awakened in obvious discomfort.

"Come, Ethan. Some air, por favor."

"Please," Jack implored. "Try to come with us."

They made their way slowly on deck, Jack leading the way.

The ship was hard aground, almost perfectly level and very stable as she rested on her substantial keel. A working party was formed to repair the rudder. The men lowered the small boats. Lanterns were rigged over the fantail and an eerie light spread over the sound.

Jack stood with his parents by the port rail, breathing in the aroma off the shrub-laden dunes. In the shelter of the sound, the wind had slackened and the rain turned into a mist. The sun was gone but the twilight lit the figures moving about the deck. His mother seemed to revel at the light rain on her face.

"The boat has stopped its infernal movement and I have decided that I may live," said Ethan as he looked out at the sound.

The three figures stood silent, gazing out at the darkening lagoon.

For the first time in over a week Jack felt at peace in his bunk. His parents were sleeping soundly; they seemed to have regained their strength and hope in the four or five hours since the ship had gone aground. His thoughts drifted lazily over the past weeks' trip from Hamden to Salem; the confrontation in the tavern; the pretty Colleen—he could still recite verbatim her directions to the wharf. Wrapped snugly in his blanket, he felt warm, safe. Long tendrils of a strange sea creature flitted just outside his consciousness and with his hands he moved them aside, to see its red hair drifting silently across a pale face. He gently moved a curl from a cheek, and smiled in his sleep.

At just past four in the morning a thunderous crack rolled across Pamlico Sound. Jack could hear shouts on deck, then the sound of sailors running, their heels clomping the beams above his head. He rolled from his bunk. "A thunderstorm," he told his parents reassuringly, driving his feet into his boots and running to the companionway. But looking up, he saw, as he suspected, a clear night sky.

Something was wrong.

Once on deck he saw it. Almost a mile to the north, just inside the protected waters of the sound, were sails reflecting the full moon. A schooner, her sails taut with air, bore down on them at great speed. The vessel's skipper obviously was familiar with these shallows to chance such a maneuver this close to the dunes that separated them from open ocean. She was fast approaching the islet on which the *Star* had come aground. But why under full sail and accompanied by the roar of cannon, Jack couldn't guess.

Suddenly, Jack spotted a series of flashes well behind the schooner, followed by a booming report and a high screaming sound that ripped the night air and passed over the masts of the *Star.* There was another ship behind the schooner that had just fired a volley that came uncomfortably close to the *Star*. Then the schooner was upon them; it passed within a hundred yards, seemingly unaware of their presence. If it was looking for the channel to open sea, the schooner missed it, passing too far south.

It seemed all the ship's crew, with the exception of the working party in the boat, had lined the rail to watch the light-and-sound display. Jack asked Quince what was happening.

"I don't rightly know, lad." Quince resumed his trancelike preoccupation with the passing drama. "It would seem two ships have taken a dislike to one another."

Jack moved back to the quarterdeck where second mate Cheatum stood, giving orders to the working party. "Douse those lanterns and keep your heads down, lads—or you'll catch a stray ball."

Jack sidled up to two of the older hands.

"The schooner would be a privateer, I'm thinking," one said. "And from the looks of her, a right fast boat at that."

"Can you see·what flag she's flying?"

"No. Probably John Bull, English built."

Just then the schooner jibed and as she came broadside to the open lagoon, let loose with a deafening salvo. The projectiles streaked back across the bay and soon a fire was visible on the other ship. The larger pursuing ship swung east to free her guns to fire at the much faster schooner, once again rapidly approaching the helpless *Star*.

It was now obvious that the schooner was looking for the deep channel just astern of the *Star*. Mr. Quince suddenly came to life and countermanded Cheatum's earlier order to douse lights. "Fire up the lanterns, men! These buggers don't know we're here and it's a tight fit through that pass a'hind us. Be quick about it!"

The ship in the lagoon fired its volley too soon and the balls drove harmlessly into the dunes on the barrier island. The schooner bore down relentlessly on the *Star*'s position. She seemed intent on ramming the grounded boat, but at the last second must have noticed the relit lanterns and tacked to port thirty yards astern. It came so close that Jack could see the startled faces of the other crew, gaping at the beached ship. As the schooner tacked away, Jack read *Helena* on her fantail. The crew of the *Helena* were too busy between the reef

and the island to fire their cannons but were easily out-
distancing the larger ship. The shouts from her officers
to the crew sounded like French. The other boat tacked
again for a broadside at the fleeing *Helena*. The shots
this time were aimed higher and struck the *Helena*'s
mainsail gaff, tattering the sail beneath. The schooner
didn't seem bothered and tacked again across the narrow stretch of water.

As the *Helena* disappeared down the slough, the
larger ship lumbered slowly and carefully past the *Star*
in dogged pursuit. A fierce fire on deck consumed a
quarter of it. Smoke rolled out of several forward
hatches. Jack could see men working feverishly on deck
with buckets trying to drench the fire.

"The man is stubborn." This came from Quince,
who had come up behind Jack. "Break off the engagement and put out your fire, lad." He was talking to
himself, Jack realized, and watched him shake his
head in dismay. Suddenly, Jack's mother and father
stood beside him, their faces lit by the fire on the passing warship.

"What's happening? My God—that ship's on fire."
Ethan's voice betrayed his alarm. Pilar, upset by the
gunfire, shivered under the thin blanket wrapped
around her shoulders. Jack touched her arm to reassure
her. The burning warship was soon but a distant glow.

"Mind you stay out of the way of the crew," Ethan
told his son. "And get some rest." He gently guided his
wife back toward the companionway.

"Yes, Father. I'll just stay on deck awhile longer." Jack
had no intention of going below. His heart beat quickly,
the spectacle of the last half hour still too immediate to
allow him to sleep.

Shouts ascended from the working party, asking permission to resume their tasks. They were quickly answered. "Lay to!" Quince shouted, for they had less
than twelve hours to catch the evening tide. With this

knowledge, Jack decided to do a little exploring. He was more than curious to find out the fate of the two ships.

Jack climbed along the bowsprit, hand over hand, making his way to the end of the thirty-foot-long thick pole. The sprit ended well over the salt marsh, on a sandy patch of dry land. He swung from the dolphin striker and easily dropped six feet to the sand. Getting back on board might pose a problem, but Jack would worry about that later. He scrambled to the top of a low hill and standing in a hum of insects, he gazed back at the *Star*. It was a bizarre sight to see the crew milling about the deck of the unmoving ship. How would they ever get off this spit of land?

The false dawn spread a gray light over the dunes. Jack's legs were unsteady as he started south along the island. The earth felt strange after being so many days aboard ship. For twenty minutes he trudged through the soft sand, hearing the distant thunderclaps of the battle. On one of the higher dunes he saw that the fire on the larger warship had consumed her whole superstructure. Her sails were ablaze, filling the morning sky with ebony smoke. The reports he had heard a few minutes before were actually the ship's powder magazines exploding.

Jack rounded a copse of loblolly pines to be surprised by a band of wild ponies pawing at the sand. Alerted, they scattered among the dunes. It was an eerie place. You could run around on sand beaches seemingly in the middle of the ocean. Men in front of him still engaged in fierce battle were probably dying as he watched. Others behind him worked on a ship they had purposely run onto the shore and ponies cavorted about him like dogs in Hamden's downtown square. But amongst it all, it was the fire on the ship that drew him south like a moth.

He got as close to the blazing vessel as he could. The view was strange through the dead pines, the skeletal trees seeming to point emphatically away from the car-nage. The ship was sinking by the bow, fully engulfed in flames. Sailors had jumped from the inferno and were swimming to both sides of the barrier. Many had reached shore, some lying prone, others staring out to sea at the departing privateer. The sun was now rising and flashed a path from the schooner with the tattered sail to the sinking ship, hissing madly as the fire touched the rushing tidewaters of Drum Inlet.

As mesmerizing as the scene was, Jack began to fear that he might be missed back at the *Star*. He knew he had come a long way and had lost track of time. Reluctantly, he turned and started to retrace his steps at a ground-eating trot.

When Jack reached the *Star*, he waded out to the port boarding ladder. Granted, his hike down the dune couldn't be compared to Columbus's discovery of the New World, but still he felt pleased with himself; it was something he could relive in his mind for years to come. His curiosity about the battle had been satisfied. The sinking of the vessel both saddened and thrilled him. He had seen a navy pennant and American flag, just visible above the water. Twenty feet of the mainmast and part of the foremast had jutted out in the middle of the inlet, at a rakish angle. The torn remains of the flags waved limply. As Jack peeled off his wet pants and boots, he wondered about the fate of the men aboard the sunken ship. He had seen them on shore, swimming, or in boats. The proximity of land certainly saved most on board, or at least he hoped so. Very tired now, he climbed con-tentedly into his hard bunk.

It seemed he had hardly closed his eyes when a shud-der of the boat awakened him. The men must have fin-ished repairing the rudder—but how were they moving the ship? Despite his exhaustion, he donned his wet clothes and made his way topside, anxious not to miss something exciting.

The tide was coming in and the *Star* began to creak and groan as she accepted the burden of her own weight again. It was floating! Jack could soon hear the deck busy with sailors taking in lines, letting out sails, generally cleaning up and making ready for sea. The wind proved perfect, dragging them into the center of the channel. Turning, they headed south, parallel to the dunes Jack had walked earlier.

⊷ ❊ ⊶

Jack's parents appeared on deck looking much better, if not a little apprehensive about the prospects of rough seas. The day grew beautiful—clear skies and crisp fall weather embraced them.

As the *Perdido Star* made its way down the channel, Jack wondered how they would find their way into the ocean; certainly not out the clogged inlet where the ship had sunk. It suddenly occurred to him that only he had actually seen the demise of the naval vessel. As the inlet was several miles from the *Star*'s anchorage, he should probably tell someone. Going aft to the quarterdeck, Jack spotted the bleary-eyed and disheveled captain, gazing back toward the village they had seen the previous night.

"Excuse me, sir. Ah . . . Captain Deploy . . . could I speak to you, please?" The captain glared at him.

"Sir. I have information that may be helpful."

Now a grunt and short laugh from the ancient captain.

Jack wasn't sure if Deploy could hear him, so he took several tentative steps toward the quarterdeck. "I hiked down the dunes last night, sir, and saw what I think would be information, sir, that you might need."

He received a dismissive toss of the head.

"My name is Jackson O'Reilly, sir. I'm one of the passengers. Along with my parents."

The captain turned away and addressed the second mate. "Cheatum, I believe one of the standing orders aboard this—" The captain paused and squared his shoulders, as if to make a point of the next word. "Illush . . . illwus . . . illustrious ship is, correct me if I'm wrong, that passengers, even paying ones"—and now his voice rose—"are to stay the hell off my quarterdeck!" The captain turned his attention back toward the village. Second mate Cheatum motioned for Jack to move away.

Jack bounded off the quarterdeck and shouted, "Listen to me or not, sir. You'll not be seeing the open ocean at the next inlet. It's stuffed with a sunk ship and this is free advice from a paying passenger!"

The crew had been listening to the exchange and there came a roar of laughter. Jack felt the heat rise in his face. Even the captain smiled, and stealing a look at the second mate, dismissed the whole episode.

Jack stood firm. His parents watched him, waiting for an explanation of why he seemed so angry. Finally he turned to them.

"Last night I jumped from the bow of the ship and hiked along the islet. I saw the end of the battle. There is a ship sunk in the inlet. We can't get out that way. This idiot of a captain will soon see that."

"You should not have left the ship." Ethan shook his head and patted Jack on the shoulder. "Regardless, you must remember the captain is in charge and responsible for the welfare of all on board. I'm sure he'll find a way out."

Jack ignored his father, eyes riveted toward the pines hiding the entrance to the inlet. As the *Star* began her turn to port to make the exit from Drum Inlet, a lookout on the bowsprit shouted, "Wreck ahead off the bow!" All hands moved to the rails to see the masts rising out of the water. "Hard a starboard. All hands stand by to tack!" The boat began her slow turn. Jack leaned back on the port rail against his elbows. Legs crossed, head cocked, he looked at the captain standing next to the helm, and finally caught his eye. Even a ship's length away, Jack felt his wrath.

It would take several hours now to backtrack to the next inlet. Jack, still upset by the captain's dismissal, was elated by the sweet revenge. He took up his usual watch position on the bow, feeling much like one of the crew. Indeed, he thought, he was older than some of the apprentices.

When the bells rang at two A.M. he started to go below, but was stopped by the sight of something in the water, fifty yards off the starboard bow. Bobbing in four-foot waves, it looked like a small boat. The waves obscured his view and he lost sight of it. Had he in fact seen anything but a whitecap?

"Man overboard, starboard side!" The shout came from a sailor on watch. Jack stared in awe as the crew came alive, launching a gig and dragging a body onto the *Star*'s deck. No, not one body. Two. Jack was both drawn and repelled by the sight. He knew he had to keep out of the crew's way but couldn't help crowding in with the rest of them.

Smithers, a tall raw-boned seaman, nudged the older of the two bodies with his toe. "This 'un's about cooked, I'd say." The ship's doctor brushed him aside and examined the bodies.

"The older chap is dead without a doubt," he said. "Most of him is burned."

There was a slight stirring from the crew, but no one spoke.

While attention had been focused on the older man, Jack knelt to the side of the younger. He reached out and touched a wrist—and was stunned when the hand reflexively grabbed his own. The young man's eyes briefly opened, stared blankly at Jack, and closed again. The others turned at the sight of the movement and pushed Jack aside.

"This next lad just seems exhausted." The doctor grasped the young sailor's jaw, shaking him gently. "Wake up, sailor, wake up." The young man, pale and deathlike, blinked his eyes at the doctor.

"What's your name, lad?"

The sailor's mouth moved but nothing came out. He tried again: "Paul."

"Would it be Paul the Apostle, then?"

"If it pleases, sir."

Young Paul fell back, unconscious.

3

PAUL

MARTIN'S SCREAMS ECHOED in Paul's head, though Martin was dead by now, he must be. Paul had seen the burns swell his face and hands, had heard his pleas for water even as they swam from the ship.

Paul remembered the sea, hands pulling him out, the eyes of a young man gazing at him with pity. He fell back again, losing consciousness, then became aware of a crowd around him; sounds, voices, undistinguishable words. He was drenched in sweat, his tears mixed with bodily fluids and seawater. He forced himself to think clearly. How did I get here? How did I . . .

The click of heels on the marble floor signaled to Paul Le Maire that his father's wrath would be upon him. He had spent an hour alone in the sitting room waiting, watching the shadows on the polished floor grow long. The house was still. Drapes brushed against the sparkling windows. Particles of dust swirled, catching the last rays of sun. Paul knew his father had already heard of his dismissal from college. He relived the scene with anguish. Dean Nathaniel J. Clark had sent for him abruptly.

"Young man, the College of William and Mary has over one hundred years of tradition behind it. The architect of our Constitution was schooled here. By all that is holy . . . "

The dean alternately pushed his glasses closer to his eyes and dropped his head to see over them, all the while driving his hands deep into his pockets, exploring the dark interior of his pants. "What in God's name has gotten into you, man?"

Au contraire, what has gotten into *you*, monsieur? thought Paul.

Dean Clark glowed with a fury frightening to behold. The students referred to him as the Scarecrow. Long, gangly, disjointed limbs. A misshapen, unhappy face, dominated by a huge, blood-blistered nose. "You are already on probation for your last little episode," he proclaimed.

Paul could contain himself no longer. He began to laugh.

"How dare you laugh at me!" Standing righteously, the dean took a deep breath and expelled it loudly through his nose. "You, who stood in this very office and begged for another chance."

Paul knew then it was all over.

"What do you have to say for yourself, young man?" The dean's feet pounded the oaken floor. "You've acted the clown in class, ridiculed your professors, and generally disgraced not only this school but your father, who, as you well know, has given a generous endowment to this establishment. But don't think for one minute that his generosity will in any way dissuade me from expelling you if I see fit." He paused here, cocking his head, waiting for an answer.

"Sir, first of all, may I correct you on one thing? I did not try to ridicule Professor Dawes. He did that on his own," replied Paul.

"How dare you use that attitude with me!" the dean shouted. "I've attempted to give you a chance to speak in your defense and you have the audacity to correct me?"

"No, sir, I didn't mean it as a correction of you so

much as a clarification of the facts as they may have been presented to you."

The dean slammed his bony fist down on his desk. "I'm going to notify your father immediately! You have the unmitigated gall to stand there and tell me Professor Dawes lied to me about what happened?"

"No, sir. I doubt he would knowingly lie. It's just that he may not understand the reality of what was said, and was embarrassed at being dead wrong. . . . " Paul paused and with great effort contorted his face into a mask of innocence. "You see, sir, although the quotation Professor Dawes used was substantially correct, he not only used it in the wrong context, but misidentified the author. He mistakenly said it was Isaac Newton who first spoke the words, 'If I have seen further, it is by standing on the shoulders of giants.' Of course, you and I both know the phrase was first quoted perhaps as early as 1126 by Bernard of Chartres, referring to the ancients. Indeed, some would say it was Lucan, barely after the time of Christ. It was not, as Professor Dawes ineptly put it, that the architects of our Constitution gained strength from each other. That may or may not have been the truth, but had absolutely nothing to do with the quotation. So, sir, you can readily see my predicament: I was caught between trying to save the professor's reputation or engaging in a meaningful dialectic to stimulate both myself and the class."

Dean Clark had listened to him quietly. Now his eyes flashed fire. "Are you quite finished, Master Le Maire?"

"Yes, sir. I would just like to say—"

"Please, not another word." The dean sat quietly at his desk, avoiding Paul's gaze. "You obviously enjoy the fact that you're bright," he said. "That seems to be undeniable. But let me tell you this, young man." His voice rose with a tremolo befitting a tenor. "You are being expelled. You can count this as a job you were unable to finish. And I'll leave you with a quote that may give your destiny a purpose: 'In for a penny, in for a pound.' That, sir, is a true lesson for life and one that strikes close to home, for it is attributed to our former chancellor, George Washington."

The dean stood triumphantly. "You, young man, are dismissed." He stepped to the window and proudly looked out at the campus. Paul backed toward the door, torn between wanting to speak and waiting for the dean to turn and change his mind. When it became apparent that he would say no more, Paul tried again.

"Thank you, sir, for allowing me to speak." He paused. "I know that I've been a difficult student for you, sir, and that you've gone out of your way to be fair." He stopped and looked around the room for a moment, sensing he was there for the last time. "Good-bye, sir. And oh, by the way, although our eminent first president and chancellor wrote of this quote, it was actually attributed to Edward Ravenscroft in the Canterbury Guests."

Dean Clark screamed at the window, "Get out! Now. Get out. Not another word. Get out!"

"Sixteen ninety-five." Paul eased his way out the door but thrust his head back in through the opening.

"What?"

"Sixteen ninety-five. Ravenscroft. The quote. He wrote it in sixteen ninety-five."

Despite himself, Paul smiled at the memory but quickly grew somber as his father entered the room. Le Maire Senior planted himself in a spot within arm's reach of his son, who had risen to meet his fate. The particles that hung in the air quickly disappeared, as if frightened by the alien force.

"Look at me."

Paul Junior could not raise his eyes.

"I said, look at me, damn you."

"I cannot, Father, for I am too ashamed. I've let you down—"

"Ferme la bouche."

A deep-seated dread crept over Paul. He knew that when his father reverted to French he would soon be out of control.

"Tu te délectes à m'embarrasser."

"Father, I take no joy in your embarrassment."

"Je ne posais pas une question, imbécile. It was a statement of fact." The older man was smiling at the younger, but it was a mirthless, ominous grin.

"I think I explained quite clearly to you what would happen if you gave me cause to discipline you again en regard de l'université?" The man stood in front of Paul, unwavering. His eyes glinted; his chin rose and his hands worried the seams on his trousers.

Paul lifted his eyes to try to meet his father's icy glare.

"You did explain, sir, that I would be physically punished if it became necessary to confront me again on this matter. But then, that was when I was fifteen. I would hope, sir, now that I'm seventeen, that I could now speak of this with you as a man."

Paul never saw his father's hand streaking toward his face. The blow came without warning. His head spun, his cheek stung, and his eyes clouded.

"Bâtard." Blows rained down in quick succession. Paul Senior grabbed his son's coat collar with one hand and slapped him as if he were a stranger with the other. "Tu as humilié cette maison. Tu fais honte à toi-même et à cette famille." His ramrod-straight posture never varied.

"I've disgraced myself only, Father. Please allow me to make amends." Paul tried desperately to ward off the blows, at the same time wishing to take the punishment he knew he deserved.

"Ah bon! Now you wish to be treated as a man? Tu veux seulement réparer tes erreurs?"

"Yes, Father. May I speak?"

"Pourquoi est-ce que je te permettrais de parler? It is your speech that has gotten you to this place."

"Father, don't strike me again. Or I'll leave your house forever." Paul had slipped to his knees, completely submissive. He had never spoken to his father so directly before and expected a new volley of blows.

But the senior Le Maire grasped Paul by both lapels and drew him up tightly to his breast. "Tu es bâtard. Tout littéralement. Illegitimate. Your mother is the woman you thought to be your Aunt Jacqueline in Paris. I'm not your father. Nor is the pitiful woman that we both hear weeping in the kitchen your mother."

Paul gazed back as if in a dream. The older man seemed to take pleasure in revealing these secrets.

"Why do you tell me these lies, Father? I'm your son. You can't hope to punish me with false news of my being illegitimate and expect me to believe it." Paul's face still smarted from the blows. He looked through tears at this man who had just destroyed his life.

"Va à ta chambre. Vas-y. Do not speak of leaving this house until I say so." With a heavy push, Paul Senior propelled the younger man violently across the room.

This person before him, whom he loved, could not be telling the truth. Impossible. Why, he looked like his mother. Everybody said so. But yes, he also looked like his Aunt Jacqueline, who touched his face in such a familiar way when he first met her. Jacqueline—his mother? Could it be?

Paul felt he was in the throes of some fantastic nightmare. But the black dream had started well before this day; he had always felt a loneliness he couldn't quite comprehend. His father was more than New England stern: he displayed a distance that Paul could never seem to bridge, even in the most private times. He felt he could never succeed in his father's eyes, no matter how accomplished his studies or how hard he tried in his efforts at the manly arts. Paul remembered being beaten by a sparring partner in fisticuffs. He had risen to his feet again and again, blood streaming from his nose, rather than admit defeat, until the ringmaster insisted the fight stop. Glancing to where his father had stood, looking for the slightest sign of approval, he saw only the man he revered walking out in disgust.

And his mother. His mother? The lady who . . . yes, his mother. She was always good to him, but again, not the source of deep warmth and understanding he craved. Perhaps irrationally. Perhaps not so irrationally after all.

Paul stared at the space where this man who had been his father had disappeared.

You are right, sir, I will not speak of leaving this house. But I will be gone just the same.

⊨⊰ ✦ ⊱⊫

The rail was slick from the rain; salt crusted on the worn wood. Jack was tired, his legs weak from the constant motion of the boat. The deck was practically deserted, except for the helmsman and a few hands on watch. Still, he knew he had to get some sleep.

Going below was still difficult. As he made his way among the bunks, he heard a moan. That survivor's body—Paul, was it—was entangled in a blanket, stained with use. Jack stopped at the chest-high berth. The man stank of urine and was drenched in sweat. His bright blue eyes were open, focusing at the bottom of the bunk above him. He seemed to be about his own age but smaller, and delicate-looking; Jack could tell he was handsome, although right now forlorn. It's the seasickness, Jack surmised.

"The cook has told me there be salted cod and bits of cheese for supper," he said. "If you like, I'll fetch you some."

"Speak to me not of food, for I am soon to die." The words came out gravely, spoken between chapped, broken lips. There was a long pause. Jack waited expectantly. Finally, Paul's ashen face turned slowly to him.

Jack snickered but immediately felt ashamed, as he had also been sick and knew of the nausea brought on by the sea.

"I'm sorry to laugh, but you're a long way from death's door—fifty years or so, I'd say."

Annoyed, the limp sailor peered at Jack, daring him to continue.

"You'd be the fellow they fished out of the sea two nights ago, wouldn't you?"

"Fished would be the proper verb, yes."

"You looked more dead than alive. But you seem to be with the living now."

"What of Martin? My mate? Is he . . . dead?"

"Yes, I'm afraid so. His burns were severe." Jack didn't know if it was his place to tell the young man this news, but it was out and so be it.

With a sigh, the pallid seaman tried to cover his head with the blanket.

Jack moved closer and snatched a corner of the cover. "Get out of your bunk and come up on deck with me. Now." Jack knew he was taking a chance with this stranger, but there was something intriguing about him, and he was sure sternness was the right approach.

"What do you want of me?" Paul's voice was weak.

"Do as I say. Move your wet behind out of this sodden mess and we'll take a stroll." The order seemed to startle the young man.

"Are you mad? Can't you see I'm sick?"

"Nevertheless, arise, matey." Jack scooped up the body and pulled him to his feet while Paul weakly clutched the blanket to his chest. Once upright, the ailing young man promptly began to sink to his knees, whereupon his new friend quickly grasped him around the waist with one arm, then trooped him through the bunks up the companionway, out to the fresh sea air.

"I'm going to be sick."

"So be sick over the side." Jack guided him toward the rail and stood with his charge as he retched.

"Why are you doing this?" the fellow asked, gasping for breath.

"I thought you'd feel better with fresh air smacking that freckled face." Jack laughed and waved a casual hand of dismissal. "By the way, you look a proper mess, sailor."

"Please do not call me sailor. I am of late a student who in my misguided fantasy thought the sea a proper place to drown my sorrow. No pun intended. Actually, I came close to accomplishing just that." With a shiver he turned to look at the horizon. "My name is Paul Le Maire." He paused. "Thank you for your help. I'm feeling much better. But please, in the future, try not to be so abrupt. It is exceedingly rude."

Jack studied this pitiful waif, who was a full head shorter than he, and explained with as much sincerity as he could manage, "I'm Jack O'Reilly and you, sir, are as funny a sight as I've seen in a long time. Your arse is hanging out. You've vomit on your jumper, your hair is standing on end, and you smell like an outhouse in distress. So why, pray tell, shouldn't I call you sailor?"

"A sailor I am not." Paul tilted his head. "I'd only been to sea two weeks on a training vessel when we attacked a privateer in the bay off Cape Hatteras. We chased and outgunned them, but we were by and large inexperienced and were shot to pieces and sunk in an inlet close to shore."

"Yes," Jack said. "I saw most of the battle."

"We were on fire and sinking. In the smoke and confusion I ended up in a small boat with Mr. Martin, who was the third mate, and a couple of other hands I didn't know. I tried to take care of Mr. Martin the best I could." He bowed his head, continuing with effort. "The other men must have slipped over the side and swum for shore. With the tide and all, I guess we just drifted out with the current." He paused, reflecting. "They'll report me dead at sea, won't they? Maybe that will make my father smile."

Jack raised his brow at the last comment but said only, "What's done is done. You can either go on with us or go over the side. If you feel like you won't be missed, go over the side. If not, let's carry on."

Jack took the soiled blanket and shook it vigorously over the rail. The wind caught it, snapping it like a sail. The brown wool stretched straight out from Jack's hands, and freshly aired, he wrapped it around Paul's shoulders. "If you feel like talking later, I can usually be found forward by the bowsprit—trying to be the first one to Cuba."

4

HABANA

FIRST BLACK, THEN dark green and sandy white, Cuba appeared as a saddlelike hump on the horizon. It assumed different shapes during the course of the day as the *Star* beat toward it through turquoise waters, wrestling a contrary headwind. For the better part of a week there had been "nothing to see but the sea itself" as Jack had announced to the uncaring salt spray. Sea, and an occasional glimpse of low-lying sand and coral reef.

The vessel· was cautiously skirting what the sailors called the Floridas. Jack noticed the lookouts were particularly wary of hazards to starboard, or west of them, as they continued on their southern course. Ole Hansumbob told him the trick was to keep west of the northerly push of the Gulf Stream and yet stay far enough east to keep off the shallow cays.

By evening, Cuba, off the port side of the ship, dominated Jack's vision. His eyes were riveted on the tropical island, revealing itself in greater detail each time the ship's bow leaned toward shore. It struck Jack that the ship's progress was rather like that of an inebriated man heading doggedly back to his favorite pub; tacking first to the left, then reversing his bearing and staggering to the right.

Close up, Cuba was a painter's canvas, dominated by bold, verdant strokes, yet spattered unevenly with warm reds and browns. Mountain peaks seemed to attract a halo of both white and ominously dark clouds. There were thick plumes of smoke as well and Jack caught the sharp scent of something being burnt in the fields—a sailor said it was the chaff from the harvest of sugar cane.

A steady offshore breeze allowed them to tack unusually close to land as they made their way to the port of Habana. Palm trees swayed like dancers on the shore, and the light green waters of the shallows shimmered in rhythm with the trees. This same breeze made entry into the harbor difficult, but Jack enjoyed the wind's recalcitrance: being forced to approach this new world with baby steps allowed him to absorb it completely.

Finally, as night fell, they crept into the lee of the island and slipped into the harbor, dropping anchor in waters so calm that even Ethan and Pilar were able to climb on deck, beginning to breathe the fresh air of their new home. Jack noted the emergence of another figure who had been appearing with more frequency on deck during the last two days—a somewhat less bedraggled Paul Le Maire.

Jack was pleased to see the young man but fought down the urge to approach him. Paul was obviously wrestling with demons that could only be faced on one's own. Jack thought it best to grant him his solitude until he chose to leave it of his own will.

Still, he cut an amusing figure. He wore a striped shirt several sizes too large, breeches so small that they had to be slit for proper leg room, and shoes. This last was surprising, since he had none when pulled aboard—then Jack remembered Martin. He had been wearing shoes; the crew must have seen fit to let the lad have them.

Still self-absorbed, Paul claimed a perch opposite Jack on the starboard rail, out of the way of the men reefing sails and hauling what would seem to any landlubber a hopeless tangle of lines about the deck. There was obviously some arcane design to their effort, but even after all this time it eluded Jack. He noted that Paul was livelier on his perch today and the young man even started making eye contact, as if working on some inner resolve concerning Jack.

Suddenly, Paul stood and began taking a circuitous route around the busy seamen, in Jack's direction. He ventured a smile. "I decided to not go over the side, you see."

"Aye, you even look like you could be mistaken for a human being."

"Indeed. The cook let me take a pot of hot water to the scupper during that last squall and I devised a bath from the rainwater, followed by a warm rinse."

"And the clothes?"

"The cooper and bosun rounded me up some discards that work well enough."

"Well, it's easier talking to you—I mean with your not being dead and all. . . . What do you think of Habana?"

"It's a balm for the soul. Hard to stay wrapped inside yourself when there's a world like that out there."

"Yes," Jack said. "It's night and still hotter than hell's hinges, but the place seems to not slow down when the sun drops."

"There are lights everywhere. I trust that music I hear isn't coming from my own head."

"No, indeed, me hearty. It's coming from one of those drinking establishments where there are beautiful, dark-eyed ladies who don't even know the resurrected Paul Le Maire has arrived. Aye, arrived to rescue them from their otherwise dreary lives."

Paul grinned. "It's thoughts like that will make a person almost forget their troubles. When, think you, will the skipper let us ashore?"

"I believe there's inspections and quarantines that have to take place. Might be a couple of days, then they'll start lightering the passengers and cargo. Don't know about human flotsam picked up along the way, though. Might be weeks before they let you on shore."

For the first time Jack heard a chuckle from his new acquaintance. Paul was coming alive and there was something in the fellow that Jack liked. He had a seriousness and intensity in his manner, offset by a twinkle in his eye, an eye that seemed to see the world in different shades of irony.

For the next three days, anchored tantalizingly close to land, the young men passed the time together, watching self-important officials strut about their ship and accept bribes from the officers. This ritual was usually followed by the crew hauling batches of cargo topside for unloading. Hides, tallow, whale oil, and what appeared to Jack to be machined tools and hardwood lumber all made their way out of the hold. The trade goods seemed to be released in increments more in proportion to the silver flowing under the hastily erected documents table than over the top, for payment of duties and port taxes. The latter, formal transactions, were accompanied by duly witnessed scratching of quills and impressing of wax seals on stiff parchment, first by the ship's captain, then the mustachioed Spanish port officials.

Standing at a respectful distance, Jack and Paul were unsure of the particulars of the transactions, but obviously the ship's manifest and what it actually carried in cargo were two distinctly different things. As Paul opened up to Jack during these days of bureaucratic captivity, Jack felt he was watching a fine instrument being unpacked from a sawdust-filled crate. Paul carried a source of knowledge and information hard to credit in one of so few years.

The night before they were finally given leave to disembark, a simple remark by Jack regarding one of the patterns of stars that looked like a sort of wide W started Le Maire on a soliloquy regarding "a celestial seat for Cassiopeia's shapely derriere," and a flood of wisdom followed. Paul explained the planets, the constellations, the heavens as myth and physical reality. Jack had no reason to doubt his own intelligence but he was smart enough to know he was in the presence of a truly remarkable intellect. Jack resolved that he would spend as much time as possible with his new friend when they went ashore.

❈

Early the next morning, as the O'Reillys were helped aboard the boat that would take them to shore, Jack looked back at his friend who stood forlornly at the rail. Paul, a rescued, penniless refugee, was low on the order for boat assignments. If he took a position on crew as an apprentice seaman, a possibility he had discussed with Quince, he would be even lower. Paul's sad face and slight build provided a strong contrast to the robust first mate, who stood at the rail next to him, shouting orders for the men handling the boats.

Jack looked beseechingly to his parents. "Father, Mother—may Paul come with us? I'd love for him to be with us when we set foot on Cuban soil."

"No," his father said. "You'll see him soon enough, I warrant, when he reaches shore with the later boats. We have *much to do*!"

"But—"

"No, Jack!" His father's clipped voice carried a mild warning. His mother, who had been about to speak, held her tongue.

At this point the first mate yelled down to the boat, "Mr. O'Reilly, sir, would you mind taking one more passenger in your skiff?" His hand was on Paul's shoulder. "It would help us in scheduling the departures."

"Certainly, Mr. Quince, we'd be glad to, if it helps,"

Ethan replied. "Send the lad on down." Jack tried not to smile for fear his father would reprimand him. His mother gave Jack a knowing wink and raised a finger to her lips for silence.

Paul climbed down the ladder, Ethan giving him a hand into the boat. Jack ventured a glance at Quince, who, without changing expression, winked as well.

The oars slapped the water with a vigor Jack had never seen from the sailors; even these worldly seamen couldn't hide their excitement and the launch fairly leaped through the mild chop, approaching the wharf with its load of old salts and young men, all wide-eyed with anticipation.

Habana's din met them as the boat's bowline was handed to a waiting sailor on the dock. Whitewashed buildings looked like a backdrop for dingy streets that were hardly visible through the throngs of people, most wearing colorful sashes over white cotton, a brightness that Jack was sure could only be found under a tropical sun.

As soon as they were all gathered on the wharf, Paul tried to engage Jack's parents in conversation. Though Jack had introduced his new friend to them on the ship, they had spoken only a few polite words to each other. The young man quickly charmed Pilar, and Ethan seemed to like him as well; but Jack could see his father was distracted by his desire to talk to the captain who was standing not far from them, engaged in business with dock officials. And Pilar was anxious to check on the whereabouts of Count de Silva. She hoped he had received her letter. She had bribed one of the port officials to deliver it to him the day before. She knew their arrival would be a great surprise to him. As the manager of her property and its closest neighbor, the count would be the best one to give her the news about the condition of her fields, and to verify the good news about the harvest which her friend Dolores had mentioned in her Easter letter.

Abruptly, Ethan and Pilar excused themselves, moving in opposite directions.

Jack signaled to Paul that he wanted to observe his father's dealings with Deploy, so the two of them positioned themselves a few feet from the older men.

"Captain Deploy, a moment of your time, sir," Jack's father said.

The captain's weathered face was expressionless as he listened to Ethan, who might have been a fly buzzing about the docks.

"As you know, the tools of my trade are not easily moved. Since I understand you don't intend to load cargo for your next port right away, perhaps I may leave my smithing wares and gun parts in your care for a short time?"

"Impossible. We head for Boston with the morning tide."

"Boston? Sir, I—well, I . . . was told you were carrying merchandise to the South Sea whaling fleets and wouldn't leave for a fortnight."

"What in blazes are you saying, smithy? Boston? I said we head for Papeete, probably two, three weeks hence."

"Uh, well, very good then." Ethan was clearly at a loss. What had the captain not understood? "So, Captain, may I leave my wares on board temporarily?"

"Makes no mind to me as long as they're in the forward hold, out of the way when we first start loading."

"Thanks so much, sir—"

"Aye, your thanks and five dollars for lease of space will be gladly accepted."

"Five—" Ethan's face sank. "I thought it would be a simple courtesy."

"Matters not what you thought, smith. You've heard the terms. Take 'em or leave 'em."

Jack felt that a sane man would have dealt with his father more fairly. Instead, he was being swindled by this drunken old despot. They both watched in silence as Ethan walked away, beaten. Jack's body tensed, his entire being wanting to retaliate. Paul laid a hand on his arm. "Whom the gods wish to destroy, they first make mad," he said.

Jack made no move to intercede, for he knew it would only elicit displeasure from his honest father. He vowed not to let it distract him from the intoxication of being in a new land. "It's the way he is," he told Paul, who obviously understood.

❧ ✳ ☙

Across the boardwalk, Pilar located the count quite readily. One of the harbor officials had directed her to a man whose manner of dress seemed more appropriate for attending a ball than for standing around a harborfront. Outfitted in a long satin waistcoat, lustrous pantaloons matching a pink jacket, and a shirt with a fragile high-collared neck, he was surrounded by an entourage of people courting his attention. The sun reflected onto the nobleman's face and he turned toward her. Pilar recognized him from her youth. Count de Silva had not changed much, she thought, only a little older and he was more pompous in his bearing than she had remembered. With some trepidation yet resolute, Pilar approached the stately gentleman and introduced herself. Immediately the count came to full attention, and greeted her grandly. He said he had come to search for her as soon as he received her letter. He extended every courtesy, making his personal in-town villa available to her and her family until they could get settled on their own. Within minutes, he ordered his servants to go with her to collect her baggage and find her family. He sent one carriage off to the villa with their belongings and invited them to ride there with him in his own carriage; but when the O'Reillys and Paul learned it was only a short distance, they politely declined. They chose instead to walk the few blocks, finding a joyous pleasure in stumbling now and again as they tried to regain their land legs. Jack and his mother delighted in Ethan's drunken steps and apparent dizziness while the count, holding back his carriage in step with them, tried to keep up a continuous dialogue with Pilar. Jack watched as his mother conversed with this Spanish grandee. He lengthened his torso out of the carriage window, straining to participate in the O'Reillys' good mood. He tried much too hard, to Jack's way of thinking, and his elation about seeing Habana was put off by his cautious instinct about the count.

The villa paralleled Jack's imagination of the Arabian Nights more than the reality of Habana. The entry was guarded by two grand oak doors at least ten feet high. Hexagonal clay tiles led them into an enormous atrium beautifully festooned with exotic plants and flowers. Ornately carved designs framed windows and doors. Servants stood waiting with cool drinks as they were ushered to their rooms. A far cry from Hamden, Jack thought. A far cry indeed.

Settled in the count's villa, Jack told his mother that he and Paul were headed off to explore the streets of Habana. With a warning to be careful, the young men fairly bounced in their gait, their excitement evident as they took in the exotic environment.

But beneath the exhilaration, their young eyes could not ignore an underlying sense of oppression. The streets were crowded with black Africans, sometimes chained together, herded along as if cattle. Jack noticed Paul's attention drawn to a side street. An incident was unfolding, a scuffle between some overseers and a procession of African slaves. One slave protested openly to ill treatment and was quickly disciplined, two quick slashes delivered across his face by a riding crop wielded by a heavyset Spaniard. Several kicks from another Spaniard directed the slave, blinded by blood and rage, back to the procession. He staggered, his hands clutching his face, trying, it seemed, to withdraw to a world behind his fingers.

Jack was troubled by the high visibility of the slave trade. Here slavery was not simply a tolerated evil, as in New England—or an institution, as in Virginia—but a booming business, dominating all other forms of commerce. Indeed, almost all the ships entering and leaving port had some degree of investment in human cargo.

Paul had explained to Jack the problems he had with his father's keeping of slaves. Understanding Paul's sensitivity to the issue, and given his own discomfort, Jack tried to steer them away from slave-processing areas; his superior height allowing him to see further over the heads of the crowd than Paul. At one point, Jack spied an enclosure in which a number of slaves were being prepared for whipping; he quickly changed direction— and they ended up walking straight into a plaza where an auction was in progress. The vendors handled the Africans like livestock, opening their mouths to the crowd of potential buyers and voyeurs, there to see the latest crop. It mortified Jack that much of the bartering seemed to be carried out in English.

The auctioneer made the women strip and actually squeezed the breasts of one of them to show milk spurt forth, proving her healthy and of child-bearing age. The fact that the child she had borne was to be sold elsewhere seemed of no apparent concern to anyone but her. Jack could not forget her haunting eyes. Her indifference to the humiliation came, he knew, from her realization she would never see her child again.

The seller turned a "buck" to face the crowd, grabbed up his privates and winked. "Imagine as how this will serve to keep yer herd producin'."

Jack was disgusted at the laughter of the men and the red-faced laughs from some of the ladies. Yet, despite his growing discomfort, he was determined to enjoy the wonders of Habana. He knew he must distance Paul from the auctioneer before his friend's heart overpowered his brain and there was trouble. He grabbed Paul's shoulder and turned their stride toward the Casa.

There was to be a party that evening on the waterfront. The Casa, colloquial for Casa de la Contratación, or House of Trade, sat in the center of the excitement. It had been the controlling force for over two hundred years of Spanish trade in the New World, an Iberian predecessor of the East and West India companies that later developed in England and Holland. The count, a peninsulare or native of Spain—not born in Cuba—was a high-ranking official at the House. The gathering that night was to be held in honor of the newly arrived residents of Habana, who, in the count's words, would "obtain their just rewards" from Pilar's birthright. The O'Reillys were to be formally welcomed to Habana, home to people of many nationalities, much like the recently formed United States.

─═✦═─

Jack and Paul, dressed for the evening in clean but threadbare attire, sat on the sweeping veranda of the Casa, more interested in the beauty of the Spanish and Creole ladies than the venerable history of the House of Trade. The ladies had a way of either ignoring you or looking through you with measured indifference, Jack felt. He waved and winked but drew only hostile stares from the women's chaperones. It mattered not; the dark-eyed beauties were unattainable dream creatures. Jack and Paul enjoyed just basking in their presence.

Jack was relaxed conversing in Spanish—even in translating for Paul. He saw that his mother was watching a group of people at the end of the room. A large man stood with his arms spread, enfolding two men of smaller stature. As if sensing he was being spied upon, the figure raised his head and turned slowly. It was the count, who was difficult to miss, as he was an inordinately tall man and again dressed as if to attend a king. A pale cerulean blue waistcoat and tights, red leggings, and black shiny ankle-high boots. The overall effect seemed overpowering and in slightly bad taste; the blue being too young for this fifty-year-old and the leggings and the cravat overly dramatic. His eyes stayed hooded as he drifted back to conversation.

Jack's mother held tightly to her husband's arm as they nodded their way across the vast room. Upon seeing them approach, the count excused himself from the group and made his way toward the couple, who looked a bit lost and intimidated by their new elegant surroundings.

De Silva stopped them, exchanging pleasantries in English with Ethan.

Jack was put off by his superior manner and elegant clothing. He's similar to the elders of Hamden, he thought, seeming to think of himself as handsome with his slicked down mustache. But he smelled of cheap cologne and perspiration. Jack sensed he must keep close track of this man.

The count seemed distressed, unconsciously wringing his hands. He turned to Pilar and said, "Señora, may I speak briefly of our situation?" Without waiting for a reply, he plunged ahead. "I'm sorry to speak of this on so early an occasion. But I feel I must put things right." Here he paused for help, his eyes flitting quickly around the room.

"I understand you received a letter from an old friend, about the progress of the cane fields." The man was truly uncomfortable. "That is to say, of course, she is free to say what she wants, and to you especially so because of your childhood relationship. But what I am trying to say, señora—"

"My God, man, it's all right. I'm sure my wife understands that people exaggerate," Ethan interrupted. "I didn't mean to upset you when I mentioned Dolores's letter. Pilar was so happy to hear from her, and hopes to see her again very soon. That is all." Ethan turned to his wife. "Would you like a cool drink, dear?"

"Yes, Ethan, and be so kind to get our host one also." Pilar kept her eyes on the count. Jack watched as his father crossed the room toward the buffet.

"¿Qué dijiste?" she asked in quiet Spanish.

"Dios mío, señora," de Silva said. "Your friend has overstated the harvest of the cane. She has no knowledge of our business. It is my understanding that she congratulated you on the success of the farm. . . . " The count paused. "Do you feel you have been lied to about the harvest?" He proceeded without waiting for a reply. "I assure you, it's just as stated in our many letters to you. There can be no profit from immature fields, and that is the situation at present." The count turned away slightly.

Jack could not make out the rest of his words, but de Silva's repeated glances around the room were so patently helpless that he almost felt sorry for the man. A silence deepened between the count and Pilar. He bowed his head and stepped away, gracefully pulling a small dagger from its scabbard on his belt. Jack's entire body tensed but Paul calmed him with a surreptitious pat on the shoulder. With a smile at Pilar, the count moved the blade slowly to catch the light and waited just a moment before striking his crystal glass. The sound drifted throughout the room.

"Señores y señoras, please, your attention."

The crowd immediately stilled.

"As you know, this is a momentous evening. We are gathered to welcome our newest emigrants from the Estados Unidos de America. May I please present Señor y Señora Ethan and Pilar O'Reilly, and their son, Jackson."

The count strolled to the center of the ballroom with a sweeping gesture, engulfing Pilar and Ethan in his outspread arms. People applauded and shouted heartfelt greetings, and the small band started a march. Jack watched as the charismatic figure charmed the crowd. Yes, the count was definitely a man to be watched, he thought.

"Supper is now served!" the count proclaimed above the festivities. "Let us eat, drink, and think not of tomorrow, for the man who does has lost the moment!"

The crowd drifted toward the dining room and seemed delighted by the count, whose energy embodied the ambience of the party. The faint scent of flowers grew stronger as Jack entered the ornamented room. Each wall panel inlaid with a mirror stretched clear to the ceiling. A chandelier fully eight feet across holding several hundred candles danced their light off the mirrors. Each bay held a stand of flowers guarded by a black servant ready to attend to this gay crowd.

Jack and Paul were shown to their chairs across the table from Jack's parents. Sitting next to Pilar was an olive-complexioned, raven-haired young woman who immediately caught the eye of the young men. The count took his place at the head of the table, the beautiful woman to his right.

In his best sotto voce Spanish, Jack exclaimed, "¡Santa María! ¡Qué pinta trae la niña!" ending with a low laugh.

"In my limited knowledge of Spanish, I would say that you spoke of the Godlike qualities of yonder fair maiden," Paul said, sneaking a look at their victim across the table. "But I wonder if you know truly of what you speak?"

"No, I know not of what I speak, but I would like to," Jack said with a grin.

"These are universal thoughts you are thinking, my young friend. But I was wondering if you were aware of the reference in your elegant quote to the highly regarded explorer and discoverer of our homeland, Christopher Columbus?"

"You speak of exploring in the New Land?" Jack asked. "This I could understand. You're aware of the roundness of the earth, of globes dancing in the heavens, of valleys of delight, yes. I can see what you mean—she is a delightful bocadito."

"Little mouthful, yes—I see—but, no—what I meant was that 'Santa María' means Holy Mary. The 'pinta' means the fine look of, and the 'niña' I suppose means young girl?" He thought for a moment. "Or I suppose it could describe various objects on a person's body or—well, never mind. I can see that you're smitten and in no mood for philosophizing."

When Jack's attention was finally diverted from the beauty by his mother's melancholy face, he silently mouthed to her, "Are you all right?"

Pilar nodded a hesitant yes.

The attendants cleared the appetizers from the table and served a steaming soup of conejo en salsa sabrosa. The party seemed to be progressing well, the guests savoring the splendid food. The rabbit soup was taken from the table and replaced with succulent roast pig. Portions were large, and the juice flowed over the sides of the delicate china plates.

The count again tapped against a wineglass to gain the attention of the guests. Rising, he proclaimed, "I would like to propose a toast not only to our new friends—and old ones alike—but also to the king, Habana, Cuba, and to the glorious Caribbean!"

There were choruses of "hear hears" and murmured "amens." They all hoisted their glasses and drank, except Pilar, who brought her glass to her lips but, Jack noticed, didn't swallow.

"To the economy of this powerful country that has increased threefold in the last ten years!" the count shouted. The guests tipped their glasses once again and, emptying them, had them refilled. "And to our good fortune in acquiring foreign workers, without whom our abundant cane fields would lie fallow." Again, an outbreak of agreement and lifted glasses.

Paul, upper lip quivering, fixed his gaze on the plate before him. Jack could see trouble brewing. Paul waited for the noise to abate, then turned to the count, speaking in a steady, cultured voice.

"Excuse me, sir. May I commend you for your eloquence and panache? However, I am baffled."

The count sat, his attention drifting to Paul. "You don't look baffled, you look lost and unsure. Relax, young sir. Eat, drink, and be merry, for tomorrow we die."

Paul put both hands on his glass of wine. "Ecclesiastes and Isaiah."

The count took this in. "The Bible is many things, young sir. Poetry, prose, fables, truths, untruths, and more. One's perception of it is sometimes faulty."

"Yes, sir, but hope springs eternal in the human breast." Paul took a deep breath.

"Meaning?"

"That I am always optimistic about the human condition, sir."

"Go on."

"That when the English poet Alexander Pope wrote that passage, I am sure he meant many things. I mean, sir, that in the context of your toast I would hope that a learned man such as yourself would speak the truth."

A muscle pulsed in the count's jaw as he smiled, revealing to Jack a concerted effort on the dandy's part to hold his anger in check. Jack could see the count was unaccustomed at being spoken to so directly—especially by one so young.

He could also see that Paul was determined to engage this egotist in a debate. Jack was vaguely aware that Paul was in trouble, but smitten as he was by the Latin beauty across from him, gave only a desultory kick to Paul's shins when he felt he was being too brave.

"You speak of the truth as if it were your own special province." The count, although still amused, seemed intent and much on guard. "I would say this to you, niño: you are too young to speak so frankly to me. But I am a man of patience and if you think I speak not the truth, I would only say I disapprove of what you think. But I would defend to the death your right to think it."

The large party was slowly becoming aware of the contretemps starting toward the head of the table. Polite talk continued but people began ignoring their partners, intrigued by the match between the count and the upstart youngster.

"I don't understand, sir." Paul, sitting a little taller, squeezed Jack's leg to get him to listen.

"A French writer whose name I have forgotten and is of little import"—the count smiled wickedly—"explained that he would defend to the death the people's right to think as they please. To be more specific, you may think as you please, young sir. And I would defend it." The count gained some in volume and, looking around him, proceeded to put a cap on the conversation. He cupped his hands to his mouth as if to whisper. "But keep it to yourself."

The crowd laughed and applauded gently, seeming to relax.

Pilar's untouched food was whisked away and replaced by fried plantain and dark rich coffee. Jack caught her staring dismally at her dessert.

When the dinner was finished, the men adjourned to the candlelit garden to smoke their cigars.

"I am surprised, sir." Paul walked up to the count with Jack.

De Silva turned to confront this annoying youngster. "Is this a bee I see before me? Is this a wasp continuing to buzz? Surprised? I would think one so versed in the ways of life would be beyond surprise."

The men gathered in the garden, savoring the prospect of the upcoming exchange.

"No, sir, I'm always surprised when learned men misquote to serve their own purposes. For you to dismiss Voltaire as 'of little import' is no mean surprise; but most shockingly, you incorrectly paraphrased one of the great men of letters. Voltaire wrote that he disagreed with what someone else had written. Not thought. But would defend his right to write it."

Jack moved next to him, grinning benignly.

"Quite a difference, wouldn't you say?" Paul continued. The count nodded imperceptibly, not in agreement, but more as if making a decision about someone's fate. Pausing only briefly, Paul continued.

"If I've embarrassed you, sir, please forgive me. But getting back to my original question. I'm baffled at why you would use the term 'foreign workers' toiling this land when in fact it is a euphemism for slaves—pure and simple."

The count stood calmly, fingering a small pendant hanging around his neck. There was a stirring; most of the men looked as if they would like to thrash Paul and could have done so quite easily. One of the count's compadres moved swiftly in front of the young man.

"Your impudence, young man, is exceeded only by your tattered clothing," the count said. "If you were just a bit older and larger, I'd cut an epitaph in your chest and send you home to your mamá."

Paul seemed unperturbed, but Jack knew his friend was trapped. He could see Paul wanted to engage this man in a debate about which he felt deeply, but had succeeded only in making those around the count angry with him, to say nothing of the count himself. The fact that de Silva had misquoted a great author seemed of little consequence. Jack thought any further confrontation at this point might endanger his family's relationship to the count. Maybe it was time to repair relations and call it an evening.

Paul may have come to the same conclusion. He smiled at his adversary and took a step back. "Count de Silva, may I just say the following: 'Men of means who use their wealth well will have sown the harvest of prosperity for all.' I am a guest in your home and I have been well served. Thank you and good night."

Paul turned with Jack and they proceeded to leave the garden.

"Wait just a moment, little one." The count lit his cigar and stood relaxed. "Who wrote that last quote? I'm not familiar with it."

"Paul Le Maire. Cuba. Eighteen five," Paul answered, without looking back.

Jack and Paul joined Ethan and Pilar.

At the end of the evening the count stationed himself at the door to bid farewell to his guests. As the O'Reillys approached, he bowed graciously.

"Would you be so kind as to wait just a few moments until the other guests have left? I'd have a word with you." Jack observed the smoothness of the count's manner. He was repulsed; there was little except his title to distinguish him from his father's detractors in Hamden. But he could only stand patiently with his parents in the great hall, watching Paul make his way through the mass of people toward the count's well-stocked library, adjacent to the hall.

The exit from de Silva's villa seemed to be delayed by a young man, explaining to anyone who would listen how he was bringing ice in insulated ships into Cuba and other ports in the Caribbean. The guests were being polite, but most were anxious to leave.

Jack could see Paul still in the library; his back to him, hunched over what was probably some classic book. Jack called to him. Paul half turned and held up one finger to his mouth, then continued his quest. Finally, except for the O'Reillys, Paul, and the count, the great hall was empty.

"I'm so sorry to detain you like this, but something has arisen that is out of my control. There are many papers you will need to review and sign relating to your father's estate," the count said.

The O'Reillys stood waiting apprehensively.

"Normally they would take two or three days to facilitate. I've just received news that this will probably not be the case."

"But what is it that would take longer?" Pilar interrupted. "We understood the papers were in order."

"It seems it's more complicated than that, and may take several weeks. There seems to be some question about the deeds to your land. Nothing to worry about. It is my suggestion that you stay in Habana until the papers are put right. You are welcome to stay in my home as long as you deem necessary."

Paul rejoined them to overhear their last exchange. Had Paul gone too far in his baiting of the count? Jack wondered. It had been great fun, but there was still a lot to be settled between the count and his mother. Jack watched the count to see if the announcement of the delay was related in any way to the evening's events; to Jack's way of thinking it didn't seem to be.

Jack could tell his parents were puzzled at the news. With a certain resignation, the two thanked the count but stood awkwardly, unwilling to leave. Jack's unease about this man escalated, and he sensed his mother was wary, too. Although the nobleman appeared calm, Jack felt he was maneuvering them somehow.

"We are all pleased to accept your hospitality," his mother said. "We would like to visit Matanzas Province tomorrow. I wish to see the land for myself. Would you arrange a carriage for us?"

The count seemed distracted as he walked them to the door. "Your carriage as the cock crows, señora?"

"Seven A.M. will be adequate, gracias."

"Since it has been many years since you have seen the finca, may I provide you with a map?" Pilar nodded her thanks. With a snap of his fingers at a servant standing by, the count ordered pen and paper. On the large table in the foyer, he quickly sketched a map, pausing only briefly toward the end before scratching an X on the wavy line of the diagram. "Excuse this crude article, but I think it will suffice."

The count handed Jack the map. "Would you please hold this for your parents, señor?"

"Of course, with pleasure."

De Silva then turned to Paul. "Will you be accompanying the O'Reillys on their journey tomorrow?

"No, that will not be my pleasure. I must continue my duties on the *Perdido Star*," Paul answered simply.

"Pity." The count grinned. To Pilar and Ethan he said, "Your carriage is here. I shall see you back at the villa shortly." The couple nodded and made their exit, the two young men following.

During the ride back, Jack heard his father ask Pilar, "Why so thoughtful, dear? We will be guests in this house of plenty and we are on the eve of seeing your old homestead. And best of all," he stated facetiously, "I'm on the verge of becoming a farmer. Working in the fledgling red cane fields from dawn to dusk. Plowing out an existence for my beautiful Pilar with the help of my willful son. Before long, the crops will be yielding a rich return."

He abruptly ended his halfhearted attempt at humor, for his wife was weeping softly. "It is nothing, my love," she said. "I am tired from the long trip."

❧ ✳ ❧

As the carriage came to a halt in front of the great doors of the villa, Jack asked Paul, "What do you say we take a stroll before heading to bed and troubled dreams?"

"Dreams are the stuff of life. Troubled or calm, it takes all kinds to be fulfilled."

"Paul and I are going to walk awhile," Jack told his father.

"Don't be long," answered Ethan, as he helped his wife out of the coach. They bid farewell to Paul and went into the house.

The two young men walked in silence. "Do you think I went too far tonight?" Paul finally asked.

"Maybe a little. The count strikes me as dangerous. Still, that puffed up jackanape needed taking down a notch or two."

There was a wonderful peace about the deserted streets. An occasional dog bayed in the distance. A window clicked nearby, closing against the cool night air. The moon cast a soft light over the white buildings, melting them into the cobblestone street. They were both lost in the night's events and failed to hear the whistle of the wind as two heavy boards struck them on the back of their heads.

Paul bowed at the waist then plowed face first into the street. Jack spun with the blow, instinct sending him crashing into the door of a shop, his hands protecting his face from another strike he knew was coming—he could hear Paul's cry from the ground and wondered how badly his friend was hurt. The man who hit Jack immediately took another swing and missed; Jack caught the man's coat sleeve and twisted his arm quickly around in back of him. With a scream of pain, the man was forced to his knees. Using his free hand, Jack slapped him violently across his ear. The second assailant tried to swing at Jack without striking his fellow assassin.

Jack kicked out blindly and caught the man squarely in the groin. The attacker dropped his weapon and bent over, retching. Both men stumbled away in the dark street.

Jack caught up to the larger of the two men. "You're a clumsy fool," he hissed in his ear. "If you're to survive as a thief, you must learn your trade."

He spun the man around and with a resounding boot in the rear, sent him scurrying. The second man, his hands still dug deeply into his crotch, limped down the street; he looked back occasionally, shouting empty threats. When Jack took a couple of steps toward him, he dropped his belligerent attitude and hobbled after his vanishing partner. Paul sat up, blood streaming down his face.

"Are you all right?" Jack asked.

"Yes, of course. I've never felt better." Paul breathed through swollen lips, rocking back and forth in a great deal of pain.

"I'm going to lift you. Are your ribs hurt?"

"No. Just my face, head, and pride."

Jack helped Paul into a standing position. "Well, my friend, if you think you can make it, I'll walk you back to the *Star*."

They started slowly toward the waterfront.

"It was a fine evening," Jack said. "We've dined grandly, had an eyeful of beautiful women, a lively exchange with a count, and, best of all, been set upon by a pair of incompetent thieves."

"I'd agree," Paul said, cheering up. "The food was fine, the wine delicate, the women breathtaking, and the count a worthy adversary." He brushed the dripping blood from his nose. "But those weren't thieves. Someone sent them to shut my uncontrollable mouth."

"That seems a particularly violent attack just for an argument." Jack looked quickly up the street; the ruffians had long since disappeared.

Paul rubbed a spot on the back of his head. "In any case, I think we can agree that the count doesn't take well to differences of opinion."

Jack wondered if the count was responsible for this. If so, what else might he attempt in the weeks to come? He suddenly wondered if his parents had made it to the villa safely.

The two friends stopped at an intersection. They could see the *Star*'s bow peeking from behind a building at the end of the street. Paul drew up his shirt and brought out two small books, tucked in by his belt.

"I realize you've never read a book, O unlearned one, but the next time I see you, I'm going to quiz you on these."

Jack brought the two books close to the lamplight: *Paradise Lost* and *The Pilgrim's Progress*. "*Paradise Lost* was required reading in school last year but I spent so much time helping Pa with the rifles that I never finished it." He kicked a rock down the cobbled street, the noise reverberating off the buildings. "I envy you, Paul, sailing away so blissfully. A part of me wishes I were going with you."

"We'll probably be shoving off in a day or two." Paul looked down, reluctant to go on. "I hate repeated good-byes, so why don't we say our adieus now. I'm sure I've created enough tension between your family and the count so the less I'm seen around the Hacienda del Bull Droppings the better. You've been a good friend. As for my sailing away, I, in fact, envy you, old friend—starting a new life with people whom you have nothing in common with, working in the fields as a laborer from sunup to sundown. Feeling the rich earth in your hands, shoes, hair, and down the back of your neck . . . yes, I truly envy you. I, of course, will enjoy none of that. I'll be slaving away on some exotic South Sea island, being fanned by naked maidens as I weave baskets and drink coconut milk."

"Nos divertimos como locos!" Jack laughed.

"Yes, a crazy time we've had, indeed. Au revoir."

"Vaya con Dios."

Paul ambled down the street toward the *Star*, Jack

toward the villa. Jack clasped the two books to his hip. It had been a wonderful gesture on Paul's part. He wondered when Paul had the time to buy these books—then it came to him in an instant. That little thief! He stopped and laughed. Paul stole these from the count's library! Jack turned to shout at him but he had disappeared.

Jack moved onto the street that led to the count's house and heard a sound in a doorway. A dark figure sitting in a narrow doorway and wearing filthy clothes sat on the floor swaying and mumbling.

"Pardon?" Jack stopped to listen.

"No viene hoy sino mañana."

"Who's coming? ¿Quién?"

"Jesús."

The figure continued to sway back and forth and Jack walked slowly away. After a dozen strides, he heard the words "¡Cuidado, mi amigo!"

"¿Cuidado?" Jack called back. " 'Careful' is my middle name, señor." His mouth seemed suddenly dry.

5

THE ROAD TO
MATANZAS

WITH THE COUNT'S map in hand, Jack watched from his perch next to the driver as the surefooted Andalusian horses negotiated the ruts on the lonely road. The ripe scent of Cuba hung in the air. A brief rain had turned to steam and thickened the atmosphere; the fragrance of a multitude of tropical fruits and flowers—jasmine, mango, papaya—mingled with the smell of rich, wet earth.

Jack's parents jounced below him in the carriage, the sound of his father's voice occasionally trailing through the closed roof. He marveled at his mother's patience. She did not, he knew, share the depth of her uneasiness with her husband, but Jack had seen the dark rings under her eyes this morning. His father appeared oblivious to the fact she hadn't slept; instead, he maintained his conviction that legal delays were not that uncommon and there was no need for concern.

Well, perhaps he's right, Jack thought. Cuba was civilized, if not civil. Law was strictly maintained in the colony, at least for the privileged. Jack had the sense the authority might even be oppressive. If the count was up to any chicanery, the proper authorities would probably, as his father felt, set it straight. What was it his father loved to speak of in those New England town meetings? Rightful authority; aye, the blind justice of law, not privilege. Time would tell.

Jack decided to sit back and absorb the countryside.

Talk of property and taxes and money held his attention just so long when there was raw life to be enjoyed. But these sights were driven from his mind by the sudden memory—nay, vision—of red hair, blowing over a face with laughing green eyes.

The driver, a grizzled man, caught the smile playing over Jack's lips. "Sí. ¿Es muy bonito, no?"

Startled the man could read his thoughts, Jack replied, "¿Qué dijiste?"

The old man gestured toward the landscape, remarking on the low hills, the reds and greens. Low soft hills indeed—red hair over a full bodice of soft hills. God, he longed to melt under the gaze of those eyes. "Sí. Es muy, muy, muy bonito."

The old man chuckled. Jack realized the man could recognize the symptoms of a lad who had been "struck by lightning," as they put it in the old country. Just then, he spotted a stone marker on the side of the road, the number 27 engraved on it in blue.

"Pare por favor, señor. ¿Es aquí, no?"

The man slowed the rig. "Aiee, es la finca."

"What's that, Jack? Why are we stopping?" Ethan's voice from below.

"This map, it shows that marker as the northern boundary. . . . I believe we're here, Father. All the fields on the right for the next mile and a half should be mother's estate."

Ethan stepped from the carriage. "Our land." He took in the rolling fields of black-tipped green. "Beautiful. Come, my dearest, and look at our future, shining before us." He walked several steps ahead, hardly able to contain himself.

Jack felt a sudden chill pass through him. The cane! He hopped down from the seat and had his fears confirmed by the look on his mother's face; she had moved back from the window. Her hand was over her mouth, her face white.

"Mother!"

"Jack," she said evenly. "Get back on the carriage and tell the driver to turn around. I . . . I want to go back to town."

"But Mother—"

She leaned forward and said in a hoarse voice, with an intensity he had never seen, "The cane is mature, Jack. I grew up around cane. It has been so for many years." Pilar lay back as Ethan approached, but her eyes remained fixed on her son's.

"Jack, we were lied to. I am frightened. For now we will tell your father only that I am ill and must return."

Jack placed his hand on hers.

"Don't worry, Mother, it will be all right, it—" He reached through the carriage window, squeezed her hand hard and turned. He couldn't lie to her. He too was frightened. Frightened and something else. He felt rage building.

His family had been cheated again, perhaps over a period of many years. His mother had been led to believe that the cane fields had lain fallow and were just recently being nurtured toward a mature, harvestable crop. Somebody had been profiting from these fields for a long time. Somebody powerful, he thought. Worse, whoever had defrauded her would now see her as a threat. De Silva? But why would he have facilitated them seeing the finca? Jack's head spun with confusion. The rich aromas that had captured him this morning suddenly seemed sour, overripe.

When Ethan returned to his wife, she explained to him her need to return to her room. Jack sat staring darkly at the fields. The driver said they would be able to turn around at the copse of trees ahead. Until then, the road was elevated, deep berms running along each side to catch water. Jack left his parents to climb topside, next to the driver. The man must have felt the dramatic change of mood in his young passenger, but he said nothing.

They had covered no more than a hundred yards when riders came into view ahead of them. Jack watched the driver slip his hand under the seat, making sure his pistola was available. It seemed a perfunctory precaution; although highwaymen could be a concern this far from Habana, they had been assured the guardia had suppressed banditry in the area.

As the distance between them narrowed, Jack saw the old man return the weapon to its holster and visibly relax. The men were now easily recognizable in their blue and red uniforms. Guardia civil. They drew up next to the carriage.

"Buenos días." A mustachioed sergeant carried the crisp air of authority.

"Buenos días, Sargento. ¿Cómo está usted?"

The soldiers' official manner made Jack uneasy; they seemed particularly aloof, less like protectors of the people and more like keepers. He heard his father open the carriage door.

"Buenos días, Sargento, is there a problem . . . uh ¿un problema?" Jack knew Ethan had exhausted his repertoire of Spanish, but he insisted in asserting himself as head of the household.

"No, no problema, señor. Sargento Matros at your service." Then to the driver, "¿Quién es?"

"El caballero y la señora son norteamericanos." The old driver began to explain that his passengers were the owners of the estate to the right of the road when Jack's father once again interjected.

"We are the O'Reillys, Sergeant. My wife is the owner of all that you see to the east."

The man was looking at a piece of paper in his hand. "Sí, Sí . . . bueno eh, su nombre . . . uh, yore name es O'Reilly, sí? Y los otros, uh, yore wife es name Pilar? And yore—"

Jack stiffened. His father continued in his proud, affable exchange with the man; he seemed not at all curious that a civil patrol leader would happen to know his wife's Christian name.

"Yes, Sergeant, my wife, Pilar, and my son, Jack, recently of New England. We are delighted to see that you and your men are patrolling these roads. We've heard much of the . . . eh . . . bandidos."

"Sí, bandidos." The sergeant directed his words to Ethan but kept his eyes on Jack. If trouble came, he seemed to realize, Jack would be the source. Finally, he turned back to Ethan. "Bienvenidos, Señor y Señora O'Reilly, bienvenidos a Cuba."

"Gracias," Ethan said, smiling.

"Vámanos." The sergeant waved his hand as if to lead his men on, but, without looking toward them, he signaled the soldiers who had moved behind Jack on the right side of the carriage.

Jack had done everything he could to act natural, but he knew the sergeant had become wary. His friends in New England had said Jack's eyes told his emotions and they joked about not wanting to be on the receiving end of one of his "looks." When the sergeant made his gesture to the men behind him, Jack didn't need to react; his body simply uncoiled like a tightly wound spring. He heard a saber swish and chunk into the wood of the seat behind him as he rolled on top of the driver, never looking back at his assailant.

His instincts told him the blow was coming from behind, but they told him too that the brain of the beast was the sergeant. Jack saw the old driver assume a terrified, hands-over-head crouch. He was blocking access to the pistol, so Jack used what was available. Leaping up, he thrust his foot toward the officer's hip where it pounded into his left thigh, causing him to jerk violently and the horse to spin so swiftly that he was thrown to the ground. Jack himself lost his balance and went careening into the mud, only a few yards from the taller officer. "Have you gone crazy?" Ethan yelled. Jack knew his father had seen none of what transpired outside the carriage. Jack shouted from where he'd landed in the mud. "Go, Father! Take Mother! They're no good!"

"What! For God's sake, Jack, they're constables—" His father was trying to scramble out of the carriage when his wife screamed to him to come back inside and bring Jack with him.

Other soldiers were trying to approach Jack but he managed to raise himself up and bounded back to the carriage ladder. "¡Andale! ¡Andale!" he shouted to the driver. When he jumped back to the ground, he held the oaken handle that served as the lever for the carriage brake. The four-foot piece of wood with a fashioned grip had rested loose in its retainer and Jack had easily yanked it from its metal boot.

A young soldier who flanked the sergeant had unsheathed his saber, advancing on Jack. A moment's hesitation gave Jack the opportunity to step to the soldier's left and bring the plank down solidly on the soft muzzle of his horse. The creature jumped back, whinnying in pain. Jack crashed the board down violently on the arm of another soldier, leaping to the side and slashing about in the manner of a two-handed swordsman. Another of the steeds made a high-pitched sound and threw its rider when Jack smashed its left hind hock.

Pandemonium ensued among the mounted men. The young man with the flashing dark eyes had transformed himself into a demon, flailing in rage. Fighting like a cornered tiger, Jack was vaguely aware the carriage had started to move; he could hear his father's voice railing against the tide of hooves and men. "See here, damn it all, that's my son! Leave him be! Driver!"

Two of the guardia civil had fallen in a heap. Jack

had forgotten about the sergeant and a second later buckled over, reeling from a punch to the head from behind with what he guessed to be the hilt of a sword. When he turned to confirm, he took the brunt of a steel-banded fist, this time in the face. In Spanish or English—he couldn't sort it out—it came to the same thing: the sergeant had yelled to his comrades, "Kill the dog! Throw his stinking carcass in the ditch. You others, come with me."

Jack was aware that most of the men were riding off after the carriage. The ones he had injured were left to dispose of him. He felt one of them pull him to his feet. The man moaning on the horse, his arm hanging limply from its socket, screamed for his comrades to gouge his eyes and slice off his balls. The one who held him yelled for the other to shut up. Coldly, he said to the man on the ground, "Gut him and be done with it."

Spanish—it was clearly Spanish they were speaking. Jack had the curious thought that he preferred to be killed in English. He knew he was soaked in blood, from the back of his head and face. Still, he had gathered himself for another assault on his attackers when he was suddenly propelled forward by the man holding him. He looked up in time to see the other's sword swing in a vicious backhanded arc and lodge in his side. The man looked him in the eye as he followed through, drawing the sword backward in a long cutting motion. Jack felt himself spin with the retreating blade and felt another man's boot kick him squarely in the back. The water-filled ditch rose to meet him and he blacked out.

When he came to he knew only seconds could have passed, since the men were still talking about him. The man on the horse argued that his friends should at least cut Jack's throat if they wouldn't bring back his balls. Jack knew he was moments from death anyway and hoped it would happen before the screamer had his way. The others told their associate to shut up and bear his pain like a man; they didn't need to crawl in a ditch to cut the throat of a pig they had just gutted. "Let him water the soil with his blood. Let him die slowly."

No! Wait, goddamn it! My life ... it's just starting, this can't be my time to die. And these mustachioed, pinch-faced bastards ... Who's going to avenge? ... no, this can't be right.

Jack faintly heard them move off. How long does it take to die with one's entrails in one's hands? he thought. The image of what might be happening to his mother stirred him to regain a sitting position. He looked down at the bloody mess that was his side and shivered, remembering the sound the sword had made as it sliced along his midsection. Fiercely clutching his side, he tried to rise. Oh God! He was falling apart, wide slivers of red and white flesh were peeling off him like the pages of a book. He didn't understand—he had been sliced only once. And then he realized that they *were* the pages of a book, and his heart rose in exalta- tion. *The Pilgrim's Progress* had taken the brunt of the sword.

The realization that death was less imminent than he had imagined spurred Jack on. His parents! Breathing heavily, he packed a wad of the most blood-soaked and pliable pages of the book into the deepest part of the cut on his torso. Then he wrapped his tattered shirt around his middle to hold the makeshift dressing in place. Although weakened almost to the point of immo- bility, he was satisfied to see the loss of blood essentially stanched. Covered with mud, he continued pursuit of the carriage, staying in the drainage ditch that hugged the side of the road.

"See, you bastards haven't killed me. I knew it couldn't be." Jack spoke to himself in gasps. "If you hurt my par- ents ... so help me Christ, touched my mother ... Jesus,

Jesus, Jesus, I've got to walk . . . they can't see me in this ditch."

After about fifty paces, Jack spotted a bundle ahead and above him on the edge of the roadway. He reached for it hoping it might be a sack discarded from the carriage in the melee, containing something he could use as a weapon. It was the badly mangled body of a man. Gathering himself, he took a chance on being spotted from the roadway and raised himself to almost his full six-foot height to determine who it was and if he still lived. It was his father. Dead.

"What . . . have they done? No!" Jack tried to scream but the words emerged as a croak.

Fighting conflicting urges to hold his father close and push him away in horror, Jack could only stare as the image burned into the back of his brain. He couldn't determine the nature of Ethan's wounds, but it was irrelevant. His father's lifeless eyes stared at him, half questioning, half accusing. He pulled his father's hand to him and kissed it. In desperate anger he spoke softly, "Father, you have your wish. You have finally been listened to by rightful authority. Look—it has reached out to you."

Jack's mind blurred in a kaleidoscope of images: his father speaking at town meetings, his pathetic search for justice from distinguished-looking gentlemen who smirked behind his back. In Cuba injustice was not so subtle. Here the privileged cut you down in cold steel. His killers had parodied his naive faith by obscenely butchering him in front of his wife.

After closing his father's eyes, he forced himself to continue, as if in a nightmare, to where the carriage had rolled to a stop. They must have overpowered the driver, Jack thought. Voices rose from not far away.

Jack arrived at the trees the driver had evidently been heading for, and struggled to a concealed position, where he commanded a full view of what was transpiring.

The sergeant and soldiers were gathered about his mother, clearly visible only fifty feet before him. Slumped over the driver's seat next to where she stood was the body of the old man. "You bastards from hell," Jack murmured. "God give me the strength to kill you all."

The sergeant was apparently bickering with his men. They were talking about how they might take their pleasure with her before snuffing her life like she was a piece of meat.

My mother, you pigs! The woman who pulled me to her warmth a thousand times when I was hurt or frightened. You are talking about my mother.

A soldier grabbed Pilar by the hair and pulled her in the direction of Jack.

She was almost unconscious. The shock of seeing her husband killed and the sure knowledge that the same had happened to her son must have devastated her. The soldier released her from his grip just yards from where Jack was concealed. She sank to her knees, staring vacantly ahead, murmuring what Jack knew were prayers.

Though semidelirious, Jack had the presence of mind not to move. Even covered with mud and leaves in the bushes, he could still be spotted if someone looked his way. His eyes flitted about him in search of a rock, a stick, anything to use as a weapon.

The guardia were in disagreement over what to do with her. Some of them begged the sergeant to have some time with her "over the barrel." They had already pulled the water cask off the carriage for that purpose, but the sergeant forbade them. "I have my orders and they don't include that," he snapped to one of the men who had started to tear off her bodice.

Jack was powerless. He prayed for strength but God seemed to favor him no more than had the guardia civil. The group quieted as another carriage suddenly appeared from the opposite direction. Through eyes lanced with despair, he saw a man emerge and advance to the sergeant. "¿Qué pasó, en nombre de diablo, qué pasó?" The man was dressed in an elegant waistcoat and flowing cape.

"Nada, Señor de Silva. Es finito, todos estan muertos, solamente ella—" The sergeant pointed to Jack's mother as the only unfinished business.

Jack's limbs weighed him down. He couldn't act to save his own mother! He was nearly paralyzed, but his mind still worked well enough to put things in place. The map, the list of names, the fresh wagon ruts in the road—de Silva had planned all this!

"God in heaven hear me," Jack murmured. "You worthless Savior, I'll forgive you everything if you just give me a blunderbuss and the strength to use it."

His mother stopped praying and in wonderment stared directly into Jack's eyes. He saw her slowly come to the recognition that her son was alive. The joy in her face was beyond description, as was something else following it—determination, cold fury, the look of a she-wolf given back a lost chance to protect her young. Jack sensed for the first time that although his physical strength might have come from his father, something deeper had been bequeathed to him from this woman. He felt she was willing, ordering her pup to remain still.

"So, Señora O'Reilly, you are enjoying your morning ride?" De Silva had come to her side. She stared at him with such fury that he turned away in Jack's direction. Suddenly she pushed herself to her feet. Jack watched her purposefully complete the rip in her bodice. Her breasts fell out in full view of the count and all the men.

They stood transfixed by her nakedness as she raised her hand to the count's cheek as in supplication.

"Ah, my dear lady, you enchant me, but alas—"

Pilar pushed her forefinger into the count's left eye. His scream reverberated in the woods.

Taken totally by surprise, the sergeant jumped forward, grabbed Pilar around her waist, and threw her to the ground. He placed his foot on her back, her face once again pointed toward Jack, though he was hidden several yards away. The sergeant pulled her head back by the hair and pulled his dagger.

"No!" screamed the count. Clutching his eye in agony, he shuffled over to her. Jack watched the apparition pull his own knife and shove it into his dear mother's throat. He heard the rip of flesh and saw her fall, face first, to the ground. For the last time she stared at her son, life draining from her. He saw in her eyes a flash of what could only be triumph. Triumph and love. Then her eyes glazed over.

━┥ ✵ ┝━

He must have been unconscious, he knew not for how long. When he opened his eyes, the road ahead of him was empty; no mother, no guardia—of course, a dream. Yet he knew in his heart it wasn't. There was the blood-caked dirt in front of him. He tried to move but pain shot through him; but he was stronger than before and struggled to his feet.

Must go, but where? He felt some discomfort in his left, uninjured side. It was—he started to laugh. Well, how about that for symbol, Paul? *The Pilgrim's Progress* has been struck down, so what was left? *Paradise Lost*, of course. The laughing took his strength and he fainted again.

Some unknown time later he came awake and searched inside himself for strength. He rose, started to walk, began staggering through the forest, the fields. The cane cut him in a hundred places but he was barely cognizant of anything but the burning in his side. He knew only to head for Habana. Paul. Maybe he could reach the *Perdido Star*.

6

RETURN TO
THE *STAR*

"LAY-MAR, Paulie Lay-Mar. You're needed on deck ole chum. Hee-hee. Your presence is awaited, and even called for."

It was Ole Hansumbob's voice, calling out among his sleeping shipmates. "Your name drifts through the night. Paulie, arise, wherever you are."

Grumbling and sharp words shot back from the darkness. But Ole Bob was impervious.

"Over here, you idiot." Paul was awake and not in good spirits. "What is it? Am I on watch? What time is it? And the name is Le Maire. Le Maire."

"The time is nigh, and your watch is at least close enough, and I swear I hear your name a driftin' like the gulls in the mist. I thought I'd call you to work, it seemed a sign. A sign, lad."

Paul had no idea what Hansumbob was talking about; but it seemed pointless to argue. He slipped on his soft shoes, thin coat, and hat, and started topside.

A light rain dampened Habana, but not her spirits. The decks of the *Star* glistened and a northerly tropical breeze kept the old ship tugging gently at her tethers.

Paul gazed at the city night. He had grown accustomed to life aboard ship and had in fact begun to enjoy these quiet hours on watch. It gave him time to contemplate. He had sent word to his father in Virginia via clipper ship that he was safe, a curt note that displayed neither anger nor love.

The night passed slowly. A distant guitar plucked a woeful song as taverns along the waterfront began to darken. Sailors and women of the night kept company, drifting along the streets. There were arguments; several drunks were helped by shipmates to find their proper billets.

Paul's lids felt heavy. His thoughts grew confused and he was on the verge of drifting off when he thought he heard his name. Hansumbob was right! Instantly awake, he scanned the expanse of the ship. There was no one on deck. The sound of his name had been his own protective device, he decided, to keep him awake. A way God had of looking out for young sailors who lapsed easily into their civilian ways.

A mist came in from the bay, obscuring the waterfront. The few figures left on the cobblestone street floated ghostlike, feet seemingly off the ground. Paul's eyes stopped at a bent figure, standing still in the road. The man had not moved for what seemed like minutes; another drunkard, Paul figured.

He decided to make his obligatory tour of the ship, making sure the lines were secure, nothing had come adrift. The watch at night was mostly for protection from thieves, not really maintenance of the ship; as long as her bilges were regularly pumped, she'd probably float proud at the dockside for years to come left unattended. But inspection was one of the laws of the sea. His shoes padded on the wet decks as he checked each mooring line along the starboard side.

A clock struck four, reverberating from several blocks away. The night was about to lose its battle with day.

Leaning his elbows on the damp rail, Paul gazed sleepily over the bay. In another three hours the ship would come alive. Today, at last, they would set sail, catching the morning tide and making their way south around Cape Horn, then west to the South Pacific. The thought of adventure stirred him, and he shook off his stupor.

"Paul."

Again his name. Now he knew it was not his imagination. He looked out into the fog. The figure he had seen earlier had dropped to the ground. He was calling weakly, one hand at his side, the other holding his face just inches from the street. "Paul."

"Jesus Christ! Jack!"

Springing down the gangplank, Paul bolted toward his friend, prostrate on the cobblestones.

"Are you drunk? Or is it just tired you are, and find this filthy street a comfort?" Paul was amused.

No answer. Only heavy labored breathing.

"All right, me laddy. I'll just get you to your feet and walk you around a bit to sober you up."

Paul started to lift Jack when he felt a sticky wetness. Even in the dark, Paul could see Jack's shirt was torn across the front, that the stickiness was blood.

"Jack, wake up, man. What is it? What happened?"

"Ship," Jack mumbled.

"What?"

"Get me aboard."

"We've got to get a doctor for you. There's bound to be one awake. You've a cut across your stomach—and deep."

"No doctor. Just get me aboard."

"Why?"

"Please. Hide me."

"Jack. We're sailing at first light. You need a doctor."

Jack looked at Paul directly for the first time. His eyes were bloodshot; his skin hot and clammy. There were dried cuts on his face and caked dirt around his mouth. But Paul could see gratitude in his friend's look, and his own heart beat a welcome.

"Don't worry," he said. "I'll help you."

For three days the *Perdido Star* sailed along the northern shore of Cuba, making her way toward Cabo Maisi where she could bear south to the Jamaican channels and the Caribbean Sea.

Since their departure, the mates paid scant attention to the very sick stowaway Paul had been tending to between his own duties. But Paul knew it was only a matter of time before one of the officers became aware of this unwanted extra hand.

Jack's fever broke on the fourth day and, although unable to keep down solid food, he sipped some of Paul's porridge ration and a great deal of water. Paul hadn't been able to get a coherent story from Jack. He worried that, with the island of Cuba slipping away, Jack's parents would be concerned for him.

"I see you used my book to fine purpose," Paul said when he knew Jack could understand. "Good words have always been known to save a soul." He hesitated. "I think it's time you told me about this wound in your side. You've been gone four days and I'm sure your parents are sick with worry."

Jack remained silent, staring blankly.

"Listen to me. You can't just sail away like this without telling your parents something."

Jack turned to look at his friend. His eyes were clear for the first time in days. "I can't tell them, Paul."

"Of course you can. They'd understand. Just be forthright."

"You don't understand. I can't tell them—because they're dead."

Paul slumped to the floor of the fo'c'sle. He sat as if dead himself, unable to speak. His breathing became labored; he felt as if he himself had been slashed. "I—I—just saw them. But how—"

Jack turned away, back to his silent staring.

Paul made his way on deck, taking deep breaths. There seemed to be only one thing to do. Reveal Jack's presence to one of the officers, or possibly the bosun, or the first mate, and ask for help.

Mr. Quince seemed to be the fairest man of authority on board. Still, it was with great trepidation that Paul approached him and brought him down to see his sick friend.

Quince's huge stomach pressed tight against Jack's second-tier bunk.

"You look like death's cousin, wee Jack," he said, his tone compassionate. "Your color's gone and you smell of last year's dead dog. You'll be over the side if the captain gets wind of ya."

Jack eyed the first mate's girth. "Do your worst sailor," he replied. "I'll be swimming alongside this leaky tub long after you've been wrapped, stuffed, and weighted for your last bath."

Quince stared for a second, shocked, then laughed so hard he had to hold onto Jack's berth.

"I'll do what I can, Jackson." He paused. "I think that's what I heard your mother call ya. I'll do what I can with the captain. No promises." He glided smoothly and powerfully between the berths, heading toward the companionway. "If it be any consolation, wee Jack, I feel for ya." He lifted his bulk up the stairs. "There's compensation in this world, lad. Trust me on this."

Paul reached over and squeezed his friend's hand, then made his way on deck. The sky was ablaze, a pink glow reflecting off the clouds in the eastern sky. Jack's parents dead? It should be raining. There should be heavy seas and biting, bitter rain. Why Jack's parents? What had happened? Who had attacked Jack? Paul could think of several people in his recent past much more deserving of that end.

⊰ ❋ ⊱

Paul was working on deck several days later when Quince approached him.

"The ole man says he would like to put your friend off the ship at Port au Prince, Haiti."

Paul bridled. "The captain's an ass, as he has demonstrated on several occasions. I suppose I owe him a debt of gratitude for taking me on after finding me in the middle of the Atlantic, but I'm hard-pressed to understand him."

"You weren't listening," Quince laughed. "I said he would like to put him off. Not that he was going to. I've talked to him and he's agreed if Jack can start work in two days' time, he'll keep him aboard as an apprentice. If he can't do the work, you'll do it for him. You'll stand his watch and your own and generally take up his slack. Is that understood?"

"Yes, sir, Mr. Quince. Thank you. We'll do you proud, sir." For the first time since Jack's arrival, Paul's heart felt free. "We'll do you proud, sir. I promise."

BOOK TWO

Book Two

7

LATITUDE 52

ASSIGNED TO HIS WATCH high in the foremast, Jack dropped his legs over the edge of the crow's nest and let his mind drift. The breathless beauty of the sea battled the rage in the pit of his stomach, his bitterness over the count. Besieged by tormenting pictures of his mother's bloodied body, de Silva dominated his thoughts. Jack vowed to return to Cuba. A constant image of the count's neck surrounded by his hands kept him alive.

Movement below caught Jack's eye. It was Quince. The man had been his salvation. Jack and Paul had sat for hours listening to Quince's stories of the sea, but most recently they had discussed the captain's strange behavior. Sometimes the old man seemed to be drunk, at others totally mad, standing at the rail looking out to sea, talking and laughing to himself. Jack wondered what the fate of the old man would be. In fact, what would all of their destinies be on this passage?

Now Quince seemed troubled, Jack thought, as the mate stood on the quarterdeck, watching the helmsmen make the small adjustments necessary to keep the ship on course. He had spent more and more time above deck lately, looking constantly for that frayed line, loose plank, or sail not trimmed. But there was something troubling inside him too.

The *Perdido Star* had been pressing south on her dogged journey, tacking every twenty-four hours. She would change from 165 degrees south, southeast to 190 degrees south, southwest but always on her beam reach south toward Cape Horn.

Paul, who had just come up from below, looked up at Jack. He waltzed across the deck, imitating a drunken sailor, pretending to heave up his rations over the side. Jack laughed in spite of himself, for Paul's good humor had kept him alive these past weeks. Jack's passion for returning to Cuba was in direct contrast to Paul's lack of direction. Paul, for all his intelligence and wit, seemed to live just one day at a time.

Smithers, the surly deckhand, came scampering up the ratlines to replace Jack, and Jack went to find Paul, who was standing near the rail. Quince called them to the quarterdeck.

"You lads step up here. I'll have a word with you."

"Now what trouble have you stirred in that witch's cauldron you haphazardly call a brain?" Paul asked Jack.

"Pissant," mumbled Jack. They crossed the deck to the ladder leading up to the quarterdeck.

Quince's concern was immediate. "The captain has called everyone into his cabin for a set-to." Quince paused and breathed deeply. "Of course, we all can't fit into his cabin. So anyone who is not on watch is to lay below at half the hour and stand in the companionway outside. We'll leave the door open." Quince cursed to himself. "Keep your ears open. You'll learn something of the sea and of life if I'm not mistaken."

Jack, Paul, and the rest of the starboard watch gathered in the crowded companionway. Jack stood to one side of the captain's door and could see the cabin was a disorderly mess. The small table was stained and pitted with years of drink and food. The old man had attempted to make his quarters respectable by kicking his filthy clothes and meal leavings under his bunk. Three large ports looked aft to the foaming wake of the *Star* but were inoperable, so the tiny cabin stank not only of the

corky septuagenarian's body but of the crowded officers in the cramped space. The low overhead kept the
men slightly bent and uneasy.

The captain was the only one seated.

"I've called you here to get your feelings on my plans,
as it were." He took a long pull on his tankard of grog.
"I've made many a passage of the Horn, lads, and it's not
an easy thing. If you were lucky, you could do the thing in
three weeks, from fifty degrees south latitude in the
Atlantic to fifty south in the Pacific. But no one's had that
kind of luck. It be twelve hundred miles, and that twelve
hundred is as hard a thing as exists." The man's bloodshot, rheumy eyes looked expectantly at the semicircle of
men around him. He paused, apparently waiting. "Well,
don't just stand there, dammit. What's your answer?"

The men all stood mute. Each waited for the other's
puzzled response.

Jack heard Quince's voice, the most experienced and
bravest seaman on board. He cleared his throat. "If it
pleases the captain, sir—"

"Yes, man. For God's sake, spit it out."

"With all respect, sir. If you're asking if we be prepared for the Horn, then—"

The captain stood promptly, ignoring Quince. Taking
one quick stride, he turned to face the aft ports, hands
gripped behind his back. "We're making good time, I
see. If I was a gambling sort, I'd say eight knots, by
God." He turned to face the mate as if to catch Quince
in a lie. "What's yer name, sailor?"

"My name be Quince, sir." The first mate's dismay
was evident; Jack knew he had been aboard the *Perdido
Star* for five years and had served under the captain
nearly three of those.

"Of course. I know your name, man. I didn't ask you
that, you fool. I said, 'What's our present course?' "

A sailor standing next to Paul whispered, "Oh God,
he's absolutely around the bend. We're lost."

The captain looked expectantly at each man in the circle around him. A grin on his face seemed to explain to all in attendance that he had caught them unprepared and would now divulge some secret.

"None of you lubbers have made a passage and God bless you for it. But I've made more than a few and I tell you, it's pure hell. So, here's my plan. We'll bypass the Cape and sneak through the Straits of Magellan. It'll save us three hundred miles and be damned with the East India Company and its duty. Time is money, I always say."

The captain turned again to the aft ports and began speaking to the openings.

"If it pleases the board of inquiry, sir, we came not through the Straits, sir, but 'round the Horn. It be five weeks to the day as noted in my log, sir." Jack could see the old man gesturing as if speaking to a court. He mimed opening a log, showing the imaginary group how he had dutifully kept it, how it showed clearly their epic journey around the Cape. Then, in a definite change of voice to one of command, he ordered, "Mr. Quince, set a course for the Straits and keep us several hundred miles off the South American coast. I'll not have any of the East India's cutters spying on us."

The captain had just spoken to a nonexistent board of inquiry. A course change of several hundred miles offshore would put them at the mercy of the westerly winds, driving them even further offshore.

"Excuse me, sir," the navigator Boyer started softly with great care. "A course change of this magnitude, will, sir, expose us to—"

In a sudden rage, the old Dutchman flung his grog at Boyer's head. The tankard whistled past his ear and sailed into the companionway, landing in the hands of Hansumbob, who looked down at it, stunned.

"You dare countermand my orders! You stand there and deliberately try to undermine my authority with these fine officers, you slackard. I'll have your hide on a yardarm."

Quince stepped forward with great authority. "Given your permission, sir, may I take this offending sailor on deck and deal with him in the appropriate manner?"

"I'm tired of all of you. Get out of my sight." Shaking, the old devil dropped into his chair. "We'll be in Boston in a few days. I'll deal with this mutinous behavior then." The group in the companionway looked at each other and whispered as one, "Boston?"

The captain's trembling hand turned the spigot on the grog cask. He watched as the precious liquid spilled onto the deck. Quince herded everyone from the room and on up topside. The group gathered in the waist of the ship above deck. Paul and Jack, anxious to hear, stood on the fringe.

"Quick thinking, Quince." Mr. Boyer was trembling. "I don't think I've ever been in such a hellish situation. My God, the bastard is totally gone." Boyer looked at the shaken officers for confirmation; a chorus of agreement came in return.

"A contest worthy of the gods. Brave men matched in conflict with adversity," Paul said, as he and Jack drifted away from the troubled group.

Jack poked a finger in Paul's ribs. "You sound as if you're on a cloud looking down on all of this."

Paul nodded. "If it were only so, Jackson. If only."

—≡❋≡—

There was a sense of doom aboard the *Star*. The meeting with the captain was discussed endlessly. The officers seemed to be, for all practical purposes, useless. First officer Mancy relied almost totally on Quince, even though he was of lower rank. The ship was proceeding south, eventually to O'taheiti, as planned.

Occasionally the captain came on deck, sometimes

only partially clothed, taking his constitutional and mumbling to himself. Jack felt a peculiar kinship with this tormented old soul.

The weather became more brisk each day even though it was summer in the Antarctic. They prepared for desperate conditions. Jack did the work assigned to him and helped ready the old ship. They were two hundred miles off the coast of Argentina, passing the 53rd degree latitude, turning west into the Straits of Magellan.

Jack and Paul worked together on the foredeck splicing rope. Paul continued his quest to try to draw Jack out of his periodic moods of sullen silence. "So, my good friend, what do you think of the sailor's life?" Jack didn't answer but bore down even harder on the task at hand, viciously driving his marlinspike into a knotted rope. Paul tried again. "You'll feel better, Jack, if you talk it out."

He still didn't answer. Some days he could be almost cheery, others, like today, he was morose and totally into himself. Jack felt as if physical exhaustion were his only salvation.

When the *Star* was just fifty miles from Espíritu Santo, the weather changed. The winds came around, into their teeth, and the crew were forced to change direction a number of times. They ran as hard as they could hoping to find shelter close to the shore at Tierra del Fuego.

It was not to be. The winds picked up to the point where they had only two choices: turn to the open sea and hope for a wind shift or try to find a cove and wait for better weather. Finally, they found a small bay called Punta de Arenas. The ship stayed anchored for nine days. Bare poles being beaten, the savage wind tried to push them out into the open sea.

Occasionally Jack would pass the captain's cabin and hear him raving, repeating the same phrase in the high-pitched voice of a much younger man. Jack spent most of his time in his hammock. He was situated in the corner, hard by the forward gun; beside him lay a wooden box piled with iron balls. Tackle to haul the gun to the gunport was neatly laid, but glistened with tar and grease. One of Jack's duties was to keep the Iron Dog with the Loud Mouth clean and ready for action. A faithful cur, the cannon lay beneath him as he stretched out for the four-hour sleep before the next watch. The four-on-four-off schedule for nearly a fortnight had exhausted him; the sea had become a demanding school.

Jack knew Paul was trying to force him to talk more about what had happened in Cuba, but he found it hard to manage anything other than a halfhearted grunt or nod. During the brief periods of relaxation when the men sat about, retelling sea tales and smoking their pipes, he was silent and reflective.

Always at the center of the group was Quince, who seemed to have second thoughts about the authority tacitly laid upon him.

After confirming with first officer Mancy on the ninth day in the bay, the first mate decided they would weigh anchor at first light and take their chances in the heavy seas.

⊰❈⊱

Jack once again was high in the rigging of the *Star* as she rounded the long spit of land at Punta de Arenas. The ship's company were on deck and aloft, trying to drive her into the wind. After several hours the air fell still, followed by a soft rain and fog.

Unable to get his noon fix on the sun, Mancy had to dead reckon the ship's position, figuring time traveled plus their speed and direction by compass.

Jack pulled on a line; Paul beside him on the foredeck ignored the pain from his chafed, bleeding hands. Jack strained to hear Quince as he spoke with the first officer.

"Mr. Mancy, sir." Jack could see Quince was debating his next words.

The officer turned and just nodded.

"Sir, by my estimate it be the better part of fifty miles from the point where we left the bay south to the inlet of the Straits." He glanced down at the compass encased in the wooden binnacle. "I don't believe, sir, with due respect, that we've traveled with the wind in our face more than thirty miles."

Willing to listen to almost anything, the officer quickly replied, "What's your suggestion?"

"We bear out to sea until the fog lifts and we have a clearer view, sir."

"We'll discuss it," Mancy answered.

"I may in the very near future be one of only a few true landlubbers who have been shipwrecked twice in a two-month period," Paul said.

Jack pulled on the line with renewed strength. He glanced at his friend, speaking to him for the first time in days. "I find the closer to the rocks we get, the better I like it. I haven't had a swim since last summer in the creek in Hamden woods." Jack quietly asked, "Do you want to live forever, Le Maire?"

Paul looked back, inches from Jack, pale and surprised. "You scare me when you talk like that. I thought we were friends."

Jack couldn't bring himself to answer; instead, he threw himself back into his work.

The first officer gathered the other senior ranks to discuss Quince's proposition that they had not come south far enough to slip into the Straits. None seemed to have an answer. Jack and Paul glanced up as Quince brushed past them, making his way forward to be closer to the starboard watch. Just then the port lookout screamed, "Land ho!" The port man was stretched out, one leg wrapped around the rail, both hands cupped over his eyes.

"Where away?" Quince yelled.

"Two points off the port bow."

Quince ran aft to the quarterdeck. The helmsman had already started a turn to starboard. The fog lifted and the rocks on shore loomed huge as barns. They barely cleared them, and Jack was fascinated by the disquiet that ran through him; these rocks would have solved his problems.

As they made their way back out to sea, Jack volunteered for the most dangerous jobs: a line fouled at the top of the mainmast was quickly freed by him, the jib sheet caught in the bowsprit stretching twelve feet over the waves seemed an easy task to untangle. The other crew members just shook their heads in wonder.

When Jack wasn't on watch he would linger in his hammock or restlessly pace between the bunks. Sometimes he would lever himself to the ceiling by grabbing a cross brace and pulling himself to his chest and then back down, repeating this until he was exhausted.

The ship ran swiftly southwest with the wind at her back, the crew trying desperately to get back to the Straits.

Paul had stopped Quince to ask where they were and what strategy was planned. Quince replied, "We are wandering about in the Southern Ocean. Where's your friend Jackson?"

Paul pointed to Jack on the foredeck, splicing rope.

"O'Reilly, come down here. And be quick about it, lad."

Jack dropped the line and joined them.

"I'd like to bring you lads up to date as to our condition." Quince explained that they discussed several days before whether to run farther southwest and bear into the coast or try and hold station where they were. They chose to run, trying once again to get in the lee of the mountains and battled into the protection of the shore.

But they had kept slipping further south and the ship was caught between two land masses: Staten Island and the mainland. The wind and current were sending them into Drake Passage and a commitment to the Horn. "You lads keep a weather eye these next days. She'll go hard, she will."

As soon as they passed Staten Island to port, the weather changed once again, leaving them becalmed in a restless sea between Nueva and Wollaston Islands. The fog came up once again, and there was little or no wind. The ship lay adrift for days, unable to move. They were close to a number of small islets—the graveyard of scores of ancient vessels, Quince told them ghoulishly—and a constant watch was held. Quince ordered the longboat lowered. With ten men bending into the oars, they tried to pull the ship away from the rocks.

Jack and Paul sat together watching the activity, Paul with a grimace on his face, Jack with a grin.

The line strung between the ship and the longboat was lost in the fog and those on deck could not see the smaller boat most of the time. A lookout on the bowsprit called constant direction, and the *Star* slowly made its way southwest.

After a number of watch changes, the exhausted longboat crew was called aboard to rest for the night. At two bells, Jack heard a shout down the companionway hatch.

"Starboard watch on deck! Weather coming!"

Indeed it was. Above their heads a dark mass blotted out the stars, and a driving sleet hit the ship.

"All hands aloft! Shorten topgallants, reef the topsails!"

The ship came alive with men dashing up the ratlines. The long windless days and nights had lulled them into a stupor, and every yard of canvas was out when the weather hit. If they didn't shorten the sails up quickly enough, they would pay with a broken mast, or worse.

The winds shifted almost by the minute; the decks became dangerously slick from a driving wet snow. When the ship lurched, a sailor stowing a line on the port rail fell, banging painfully into the aft companionway hatch.

Quince stood next to the helm, straining to look for the rocks of Wollaston Island. The snow built on the masts and sails as he called to turn starboard. After twelve straight hours the winds from the west died—but only marginally, and the ship made little headway.

Serving his watch at the helm, Jack observed as officers gathered on the quarterdeck, shouting at each other. Jack caught Quince's eye. Quince shook his head slightly as if to say, "Learn from this." Three officers were nose to nose with each other, all constantly interrupting with a different view of what should be done.

"If we are to maintain discipline we must not allow the crew to see us in dissent."

"It has been my understanding from every source I have spoken to, that to beat the Horn you must fight her."

"We must do a combination. We must fight when it's relevant and pull back when prudent. I, for one, would bear off to the north, and in the protection of this bay, try to sneak around the inside of the Horn."

During all of this, Quince stood silently, legs apart, hands folded behind him, listening.

Mr. Mancy turned to address him. "Quince, none of us have done a passage around this devil, so you might as well voice your opinion."

Quince stared to port at the vague shore of Wollaston, not looking at the group. "I've done many a passage, sir, and it's my opinion, if indeed you're asking, that the Horn loves a fight and she'll only let you pass to port of her, and then only if you're a worthy opponent." The first mate turned to the sad group of inexperienced officers. "I say fight the bitch. Fight her tooth and nail."

Hiding his smile, Jack bent over the binnacle, pretending to study the compass.

Mr. Boyer was the first to speak. "It was my understanding, Quince, that in our recent contretemps with the captain, he stated, and I thought rightly, that none of us 'lubbers' had made a passage around the Horn. Was that not so?"

The first mate brushed the snow from his red face and blew on his frozen fingers. "May I speak frankly, sir?" he asked.

"Of course. By all means."

"First of all, none of us would be standing here jawing about how to get around the Horn if the captain was right."

There was immediate concurrence among the three officers.

"Secondly, I think we would all have to agree that the captain was not dealing with a mind that was fully functional."

Again a murmuring of assent.

"I've made ten passages of the Horn spread over the last fifteen years. None of them easy and two of them with Captain Deploy. The fact that he didn't remember my name or that we had even sailed together grieves me." Quince stepped up to the helm and scanned the compass. "You've drifted two points off your course, sailor; bring her up into the wind."

Jack quickly responded.

The officers stood braced, waiting for Quince to continue.

"If we're to survive this trip—and I see no reason why we can't—I say do as Captain Deploy would have done in better days. Treat this passage as a difficult one, but approach it as a sailing problem, not as a myth that needs to be conquered." He waited a moment, then continued. "The wind'll blow in this quarter of the world from every direction and seemingly all at the same time, so to hide in the lee of this island with chances of going on the rocks seems foolhardy. We have to be out there driving to windward for all we're worth. Changing the ship every minute if need be, but pushing, pushing till we can make enough seaway to turn the corner. If we have to beat halfway down to the Antarctic, so be it." Quince looked at each man in turn. "To honor Captain Hans Peter Deploy, let's not hide here like frightened apprentices, but stick our noses in this thing right and proper."

Quince's reasoning and knowledge of the sea touched Jack in a surprising way. He felt a strange uplifting and sense of pride at being on the *Star* with this man who had never lost his temper among the group of weak officers. Maybe it was worth staying alive, if only to see how it would play.

It didn't take long for the men to make their decision. The *Star* swept out from the lee of Wollaston but couldn't make her way west, so she showed her beam to the wind and beat south, toward the Antarctic. After several hours of relentless sleet, rain, and snow, she came about and started back toward the Cape, hoping to make at least a half mile on her long tack. But the winds picked up even stronger and she was forced to shorten sail, only to lose a mile instead of gaining a half.

On the quarterdeck the officers were grim with determination. They tried time and again to gain seaway at this famous corner of the world. Finally, they stood down, just before darkness set in, hoping to try again at dawn.

The sun never rose the next morning; the sky just became a shade lighter. But it was enough to see the rocks of the Cape, so once again they set out. When the Antarctic coast lay just twenty miles away, they tried a direct westerly charge, but the five thousand miles of open ocean ahead allowed the seas to build to enormous heights, beating them back to the east. This time when asked his advice, Quince suggested more sail, not less, so they would be more maneuverable—and it seemed to work. They were able to point further up into the wind and were fast approaching the Horn from their extended tack when one of their jib stays parted. It flew to the east like a giant pennant, cracking in the wind.

"Cut that sail, lads!"

Jack and Paul shot up the ratlines.

"Cut her away and be quick about it!" The Horn, less than a half mile away, loomed heavily on the horizon. If they could stay pointed up they would be able to tack just west of the Cape and with luck be through safely.

The officers stood together, transfixed by the event before their eyes. If they made it, they would still have heavy sailing for a bit but they would be able to round the coast of Chile in a few miles and then beat north along the archipelago.

The seas churned the ship. Groaning from the enormous strain, her bow alternately pointed above then below the Cape. They seemed to be headed directly for the rocks; it would take a combination of a quick wind shift and a friendly sea just to get them through. Then they had no choice—they were committed. With just a hundred yards to the rocks, it didn't look like they would make it.

Quince stood braced on the quarterdeck rail. When it seemed the officers behind him were losing faith, he yelled to the helmsman, "Steady as she goes, lad. Don't point her any further up or we'll be in irons. Steady as she goes!" They could hear the surf crashing against the rocks as the old ship caught a wave and brought her bow further west.

Then, as if by magic, the wind swung to the north and brought the ship around. They were past the rocks of Cabo de Hornos, heading west.

One of the younger officers leaned over the lee rail,

sick, as the rest just stood, looking at the rocks receding in their wake. If they could have seen Quince's face, they would have been ashamed, for the stout old sea dog wore an enormous grin. They had beaten the Horn. As Quince had said, it was just another sailing problem.

—≈✦≈—

Jack pulled steadily on his oar, relishing the feel of the muscles in his back. Hansumbob stood in the bow of the longboat, one hand stuffed into his coat-front, the other gesturing toward the approaching beach.

> *In the spring of '76, there was ice upon the sea.*
> *A bunch of us went whaling, upon this we all agree.*

The rest of the men, rowing to shore, groaned as Bob recited his doggerel. The old man just continued as if he hadn't heard their protests.

> *But nothing else about that trip was normal—don't*
>   *ya see.*
> *For Jim Larue and his brother Bill were lost and woe*
>   *is me.*
> *We searched the night till break a day. A plenty of*
>   *whales there be.*
>
> *But we let them go.*
> *We let them live, for the sea had snatched at we.*

"It don't rhyme so good, Bob. It don't make no sense," Smithers grunted, as he strained against the oar. The rest of the crew were silent, for there was nothing so entertaining as having sport with Ole Bob.

"It don't need ta, ya idjut." Bob sulked, both hands deep into his jacket pocket. "It 'spose to be a story, Smithers. It ain't 'spose to be no poem what rhyme, like perfect."

"Well, ya got that part right."

Bob waited a moment, obviously thinking about how to defend his poetry.

"Your trouble, Smithers, is that you got no sensitive in ya."

"Hallelujah to that!" Smithers laughed, encouraging the crew to follow his gaiety.

"I could tell ya tales what would make your hair stand on end." Bob stopped for a moment and quickly snatched the hat from Smithers's head. "If ya had any."

The crew roared. Bob had touched on Smithers's soft spot; Jack knew this man's baldness was not to be tampered with.

"The point of the story be, there's these men. An' they all take to whalin' and a couple of them get lost in the sea and the rest of them take to a lookin' for 'em and it ain't to be. They see plenty a whale an' course, that what they lookin' for too. But they don' have the heart to kill the whales when they lost some of their own kin. Ya see, that's what the 'we' is about. Well, anyway, if ya haff to explain a story, it means your audience not be up to your standards no how." Bob turned back to the approaching shore. "It be a hot day on old Cape Horn the next time I tell ya lubbers a tale—and ya could bet your grog rations on that." Ole Bob punctuated his speech with a heavy tobacco spit over the side and the longboat beached in the soft sand.

Quince made up a working party to find fresh water. The high cliffs of the archipelago created enormous falls, which in turn made pools where the sailors filled their casks. A mist kept the cliffs shrouded so that the streams of water seemed to fall straight out of the sky. The men were relaxed and feeling good after the ordeal of the Cape. They had pushed on to get well away from the bad weather, a hundred miles up the Chilean coast to Desolation Island, which guarded the west entrance to the Straits of Magellan. It was here that they had anchored in a small cove, to replenish their water supply.

Jack rolled one cask down to the boat and started back for a second when he heard shouts from the men around the pool.

Bosun Ben Mentor danced a jig, pointing to Hansumbob, who was exploring the beach. "Bob!" he shouted, breathless from his dance. "You be lookin' for whale down there?"

Bob picked up a tusk. "Not a whale at all if ya need to know, but maybe a sea lion."

"Well, is it still good to eat, Bob? Or do it need a bit a cookin'?" Smithers asked.

Jack could tell he still smarted from the crew's laugh at his expense. Smithers reminded Jack of an older version of Billy Slocum, Jack's schoolyard nemesis. Always looking for a weak spot in someone's character, the victim would usually be someone smaller or weaker. Jack took a deep breath, determined to mind his own business.

"Bob, what ya say you and me Indian wrestle?" Smithers called.

"Nope. Don't wrestle, don't care to. Specially with no bald man, what's thick-skinned."

"I say we Indian wrestle, ole-timer. If ya can wrestle like ya can pass the insults, you should be fine and dandy."

There was a rustle, the men sensing a fight in the making.

"Thankee, Mr. Smithers. I appreciate the offer but I'll decline respectful, sir. And I'll drop my comments— they all be in fun. Just fun." Ole Bob delivered his speech quietly and sincerely. Jack knew men cooped up in tight quarters needed an outlet sometimes, and that Hansumbob didn't wish to be on the receiving end of Smithers's rancor.

But Smithers felt wronged and needed some satisfaction. He stood hands on hips, legs apart. "I called ya down, Bob, I called ya and ya slithered away like a dog. Now take my hand, dammit, and be a man."

Smithers extended his right hand. Bob looked around for support, smiling in a way that would make any man think twice about harming this gentle soul. He walked slowly up to his opponent.

"I'll gladly shake your hand, but to say I'd wrestle would be a lie. It wouldn't be much game for ya."

He extended his hand. Smithers pumped it and Bob flew ass over tea kettle into the sand, face first. The men shouted.

"Once more, Bob. I'll give ya a better chance. Stand up, man."

The men roared again. Smithers hauled Bob to his feet.

"Right foot against right foot, Bob. Right hand clasped right hand."

Bob pulled back.

"Give me your right hand, dammit!"

"He said it wouldn't be much of a game for you." Jack's sudden interruption shocked the crowd, which quickly fell silent.

"Who's that?" Smithers turned in rage, more than ready to take on the whole ship's company.

The seamen parted, revealing Jack O'Reilly sitting quietly on a mound of sand.

Smithers bared his teeth, a mirthless split in his face. "Shut your young mouth, lad, or I'll stuff it with sand and paddle your pink behind."

The image of this enraged bully took Jack to a violent road in Cuba. The young man's eyes narrowed into a penetrating force. In a voice chilling in its intensity he said, "I dare you to try it."

Smithers froze, then looked with amazement at this new, somehow overpowering figure. The rest of the men were silent, equally astonished. Above them on the mound, Jack continued to pierce the man with his stare. Smithers's offensive stance gradually dissipated, and he finally ended the standoff with a grimace and a spit to the ground directly in front of him. "Aagh, a pip-squeak like you ain't worth the effort." The other men broke their silence and slowly returned to their task of replenishing the water supply.

The casks all filled and stowed, the crew reluctantly pushed off the Chilean shore. As the men settled into their oars, Smithers dug his elbow into Jack's ribs. "Excuse me, old salt, didn't see ya there." When the crew pulled themselves up the rope ladder to the *Star*, Jack positioned himself in front of Smithers. Halfway up the side of the ship, Jack grabbed a rung of the boarding ladder with both hands and drove his feet hard into Smithers's face. They both fell back into the boat, Jack landing on top of Smithers, his knee planted firmly in the sailor's chest. The groaning man's lips were split, and a tooth hung loose from his bloody mouth. Jack never spoke but just glared into the sailor's eyes. There was death there, and Smithers saw it.

⊰❈⊱

New Year's Day, January 1, 1806. The *Star* had finally been blessed with good weather; a fair breeze lifted her onto its shoulders and practically skipped her along the waves. Plunging gracefully into soft seas, she averaged nine knots, covering nearly thirty-five hundred miles toward the Society Islands in the thirty days since leaving Chonos Archipelago on the Chilean coast.

The crew were in grand spirits, as they had been given an extra ration of grog to celebrate the new year. The added pleasure left everyone elated and content—with the exception of Jack, who brooded. His brief encounter with Smithers over a month ago had left him depressed and vulnerable, walking around mostly in a state of trance. He couldn't seem to shake his feeling of helplessness. Nor did he want to. He found comfort in his obsession; it kept him striving to be better than the rest of the sailors, but his growing fear of the dark and perpetual nightmares kept him in a constant state of unrest, his inability to express his burden gnawing away at him.

With favorable winds, they would be in Papeete in seven days' time; the old ship seemed to sense this and kept herself upright and proper, like a gallant elderly woman. The decks shone from the pumice, and the rails glistened with a new coat of varnish. The sailors gathered in small groups on the decks, repairing sail, splicing rope, or polishing brass, just for something to do. The sails had been badly beaten by the Cape but were starting to show some style. The brass was pitted but serviceable, and the broken lines were slowly being mended from their long ordeal around the Horn. All in all, the ship was being made into the sailing machine she was meant to be.

Paul and Jack were aloft in the mainmast hauling sail. "Six months ago, we were both in school," Paul said. "Did you ever dream you would be one hundred feet in the air, swaying in balmy breezes?"

"I don't know," Jack grunted, continuing to pull in the heavy canvas hand over hand.

"It speaks!" Paul feigned surprise. "Only eighteen years old and words come tumbling from its lips!" Paul called to several of his shipmates dangling on the foot ropes, hauling sail. "Did you hear, lads? It said, 'don't know' or something like that." Paul addressed Jack. "There may just be hope for you after all, you talkative little dickens, you."

Jack cleared his throat. "I want to kill someone or something or smash a belaying pin into a grinning Cuban face or rip off an arm and beat someone to death with it. I can't stop these terrible images from coming into my head. I hate them but at the same time, I can't do without them. I . . ." Jack stopped to prevent a sob from coming up his throat.

Paul felt ashamed then, to have made a joke of Jack's

suffering. But in some ways, it had worked. He continued to pull on the wet sail. "Were you ever happy,
Jack?"

"No."

"I don't believe that." Paul tried again. "There were
times since I've known you when you were full of jokes
and fun. Go on, admit it to yourself. Say to yourself, 'I
was happy once and I will be again.' "

"All right, I guess I was happy once—so?" Jack shot
Paul a dirty look.

"So in order to get through each day as best you can,
in order to survive this voyage, without becoming a
blithering idiot, think of happier times."

Jack disgustedly turned back to his work.

"Yes, think of happy times and grow stronger, so that
you will be healthy of mind and body when you get
back to Cuba—*then* you can rip off someone's arm and
beat them to death."

8

O'TAHEITI

THE *STAR* LAY ANCHORED in the harbor of Papeete. Both watches had been allowed to go ashore and the ship was practically deserted. The only men aboard were Jack, Hansumbob, and a couple of the cooks.

Hansumbob sat on the top deck, his back against the main mast carving on a small piece of bone. Jack liked the old sailor, but each time Bob attempted to speak to him, he felt himself withdraw. He had not exactly been rude, but he tried to discourage any contact. Nevertheless, Bob persisted.

If ya need a soul to talk to
and ya doesn't know how to start,
just let your poor heart wonder,
you'll look and feel right smart.
I've sailed the seven seas by gar
and I've seen and done it all,
but I never met a sailor man
who failed a supper's call.
They fight and drink and make one fret,
'tis awful sometimes to see,
but I never met a sailor man who was late
for a cook's entreee.

Bob giggled and tapped his feet, but the harder he tried to get a response from Jack, the more distant Jack felt. Finally, Bob settled back silently against the mast and resumed his carving.

I oughta dive into these waters and swim to shore, Jack thought. Laugh, drink, and forget my troubles. I'm sure everyone on board is tired of me. Better yet, maybe I should say good-bye to this old fool Bob and head out of the bay, see how far I could get toward Cuba. If I swam two miles in one hour and rested every three hours, in twenty-four hours I would cover about forty miles. If I kept that up for ten days that would be four hundred miles. About then, I would just call it quits. And take Paul's advice and die happy.

Jack reveled in these thoughts. It seemed his troubles were his only companions these days. Loyal and readily available.

He had smelled something cooking for quite some time. The wood smoke, mixed with the fragrance of the tropical flowers, eased his mind. But the afternoon still-ness was quickly shattered by a scream from the bowels of the ship.

Bob leapt from his position and raced to the companionway hatch. Throwing it open, a cloud of dense smoke billowed out and, choking on the fumes, he backed away.

The outcry startled Jack out of his brooding. A sailor stumbled on deck, coughing and vomiting. When Jack reached the companionway, he found the man's clothes smoking and badly burned.

"The cook's down there! Get him out! Oh Christ, get him out!"

Jack grabbed a piece of sailcloth and covered his head, not knowing what he was going to do but realizing he had to do something. He plunged down the narrow stairs, his view limited by the smoke, and crawled toward the galley. As he reached the cook, flames were licking violently against the overhead, wanting to consume everything in sight. The cook lay on the deck kicking desperately, trying to extinguish the fire burning him alive. A large kettle lay overturned on the floor and grease bubbled around his head.

Jack reached under the cook and lifted him, the oil searing his arms. A hazy light guided him as he made his way up the companionway ladder with his hollering bundle. On deck, the cook's clothes seemed to ignite in Jack's face when the air hit. They were both ablaze.

Jack took three quick strides and cleared the starboard rail, his burning shipmate in his arms. He caught a glimpse of the astonished faces of the men in the longboat as he passed just inches over their heads. The sailors on shore had seen the smoke even before Bob and Jack and had been on their way back to the ship.

The two men were quickly fished from the water and hauled aboard. Jack bathed his own burns with cold water and watched as Cookietwo sat with his back to the port rail, trembling. After several hours, he could hear only an occasional moan. Cook's eyes, when they were open, fixed on some distant unattainable salvation. Jack dipped a cloth in the cool water and laid it gently on the man's forehead.

"You may not 'ave done me a right good turn, young Jack," he whispered, his voice shaky.

Jack nodded and continued to cool the reddened face and limbs of the suffering cook, the older man lost in a mumbled prayer.

In the weeks to come, Jack's burns healed without a trace, while Cookietwo's face and arms were horribly scarred, the raw skin angry and full of infection. But it appeared that the cook would live.

⊰✸⊱

Several of his shipmates tried to thank Jack for his attempt to save the cook, but he remained resolute in his determination to keep to himself.

The officers eventually took the longboat into the settlement to hire a new cook and returned with a small dapper Chinese gentleman named Quen-Li. Jack stood on the foredeck, watching the Oriental swing effortlessly up to the rail, glance around, and vault to the deck, as graceful a move as Jack had ever seen.

Jack observed this slim Chinaman for several days; he was fascinating in that there was a physical strength about him that belied his years. He moved as if gliding, his head never bounced, and most intriguing were his eyes; they were penetrating and yet kind.

"Methinks this fellow may be a man of many parts," Paul told Jack, who nodded assent as the pair watched the Chinaman chop vegetables. It was apparent he had many years of experience with a knife in his hand and not just in a galley.

9

STORM

TEMPERS WERE GROWING increasingly short as the weeks passed. The starboard crew had just finished a grueling watch, and several hands shouted around the mess table as another serving of tasteless hardtack was passed around with a half pint of rationed grog. For two days they had labored without a hot meal, the weather too rough to light fires in the recently repaired galley.

As Jack reached his hammock and seabag, he was overwhelmed again by the strong smell of the fo'c'sle. The tight crew quarters on the gun deck made for spartan living; tallow lamps blackened the overhead and the deck under his feet was sticky from tar and salt. The pitch of the ship seemed to be getting worse. She rose, then plummeted, taking white foam over her bows that washed down the foredeck. Next, a foot of water spilled over her gunwales, momentarily backing up the scuppers.

The constant deluge of waves soon found the imperfections in the foredeck hatch, spraying hammocks and seabags that already stank of mildew and stale clothes. Jack peeled off his wet jacket and rigged his hammock. Several of the crew on his watch were already asleep, looking as if they had passed out the moment their bodies became enfolded in the netting.

The old ship's wooden bones creaked in protest as she crashed through the rough seas. She swung through a 30-degree arc on the highest rollers and the captain still hadn't shortened sail. No one besides Quince had seen him for days.

As he lay in his berth, Jack's limbs ached from the beating he had received two days prior as penalty for being late for watch. Images of the experience replayed in his mind, keeping sleep at bay. There was no order to them; sometimes he was himself a spectator.

"Well, strike me pink. What have we here?" He had been confronted by the second mate, Cheatum, who spoke in questions as the Lord spoke in parables and at this moment had more control of Jack's destiny than the Lord. Jack hurried to his place in line as the rest of his shipmates tried to quell their laughter. They loved a confrontation, anything to break the monotony of life at sea.

"I asked you a question, wee Jack. Or would you be dreamin' again?" The "wee," Jack knew, referred not to his physical stature but to his youth and status in the hierarchy of the ship. The second mate eyed him for an instant, then stepped forward and backhanded him, bringing the taste of blood to his lips.

Jack hit back with such speed that the two blows sounded almost as one. Cheatum was stunned, as was everyone on deck. He was so taken aback that he stood for a long moment, mouth agape.

"How dare you hit a superior. I'll thrash you within an inch of your life. Drop your britches and grab your ankles."

"Never," Jack replied.

"Am I hearing correctly? Did you say 'never'?"

Jack surveyed the mate, a silent challenge stance. Muffled talk rose from the other sailors, some actually on his side, others clearly troubled by the threat.

"O'Reilly, you've been a pain in my arse for a long time now. You've walked these decks kinda proud and aloof and I for one am sick of it. You're a brave one, I'll grant you. Sticking your nose in the fire and all. But mind this, you'll drop your pants for your beating, lad, or you'll take it on the back with the cat till you beg for it on your butt."

Jack never blinked. Cheatum signaled for two sailors to tie the young man spread-eagled against the pulpit, hard by the mainmast.

Jack heard Paul's voice from somewhere behind him. "The Bible says, 'Take an eye for an eye, a tooth for a tooth.' Following the Good Book's sayings, doesn't it make sense to mete out punishment in the same way?"

"Shut your teeth, Le Maire, or you'll be next," barked Cheatum.

"For instance," Paul continued, "if one is late for duty or roll call, or what have you, then it follows one should be forced to be late for one's foodstuffs or one's grog ration or—"

A blow on the side of Paul's head flattened him on the deck. Cheatum stood over him. "That should close that yap of yours, laddy." He returned his attention to Jack. "I'll say it once again: on your back or your butt? What's it gonna be, me hearty?"

Jack didn't answer, but he saw the seaman named Red Dog hand Cheatum a cat-o'-nine-tails which he dipped in a bucket of salt water. The moist leather dripped on the deck of the *Perdido Star*.

Jack never wavered as Cheatum laid into him heavily. At fourteen strokes, a shout was heard from the quarterdeck.

"Mr. Cheatum, that will be quite enough." Jack recognized Quince's voice. "Stow the cat and release that man."

The word "man" seemed to echo throughout the deck of the ship; a quiet pervaded the event as each sailor on board seemed to realize that this boy had stoically taken much more than many of them could have endured.

Jack's face was red, and tears flowed down his cheeks, despite his efforts to stop them.

"They be salt of the earth, wee Jack. Lick them away," shouted some disconnected voice. But Jack refused the invitation. Something black was growing in his soul. Something that comforted and frightened him at the same time.

Now in his hammock, Jack repeated his mantra: I must find a way of surviving this voyage. A way back to Cuba. Drifting into a slumber, his thoughts found purchase on that new hardness in his soul. *I will live. I will find a way to confront the count, and in the meantime I will not allow him to destroy me.* The face of the count drifted mistlike in front of him, tantalizingly out of his reach. He could hear only vaguely the sounds of sleep about him, the ship's hull sliding through the endless sea.

"Starboard watch on deck!" Cheatum's booming voice rang through the crew's quarters.

Whether it was minutes or hours later, Jack hadn't a clue.

"All hands show a leg. Look lively now, bear a hand to shorten sail, she's blowing a norther real proper." Cheatum paused to boot a laggard, still intact in his hammock. "We're awash fore and aft, so it's foul weather gear and all hands bear to."

His back stiff with pain, Jack bolted out of his hammock, cracking his head on a stout oak beam. He took a deep breath and reached a handhold on a stanchion, the wood worn smooth where many had grabbed before him.

The ship was violently alive; her heel was to port and seemed stuck there. Jack felt his feet and lower legs growing suddenly heavier and knew the ship was rising with a huge swell. The weight left just as quickly and the ship plunged.

Paul was being sick in a port scupper as Jack came on deck. Jack knew the feeling; the queasiness had been with him since they had departed O'taheiti three weeks ago.

"I don't think I can make it, Jack." Paul couldn't meet Jack's glance as he approached. "I've been sick for two days and can't get my strength." The gray of his face matched the lightest part of the sky.

Cheatum pulled himself expertly up the companionway to the main deck. "Lay aft, you lubbers, and report to Mr. Quince—or would you prefer my boot?"

Again the mate asked questions without answers; perhaps it made life simpler never to commit to a direct statement.

Jack covered for Paul's sickness by stepping between him and the mate. The air crackled, an acre of canvas bursting with the mean wind. Sheets and halyards snapped against the mast and sharp gusts tore at their clothes. The two young men made their way aft by the lifelines, rigged by the port watch while they had slept.

Quince was shouting orders as Jack and Paul arrived. Helmsmen Peters and Smithers battled the wheel. Like a spooked horse, the ship attempted to buck herself free of human will. The helm was alternately down hard to starboard and then sliding quickly to port. Jack knew this was a dangerous situation, as the ship jerked 20 degrees on either side of her course. If she was pooped and a huge wave came over her fantail, she would be in danger of drifting sideways, into one of the huge rollers breaking ten feet above her bowsprit. Once in the trough and hit by a huge wave, she would surely broach.

Jack and Paul awaited instructions with a group of seamen. Finally Quince ordered them topside on the foremast, to begin taking in sail. The wind seemed to be coming from several directions, and the air was heavy with water. The pounding of the boat and the wind and the waves made for a hellish noise. A nightmare of conflicting colors darkened the sky in the north. To the south Jack could still see some patches of blue, and the west was spotted with the red of the setting sun. But the north was pure black, purple clouds boiling and expanding in plumes that lifted for thousands of feet.

The wind increased to forty knots, and the big ship dove and cut from one wave to the next.

"I don't like it much in the trees when it's like this." Paul grabbed a ratline and pulled himself up till he stood on the starboard gunwale. "I'm feeling bad, Jack. Real sick."

"Well, look at it this way." Jack was following Paul up the ratline. "Quicker we get her shortened up, the quicker we'll be back in the sack." Jack had started to feel better; his rage had not diminished, but now it was tempered by his will. He felt an enormous kinship with Paul and would always be in his debt for his understanding.

Jack loved being aloft in foul weather. "Remember, one hand for the ship, one hand for yourself."

"I'll have two hands for myself, thank you." Paul attempted a grin.

They approached the first spar. Some members of the port watch had secured the fore gallant sail and had started up before them. All hands turned aft to a loud ripping sound; the lower fore and aft sail on the mainmast had split. The wind backed around and the boom broke free and swept across the bridge deck.

A sailor who had levered himself up on a backstay above was swept overboard. Jack could see him thrashing in the waves, swimming after his departing ship. A line tossed to him fell short as a bolt of lightning split the sky. Again the line was tossed and again it fell short. The drowning man's head, covered with foam from the pitching waves, reared one last time before disappearing into the sea.

Jack fought down his bile. He could not rid himself of the look in the drowning man's eyes—questioning as much as terrified. Paul's arms gripped the spar.

Mr. Quince turned from the doomed sailor and shouted orders. "Look lively, you men. Up the mast you go and be quick about it, or I'll have your hide!"

Faced with adversity, Jack felt his senses sharpen. He could smell the fear on Paul.

"My God. That sailor—he didn't have a chance." Paul's legs were failing him. "Did you know him?"

"No." Jack remembered only that he was an older hand and from the port watch. "Get topside or it's going to go heavy on us."

Paul squinted down at the deck below, took a deep breath, and proceeded up the rope ladder. When they got to the spar just below the topmost one, they were ordered to spread out and begin taking in sail. Jack's purchase was outermost on the spar. The ship heeled badly and the distance from the deck to the spar accentuated the movement.

Forearms and backs aching, they strained against the heavy sails and slippery reef lines. Jack sometimes forgot to keep a hand for himself in the heat of keeping up with the older mates. He was relieved to see Paul close to the mast, one leg looped through the ladder and the other placed firmly on the stepping line. The wind backed clear around and came in from the southeast.

In his brief time at sea, Jack had experienced Cape Horn. But this weather seemed heavier; his back was wet from the blood of freshly opened scabs and scalding from the cold seawater, but this, to him, was exciting. He felt alive. One of the older men was frozen in place next to him, fear-filled eyes peeking out at the storm. He appeared incapable of moving on his own.

"Come out of it, there's nothing for it but to put your back into it," Jack said.

Without changing expression, the man started down the ratline.

"The mate will have your ass," Jack yelled.

The deckhand never looked back. He had taken two steps down when a sudden gust snapped the mast above Jack's head. The crack of the breaking wood was followed by a shout from the working party on the top spar. The mast had parted.

The spar seemed to pause momentarily in midair and then mast, spar, ratlines, sheets, and halyards all passed in front of Jack on the way down to the deck. Jack reached out for a sailor falling in front of him who flailed at the air as if he would climb the wind to salvation. Jack grabbed the man's sleeve, his hand jerked once, and the apparition was gone. It could have been a dream except for the torn piece of blue-and-white-striped shirt Jack clutched in his hand.

The tangled lines slowed the progress of the spar. But each time it stopped, the accompanying jolt loosened another sailor's grip and he plunged to the deck or over the side. Jack found himself withdrawing to a place deep inside himself, disconnecting with the mayhem around him. He felt a strange calm. For a brief moment he dispassionately considered his recent beating, his mother's courage, his father's face. Seconds later he was back to the reality of his predicament.

Jack quickly pawed his way down the ratline until he found himself next to Paul. It occurred to him that as he came down the line he should have passed the older sailor. He hadn't. He too must have been swept away when the mast parted. In fact, there was only he and Paul—and something had happened to Paul. He was lying limp, one arm through the batten hole and a leg through the ladder. It had kept him from being swept away.

"Can you hear me?"

No reply.

A shout from below asked Jack if he was all right.

"I'm all right, but my mate is bad hurt."

"Is he dead?"

"No sir, just banged on the head. I'll try to tie him and lower him down."

"Well, be quick about it, lad. We're in deep trouble here and need every hand." Jack understood that Quince thought Paul dead, but knew it would be quicker for the first mate to humor him in his attempt at rescue than talk him into deserting his friend. Below was a scene of snapped timbers, twisted canvas, blocks, lines, blood, and broken bodies—at least five on the deck, and more over the side.

Jack saw one man in the water holding to a bit of spar attached to the debris on deck. The sailors on the quarterdeck clearing the wreckage couldn't see their comrade. Jack shouted but the wind picked up and he couldn't make himself heard. The man clung to the spar then broke free and drifted away, swallowed by the sea.

Jack turned his attention to Paul, talking to him. A conscious man would be easier to lower to the deck through the confusion of timbers. Paul was incoherent and Jack knew he would have no help. He stepped from the spar onto the ladder just below where Paul's leg extended between the rungs. A line from the now missing upper works had draped itself over the yardarm next to him, and Jack looped it under Paul's rear and around his back, taking an extra turn to widen the strain on the makeshift chair. He then cut the line, looped it, and tied a bowline in front of Paul's waist.

He threw the line over the spar and then wrapped it again to get more friction. Pulling Paul's leg from the ladder was difficult, since Jack had to lift his friend's weight to free it. This done, he pulled him up once more and extracted his arm from between the sail and the spar. Now his body was free and swinging with the movement of the ship. The line around Paul's back was too low and he hung doubled over. He swung away from Jack as the ship heeled and then was on his way back, head first. Jack lunged himself between the mast and Paul.

Suddenly, the line over the spar holding Paul's weight slipped from Jack's grasp and his friend dropped six feet before Jack could stop him. Jack forced himself to ignore the rope burns on his hands and kept lowering Paul to the deck. The sailors below couldn't help, for the ratline ladder had parted fifteen feet from the deck when the mast had broken.

Jack tested his strength by holding fast with his left hand and feeding out the line with his right. It was going to work, if he could just keep Paul away from the mast. He waited till the ship shuddered and righted itself in a trough and then quickly played out the line, hoping to drop Paul to the waiting hands below. He inched his way up closer to the spar and let the line out. Still fifteen feet short, Paul's body swung dangerously close to the mast. Jack grasped the spar with the rope around it and let go more slack. Paul dropped again, but was still several feet from the sailor's grasp on deck. The ship heeled suddenly and the limp body swung aft.

"Catch him!" Jack screamed. Quince, on the bridge deck above the sailors, grabbed Paul with one arm and lowered him to the deck. Relief washed over Jack as he could see Paul was safely down. As the pain from the ripped skin on his hands began heating its way into his consciousness, he took a moment to rekindle his strength.

"Take a wrap under your arms and get down here!" bellowed Quince. But Jack had already begun his rappel down. Again his line was too short, but Jack dropped into the arms of a half dozen waiting sailors. A few men whispered "well done" before hurrying off to deal with the carnage about them.

Jack looked to the bridge deck where Quince and Hansumbob had propped Paul up against the compass binnacle. Paul met Jack with a blank-eyed look.

An eerie quiet settled over the ship. Jack noticed the water had become calm; several sailors stopped their work and gazed seaward. Black clouds billowed about them, but just scant miles away the sea still boiled. Jack could see the stars straight above him, as if he were peering up from the bottom of a deep bowl. They were caught in what appeared to be a lake, surrounded by towering mountains of water. Jack fell to his knees, more tired than he had ever been in his life.

There was a stirring on the bridge deck. Jack saw a figure all in white—it appeared to be a ghost climbing up the aft companionway. After a moment, Jack realized he was looking at the captain, naked, his pale skin silhouetted against the dark skies behind him. His long hair was disheveled and he had a large, blood-caked welt on his left temple, like a piece of old jewelry. Dried vomit adorned his chest and in his left hand he held a jug of grog. His right hand held a saber, still sheathed. He seemed unaware of the bodies and debris about him.

"Mr. Quince, why are we running with short sails? Damn it, man, we're almost becalmed. Lay on the canvas, mister."

Several of the crew dropped their heads. Jack realized for the first time how much his fellow sailors had come to believe in the hierarchy of the ship at sea. The raging of the storm and the death of their mates had shaken them, but the recognition that they were truly without a captain was crushing.

"Smithers, see that the captain is safely back in his cabin. Lash him securely in his bunk," Quince said. He stepped toward the old man and took the saber from his hand. The captain sputtered a protest.

A rogue wave from the stern lifted the entire ship and spun her. The water carried Jack halfway across the quarterdeck. Coughing seawater over the aft rail, his hands gripped the rough carving he had seen the captain working on while docked in Massachusetts and Cuba. Salem seemed to him a lifetime ago—when he was just a boy. He ran his fingers over the intricate letters: "Captain Hans Peter Deploy. 1730–1806." The captain knew this was his last trip.

No one manned the wheel. It spun lazily, as if detached. Then Jack realized that, in fact, it was. The pintles were sprung from the gudgeons and the rudder had come unshipped. My God, thought Jack. We're sitting in this pond like a toy boat.

Quince bellied up to the starboard rail and stared into the blackness. In a voice full of dread, knowing he was the only one capable of command, he addressed the crew. "Quickly do what you can for the ship, lads. Then lash yourself to the pulpit around the main and foremast and pray . . . for we are surely in the eye of the typhoon."

⇥⟡⇤

Jack secured Paul onto the pulpit surrounding the mainmast, jamming in the belaying pins upside down so that a quick pull down would release the line he had secured around both of them. Then he sat quietly against the wood as sailors all around him tied themselves to masts, stanchions, and cannon.

Talk was scarce as the sailors prepared. Quince took one last survey of the ship and tied himself in. The winds started to pick up.

Debris from the wreckage over the side pulled the ship to port, but the winds and seas were pushing back to starboard, and it was in this pattern that the typhoon found the *Perdido Star*. She was helpless in the heavy seas.

The seawater came over the bow in housefuls. It hit the quarterdeck then burst upon the sailors on the main deck all tethered in their spots, helpless to ward off the tons of water. Jack could hear screams as the men gasped for air and prepared themselves for the next wave. The relentless pounding loosened some of the timbers, and the noise of the waves was countered by the sound of the parting of the ship's main cross members. She was beginning to break up.

Waves struck the cabin on the quarterdeck, sounding to Jack like the felling of trees. Tons of water rushed into her companionway hatch, spilling into what was once the captain's cabin. The water would shoot over Jack's and Paul's heads, slam against the quarterdeck bulkhead, and disappear into the cabin area. As the *Star* pitched again, it would dump the water, along with debris from the aft cabin, back on deck. The returning water lashed against the new wave coming over the bow, meeting in the middle of the main deck where the sailors were struggling for life.

Jack now thought that strapping in was not such a good idea. He could barely catch his breath between waves, and looking about him, he could see some of the mates were struggling mightily to keep from drowning.

At one point between waves, Jack raised his head above the pulpit stanchion to look aft, when he heard a loud shout. "Jack, above!"

A spar in a tangle of lines came screaming down in a large arc toward the pulpit, crashing just inches above Jack's head. The concussion alone was enough to deafen him and he had pulled Paul down with him. They were shaken but unhurt, as yet another wave washed over them. Sputtering, Jack looked to where the warning had come from. There lay the drowned body of Cookietwo. He had repaid his debt.

Across from Jack, three sailors secured between the cannons were trying to untie themselves, for one of the cannons had come adrift and was running to the length of her securing line and then back again, swinging like a pendulum from the end that still held. The sailor closest to it was unconscious and in the path of the two-ton, cast-iron killing machine. Jack could do nothing but watch helplessly as the man was reduced to pulp. The damn thing didn't need to be loaded to take seamen's lives.

"Are you all right?" Jack shouted to Paul, hearing his voice.

Paul must have been delirious, for his answer didn't make sense.

"Say it again. I can't hear you."

"I said, never let me find you again, old sir, near our hollow ship. . . . " Paul pointed toward the ocean, laughing.

There, tied securely onto what was left of his oaken bunk, floated the captain, holding an oil lantern, silver beard and hair wild with water, gazing into the black sky. He lifted a hand to wave briefly as the sea carried his bier into the night.

"Are we dead yet? Do we deserve this?" Paul asked, suddenly cogent, his voice matter-of-fact.

Jack spit seawater and replied, "Not dead yet. But close. Very close, Paulie."

"Paulie? Only Hansumbob calls me that. I remember the first time I heard that name, it was the night I peeled you off the street in Habana. Do you remember that night?"

Jack watched the violent sea. He remembered.

The storm wrenched their bodies from side to side. After the endless hell of drenchings, the water tearing at his bindings, Jack was beaten so badly, he was barely conscious. Then the wind's fury began to ease. The ship seemed to right herself, slowly circling in her own debris. Stars appeared not only overhead, but across the entire sky. The decks were now awash, fore and aft; the port rail was four feet underwater, and the ship lay as a tilted whale. But they had survived the storm.

It occurred to Jack they should be sinking. The seas had calmed beyond what seemed reasonable from just moments before—they must be in the lee of land, given the odd lurching of the ship.

Wounded and drowned sailors were all around him; some of the stronger ones started to move. He knew the sailors tied to the port rail were all dead, for he saw that part of the ship submerged most of the time.

Jack became aware of a wild joy coursing through his veins. It was the most exciting and terrifying thing that had ever happened to him.

Quince untied himself and began giving orders to the mates who were able to move. A grinding, unearthly sound stopped him. He made his way aft along the starboard rail, shouting, "We're hard aground, lads. Quickly grab anything that floats and prepare to abandon ship."

Jack pulled out the belaying pins, untying Paul and himself. He grabbed the door to the captain's cabin.

"What's happening? Are we home?" Paul's face was intense with pain.

"No, Paul, we're not home yet. We're going to take this piece of wood and begin paddling. We've gone aground on a reef, or a spit of land, and if we're lucky, lad, maybe there's an island attached."

10

WRECKED ON A SOUTH SEA ISLE

JACK AND PAUL CLUNG TO the safety of the door, drifting away from the remnants of the ship, praying to find solid earth. They could hear the surf breaking somewhere on a distant shore but the heavy seas and dark night made it impossible to know which direction to swim. They were exhausted. Jack had left the safety of their life raft twice to go to the aid of a sailor crying for help—each time finding nothing. The sea was exacting a heavy price this night.

A dozen or so sailors were shouting to one another, assembling slowly, scrambling over jagged rock and coral shallows, desperate for land. They knew from the pounding of the surf that it was near; but getting there was frustratingly difficult. They would be atop a coral head, in two feet of water, and moments later flailing in water over their heads. Jack and Paul were too busy keeping the door from splintering on the coral to pay attention to anything else. Finally, they made it through a break in the reef, landing in a tiny cove, and could see a foam line ahead. Jack thought he saw movement at a point where the mangroves were thinnest, perhaps a large animal or a man.

At last staggering onto shore, Jack noticed signs of human use, in the form of a fire-blackened hearth mere yards from the water. He and his friend continued dragging valuable flotsam to shore, even the occasional bedraggled sailor.

"Look, Jack, there's charred animal bones in some of these things," Paul said. He pushed a barrel full of something he couldn't identify to higher ground, past the water's edge.

"Yeah, looks mainly like fish."

The moon had broken through the clouds, and the men were making shore more easily. They arrived in ones and twos, collapsing long enough to catch their breath. Suddenly Quince seemed to appear from nowhere, relatively unscathed and already shouting orders.

"The *Star*'s awash and down at the gills, men, but there's a passel of junk floatin' around out there that's gonna seem like treasure tomorrow—so look alive!" He had apparently made it most of the way to shore in the ship's launch but waded a different route over the last few reefs. He had clutched in his huge arms an odd assortment of personal treasures, including a pistol case, a cutlass, and a bunched-up red sash which Jack had seen hung over his hammock in the *Star*.

As Jack waded out to grab a floating box, he tried to take in as much of his surroundings as possible in the moonlight. The islet they had landed on seemed small and not readily approachable except through the break in the reef they had discovered. Hands occupied, he jutted his chin seaward and remarked to Paul, "Look at that." Paul, dragging a timber to shore, turned. Even in the dark they could see outlines of larger islands nearby. Jack's imagination ran with possibilities as he harvested pieces of the *Star* from the sea. Indians, cannibals, stories of castaways.

"Okay, take a break, men." Quince motioned the survivors to gather several yards inland, away from the beach. Most of the easily salvaged flotsam had been collected, and Jack figured Quince thought it more important now for the men to take stock, rest, and if possible, get warm. Getting warm was the issue. Even in the tropical night the men were seriously chilled from their long exposure to the sea.

"Men, we need a fire."

"The natives will see us," Smithers croaked from where he had sprawled on the ground.

"True enough," answered Quince, glancing toward the nearby islands. "But there's no point in not building a fire to hide our being here, since by morning the mast of the *Star* will be visible for miles."

He's right, Jack thought. The ship might be under but her mainmast wasn't, and the soaked, weary men needed warmth and rest before they could defend themselves.

"The smoke oughta give us some protection from these damn insects, too," muttered Coop, the ship's cooper and chief carpenter. "But how we gonna start one? Everything's soaked through."

"Anyone bring a serviceable pistol or rifle to shore in all that mess?" Jack asked.

Bosun Mentor answered that there was one in Quince's kit, to which Quince nodded, then said, "But so what?"

"Let me try something," answered Jack. He explained his plan, and soon Quince had the men laboriously carving a pile of wood shavings from the comparatively dry inside of otherwise-soaked ship's timbers. They scooped gunpowder from the center of a damp cask that had floated to shore, while Paul removed oil from the reservoir of a broken ship's lamp he had salvaged. The men's shivering was noticeably increasing; the intense excitement of their survival effort was waning, the effect of their long immersion catching up to them.

They sprinkled the mound of wood splinters on a plate salvaged from the mess, and heaped gunpowder over it. Paul poured the oil so it pooled under the shavings.

"Stand back, fellas." Jack had removed the ball and

charge from the pistol and with powder only in the flash pan, he held the pistol sideways, flintlock almost touching the flammable concoction in the plate. He pulled the trigger and a bright flash hit the plate. The men cheered as first a sizzling flame, then a steady fire, took hold. Paul placed the plate on the ground, in one of the old hearths. It worked on the first try. Many boxes had been brought ashore or floated in of their own accord. They were pried open and anything that would burn became an offering.

Quen-Li, whom Jack had not noticed in all the commotion, appeared with his arms full of old coconut husks, gathered from a nearby stand of palms. An excellent idea, thought Jack. They burned beautifully and kept them from using something they might need later. The men's spirits rose in direct proportion to the height of the growing flames. Jack knew the light and heat restored some sense of control in a world that had fallen apart beneath them.

"Well, maybe the savages will find us and eat us by morning, but at least we'll make them a warm repast. I do so hate a cold breakfast," Paul said.

The men, slumped around the fire, blankly considered Paul's comment for a moment and slowly started to break into smiles. The smiles grew into low chuckles, into general laughter, and finally, insane guffaws. Jack, unable to keep his own reserve, joined them.

The evil spell had been broken. Jack marveled what a fire and some offhand humor could do. By bleeding, goddamn hell, they were alive! They were somewhere with earth beneath their feet and blood still in their veins; not still, pale forms on the seabed. Or worse, flailing in the waves, trying desperately not to drink the ocean.

Quince let the men calm from their outburst of nervous energy and told them they would have to take stock of their predicament before they could sleep. Jack and

Quen-Li seemed to recover some strength the quickest, and they rose to help Quince assess the number and condition of seamen sprawled about the clearing.

They counted sixteen survivors of the *Star*'s demise, two seriously injured. Jacob, the ship's youngest able-bodied seaman, lay in a state of shock. Shreds of skin remained where his little finger used to be on his left hand. He was badly bruised from head to foot, and his right leg appeared to be broken.

Mancy's head was partly stove in from the mainmast boom, which had swung free from its stays and fetched him a glancing blow in the last moments of the storm. His left eye bulged partly out of the socket, and his head on the left side was a confusion of blood, bone, and scalp. He seemed alert and followed the movement of his mates with his right eye. He had not uttered a sound since the wreck, but his mates weren't sure if this was due to disability or disinclination. His drool flowed and the right side of his face—the undamaged side—twitched uncontrollably. Paul whispered to Jack that it was due to the damage to his brain. The men tried their best to make him comfortable. Everyone seemed to know that Mancy was only with them for a brief stopover on his way to eternity.

Quince believed Jacob would live if no infection set in and if his leg was not badly broken. The young sailor had no recollection at all of how he had lost his finger, but knew it happened when they scrambled to get a keg of drinking water and other essentials into the ship's launch for the last run to shore.

Besides Mancy and Jacob, Quince counted Jack, Paul, Cheatum, Mentor, Smithers, Hansumbob, Coop, Peters, Klett, Brown, Red Dog, Dawkins, and himself among the survivors. Quen-Li also. All told, eleven had died in the wreck of the *Star*. All of those who lived were seeping blood from the cuts they had sustained on the jagged coral outcrops, particularly around their legs and hands. Jack noted that the coral abrasions tended to leave a nasty red flare about them. They'd be slow healing for sure.

The men soon collapsed around the fire, most falling asleep. A watch was kept all night on the quiet water leading to the cove. The guards were relieved frequently, the exhausted men only capable of keeping their eyes open an hour at a time. Each, in his turn, happily passed the one usable pistol over to his mate on the turn of an hourglass. Salvaged from the ship, the simple time-keeping mechanism was a comfort in itself, somehow providing a familiar touchstone to the *Star*, governing their routine.

⊰ ❈ ⊱

The next morning broke gray, attended by a warm drizzle. As the sun began to break through, the heat of the South Pacific day engulfed them. But at least with the sunlight, the insects that had tortured them throughout the night dissipated. It was now easier to wander from the protective smoke without "losing a quart of blood to the damned winged furies that, by the saints, were a cross between a friggin' fly and a mastiff," in Quince's reckoning.

Quince had the men tally their resources and comb the beach and shallows for anything more that might have washed up. Jack was glad to see that the first mate had managed to salvage a load of shot and several horns of dry powder for the pistol, and the sea, at its own whimsy, had tossed more than a dozen kegs of gunpowder onto the shore.

The *Star* had released a fair amount of bounty to the shipwrecked men, but the ship's remains had settled to the lagoon bottom and anything else would have to be outright salvaged. Very little in the way of food had been rescued. As the day drew on, they managed to save a barrel of flour and several bags of rice—all of it wet. The rice started to swell, so Quince ordered it cooked. The salt water, with which it was impregnated, made it almost inedible. The islet held little food. No citrus fruits and only a few coconuts that weren't so old and dried out as to yield white meat worth the effort of splitting them. Of great relief to the men was the presence of a full hogshead of fresh water that Quince had ordered salvaged at all costs.

The men preserved the coals from the day's fire and added more dried wood to a pile growing steadily under a piece of sail canvas. There were plenty of fish in the lagoon but catching them was harder than expected. Knowing thirst would be the real killer, Quince had Jack, Paul, and Coop rig a rain catchment; but they lacked suitable containers to hold the water once collected.

By the third night the men settled into a routine, priorities being to maintain water, obtain food, and keep guard. At night, they could see fires on neighboring isles and knew the natives could certainly see theirs. The nagging cuts on their feet and hands became more than a nuisance. They were becoming debilitating.

On the fourth day Mancy died. Because his one good eye remained always open and his breathing shallow, it was only when Paul noted the drool had stopped that he took the initiative to check on the man. He was aghast to realize that rigor mortis had already set in, which meant the men had been murmuring comforting asides to a corpse for the better part of the day.

Disposing of the body proved no easy chore. It was impossible to dig an adequate hole in the thin mantle of soil covering the coral and limestone surface of their new home. Burning the seaman would take more wood than they could spare, so burial at sea seemed the only option. Most of the men were weak. Dragging their mate to the beach and out to the launch took precious energy and several hard-won links of chain to weight him down. But a putrefying body could spell real trouble for the men's health on this tiny island, so Quince said it had to be done. They removed Mancy's jacket when the rigor dissipated and his arms became pliable. Minus his clothes, which they all agreed would be of more use to the quick than the dead, Mancy's remains were rowed to the edge of the reef and consigned to the deep.

The procurement of fish in any quantity proved a significant challenge. The men were sometimes successful with hook and line, but the bottom constantly snagged their tackle. Paul and Jack came up with an imaginative attempt at a solution. They designed an explosive charge that could be detonated in the water, hoping the fish would die in the concussion. After all, if there was one thing they were rich in, it was gunpowder.

Given the right conditions, Paul said, a fuse could be designed to discharge underwater. It had something to do with boiling the saltpeter.

"No, it's the whole mess you boil," Jack answered. "Nitrate, sulfur, charcoal, and all. I've heard it was done during the war, when the army and that Bushnell fella were experimenting with mines and submarine torpedoes in Boston harbor to break the Redcoat blockade.

"My father said there was nothing to it if you made a slurry of the gunpowder and coated it on the fuse. The fire burns from bubble to bubble, using the trapped air to keep the flame alive."

"Did he ever do it?"

"Never had a cause to. But if he said it can be done, I'm sure it's possible."

They worked on the project all day. Finally, after boiling a concoction in the one pan not being used for collecting water, they dipped some twine in it and hunted for a proper container to use as a bomb. They settled on an apothecary jar, which they filled with dry powder and sealed with candle wax. Homemade fuse in place, Jack and Paul took it to a shallow reef near their cove where they had seen a bunch of fish congregating. They lit the fuse and tossed it amongst the fish. It sparked mightily and kept burning in the water, making a strange trail of white smoke as it sank, and finally fizzled out. Failure.

Next they tried a drill from the remains of the salvaged surgeon's kit. Although it proved useless for Mancy, it contained a trephination bit for releasing fluid from beneath the skull in head wounds. They used it to drill a hole in a deadlight, wrenched from ship flotsam, which they then crammed full of black powder. "Shove it in there as hard as you can, compress the hell out of it," urged Jack.

Paul looked at him doubtfully. "Isn't that a little risky?"

"Come to think of it, be sure to use wood to ram it. Metal against metal could create sparks and that would be a problem."

"Thanks for the warning." Paul tossed aside the bent iron spoon he had been using for the task.

They finished the tamping, inserted the string through the hole, waxing it in, and finally tossed the latest design into the turquoise water. There was a muffled whump. Within seconds a number of small reef fish flopped on the surface. Their only catch. A semifailure. It appeared this approach would be inadequate for feeding the men, even if they perfected their technique.

That evening around the fire, Jack offered to reconnoiter one of the neighboring islands at night and perhaps do a little foraging.

"Ya figger the savages won't know yer coming 'cause it's dark out?" Quince asked. "No, Jack, for lawd's sake I need you too much to lose you on some fool's errand. They know we're here—no way they couldn't, with our fires and all. Christ knows why they haven't shown up . . . for better or for worse."

Paul grinned sardonically. "Greet us or eat us, the poor devils can't make up their minds."

"Enough, Paul. See if you can rig some more shade cover from that sailcloth, lad."

"But," continued Jack, "if they know we're here, what's the harm in paying them a visit?"

"No." Quince sounded irritated but Jack knew the question needed answering; for the others as well as himself. "We're a force to be reckoned with here, even with only one gun. We've cutlasses and we're together and there ain't but one way of gettin' at us. We split our forces and we've lost an edge."

"What if they're friendly?"

"They might be, but I'll believe that when we're shaking hands and dancing the minuet with their ladies—not till then."

Jack knew Quince was right, but patience and inaction never came easy to him, even when warranted, and he chafed under the mate's restraint.

"Another thing, Jack. Those fires are probably from natives all right, but what if they're not? Malay and Chinee pirates range the coast of Asia only a few days' sail from here and they probably set up for their raids somewheres in these waters."

Jack nodded his understanding. Paul added, "Could be Europeans, too, Mr. Quince. The John Company's packets also range these parts. The bastards could dye us black and sell us like they do anyone else they can't exploit in some other way."

"Enough. Get that sail rigged for shade." Jack hid his smile when he heard Quince mutter, "Sometimes that lad can be insufferable."

Quen-Li proved invaluable in procuring what little vegetable matter the group could consume. He obtained tubers and green pulpy leaves scattered in the mangrove flats and made a mush that provided some nourishment even though it tasted "like something that had been et twice before," as Coop put it. The Chinaman seemed to thrive on the gruel himself, being one of the few survivors showing no signs of physical or mental distress. Jack was increasingly intrigued with the calm strength of this man, certain there was something in his past that had little to do with a life spent slopping gruel for sailors.

Jacob seemed to be taking a turn for the better. His hand, soaked in hot salt water by Quen-Li and lanced when necessary by Mentor, was healing. Again, their surplus of gunpowder helped them in odd ways. From the start, Mentor had insisted on pouring some of the powder into the open wound. When it worked, even Jack became convinced the old folk tale was right; no infection was setting in. Paul, particularly intrigued with the development, opined that maybe the sulfur or potassium nitrate, which made up significant portions of the powder, was responsible.

Jacob's leg had not been broken as originally feared. He started hobbling around a bit, and the swelling went down. The young man's physical improvement seemed to help him combat the profound depression he had been suffering over the loss of his finger. Life without a little finger was no big deal, his older mates assured him, with their own brand of rough humor. Klett, a sailor of Scandinavian extraction, had a particularly interesting perspective to share with the boy.

"Jaysus lad, could of been yer pecker ye lost. Think of it. Hell, peckerless ye'd of been better off dead—but a finger? Lad, it's nothing. Just got to reach farther back to wipe yer arse."

"Eloquently put, my dear Klett," Paul said, laughing. "Such soulful commentary, sublimely expressed . . . perhaps you'll consider a career in letters once we've made it back to civilized land?"

"Stuff it, Paul, 'fore I cuff you one," muttered Klett.

"Easy," Jack added. "Paul's just letting his tongue get ahead of his brain, which is his habit. I believe your views have been a true comfort to Jacob."

To Jack, Klett was another interesting sort. Aboard the *Star*, he had paid little heed to the huge Scandinavian, who was naturally quiet and a bit simple. During and after the storm, however, the man distinguished himself in Jack's eyes for his courage, positive fatalism, and great strength.

Their second week on the island found them all surviving and in reasonable health, but no significant improvement in their situation. The constant rain allayed their biggest concern—fresh water. Food remained a problem, particularly fruit and vegetables to keep scurvy at bay. The lagoon teemed with fish, but their ability to catch them was still marginal. And most of the men had some degree of festering sores, particularly on their feet. The overall energy level, which had risen from survival of the wreck, was dropping. Jack could tell Quince was concerned. What if the natives finally made their appearance and the men gave an obvious impression of helplessness?

But Jack was not as alarmed. Although their position was still precarious, the shock of being shipwrecked was over and they clearly weren't in any immediate danger of dying of thirst, hunger, or hostile savages.

Jack began to venture further away from camp to investigate their surroundings. On a sunny afternoon with exceptionally calm water, he paddled out to the *Star* on a raft he constructed from several wood planks that had been washed ashore. He climbed the *Star*'s half-sunken mast to get a better idea of the extent of the surrounding islands. They were on an extensive archipelago. Jack could see no end to the island chain, a flat expanse of larger and smaller land bodies, fringed by a reef that flashed white with a necklace of breakers all along the windward side.

Who were the people who made their homes in this strange land? Jack wondered. Would they be helpful or hostile? Would they look like the natives from Polynesia? He had heard these lands were less known and more primitive than Fiji and the other southern isles, but he knew that was conjecture. He had been told that only a few whalers and missionaries had visited the islands in these parts and, as Quince had said: "Whalers—half of 'em lie and the other half don't tell the truth . . . on the whole, though, they're more honest than missionaries."

When Jack described to Paul what he had seen from the mast, his friend said he suspected that they were on an atoll, maybe the Pelews or something north of them. The absence of any volcanic peaks meant they were probably not in the eastern Carolines but further west, "damn near to Asia," as Quince had put it.

"The water is real shallow where it's light green, inside that wide fringe of breakers you described," Paul said. "Probably no more than ten to thirty fathoms at most. The dark blue, outside the white surf, is Davy Jones, thousands of fathoms—we're lucky the *Star* made it through before sinking, else she'd be way beyond our reach . . . in this life anyway."

Jack didn't want to think about it. "How long do those books say it takes for all this coral to build up? You said yourself the water's thousands of feet deep all around it."

"Ah, my friend, that's a question isn't it?"

Jack listened to his learned mate tell him of the latest ideas coming from folks called "uniformitarianists," especially some fellow named James Hutton who wrote a book called *Theory of the Earth*.

"They'd say the base of these islands is volcanic," Paul told him. "It rose above the surface once, then eroded from the forces of wind and surf, then coral built up on its remnants as it sunk."

"Wind and surf? That'd take thousands of years!"

"More like millions. Yes, if you take the Bible literally, you'd have to believe the earth was formed in about 4004 B.C., according to the Ussher-Lightfoot chronology."

"Ussher-Lightfoot?"

"It's two fellas, religious types that added it all up from the Bible. But the point is you'd have to believe the world was created by God just as you see it, as there wouldn't have been enough time for much to change in less than 6,000 years; unless there was a whole series of catastrophes, huge floods and the like. But those other people say that everything happens in gradual changes, little by little over the ages. Anyway, whoever's right, I've got kitchen duty tonight . . . see you at the trough."

Paul left, and Jack sat on a piece of driftwood reflectively moving his toes through the sand. He tried to imagine the sand being just broken-up bits of coral and rock and what it meant to live in a world millions of years old. Did it make him more, or less, important? Did it make what happened in Cuba to his parents insignificant, in the grand scheme of things?

He wished that thought hadn't entered his head. "There is compensation," Quince had told him. How? How could there ever be enough? The blackness in his heart threatening to take over, he quickly jumped up and started to walk down the beach, trying to get focused on something constructive, alive. Colleen, now there was something alive.

She seemed so far away now . . . hell—he hardly knew the girl. Why did she walk through his imagination like she owned it? He had hardly talked to her, except, dammit, that girl spoke volumes through her eyes. The twinkle, the softness . . . like his mother in a way. Her brogue. It puzzled Jack why his memories of the girl weren't dimming with time. They were growing stronger.

He passed one of the long-deserted native hearths and said out loud to no one, "Hundreds of years, thousands, millions? I'll bet you folks never read *Theory of the Earth*. . . . Why don't you show yourselves?"

11

THEY MEET
THE NATIVES

FIRST CONTACT WITH the natives was not much longer in coming. In the early light of the next day, a man materialized out of the morning mist, right in front of Jack. He appeared from the brush bordering the rough windward side of the islet, the exact opposite direction the sailors had expected. Jack had finished relieving himself on the fringe of the camp when he realized that the man-shaped bush he was studying through bleary eyes was, in fact, a man.

The native watched Jack with no discernible expression. The spear in his right hand was held butt to the ground and what appeared to be some form of battleaxe rested easily on his left shoulder. The native seemed to harbor no threat but rather maintained a cautious, noncommittal demeanor. Jack took a step back. He instantly felt certain the man was not alone; his suspicions were confirmed as other forms began to appear out of the rapidly dissipating morning fog. Jack couldn't help thinking they were the strangest looking people he had ever set eyes upon. He wondered how he and his shipwrecked comrades must appear to them.

The natives were dark copper in color and appeared to be wearing even darker clothes. But seeing their exposed genitals, Jack realized they were actually completely naked and used some sort of body paint.

He dared not rush back to alert his comrades—he feared it might be seen as a defensive, or worse, offensive, act. Instead he stood quietly, taking in the details of the bizarre apparitions while they seemed to do the same with him. It occurred to him that he had been wrong again; it wasn't body paint he saw, it was tattooing.

Their hair was jet black, rolled back on their heads into buns. Jack looked into the eyes of the man closest to him for some sign of mood or intention. The dark eyes met his own without blinking. But he felt they projected neither fear nor threat—if anything curiosity and maybe a hint of amusement. Whatever his intent, the man cut a formidable and fantastic figure.

As this new knowledge sank in, Jack realized that the activity behind him that had been swelling with the onset of the day had silenced. He knew without turning that his shipmates were aware of his situation.

Being closest, Jack figured it fell on him to make the first move. He raised his hand palm outward, smiled, and gestured to the visitors to follow him. Then he deliberately turned his back, which he assumed could only be interpreted by any race as a sign of trust and nonaggression, and took several steps toward his fellows, praying his next sensation would not be that of a spearhead through his body. He sensed the natives had not moved and motioned again to them, resuming his calm stroll toward his shipmates. He was relieved to see the watch had been recalled from the cove, the pistol wisely kept from sight.

With apparent nonchalance, the leader stepped forward, spear now resting on his right shoulder as the axe rested on his left. Quince moved parallel to Jack and uttered the first words of the encounter.

"Uh . . . okole maluna. Friends."

Jack knew Quince had experience from earlier voyages of the Sandwich Isles, but could tell his words meant nothing to the tattooed man. Quince followed his statement with a gesture that to Jack seemed a happy choice. He removed the red scarf from his neck, the one he had managed to retain through the ordeal of the shipwreck, and offered it to the visitors' apparent leader.

The man broke into a big smile, took the cloth, and waved it at his fellows, accompanied by a wild language sounding of another world. The others visibly relaxed in their demeanor; from nowhere, one produced a good-sized fish. Jack marveled that they had so easily come prepared for battle or barter.

The leader pointed to himself and said, "Gan Jawa." Then he pointed to Quince questioningly. On impulse, Jack responded before the first mate. He pointed to Quince and stated in a firm voice: "Gan Quince." A long shot, but it seemed to work. The natives milled about the camp but glanced at Quince for approval as though they were in the presence of a foreign chief. Jack reasoned that a firmly established hierarchy, in a motley group such as theirs, would elicit more respect. We might be wrecked, but we're not leaderless or undisciplined, seemed the correct attitude.

The natives were either extremely cunning or truly inclined to friendship. They were most fascinated with the hairy chests of the Americans and Europeans that had never been darkened with inked decorations, and many stepped up to examine them. Although barefoot, they walked with apparent impunity over the sharp coral that cut the feet of sailors. At one point, Gan Jawa walked back to Quince and waved his arm in a circle encompassing the nearby islands, ocean and sky, and said easily: "Belaur." Quince nodded knowingly, but when Jawa turned away, he shrugged his shoulders. They now knew the name of the place they were in, although Quince had apparently never heard of it.

Jack remarked quietly to Quince that he counted only nine natives all told. But Quince spotted several canoes making their way into the cove they had been guarding. Each had three men in it and a noticeable lack of women. In American Indian parlance, this would be called a war party. It did not escape Jack that it had been intelligently deployed. The men in the bushes must have gained the island in some fashion he didn't yet understand, ready to call in reinforcements from seaward at short notice. The newly arrived group disembarked smoothly. The last man in each canoe stepped out and held it steady before the others took their eyes from the white men even for the instant required to shift their weight and ease out of the sleek craft in water less than a foot deep.

Jack also noted that the newcomers deferred to the original leader of the group. That meant that the leader had chosen to expose himself to the danger rather than allot the role to some lieutenant.

As the two groups examined each other, making cautious signs of goodwill, a few objects were exchanged. Pieces of scrap metal and nails from a keg went for woven mats and bone fish hooks. This soon turned into a brisk trade; but Quince, concerned at the undisciplined give and take, ended it by flourishing a feathered hat above his head to get his men's attention. Teeth gritted, but with a smile on his face, he announced firmly, "Avast you dumb sons of sea whores, don't be giving away what we might need to live on." But at the end of his order, he presented the hat to the leader, gathered his men in a line, and had them salute. A smart move, Jack thought. The trading had been curtailed, but no feelings hurt.

The natives stayed for most of the day, inspecting the wreckage of the *Perdido Star*. The forward section was easily visible in shallow water; they gazed at where the broken masts protruded from the sea. Small clusters of dark men and eventually women and children arrived to observe the activity of the whites, as if witnessing an incredible spectacle. Gan Jawa occasionally motioned his fellows to help in some of the more labor-intensive work of the Americans when it appeared extra hands would be helpful.

The native leader seemed perplexed when the white men turned some of their efforts to cleaning the fish they had been given. Soon another canoe arrived and several women walked over to the fire and unceremoniously took over the preparation of food. It became clear that in these parts men might do the catching of game, but it was definitely women God meant to cook it.

By evening, the natives, much better swimmers than the sailors, had helped the shipwrecked men gather more items from the wreck, cooked a meal, and even produced some fresh fruit—a matter of no small joy. Pacific isles were notoriously variable in abundant edible fruits. If these were plentiful, there was no threat of scurvy.

At some signal Jack didn't catch, the islanders began slowly repairing to their canoes, the grateful hosts walking to the water to see them off. At this point their good fortune became even greater. A departing native man yelled something to one of the women that caused a flurry of excitement from Brown. Brown was just that— a brown-skinned Malaysian, hired on in Papeete, whose real name was unpronounceable to his mates.

"Quince!"

"Aye, what's yer problem, Brown?"

"No problem, sir. That man told the woman to hurry up with bringin' 'im the paddle."

"Well, so bleedin' what—" Quince paused. "You understood him?"

"Aye, sir. It's Malay—he's talkin' a dialect I can understand."

Quince turned quickly to Jawa and indicated he would like to have the last canoe return.

When it did, Brown excitedly rattled off several statements in a singsong language foreign to all but the man who had called out. Immediately, the Belauran replied in the same tongue.

"Mon dieu," muttered Paul to Jack. "We've found a bloody human Rosetta stone."

The shipwrecked men had indeed received a bounty of blessings that day. With the leaving of the last canoe, Quince called a council around the still glowing coals.

"Well, lads, I'm not a religious man but we need to start by giving thanks. Our futures looked sad indeed last night, and now we're sitting here with full bellies among friendly people and thanks to Brown here we can even talk to them."

The men bowed their heads and Quince led them in a small prayer, lamenting the loss of their mates and thanking the Lord for their good fortune.

"What's the next step, men? What do we need the most and how do we go about gettin' it?"

"Shoes." The answer from Paul came immediately and was seconded by several voices.

Most of the men, if they owned boots at all, had shed them swimming to land. Even the Jack Tars accustomed to scrambling barefoot up ship's rigging were hard put to deal with the jagged coral piercing through the sand on most of the islet.

"There's hardly any damned sand or soil on this rock, Skipper," one said. "Christ, it's like we're walkin' on broken glass."

Jack noted the man's reference to Quince as "Skipper," carrying with it an unintended import: the men were informally changing the ship's hierarchy. Quince noted it, too. No one had challenged the first mate's leadership all along, but the simple use of that term in a seaman's world was tacit indication that Quince had been promoted.

"You're calling me 'Skipper,' lads, but there's nothing says that has to be, since the *Perdido* is a merchant ship, not a sovereign vessel, and we're well past any imminent peril from the sea. So . . . is there any objection to my being in charge?"

A general silence ensued. All seemed to feel no reason to disrupt a working system, and none harbored against Quince more than the usual minor grudges one might have for a superior.

"Okay. Shoes it is then. We've got water and food and we're going to damn soon need something to protect our feet."

"We can make some moccasins," Red Dog said, "but it's a bleedin' shame we can't get to the cargo, where I know we're carrying at least one whole damn box of them."

"Tools, too," Mentor chimed in. "We've got some but could use a lot more."

"And guns," Coop added. "Don't forget that. The savages have been square with us, but what if that changes?"

"Aye guns," said Smithers. "We've got plenty powder and lead but we're at anybody's mercy till we have more than one pistol to defend the lot of us."

"We had a good dozen musket on board," Quince observed thoughtfully, "but they were locked in the captain's cabin and that went into the abyss when that wave took all the aft superstructure. Most of the hull seems in shallow water; the rest's in the bluest part of Davy Jones."

"I might be able to help," Jack said.

They all looked at him.

"The fo'c'sle is sunk shallow and intact. It probably still contains my personals."

"You aren't sayin' you were keepin' guns in the crew quarters, lad? You know darn well that's against ship's rules."

"No, I wasn't keeping guns, but my most valuable possessions were there and that includes a bag of brass parts to twenty of the finest rifle mechanisms ever made. I know because I helped my father make them. I took the liberty of removing them from the hold one day when I spied them among my father's possessions that he had left with the captain in Cuba."

The men were all silence and raised eyebrows.

"And barrels—" bosun Mentor broke in, "—yea, I know what you're going to say"—he worked belowdecks, often checking the stowage—"there are twenty fine barrels still in the second hold. Your father's."

"Yes. I suppose it's my inheritance of sorts. The mechanisms are made of brass, of course, so they should suffer little from exposure to seawater. The barrels are thick gunmetal and well oiled, so they will also fare reasonably—for a time at least. Given our present circumstances, they would be worth their weight in gold if we could get to them."

"Jaysus," Coop said. "With stocks made from the mangrove wood and those parts, we could have twenty operational muskets. We could hold our own against all the savages in creation. Think what we could do with some of the cannon."

"No, Coop," said Quince. "It's the muskets that would do it. Cannon are good to defend a ship, or if we were making a fort, but they're too damn heavy to lift and move for our purposes. No, the muskets would be the thing."

"Even better than that," Jack continued. "These gun parts aren't for your ordinary musket. They're mechanisms and barrels for Kentucky long rifles: we could shoot the eyes out of mosquitoes at two hundred paces."

Quince fumbled for his pipe and tobacco pouch. "Maybe so," he said, nodding his head toward the *Star*. "But they may as well be on the moon for all the good they do us out there in five or ten fathom of water."

"Aye, and what about gettin' home?" Smithers asked.

"What in the name of God are we doing about that, I ask ya?"

"Easy, now," Quince answered. "We're going to be here a good spell and need defend ourselves in the meantime."

"He's right," came from Mentor, looking pointedly at Smithers. "We has to live one life at a time, we do. Don't know when we're leaving these parts but it's more likely to be on our own terms, if we got shoes on our feet and guns in our hands."

They all stared seaward and said nothing; the subject dropped in favor of sleep. The men retired, feeling better than they had in a long time, despite nagging questions of the future. Soon the camp was quiet, the *Star*'s surviving crew sleeping more peacefully than they ever had since the wreck. But Jack was awake, unable to keep thoughts of the count, or of Colleen, from his mind. He was determined with an almost fearsome intensity that he would meet both of them again.

12

SETTLING IN
ON BELAUR

A FEW DAYS LATER, ideas of the salvage of guns or shoes were all but forgotten in order to move camp to the Belauran village. The islet they were on was limited in resources and access to the lagoon. Beyond proximity to the *Star*, it had little to recommend it. Jawa felt it would be easier to offer the protection of his own clan—and that of the chief of the entire island chain— if the men of the *Star* moved to Belaur proper on the main island.

The day was spent strapping cargo from the *Star* to the native outriggers for the one-hour paddle to the main village.

Of great value were sailcloth, needles, and thread. A fair amount survived, although much remained in the hold of the sunken ship. Most of the cooper's wares were easily accessible, including his mallets and a wide assortment of hoops and staves that would probably prove useful for fresh-water storage and other purposes. Of less immediate utility—but the subject of considerable mirth—was an unmarked crate which, when eagerly opened, revealed over four dozen hoops for women's dresses, and another forty pounds of horse hair for use in making toothbrushes—enough for a small army.

Most of the gunpowder was left at the islet to dry out, there being no purpose for it in the immediate future.

The men spent the first three days on the main island

sorting through salvaged material and resting from their ordeal. They were camped on the outskirts of the village, but the women and children brought them food and drink and helped them construct lean-tos as temporary shelters—though the weather was so pleasant this seemed hardly necessary. They were told not to enter the village because that triumphant moment needed to be attended by great ceremony. Thus far, all communication had been through Gan Jawa. The meeting with high chief Yatoo would symbolize their formal acceptance by the Belaurans and their official induction into village life.

On a Sunday, the survivors dressed in their best clothing remnants, including some modified women's wear found in yet another crate. The natives were resplendent in shells, beads, and feathers. Jack was intrigued that, even in their most formal attire, it was only by chance that the islanders' "privates" were covered. The younger women made designs with paint that served to enhance rather than hide their breasts and sexual organs. A drum beat, and the entourage was escorted into the village by Jawa, whom the sailors now took to be some sort of underchief or warlord.

Jawa wore the feathered hat that Quince had given him and carried his axe in his right hand, with no spear in his left. Jack noted also that the warriors who accompanied him carried spears but no axe. Jawa's axe must have some ceremonial significance, Jack thought, the razor-sharp shark teeth inset along two sides wickedly reflecting the bright sun.

Brown, the newly designated chief interpreter of "The Right Honourable Brotherhood of the Shipwrecked Men of the *Star*," stood importantly one pace to the left and behind Quince.

When the procession reached the largest of all the huts, they stopped and waited. Chief Yatoo emerged and stepped forward to within a yard of Quince, who wore no headgear but sported an officer's jacket with brass buttons. No one seemed to notice that it was too small for him, having recently been removed from the body of the late first officer Mancy. Quince's cutlass and scabbard hung over his shoulder with a bright red sash. Jack knew it was a fine cutlass, though not his favorite, which, given Quince's intentions for the ceremony, he had left in their makeshift camp outside the village.

Though shorter than Quince, Yatoo almost matched him in girth. His left ear was pierced, a ring of bone or shell thrust through it. Covered with tattoos like the others, he also had dark brown stains on his teeth, two of which seemed artificially sharpened. What amazed Jack was that a man adorned in such a bizarre fashion should have such a regal bearing. He felt an urge to bow in his presence—a feeling he never had around the high and mighty gentry of Hamden.

Yatoo held both his palms upward and, through his man, the Malay speaker Graman, and Brown, told Quince that the crew was welcome to his village and to the chain of islands called Belaur. He noted that the white men had come in a fine ship and must be from a great island far away. They had never seen such a marvel up close, he told them, although twice they had seen white sails of giant canoes in the distance and wondered from whence they came. They had heard of men with white skin and great pigeons that walked but could not fly. There was even a legend of a giant man with four feet and two heads who had walked upon the beach sands and breathed fire from noisy sticks. Did Gan Quince know of these things?

Indeed Gan Quince did, and said he would be glad to share what he knew of the world beyond the reach of war canoes. Gan Quince was, in fact, a prince from a land far distant, he explained, and he expected that a great fleet of vessels similar to the one that had wrecked on the islet would be sent in search of him by the king. There would be great rewards for those who helped him and ghastly reprisals for any who had harmed him or his men. He was grateful that Chief Yatoo had shown him and his men such courtesy.

Yatoo made a sweeping gesture with his hands toward the furthest portion of the compound. There were eight huts with newly thatched roofs waiting for their new occupants, seven for two sailors each and a private one for Chief—indeed now "Prince"—Quince.

"Can you imagine?" Paul murmured quietly aside to Jack.

"What?"

"Can you imagine, old friend, if these people had wrecked a great canoe in our land, or Europe, being treated with such grace and humanity? Makes you wonder who the real savages are." Jack nodded thoughtfully at Paul's remark, never taking his eyes from the happenings. Yatoo stated that he and his people would help the Americans with the further salvage of materials from their ship and assist them in constructing another if they wished. He asked only in return that they be friends, teach some of his people their language, perhaps donate some metal, and help in defense of the village from attack by Yatoo's enemies.

Quince immediately agreed to Yatoo's terms. As a gesture of friendship, he stood at attention while Mentor came to his side in a well-rehearsed move. He removed the cutlass and red retaining sash from Quince's shoulder and placed them in Quince's outstretched palms. The old sailor then clicked his heels in as military a fashion as he could muster and returned to his place in line. Quince bowed his head and handed the cutlass to Yatoo.

The chief was obviously greatly impressed by the sword. He stepped back, slowly removing the shiny blade from its sheath and walking purposefully to a retaining pole on a nearby hut. Grasping the hilt tight in his fist, he swung at the pole in a clubbing motion, simultaneously uttering a loud war whoop. The pole split in half and collapsed, along with much of the hut. Yatoo dissolved in laughter, accompanied by guffaws from his followers.

The entire village yelled wildly. The chief then replaced the sword in the scabbard, handed it to a retainer, walked to Quince, and with tears in his eyes grabbed him up in a great bear hug. Soon the villagers were cheering and escorting the whites to their huts. Runny-nosed children, loudly imitating the chief's sword slashes and war whoops, ran in their wake.

Paul glanced at Jack. "I believe the formalities are at an end."

"Yes, it's eat, drink, and be merry time." They came to an empty hut. "How about this for an elegant hacienda? And will I do for a hutmate?"

"I would be most honored, Lord O'Reilly," Paul remarked. "If Quince can be a bloody prince then we can sure as hell be lords."

"Aye, Lord Le Maire."

The dwellings prepared by the Belaurans were comfortable and most functional for their tropical world. Jack lay on a pallet, elevated from the centipedes and other vermin, and noticed how the thatch permitted a breeze to enter from the direction of the prevailing winds, passing lightly over his body. Before they left to join the others, Jack remarked to Paul, "You know something, old bean. This really is an elegant hacienda."

"Tu as raison, mon ami," Paul responded. "Keeps out the rain and sun, lets in the breeze, handy hearth, and you don't have to sweep the dirt off the floor 'cause it *is* dirt. Only problem is it's going to be hard to bang nails into the thatch to hang paintings and the like."

"Come, you fool." Jack cuffed Paul playfully. "It's

time to join our associates—even lords have social obligations."

The revelry went well into the night with a plentitude of food, song, and a strange drink ceremoniously pounded from what seemed to be the roots of a pepper tree and strained through hibiscus bark. It was passed around in a coconut half shell to the sailors. The men, used to rum, thought it a comparatively mild party beverage until their lips turned numb. The natives called it sakau, a narcotic home brew that, when consumed in quantity, could make the average shipwrecked sailor forget his troubles and perhaps his name.

At the end of the evening, many of the men found that they had women returning with them to their huts. This included Jack and Paul, but while the young Le Maire seemed as if he had been blessed with manna, Jack was strangely subdued regarding the attractive young lady, Wyalum by name, who joined him. But she soon tired of his shyness and left—to find a willing host in another hut, he presumed.

Jack lay on his pallet long after she had slipped away. It wasn't that he didn't want her—his whole being craved the woman; he just felt sad to the point of paralysis and didn't know why. Finally, he left the hut so as not to inhibit Paul. There were no separate sleeping areas in their hacienda; and although Paul's consort seemed to be oblivious to Jack and was consuming his friend like a one-woman orgy, he knew Paul would appreciate the privacy.

Jack walked a deserted section of beach, the sounds of revelry growing distant. He still could form no really coherent thoughts but felt tears making their way slowly down his cheek.

Something had happened to him in Matanzas that went so deep it affected him in ways he couldn't begin to understand. The women would be a great comfort, he knew, but not this way. The carefree lust the women showed panicked him for some reason. Images of his mother, the guardia leering at her breasts, her nakedness purposely exposed to save his life. The irony of it was almost too much. He could swallow fear to face any enemy; but women, they frightened him with their power.

He would later realize it was July 4, 1806. With sunup, the village returned to a semblance of normalcy although in three-quarter time. Most of the Americans were loath to leave their huts. Hungover and satiated, they spent the day recuperating from their good fortune. Quince decided in retrospect to declare a holiday, in respect for American Independence Day. Paul remarked that this sensitivity to republican democracy was indeed remarkable, coming as it did from "royalty."

13

SIZING UP THE
SALVAGE PROBLEM

JACK HAD NO IDEA how long two and a half minutes could be until he watched the minute glass and noted he wasn't the only man holding his breath and, after a lung-scorching period, was forced to let the air out in a sigh. The men were all staring expectantly at the water beneath them. A native man had been under for three minutes now, having disappeared into the midships hold of the *Star*, resting precariously on an incline in twenty to twenty-five feet of clear water.

When it seemed as if he must have drowned, there was a hint of movement: a flurry of tiny bubbles preceded a form unhurriedly making its way to the surface. He broke through, took a huge intake of breath, which, Jack noted, was not preceded by exhalation. The man must have let out a huge lungful of air somewhere during the dive.

Paul noted this, too. "They get rid of the stale air slowly on the dive—probably helps reduce the urge to breathe . . . interesting." He was deep in concentration, speaking half to Jack and half to himself.

Jack knew that when it came to anything literary or theoretical, it was always worth listening to his friend. Paul was hopeless when it came to engineering and mechanics, but he had been talking about gas laws and physics studies he had read.

"How could that help?" Jack said. "Seems like it would just mean less air for the man's lungs."

"It's not the air that keeps you alive, it's the oxygen in the air. Once you use it up, the air is toxic and makes your body want to get rid of it, at least that's what Lavoisier says. Now, in old Priestley's words, that would be dephlogisticated air—you know, and still combustible . . . or something like that."

"Something like that? Why couldn't you have studied less Shakespeare and more physics?"

"Now, now, it's doubt that shapes the man. Descartes never said 'I think therefore I am.' He said 'I doubt, therefore I think, therefore—'"

"Oh damn it all." Jack was in no mood for philosophy. He could taste those gun parts.

The majority of the *Star*'s survivors and many of the villagers, including the best divers, were back at the islet, pushing the limit of their abilities to see what could be retrieved from the sunken ship.

Many useful items had been brought to the surface, including a few hundred feet of hemp rope, a dozen blocks, several deadeyes, and odd pieces of chain rigging. Some of the oaken timbers themselves were removed with the use of ropes. They had even retrieved an axe, some adzes, and a mystery box. The latter was opened anxiously on shore to reveal a setting for twelve of prime Chinese porcelain.

"Christ, you idiots, look at markings before you risk a man's life to salvage the makin's for a bleedin' tea party," Quince said.

His lack of appreciation for the table setting notwithstanding, Paul and Quen-Li carefully removed the crate from the other piles of trove and took it to the cook tent.

Shram and Maril, two of the better native divers, had been able to tie the end of a hemp line to a link of chain rigging stowed in the forward hold. Steady working of the line from the surface had managed to dislodge and raise almost a hundred feet of iron links. The line was presently hung up again, but Shram returned to the hold to free it from whatever obstacle had snagged it.

Still, with these considerable accomplishments, the sailors were frustrated that only one kit bag had been found and that it contained only a single pair of barely serviceable boots. The crew's quarters, with its precious footwear and gun mechanisms, were in about ten fathoms of water and seemed out of reach. The native divers could spear fish at sixty feet for short periods, but expecting them to work at that depth searching through a tangle of unfamiliar gear to find boots and intricate brass firing assemblies was out of the question. Due to the way the wreck lay, the aft hold with the gun barrels was the most accessible. "Full fathom five thy father's gun barrels lie," Paul declared. "We needs retrieve them before they suffer a sea-change into something rich and strange."

As the natives were excellent breath-hold divers, they might eventually find the barrels, a job much easier than retrieval at the crew's quarters.

Jack retired to his housing, watching Quen-Li for some time. The cook was expertly working a blade through a filet of fish and had a pot boiling for his latest concoction of island gruel.

"Good day, brother Li. How go the cooking wars?"

"Quite well, Jackie. Quen-Li have some good fixin's by evening—don't need no wahine wogs cook for us."

Jack smiled. Although Quen-Li deferred to native women for preparing meals at the village, he was loath to give in to the island custom when on "Star Islet" where the ship had wrecked. He was the ship's cook and culinary master of the islet, which was just an extension of the ship in his mind. Quen-Li kept to himself most of the time but responded to Jack's friendliness and Paul's irrepressible humor with more openness than he did to any of the others, who saw him simply as a Chinese cook. Jack and Paul treated him as a man who cooked and was Chinese.

"Do you long for home sometimes?" Jack asked, as the knife chunked through breadfruit at mesmerizing speed.

"No, Jackie. I *am* home. And you?"

The question took Jack by surprise; it was simple enough, but he realized he didn't know the answer.

"Yes, of course I do . . . well, in a way. . . ." Jack considered that he wasn't really sure where home was. There, with the knife still making a rhythmic chuk-chuk in the background, he thought of the Chinaman's own assessment. "I am home." It seemed to Jack this Chinese cook wasted no energy in his movement or his words; his mind was as sharp as that blade he wielded with such precision.

Jack spent as much time as he could away from the village, partly for a reason he had trouble acknowledging. Women were readily available on Belaur—unbelievably so. For some reason, however, his flesh did combat with his soul in their presence. His urges were powerful and dominated his dreams, but since the dark happenings in Cuba, he couldn't even attempt to start sex with a woman. Wyalum, in particular—Maril's sister—had taken a liking to him, and the push-pull in his soul when she was around tormented him. He desperately wanted to sink into her soft brown flesh. The thought of Wyalum's tiring of his strange debility and joining other sailors disturbed him deeply, but he could not release himself to nature's insistent call. He could not even talk of it with Paul. Jack knew his hutmate was aware of his problem, but it was not something he felt ready to discuss.

One night he fantasized Colleen holding him to her in his half sleep, and she had magically transformed into Wyalum sitting astride him, moving rhythmically over his groin.

⊰✦⊱

Jack pondered again the problem of the salvage. Quince had seen to it that the capstan was to be recovered, so he could exert mechanical leverage; that was probably a good idea, but it would be of little help in getting to the most important materials.

Quen-Li had arranged a number of the recovered porcelain cups on the table, Jack noted. That would be a spiritual lift for the men, returning for supper to find the formality of an English teahouse. His eye caught the teapot and the metal chain that suspended an iron sievelike capsule for the tea from its lid. There was something about that gadget . . .

He walked over to the makeshift cupboard, picked up a drinking glass, pulled a dry piece of cloth from a box, stuffed it in the bottom of the glass, then inverted the glass and stuck it in a bucket of water, sure he had seen this done as a child. He withdrew the still-inverted glass and checked the cloth. It was dry. An idea began to form in his mind. He left the hut.

Jack's train of thought was interrupted by the arrival with great fanfare of a war canoe. Apparently, a fleet of canoes from Papalo, thirty miles to the north, had been spotted on the other side of the village. They had raided before in Belauran waters. All the natives working at the islet prepared to return to the main island. After a quick parley among the whites, Quince ordered the pistol loaded and primed and brought back with them, but kept well hidden.

He had decided to make good on their promise to Yatoo. Jack heartily approved, sticking a knife in his belt and hoping there would be some more appropriate weapon available at the village, such as a spear or an axe. He felt queasiness but part of him was gladdened at the prospect of defending the people who had taken them in as family.

The plan was for their small group to hurry through the shallows and reinforce the village. From the gestures and quick translation by Brown, Jack gathered that another canoe had by now alerted the village where

Gan Jawa and most of his warriors were located. Three canoes were quickly emptied of fishing gear and other nonessentials, so, counting the one sent to alert them, the group could muster four good craft.

—=I❀I=—

The canoes surged fluidly through the water. The Americans, distributed evenly among the four, had shipped their paddles, unable to add to the effortless coordination of the natives, whose faces shone with excitement and apprehension.

Blood boiling in anticipation, Jack glanced at Paul in a nearby canoe: he was pale with fear but would not be left behind. With the tide high, they chose passages through swampy areas, impassable at low water. At times they seemed to fairly skim over the tops of reeds and coral that lay inches from their hull bottoms.

The smooth, quiet movement of the boats resulted in an unexpected encounter with a dozen Papaloan war canoes that had taken cover in a cove. The warriors had spread along a shell bank, a scant quarter mile from the village; some of them had already climbed the mound, peering in the direction of the village compound to see if they had been detected.

The appearance of the small Belauran force was a total surprise. Both groups froze. It didn't take long for the Papaloan warlord to make a decision; the Belaurans had not been fishing: they were armed, ready to attack. Someone must have alerted them. He had obviously lost the advantage of surprise and now had to choose between a fight with an inferior force of four canoes or with a large village that he could only assume had been alerted to their presence.

The large man whom Jack took to be the Papaloan leader uttered a savage scream, waving his club to motion his men to attack.

After a short hesitation, the outnumbered Belaurans and whites back-paddled to the beach, where they could disembark to make a stand—or flee, if the situation deteriorated. The first to reach the beach yelled back defiantly at the attacking Papaloans and readied their own slings, as darts and spears whizzed in their direction from the enemy.

Jack wondered where Yatoo's main force was. They obviously had time to organize a defense, or the canoe would have never been spared to retrieve the men at the wreck. Jack hoped Jawa hadn't missed the developing confrontation by passing on the open-water side of the island chain, thinking the enemy would choose to keep open water at their backs. Gan Jawa would surely be leading the force and he wasn't the kind of man to make that sort of mistake. At least Jack dearly hoped so.

A rock passed within inches of his temple and a hail of missiles started raining around him, thrown by the men in the middle of the attacking canoes, while the fore and aft men paddled. Jack could feel the uncertainty about him; the men sent to retrieve the Americans had no leaders among them, being simply reinforcements for Jawa's men. Two of them had already been hit and the others, including the Americans, were in a near panic—it had all happened so damned fast. Quince, in the absence of any display of authority by their Indian allies, yelled for his men to draw their swords and close ranks—this last especially important, since not all the men even had proper weapons, Jack thought.

Although his heart pounded at an impossible rate, Jack found his head clear and his concentration total. The mundane uncertainties of life had disappeared. There were enemies in front; some, he noted, were breaking off to another point of access to the beach. He thought he heard Quince yelling to him, but his mind now fixed on the face of the man in the lead of the first attacking canoe. A fierce-looking Indian, he was almost on top of two of the Belaurans who had fallen trying to make land. One of the stricken men Jack recognized as Maril; the other was a heavyset man with a contagious laugh who had helped pull objects from the ship.

Now the heavy man bellowed in pain as a spear passed through his right thigh. Though Maril would not desert his comrade, he could do nothing but watch as the first Papaloan dropped his paddle, grabbed his club, and with a brutal swipe, smashed in the side of the wounded Belauran's head. The attacker then looked straight at Jack, grinning fiendishly, obviously trying to decide whether to turn toward Maril or the odd-looking young white man who had not joined his comrades on shore. That toothy grin, that murderous look . . . somehow Jack knew that look. Something in him snapped.

In a move that took even him by surprise, Jack sloshed quickly through calf-deep water, straight toward the enemy, and dove into the canoe Quince and his men had just abandoned. As he expected, the pistol was still in the basket that had been deserted when his comrades had tumbled pell-mell onto the beach.

Jack pulled the weapon out, drew back the lock, and took two steps toward the enemy's lead canoe. The wild, gap-toothed smile returned to the Papaloan's face as he looped a foot over the side of the canoe and raised his blood-smeared club in Jack's direction. Jack waited with a strange heart-pounding calm until his assailant was almost within striking distance. Just as the warrior raised his club to let it smash down on the young man's head, Jack pulled the trigger. The report was enormous. The metal ball pierced the man's chest and he let out a shattering wail as he fell to his knees.

"Smile at that, you murderin' dog."

Jack stepped forward in the stunned silence, grabbed the hair bun of the fallen native, and smashed the butt of the pistol into his head again and again.

His white comrades, less startled than the natives by the sound of the gunshot, charged back into the water to Jack's side. They were led by Quince, who wielded his cutlass in his left hand. The second Papaloan canoe had pulled into the fray, but the attackers were still confused by the noise and nature of their opponents. The momentum of the charge had been broken, and a hail of Belauran spears from behind the white men pierced several of the attackers in the second canoe.

For a moment the newcomers backed off to gather their wits. The first arrivals sent to flank the Belaurans on the beach now returned to their canoes, apparently to join their comrades; but as they paddled furiously for open water, Jack saw the real cause of their retreat. The main Belauran force was coming to the attack.

It ended quickly for the men in Jack's party. Quince finally took the pistol from his hand. "It's okay, lad," he said. "I think you've killed him enough."

Jack made his way back to the beach with great difficulty. His feet were shredded by the coral, and he couldn't fathom how he had charged to the canoe over the sharp bottom. He sat on the ground, drained of emotion. He was bleeding, but had not a scratch on him from an enemy. And much of the blood and slime covering him, he now realized, was not his own.

He and his mates looked seaward, watching the drama unfold. It was largely anticlimactic; the Papaloans yelled belligerent threats at the Belaurans and came near enough to throw spears, but they clearly were not going to engage Gan Jawa's superior force. Jack's mates asked how he was doing and patted him occasionally on the back, except for Cheatum and Smithers. But things were different for them now regarding wee Jack. He could see it in their faces as he boarded a canoe for the islet.

Jack knew there would be great feasting in the Belauran village the next day over the victory, and their party would be the center of the celebration. After all, they had repelled a surprise attack and, though one Belauran was killed, a Papaloan warrior had been sent to his maker by Jack, and at least two others seriously wounded by Jawa's men. Jack, for his part, felt relieved to be heading back to their sanctuary.

"Paul, I didn't ever think you'd be speechless," he said when his friend drew alongside, pale, white, and shaking. Jack felt nothing but a numbness and didn't know if that was a good thing or not.

Paul leaned over the side of the canoe and vomited. The paddlers slowed while he gathered himself. Jack leaned forward and gently laid his hand on Paul's shoulder. But even as he did so, he knew it was he who needed solace.

There were no mosquitoes in the evening breeze, warm off the water. The night wrapped itself about Jack and his lids grew heavy. This is a strange land, a foreign place, he thought. I have never been in a place so foreign. A high cloud must have passed because there stood the Southern Cross, suddenly in bright relief. You know you are in a different world when there are even different stars in the night sky. I killed a man today. Strange. It is a strange thing to kill. In the heat of battle I felt rage, then what? Desperate joy that this man would smile no more at the thought of killing me or my friends? But now why do I feel so empty? No joy, no sorrow. And the warrior I killed, where is that man now, only a memory, a thought? My mother and father, are they just memories? This morning a man breathed the moist air of this land, with that smell I love of the mangrove coals burning in the hearth. Tonight, he nourishes worms. He will never feel his stomach growl, tell a joke, have a woman. . . . I feel no remorse, but somehow it is sad.

My friends think me fierce now, a great warrior. What would they think if they knew all this great warrior wants right now is to crawl into bed next to his mother? Have her hold him, as she did when he was six years old. "Mi hijo," she would tell him, "all will be well." It is a strange thing to kill. But I live to kill, don't I? To do to the count what I did to this man.

14

SALVAGE

IT WAS LIGHT and Jack was awake, disturbed by a noise. It was Wyalum, rustling about the palm frond pallet. She had a half coconut shell full of a wonderfully soothing ointment that she began applying to his cuts.

Moments before she was in his dreams, caressing him in a way that made it difficult for Jack to now keep from blushing in her presence. She finished with the ointment and began straightening the bed around his midsection, watching curiously and shamelessly the movement in his trousers. Jack reactively pulled his knees up and covered himself clumsily with his hands. There was no reaction from the girl but he knew his face was now crimson.

The girl's eyes were brown, her hair raven black. High cheekbones topped an almost continuous half smile, accentuated by full lips. She placed a hand on his chest. He tried to ignore the stirring in his loins, the tightening in his stomach. He took her hand and gently pushed it aside. "I have to go." He pointed toward the beach.

Still only the half smile.

Jack rose shakily and backed away from the pallet, leaving her sitting there.

A new arrival had taken in the last of this encounter, but Jack knew who it was before he heard his voice. This would be no islander: the sound of the heavy boots and the fumes from his pipe had already announced his identity.

"Well, lad, yer having a time of it, aren't ye?"

Quince was smiling. Humiliated, Jack realized that, to the mate, he was still wee Jack in one respect. Jack O'Reilly—runaway, sailor, survivor of shipwrecks, warrior, apparent leader of men—had yet to realize his manhood. Quince puffed his pipe thoughtfully and remarked more gently than Jack might ever have thought possible, "No belly-warmers for you, eh, Jack? Never parted a woman's thighs?" He continued his soliloquy without regard to Jack's lack of response. "There's time lad. Take her easy, slow and easy." He turned and with a jerk of his head motioned Jack toward the beach.

As they made their way, Jack became aware of the sharp sound of lumber, wrenched from iron fittings. The capstan was free from the wreck and being attached to a makeshift raft by the Belaurans, working under Mentor's supervision. Most of the *Star*'s crew were clustered about the water, deep in discussion. Quince and Jack passed close enough to hear their words.

"The aft hold is sixty feet deep. May as well be a thousand," Dawkins muttered.

"Remember them wogs gettin' the fish? Bet they could get down there," Red Dog added.

"Maybe," Quince said as he joined the group. "But they wouldn't have time for more than a quick Hail Mary before they'd have to come back up."

"Aye, I saw something used in England on a ship salvage that'd do the job," said Mentor.

"What's 'at?" from Brown.

"A Lethbridge they called it. A kinda barrel a man could get in like his own coffin. They'd lower 'im down to Davy's Locker and he'd grab things or rig lines for liftin'."

"How'd he grab things if he was in a barrel?" asked Jacob.

"Had armholes, it did." Mentor ran his hands up and down his own arms to illustrate his answer, obviously enjoying the attention from his fellow sailors. "The bloke'd stick his arms through the holes, and leather sleeves'd keep the water from going in and drownin' his arse. He could see through glass, mind ya, a glass port right in the bottom of the barrel. Yeah, stay down for hours, he could."

Jack let the image form in his mind. He doubted a man could stay down for hours, but the idea of a diving machine was intriguing. All seamen knew that a host of suicidal contraptions had been used from time immemorial in the attempt to salvage valuables from sunken ships. Few knew anything about them and most thought anybody who would purposely venture beneath the ocean's surface was a lunatic. In fact, very few of Jack's fellows could swim more than a few strokes to save their lives—and saving their lives was the only sufficient motivation to swim at all.

The Lethbridge story captivated Jack. The others moved on to other tales of daring and shipwrecks, but he was fascinated by Mentor's account. He noticed that Quince was also preoccupied; he, too, had heard of the device.

Jack knew it would be impossible to manufacture such diving hardware on a primitive island, but he had a basic idea of how a diving bell worked from illustrations he had seen in a book. There was a cooper among the survivors and there were the makings of hundreds of whale oil barrels as part of the ship's cargo. His mind wandered back to his little experiment with the drinking glass and piece of cloth in Quen-Li's pot.

Jack approached his mates. "We could make a diving bell," he said matter of factly.

The subsequent silence was complete.

"What's 'at now, lad?" Mentor asked.

"A bell, a diving bell. Maybe we could make a diving bell." The men were slower to laugh at Jack these days. While some smiled and shook their heads, Cheatum and

Smithers outright scoffed; others looked at him expectantly.

Only Smithers had a comment. "Sure, O'Reilly, we'll just open up a factory, make a dozen of 'em, and sell the ones we can't use ourselves."

Cheatum joined Smithers in laughter. Jack didn't even look up.

Quince also ignored the gibe. He looked at Jack over the top of his pince-nez. "Out with it, lad."

"All we need is a big cask full of air for a man to breathe down there. The cooper can make it, can't you, Coopie?"

His mouth open at being the new focus of attention, Coopie responded that "a barrel's a barrel I guess." As he still held the floor, he went on. "Got all sorts of hoops and staves already pulled out of the *Star*. Plenty of makings for oakum. If me barrels can keep water in, I 'spect they could keep water out."

"How in hell you going to get it to stay down?" asked Quince. "You ever try to sink a barrel of air?" The questions came quickly.

As Jack had suspected, Quince had been following the same train of thought.

"Never had a need to sink a barrel full of air before," Jack mused. "But I bet we could figure out how if it meant we could keep a man down there for an hour, instead of two minutes," he went on.

"What if we hung some cannonballs from it with rope mesh and chain links?" The last from Mentor. "We could run it with fairleads over the top—yeah, iron balls is the thing for it. Jesus, a man down there for thirty minutes could do a lot of tyin' and riggin'."

Jack felt a new exhilaration in his heart.

"He'd take a breath of air from the barrel and do a minute or two of work, then swim a few yards back to the bell," Mentor continued. "He'd take a few breaths, then, back at it again. Think about it: he could do an awful fine amount of work, maybe even find the kit bags with gun parts and shoes."

Quince sighed. "The damn bags and best materials is over ten fathom down. Jack, you think we can talk the damn wogs into breathing from that coffin down there?"

"No, and they wouldn't know what they were lookin' for either. I wasn't thinking of the Indians . . . I was thinking of me. I can swim, you know."

"Ten fathom is awful deep. You'll drown your fool ass." A solemn declaration from Coopie.

"They was going that deep in Southport," announced Mentor. "They was going so deep and it was so piercin' wet and cold they was gettin' the rheumytism down there somethin' fearful."

"Well, at least there's no fear of that here," Coop said. "It's warmer'n a lady's muff in these waters."

Quen-Li's gong sounded behind them. The men trooped to dinner, Jack and Quince bringing up the rear. Neither spoke, but Jack knew what was in the mate's mind.

✃❈✄

The pain in his ears was unbearable. If it kept up he would have to drop the steel ball hanging from the lanyard around his wrist and bolt for the surface. From where he was, he could dimly see the top of the bell, beckoning to him from fathoms below. He kept trying to relieve the pain the way the natives had showed him, by wrapping his left arm around the hemp line tied to the bell, and using his right to pinch his nostrils and blow out. When his best efforts failed, he pulled himself several feet toward the surface and was about to release the weight and scramble for the sun when his ears suddenly responded. There was a screeching sound and the agony in his head disappeared, leaving his ears sore but unburdened with the weight of the sea.

Now Jack had to decide whether he could make it to the bell or head for the surface. He was almost out of the air in his lungs. Suddenly, the grip on the line with his left hand came loose and the steel ball started pulling him down. He could have let go but it was almost easier to let the weight make the decision for him. He saw the bell getting closer and felt the pain starting to build again in his ears.

He became panicky from his need to breathe but fought the urge to lunge for the surface. Suddenly, he was there. The top of the cask was a familiar friend in an alien world, and he let himself slide down the smooth wooden shape with which he had become so familiar in the days spent helping Coopie construct the marvel.

He grabbed the rim of the barrel and tried to pull himself under it and up into the life-giving air. Then, to his horror, he was dragged several feet below the rim to the seabed. He seemed trapped. Looking up now he could see the barrel suspended only a body's length above him.

It was his subconscious that told him he wasn't stuck; he was simply holding the weight in a death grip. He relaxed his hand as if in a dream and kicked upward with his last ounce of energy. Suddenly, he was inside the bell, and he breathed in a huge wheezing gasp of air. Unbelieving, he sucked in the sweet vapor, stolen from the world above. Somehow, his ears in all this had once again released, and he realized that he was now ten fathoms deep and still functioning.

For the first moment, all he could think of was to catch his breath enough to bolt to the surface and never again attempt such foolishness with his God-given life. But his head cleared, his wits returned, and with it, his courage. He took stock of his surroundings in the artificial air pocket formed by the barrel. It was dark, but light reflected from the coral provided dim illumination to the interior. He could make out the form of an axe and a lever bar still hanging from the makeshift racks where they had been placed before submersion. He reached tentatively toward the lever and it came off easily in his hands.

He braced his feet on the bell's rim below him and, pushing lightly with his back, secured himself with no effort in his new confines. Here was an advantage to being underwater he hadn't thought of—as long as he didn't fully rise out of the water, his body had hardly any weight. Soon, he had almost completely caught his breath and his mood swung to euphoria. He was safe, and he was going to give it a try.

Jack took a deep breath and ventured a body's length from the barrel. Everything was blurry but there was plenty of light and he happened almost immediately upon a sea chest, probably from the fo'c'sle. After several excursions he noticed he could hold his breath longer when diving from the barrel than when diving from the surface. The experiment was a success; he grabbed a cutlass and a bolt of cloth, the most valuable items in easy reach, tucked them under his arm, and pulled hand over hand for the surface.

⇒※⇐

The whole village crowded the shallows around the diving operation. It seemed to Jack that whatever wonders the Americans had so far demonstrated, none matched in the Belaurans' eyes the ability to stay so long in the depths. The Belaurans lived their lives with the pulse of the tides; they were part of the sea, which made the white men's apparent mastery even more astounding.

Jack, Paul, Coop, and Mentor labored like men obsessed. Quince was nominally in charge, but gave Jack room to pursue his tack. Since the first attempt, the system had been modified: a regular hogshead-sized cask now hung at five fathoms, rigged similarly to the giant one at ten fathoms. It was a place to stop and breathe if one's ear pain became unbearable or if one ran out of wind, as Jack almost had on his first plunge. Still, only Jack and one other sailor, Klett, would attempt the dives. Paul had volunteered and had even tried, but his indomitable spirit fell prisoner to his weak flesh. Shram and Maril, the best of the native divers, would assist in the deeper forays.

They still hadn't devised a satisfactory solution for the vision problem. Everything was quite blurry, adversely affecting the operation's efficiency. Salt water burned the divers' eyes—particularly the Americans'. They tried a leather hood, with two pieces of carefully ground glass from the captain's window inserted as eyepieces. The first attempts leaked hopelessly. Then they tried a carved inset of wood, with a salvaged lens from a pair of broken spectacles in one side, and the other sealed over. Sort of like goggles for a one-eyed man, remarked Coop. It stayed dry and worked wonderfully for about two to three fathoms. But then Jack felt his eyeballs being sucked out of his head and had to abandon the invention to go any deeper.

Each success, however, spurred them on, and they found themselves able to venture greater distances from their bell and accomplish even more complex tasks. Eventually they decided that two men operating from the bell together could remove larger obstructions, hoist larger items, and help each other in emergencies.

Then the accidents began.

15

PROBLEMS

"SWEET JESUS, NOT AGAIN!" Quince dropped his pipe and splashed through the shallow patch of sand to help two Indians raise Jack from the water. His eyes were bugging out, slime running down his blue face. The Indians threw him over a barrel and started life-breathing him, pushing on his back and rolling him back and forth. He coughed almost immediately and began labored breathing, violently vomiting between breaths.

Later, Jack recounted to Paul what he could remember of his almost fatal accident. The support divers were hauling at least twice as much fresh air to the bell as they had in the past. That should have easily made up for Shram, the extra person they now had assigned to the diving. Why, then, the two incidents of severe dizziness and nausea in both men? The first had resulted in an emergency in which Shram had to be carried to the surface unconscious. And now it was Jack himself, though Klett above him had suffered no ill effects. Paul was totally baffled.

One factor had to be common to both—but what? If the gains weren't so important, they would have considered stopping because of the risks.

"Damn it, Jack. You had to have done something different this time, something that Shram did earlier this morning. What was it?" Paul was exasperated, obviously shaken at having almost lost his friend. "Tell me again exactly what happened, step by step."

For the fourth or fifth time, Jack described his last

dive, the arrival at the bottom, handing the pry bar up to Klett, the taking of a series of deep breaths in what had now become a ritual exercise before the swimmers would exit the barrel on their mission. He stopped his recitation when he saw a change of expression on Paul's face. "What?"

"You said you took the pry bar from Shram on the first dive."

"What in hell would it matter who handed who the lever?"

"You said he handed it *up* to you."

"Of course he handed it up. I was sitting above him. He—" Jack stopped and absorbed the implication of Paul's question. "Well, it's true I suppose. The second time I was on the lower rest bar but . . . what could that have to do with it?" He reflected a moment more. "And it's true that Shram was on that bar the first dive, but really—"

"That's it! Shram was below you on the dive that almost killed him."

Paul was right, but it only increased Jack's frustration. How the hell could it possibly matter?

"And where are you when you take your breaths? Still on the rest bar?"

"Yes."

"You were lower than Klett, and Shram was lower than you when he took his breaths?"

"Yes . . . but . . . "

Paul began to pace. "That's it. Somehow the stale air must be collecting in the bottom of the barrel."

Jack thought. "I believe you're right."

Something else had happened on that last dive, something that Jack had thus far kept to himself. "I believe I saw your kit down there." Paul looked as excited as Jack. The significance of this, they both knew, wasn't that Paul's bag was accessible but that Jack always kept his bag close to Paul's: unless some accident had separated them, the gun mechanisms were not far away.

⊲⊐❈⊏⊳

They pondered the problem all the next day, discussing the issue with Quince, Coop, and Mentor. Paul summed up what they had learned.

"Before the troubles set in, we learned that the air squeezes down to about half its size from the weight of the ocean, somewhere around three fathoms. This makes the bell heavier at that depth, and it takes lots of work to keep the air resupplied with buckets from the surface."

General nods all around.

"This reminds me of some of Robert Boyle's treatises on gas laws. He summed up the work of Galileo, Pascal, Torricelli, the Mediterranean crowd who—" Paul stopped as he met blank stares all around. "Anyway, the point is that the weight that all the air in the world exerts on you gets doubled when you go underwater, around two and a half fathoms."

"Right," Quince said. "So what?"

"Okay. We found out the thick air helps because it means the divers can stay longer if they breathe it from the barrel rather than taking a breath from the surface, right?" Nods again.

"All right. We know the divers must fill their lungs higher in the bell's air pocket. The question is, how do we get rid of the stale air? Do we winch the whole damn thing up and dump it every time it goes bad? Maybe we can make a hole with some device that lets us release the stale air?"

"But it seems like the problem we need to solve before knowing how to release the air is knowing when to release it," offered Jack.

Quince lit a match and made a dramatic production

of blowing it out. "Lads"—he looked pointedly at Jack and Paul—"what we need is a damn canary down there."

"Aye, Skip, the mines, eh? That's what yer thinkin'." Mentor made the comment, leaving the lads unsure where their education had failed them.

"Canary?" Paul asked.

"Aye, these fellas as spent time in the isles around miners'll tell ya. They takes a canary and keeps it down there to let you know when the air goes bad."

"How do they do that?"

"Why, the little bleeders stop singin' and lay down and die."

"Presumably before the miners stop singin' and lay down and die."

"Exactly, Paul, they're more sensitive—"

"But, Skipper." Klett had warmed to the conversation. "Thars birds like 'em canaries 'ere in this island there is, but the little fellas would never make it down two fathom afore drownin'."

"True enough. But maybe we can make our own canary," said Paul, staring hard at Quince.

"Yer lookin at me wide-eyed as a hoot-owl, son. What's your problem?"

"Not an owl; I'm looking at a possible canary."

Before Klett could interject that it wouldn't be right to keep Quince in the bell to see if he died, Quince smiled at Paul and said, "It's me pipe, eh? You're thinking my pipe might work somehow?"

"The match, Skipper," Paul said. "What if we lit a candle and kept it down there? If the candle is more sensitive to the bad air than the divers, it will serve us as a superb canary."

"But how do we know—"

"Indeed, how do we know the flame is more sensitive?" Paul's mind was running now like a clipper before the wind, and his mates had to struggle to keep aboard. "Point of fact is, we don't. But I think I can do an experiment to find out."

"What about the candle using up the air?" Mentor asked.

"Don't think it's a problem, but we can check for that, too."

Quince added, "Even if it does use up too much air, that's a problem that will correct itself. The damn thing'll go out and our divers will know it's time to leave."

"It's going to be a big job lifting the whole bell just to put that candle in there," offered Coop.

"Don't need to," said Jack. "We'll stick the candle and matches in a cloth and cram it into the top of one of the air buckets the natives carry down. Instead of dumping the air, we can lift the bucket, still inverted, into the bell's air pocket and remove them without getting them wet."

"Okay," from Quince. "We're back to it then. How do we tell if the flame will go out before our divers collapse?"

All eyes to Paul.

"Gentlemen, please bring one of those wine casks that washed up the other day down to the beach, with some of our match and candle supply, and we'll engage in a scientific experiment."

❧✦❧

"Is it out yet?"

"Not yet, Skipper," came Paul's reply.

Quince was seated regally on a rock, his empty pipe dangling from his mouth. Paul's voice emanated from an inverted wine cask, the bottom immersed in a foot of seawater and stabilized by the weight of several large rocks.

A small group of Belauran men watched silently,

some chewing betel nut, others staring with arms folded, all as if they were witnesses to some bizarre alien ritual. On each turn of the minute glass Jack tapped the barrel if they hadn't heard recently from Paul. In most instances the precaution proved unnecessary, as Le Maire couldn't contain himself a full minute before announcing his status, and that of the flame, to his fellows.

Just after the twenty-eighth turn of the glass, Paul declared from inside that the flame was out. "I'm still okay, though I'm feeling a bit breathy."

Eleven minutes went by before Paul rapped on the barrel from the inside and said, "Okay fellas, let me out." Paul emerged from the barrel sweating profusely and a bit pale, pupils dilated from the dark. He squinted his eyes shut to the glare and announced in a high-pitched voice, "Boys, I believe we have a canary."

"Bravo for Benjamin Franklin Le Maire," yelled Jack.

16

SUCCESS AND
TRAGEDY

THEY WERE READY for the big push—an attempt at
the trigger assemblies. The sense of urgency escalated when Quince explained that Jawa told them of
Yatoo's wish for a retaliatory raid on Papalo, to be exe-
cuted before another moon had passed. It was now im-
perative they have those firing mechanisms. Jack didn't
relish the thought of engaging in another battle as ill-
equipped as they had been the last time. They needed rifles. Quince convened a council of the men to discuss
the issue. He explained that he had made a command
decision on the spot, when Jawa arrived, to appoint Jack
the Americans' warlord. That way he could remain ap-
propriately aloof from the proceedings and convey his
final decisions through Jack. This kept Quince on par
with Yatoo, and he thought that was an important distinction to keep.

The men signaled their approval. Young though he
was, most thought it appropriate to see Jack placed in a
position of command, particularly after the way he had
comported himself during the wreck and subsequent
fighting. Even Smithers and Cheatum were silent on the
issue in the face of the others' obvious support. Jack was
touched by the men's vote of confidence but was unsure
of himself. He knew the men saw him as a shrewd and
bold fighter, but they didn't live with his dreams each
night. In some ways taking life sickened him.

Quince summarized his negotiation: in essence, he

had agreed to let his men take part in a reprisal, since they had already agreed to help defend the village—a preemptive strike against an obviously belligerent enemy of their hosts simply meant using offense as an aggressive defense. Paul, Coop, and Mentor were ambivalent about the decision, until Quince let Jack relate the stipulations they had put on the raid.

"I asked that there would be no torture of prisoners, no rape of women, and no ear or head trophies taken. I know our friends have a different view of life and warfare, but I simply can't abide cruelty to a beaten foe and don't think we need to give up on our principles. Jawa had agreed to all but the last. I figured that was the best we could do. I don't like mutilating the dead but it's not near as bad as torturing the living. . . . So what will it be men, yea or nay?"

After little discussion, the men agreed to the terms. Paul was the most reluctant. His final comment when he consented to a unanimous approval was, "When in Rome, I suppose . . ."

<hr />

When Jack worked from the bell, he felt on the fringe of some extraordinary realm, some blue nether land between the surface world of men and the black abyss haunted by creatures of endless night. The wooden device itself felt different now that a candle had been installed. He could see Klett, the perspiration and water forming a glistening film over his face. Sound too was different in the container as they rested together between dives; both loud and intimate. Their voices sounded strangely resonant in the thick air, as if their vocal cords were tuned an octave higher.

This was to be a big day. The previous afternoon had provided great excitement when the five-fathom team found the gun barrels. They had been swimming by them for weeks, as it turned out. No one knew or remembered the fact they were in a wooden crate, as well as being wrapped in cloth and twine. The natives had looped a line around the unmarked box to get it out of the way of their search for tools, and it was raised to the surface.

On opening the box, the stunned Le Maire could only gasp, "The barrels, God's blood—the rifle barrels!" It was the only time he could recall seeing the pipe drop from Quince's mouth.

"Sweet Jesus, look at them," Quince said in awe.

Mentor and Jack reverently removed each long tube from the box, as if handling priceless porcelain. Quick inspection by Jack confirmed that their immersion had caused no significant harm. The barrels were boiled in fresh water for more than an hour to loosen the oil and salt, then periodically removed and a cloth drawn through with a wire.

As Jack and Klett readied themselves for their undersea excursions, they knew the barrels were being attended to above and that Quince had Coop, Mentor, and Hansumbob whittling away at mangrove wood blocks to fashion stocks for the weapons. They would leave the forward portions, which accepted the trigger mechanisms, unfinished until they had the triggers in hand. Then they could custom-fit each of the flintlock trigger assemblies into one of the wooden stocks.

"I'm going to run a line to where I think I saw that sash," Jack told Klett. "If I'm not back by the count of thirty, pull me back in."

Klett nodded. The men knew that once they strayed from the barrel they were at considerable risk of not finding their way back, since their vision was blurred and it was impossible to guide the swimmer home with sound signals which they found couldn't determine direction underwater. Such an event could be highly dangerous, as they usually expended their lungful of air by the time they turned for the bell. A complete miss would mean having to claw for the surface before they drowned. Although this had almost happened on several occasions, they had always found the bell. One time a support diver, seeing Shram searching for it, dropped his air bucket to guide his fellow villager to the wooden sanctuary.

Jack took the bitter end of the line and dropped through the rim of the bell, slowly making his way across the bottom. The more deliberate his movements, it seemed, the longer he could hold his breath. He used familiar bottom features to guide him to the sash. A clump of large, lettucelike coral to the left; next, a rock that, when used as a handhold, had something under it that burned his wrist, much like a jellyfish sting. Finally, the wreckage itself loomed about him and he swam three kicks to the right and over a collapsed bulwark to regain the crew's quarters, where he'd seen the sash. On this trip he noted a white canvas bag with rope weaved through it—one of the other men's kits.

Knowing his time was almost up, Jack decided to loop the line from the bell over a sturdy timber before being yanked unceremoniously back, and fashioned a quick bowline knot to secure it. Almost instantly it grew taut, the sign that Klett was applying his considerable strength to bring Jack in. Hand over hand, Jack made his way down the line, amazed at how soon he had recovered the distance to the bell. He wondered why it had taken so long for them to think of this obvious technique.

Since the line was secure to the wreck, Jack told Klett to have a go at grabbing the kit spotted on Jack's last trip. Meanwhile, Jack would drop to the bottom, under the bell, and secure the home end of the line to a coral head. That way it didn't have to be held by a diver.

Moments later Klett burst through the bottom of their wooden air pocket and gasped for air. "Got it, and blimey, I think it has boots in it." Jack's spirits soared.

Now they were getting somewhere. After all their efforts, the barrels yesterday, the shoes today, and a line laid toward the grand prize—the triggers.

"Do you think we should be getting up? We've been here well over an hour, lad." Klett, usually as adventurous as his companion, was fatigued.

"Not me. We're too close. I know I saw that damned sash—and we need those triggers now."

"I'll stay too if you're stayin', Jack."

"No, let Maril take your place and have Shram stand by."

"Jack, you'll be killing yourself for those guns—"

"Go. You're just wasting air down here. You're tired and need a break. Tell Maril to come down. Anyway, I need you up there in case anything goes wrong. I figure you could lift the whole damn bell by yourself if you had to." Hesitantly, Klett took a gulp of air and made his way to the surface.

Jack rested from the exertion of swimming and talking. He felt resolve building in him. It was so close. He was becoming dizzy and it took longer to catch his breath, but he noted that the flame in the bell still flickered. Their canary's still aflutter, he thought, smiling. Look at it, flapping its wings—hell, it's out. Must be the commotion of Klett leaving. It's gone out before, from disturbances in the bell; when I relit it, it lasted a good half hour longer. Should relight it but . . . bloosh . . . another bucket of fresh air released by the Indian divers. Aye, that's it, lads, we're hopping now . . . what the hell, okay, yeah, the sash.

Jack took in another lungful of air and dropped to the line. Here we go, down the hemp highway. Time had changed with the use of the rope. It seemed he was back to the wreck in two kicks. Hell, that piece of bulwark, that's the one near the sash. He left the line and swam to the bulwark, and indeed, right below him was Le Maire's kit! Marked with the telltale decorative sash.

He grabbed for it. Missed. There, got it! Come on you bastard, there. I've got Paul's bag. Going to be hard to make it back, feel sick.

How much later he wasn't sure, but he was back in the barrel now.

"Dyak, Dyak," Maril said.

"Aye, it's me, friend. What the hell are we doing here? Where the hell is the bag, Paul's kit? Why the hell is it so dark? Feel kinda sick."

"Dyak! No fire! Must go!"

"Yer a quick learner, Maril. You know, I'd like to drill your damn sister till she talks English good as you, hell good as the bloody damn king of England. Dick won't work though, sorry."

Another bucket of air splooshed in, followed almost immediately by another.

"Ah, me head's a little clearer. Two buckets . . . Le Maire must be having a bit of anxiety up there." More scrambling and scratching against the wood, and Jack felt the presence of another person in the tight confines.

It was Shram. He could hear him talk to Maril in Belauran, then, "Pol say, 'Up! Go up!' say Pol."

So, that's it; these wogs are going to drag me to the surface. Damn Le Maire. My bag is right there, I saw it under Paul's. Jack grabbed the bottom of the barrel, pulled himself under the two Indians, and then wildly propelled himself along his guide line. He looked back. They're following me. No time to talk . . . need guns now. Jack reached the wreckage, pulled himself over, and dove straight for the bag. All of a sudden he was frightened. He turned quickly and found Maril's outstretched hand. He pulled it down to the top of his bag, placed it there in no uncertain way, then turned and started back. He saw Maril hesitate and motion to Shram, who grabbed Jack and pulled him back to the bell. Jack surfaced in the pocket and gasped, hoping Maril had retrieved the kit. He was in air but couldn't get enough

to breathe. Jack vomited and blurted out the word "up."
He felt Shram grab him and assist his ascent to the surface. Lord, it was so far. . . .

A fire was crackling nearby. Jack could hear the
sound of mosquitoes and smell the burning wood. He
felt awful, more tired than he could ever remember
being. His shirt was off, and Paul and Quince were peering down at him.

"Ya hear me, lad?" Quince said.

"Aye."

"I've made Master Le Maire here promise not to kill
you."

"Thanks, but I think I'd appreciate it if he did."

Paul had obviously been terrified. Jack tried to smile.
"Old friend, don't be cross with me. It had to be done."

"Your whole damn chest is covered with a rash," Paul
said. "Are you okay?"

"Kinda feel pins and needles all over, head aches real
bad and tired, uh, real kinda tired." Before he fell back
into a deep sleep he heard Quince say, "No point in having a canary if you don't listen when he sings. But we got
'em, lad. Maril brought up the mechanisms."

⊰※⊱

For the week it took Jack to recuperate from his dive,
he watched the labors of Mentor and Coop as they used
their carving skills to set the brass parts into the stocks
they had already started. Much of the first day they
brought the barrels and mechanisms to his bed, to get
his assurance they were assembling the parts correctly.
He had little to say; the parts fit together well and Coop
was adept at preparing the resting pad for the barrels.
The men were better carpenters than he.

Jack felt strangely despondent. His mood wasn't
helped on the third day when an accident occurred.
Quince decided, as Jack had expected, to raise the deep

bell. It needed to be aired, and design flaws corrected in the resting platforms. And, their main diver had "diver's rheumytism," according to Mentor. Paul, though not sure it was rheumatism, believed it true that Jack had some kind of diving ailment.

Besides, they had salvaged the most needed items. Several of the men, Jack noticed, were now wearing shoes. His own boots from his kit were lying at the foot of his bed. They had been soaked in fresh water and well greased with animal fat.

They figured raising the bell to be an easy task. Hell, if it wasn't weighted down, it should come up on its own. Shram and two of the shallow-water team dove down to cut the lines from the biggest weights. After only two cuts, the bell started to move. But once it started, it gained momentum at a speed none of the men expected. Rael, a young native diver who had been practicing breathing from the bell, was snagged by a piece of the barrel rigging halfway up and dragged to the surface at great speed. Jack watched in amazement as the huge barrel hit the surface, half of its height actually clearing the water.

Rael was thrown free. The men helped him to shore, where he suddenly started to reel, his knees jerking.

"He fainted and never woke up," Paul told Jack an hour later.

"But why, damn it?" Jack lamented. "He wasn't down but a minute. He can't have any diver's disease and there was all that blood frothin' out of the poor bugger's mouth. What the hell happened?"

They never were sure. After much agonizing, Paul's best guess was that for some reason the young man couldn't release the air in his lungs when he was pulled up so fast—they literally blew up in his chest. Why it didn't happen when other people came up fast, he couldn't say.

It seemed that every triumph in this diving game

came with a price of pain or death. Rael's fatal accident deeply disturbed Jack, as he was developing an increasing sense of kinship with the Belaurans, particularly the young men who shared his diving adventures. Why Rael? Strong, bright-eyed, a young warrior with an easy laugh and ready courage. What a waste. Jack dearly hoped the gains from their underwater travails would justify such a tragic loss.

17

AN EYE
FOR AN EYE

J ACK UNDERSTOOD the need for Yatoo to take revenge
on the tribe that had attacked his village. With the
passing of another week, he seemed sufficiently recovered from his ailments to take part in the raid, second in
command to Jawa; and after a proper funeral was con-
ducted for Rael, he undertook his first military assign-
ment. Five of the twenty rifles were now ready for use,
and he had taught four of the sailors to use them with
moderate competency. A call to action against worthy
adversaries tapped the wellspring deep within him; he
found his excitement build at the thought of impending
conflict.

With a certain satisfaction, he watched sweat form on
the brown back in front of him, and he picked up his
pace slightly, enough to subtly pressure the leader. Soon
perspiration covered his own torso. The strong, young
warrior kept a fast pace until they reached the swamp.
From here on they would continue by canoe, several
having been brought around through the lagoon side. A
war party waited, composed of men from nearby vil-
lages that owed allegiance to Yatoo.

Suddenly unwilling to let Jack take the entire risk,
Quince had decided to head a party of his own men.
When his party caught up with Jack's, the group built a
fire and smoked pig meat on hot coals. Wordlessly, they
set about preparing their bedding. The smell of rotted
vegetation hung heavy in the air. Jack felt energized at

the prospect of action. His self-doubts, depression, uncertainties ... they all seemed to evaporate when conflict loomed.

Jack slowly unrolled one of the Kentucky long rifles from its fold and carefully rubbed the barrel with pig fat from the fire. The men around him talked in low murmurs; dark or white, all handled their anxieties in roughly similar ways. They walked with chests out, spoke confidently; yet Jack observed them staring longer than usual at the coals in the fire. They were men of different races, different worlds, but they knew death was a handmaiden to war. They intended to win tomorrow, but they also knew that this could be the last smoke that ever burned their eyes. Jack polished methodically, then lay down and seemed to drift off to sleep immediately. But he did not nod off before hearing Quince's words whisper in the dark: "Bless you, O'Reilly. You love it. Dancing with the devil. It remains to be seen whether you end up being a blessing or a curse to the rest of us."

◄─❈─►

With the morning light they proceeded by canoe. Maril was positioned in the prow of Jack's boat. It seemed to Jack that the ocean spoke to Maril in measured tones. It slapped against the side of his boat in rhythms born of wind and distance, allowing him to slip his paddle through its surface without sound.

An island of steep shores lay on the left. They approached a long, low reef, where sharks stayed near the surface. Here they had to dig their paddles deep and pull hard to the right, or be slowed by a crosscurrent that carried them toward the setting sun.

There was much to learn from the dark-skinned men, and in many ways Jack admired them. From his position behind the islander, he watched silently and learned. Though he had felt as clumsy as a child when they set out this morning, he could now feel his oar sing in tune with the water as he fell into harmony with the movements of his partner and the pulse of the sea.

A flying fish crossed their bow, then another. Then one landed in the boat. Without breaking the rhythm of his paddle, Maril tossed it overboard.

Jack's reverie was disturbed by movement far in front of them. Something not right on the waves . . . a canoe, maybe. Maril bowed flat and warned Dyak to do the same. No words were spoken. Maril let the current take the canoe toward a mangrove patch on a small island. They would appear from this distance as a log, if seen at all.

After many minutes they scraped bottom and Maril peered over the side, motioning to Jack to look as well. A war canoe was easily visible, but the occupants had not spotted them and the mangrove shadow would give them no silhouette.

The Belauran canoes, rounding the previous islet, slowed upon seeing Maril's maneuver. One by one the men ducked low in their sleek craft. They could tell that Maril had spotted something and were quick to join him in the little cove. Even as they reached Maril, Jack could see Jawa's two canoes, scouting seaward of the main force, making their way carefully back to them.

Words in Belauran flew between principals for several minutes, then Jawa indicated to his interpreter to convey their observations through Brown to Jack.

"They're a bit worked up over that canoe you guys spotted to seaward, Jack."

"How so?"

"They don't like that it's heading at high speed toward the south in open water. Papaloan warriors would be more cautious than to do that." Even more puzzling, Brown went on to explain, they could see women in the canoe with the men. Too, there were several other small craft in the distance—and they saw smoke coming from the Papaloan village.

"Ask Jawa if we should proceed."

"He already said he wants to head toward the village through inland waters, hide the canoes, and proceed by foot. There's too much activity on the open water up there and he thinks we'll be spotted."

Jack looked around at the sailors, who had been listening to the exchange. "Tell him okay, but two of our men still don't have shoes that fit well and I want them assigned to guarding the boats."

"Right enough." A brief flurry of conversation ensued, and Jawa poked his chin out toward Jack in Belauran assent.

Within moments they were gliding through the mangroves, not a word spoken, and only Belaurans manning the paddles, to ensure silence. Jack listened to the hum of mosquitoes, the scuttling and splashing of marsh animals—and distant thunder. Squalls approaching, he thought.

After thirty minutes of labored and humid travel, the flotilla stopped at a steep embankment. There were signs that others had entered and egressed here, but nothing that forebode ambush. As they disembarked and the guards, including Jack's soldiers, took their place beside the boats, Jack thought he could hear voices. He noticed Quince urgently beckoning him to one side.

Jack approached questioningly. Quince grabbed him by the shoulder and looked him in the eye with an intensity the reason for which he couldn't understand. "Ya hear it?"

"What? The storm?"

"It's not a blasted storm! We've been looking at each other the past fifteen minutes, afraid to say what we know to be true. Lad, that's cannon. Cannon yer hearin'. God knows, I've heard enough of it in my life."

"Cannon? Are you sure?"

Except for the incident he witnessed off Cape Hatteras,

Jack had never heard a cannon in his life. What in blazes was going on?

He had no time to consider the import of the revelation; he was summoned to lead the advance with Jawa. Jacob and Paul were near the front of the group, Paul carrying the pistol that had become a defensive weapon now that there were rifles in the Americans' arsenal. In addition to Jack, Jacob, Red Dog, Brown, and Hansumbob, two Indians had been trained to use the rifles. Jack wanted two more riflemen than rifles—in case they took losses among the men, they would have replacements capable of effectively using the shoulder arms. They carried them gingerly, well aware of the value of nineteenth-century weapons in a stone age army. Coop and Mentor were purposely left behind so they could complete fitting the remaining fifteen rifles with their firing mechanisms.

After an hour's slow but steady progress, Jawa's scout reappeared, signaling them to hide. Someone was approaching.

❧❀❧

Paul could hear the yells of natives coming toward him through the brush. A nervous sweat added to the perspiration pouring down his face from the heat; even the insect bites couldn't distract him from what he knew would be a violent drama. The first murder he had ever witnessed was in the skirmish several months past—it had deeply shaken him. He could see forms running through a deep ravine, breathing heavily, very stressed, if the sharp intakes of air were any indication.

Suddenly, a native woman, young and entirely naked, burst through the brush, though still some distance away, and collapsed. She carried a bundle. A small child. A Papaloan man followed, bleeding from his shoulder, trying to help her. A shot rang out and the man catapulted onto his face. Paul, stunned, was about to protest to his comrades that there was no call for having done that, when he realized that they hadn't. The shot came from behind the man; the Americans and Belaurans were still frozen in their places in the brush.

A man in Western clothes stepped into the clearing, passed the woman without glancing at her, and kicked the Papaloan over onto his back. Satisfied he was dead he turned to the woman.

"Get up, you kaffir bitch." The man began reloading his musket. He was dressed entirely in black: long sleeve shirt, pantaloons covering his legs disappearing into black boots.

A second man appeared, possibly Arab or Oriental, in part-Western dress, and pulled the woman to her feet. This man wore a white tunic with a red sash and headband. He took the baby from her and said something to the Westerner Paul couldn't make out. The latter shrugged and the second man shucked the baby out of the bundle like a piece of corn and smashed the child's skull against the trunk of a tree.

Paul gasped out loud. The men in the clearing looked in his direction, ignoring the frantic wails of the woman.

"You blackguards! You murderers!" Paul yelled.

The first man looked up, raised his musket, then spotted Paul, unsure of what to make of such an apparition. Paul pulled his pistol up and fired without any attempt to aim. The bullet passed harmlessly over the man's head. The Westerner sneered and again brought his weapon to bear on Paul. He fired; the noise was deafening. Paul felt nothing, though his knees started to buckle and he knew he was about to lose consciousness. His last memory was the Westerner's eye, which had grown strangely large and red. As he fell to the jungle floor, Paul could hear the plaintive wails of the Papaloan woman.

-=❊❊=-

Jack saw it all with mounting horror. He looked at the second man in the clearing who was starting to edge backward, casting sideways glances at his leader who was sprawled on his back, shot simultaneously through the eye and the throat from two different directions.

The man's hands shot up in surrender. He was even more confused when the first to step out of hiding was a native, armed only with a club. Three more brown faces appeared. Jack watched without moving from the place where he had fired. He hardly breathed while Jacob and one of the Belaurans examined Paul, afraid to hear what had happened to him.

"Paul's okay, Jack. Just fainted—ain't hurt a bit," Jacob said.

Jack exhaled in relief, then approached the stranger. "That's good for you, animal. It means you might survive long enough to quit pissing down your leg."

The man looked down, flushed. "Who in hell are ya?"

"The angel of death, baby killer. Tell us what you're doing here and don't even stop to breathe. If you lie, I'll know, and we'll cut your tongue out."

"Why, we're just doing company business. You—you've just killed a representative of the—why, the crown."

"What crown? The kingdom of murderers?" This from Quince, who had stepped into the clearing.

"We're lawful traders, consigned by the British and Dutch East India companies to obtain cargo in these parts."

Jawa walked up to them, staring at the woman, who refused to be distracted from her grief. He placed his hand on the "lawful trader's" chest and pushed him gently several steps backward. Then he swung his club upwards, catching the man on his jaw, smashing it to pulp. A downward stroke finished the job.

"I guess the interrogation is over," Quince muttered to Jack.

Jawa talked rapidly. Passed through Graman and Brown, it boiled down to: "These people are bad and have fire sticks. They must never know who did this to them. We must return to Belaur. We will not fight Papaloans until we speak to Yatoo."

He looked again at the woman. Jack knew Jawa felt obliged to kill her, lest she inform on the intruders. Finally, though, he simply motioned his men back toward the canoes. Jack told the American contingent to follow, relief in his heart. Paul, weak and dazed, was now on his feet. He walked beside Jack, back to the cove.

18

RESOLUTION MADE, UNEXPECTED ALLY FOUND

IT WAS A SOBER GROUP that arrived back on Belaur.
Jawa left to report to Yatoo the unexpected turn the
expedition had taken, and Quince convened a council
of his men, including Quen-Li, in his large chief's hut.
He asked Jack to relate the details of the encounter. For
the first time, Paul understood what had taken place
during the exchange of gunfire. The Westerner never
got off an aimed shot. Jack had widened his eye with a
rifle ball that subsequently penetrated his brain and
created a considerably larger hole on exit. The man's
musket discharged harmlessly. Jacob had also been
keeping the man in his sights, from the other side of the
clearing, and pulled the trigger before he realized Jack
had fired. The man would have died from Jacob's shot
through the neck if he wasn't already dead before he hit
the ground. Paul had simply collapsed from emotional
distress.

Jack relaxed. Even the newly learned fact that a
Belauran canoe had scouted the outside reef of Papalo
and saw the top of a great white sail did not distress
him.

"Blackbirders," explained Quince. "They're raiding
the islands for the John Boys and Dutch. Don't like to
use company ships because the business is gettin' a bad
name on the Continent. They use 'country ships,' as they
call 'em. Company reps and renegades do the dirty
work and the profits go to the East India Company tills.

They do the same with opium. Those buggers are probably carrying black cargo and white dust for the China trade. Damnedest thing is, they're legal—even if they are the scum of the earth."

"Legal! That's the most sickening thing I've ever heard." Paul's voice trembled. He took a deep drink from a bottle of grog.

"Aye, it took us all that way, but we can't go shooting merchants plying a legal trade, even if they're engaged in an ugly business—least not without being labeled brigands ourselves. That child woulda' chinked their profits—a bit older and they would've kept it, and a woman pregnant would've been fine—but the baby was just the wrong age for a sea . . . well, they saw the child as a burden."

"Blast to hell what they saw it as. It was a child they murdered!"

Quince hardened his tone. "Now look here: no one's arguing with you. That's why Jack and Jacob killed the blighter, in addition to defending your own dumb ass. By the way, lad: you don't kill a man with the noise and the flash of a gun, you hit him with the damn ball. Now I know you was upset but you kinda reduced our options out there. From now on, mark my words, Paul and all of you—nobody makes a move during a scrap without my say-so, or the command of my duly appointed warlord. Understood?"

The men's silence indicated assent.

"He's right," Paul said. "I apologize for endangering the lot of us. I also thank you all for saving me from that smirking piece of scum."

Jack reflected quietly on the exchange. It struck him odd that none of the doubts that had accompanied his killing the Papaloan months before had set in over his shooting the Dutchman. Perhaps it was because it hadn't involved a real choice, just a reflex action in defense of Paul's life.

"I think it's awful what they done," Mentor put in, pausing for effect. "But let's not forget something: them blackbirders might be our only way of gettin' home. There ain't nothin' but an occasional whaler that comes through these parts and East India Company packets that don't stop for nothin' if not paid royally by missionary societies or the like. Hell, if those country ships figure out what we done, they'll be comin' back here for our hides—not to help us."

"True enough. But I don't think they'll know unless they find out from the woman. She ain't too likely to help 'em."

"Hell, Skipper, it ain't her I'm worryin' about. Sure, the gunfire was covered 'cause there was lots of shootin' going on anyway. But they ain't so dumb not to know bullet holes when they see 'em in their man's head and neck."

"Uh, men. Jack's told me that he's taken care of that eventuality. He reminded Jawa on the way back that they had made no stipulations about trophies. The, uh, head of the gentleman in question, including the relevant portion of the neck, is presently in Yatoo's hut."

The group took a moment to absorb this piece of news. "I'll be damned," from Coop.

Jack added, "The Dutch'll know we're here from their Papaloan captives but they won't have proof we killed their man."

Mentor cleared his throat. "Ya know I never considered these 'ere tattooed blacks and Chinee as human a'fore we got to know 'em—no offense, Quen-Li."

The Chinaman shrugged.

"But what do we do?" Mentor went on. "Them East India Company scoundrels . . . they're still white men like us. Do we kill our own kind to protect them natives? And if they're raidin' Papalo, they'll be raidin' here soon. . . . What do we do?"

Half dreamily, his thoughts in a choir loft in New

England, hearing his father's voice, Jack said, "Our own kind, Mentor? Do you really think they're our own kind?"

"Aye, Jack's right," interjected Dawkins. "They are a way home for us—and I miss home terribly—but man, I'll be damned if I haven't gotten to like it here. These people, savages or not, have saved our lives, warmed our beds." He bent his head, face turning crimson. "I think I might even have made a child with Mele, who's been keepin' me company the last few months. I don't think they're any less our kind than them murderers."

Quince turned toward Jack. "What's our warlord got to say?"

Jack believed he had to play his hand carefully. He did not want to let on to the others the surge of excitement he was feeling over the fragments of a plan whirling in his head. He also had a conflicting emotion. Dawkins's words had touched him. The mention of his intimacy with the native girl had sparked a deep feeling of loneliness, dampening his desire to express himself forcefully in the discussion. Images of Wyalum and a green-eyed fantasy standing on a dock in Salem merged in some kind of confusing combination. He needed time to think. The plan, the seed of which was taking form in his mind at the moment, was not something to speak of half-baked. No, he would be noncommittal. His instincts told him that, for the moment, it was best that others be in the unusual role of convincing him to take action.

"I don't know . . . I respect the savages more than the scum we dealt with today. But taking their side against the whole civilized world . . . we'd be labeled brigands like you say, Skipper. Hell, we'd probably qualify as pirates."

Jack saw the level of respect he had achieved in the men's eyes. Despite himself, he had become a leader.

"Savages?" Paul was back into it. "You think one of

these savages would have been so outrageously cruel as to steal your land and murder your family for power and prestige, Jack?"

Jack's face was expressionless but his eyes turned into two cold pools of gray. The others tensed uncomfortably.

Quince said to Paul, "Easy, lad. You're treadin' perilous ground."

Paul, not ready to back off, had a point to make, and he always drove his points home.

"Why'd you use that example?" Jack asked softly.

"Because sometimes it's the only way to get through to you. Damn it, these refined, bewigged, besotted Europeans of ours are decidedly our own kind. It is clear to me therefore that they are, in the most sophisticated, genteel way, going to do atrocious harm to these people. They're going to steal their land, mock their dignity, sell them as chattel. It's the civilized thing to do. It's the damned British, Dutch, Spanish, and American thing to do. And I despise it!"

Jack ran a finger thoughtfully over the rim of a coconut shell. "Seems these savages here have found plenty of reason without our help to butcher each other. Does your friend Rob Pierre have anything to say about that?"

"Aye, Paul, he's got you there." Coop raised his glass with some of the others in appreciation of Jack's point and to lighten the mood. But Paul would have none of it.

"In a bloody pig's eye. Don't you swab my words away with cynical remarks, Jack. You know damn well I'm right. Are you going to have clever words for Maril and Yatoo when Wyalum gets carted off in the hold of a blackbirder because they trusted in you? And, it's Robespierre, you idiot . . . Rob Pierre, indeed. . . ."

Jack placed his hand on Paul's shoulder. "I know too that you speak from the heart and not just from that bottle. But I don't want to argue with you now. You're exhausted and near drunk." Turning to Quince and the others he continued. "Let's enjoy our grog and talk again on this in the morning. What do you say, Skipper?"

"Very well, men. Sleep on it and decide by morning."

⊶⊰❈⊱⊷

In the morning Quince reconvened the meeting.

"Men, you've had the night to think it over. Yatoo knows we're in a spot over what's happened and he'll want to know our feelings. We owe it to these folks to be straight with them, what say ye? Do we try and signal one of the blackbirders and ask their help, hoping they haven't figured out who popped two of their men? Or do we stand square with the Indians and fight 'em and hope for rescue from some other source?"

"Wait. Now, Skippee, we haven't heard your opinion—I want to know it a'fore I give my vote," said Hansumbob, an odd smile on his face.

"Fair enough. I was up all night pondering, and I'll tell you my personal opinion, though I came to it reluctant-like."

"What is it, Quince?" Coop asked.

"Well, it's them as do things wretched with snuff in their nose and blood in their eyes as bothers me most. A powdered wig on the head of one who tortures and destroys life for profit, then settles in and reads his scriptures at night. That's all I'll say now. Dawkins, what think yer?"

"Blast them blackguards to hell, I'll take my chances with the Indians."

"Mentor?"

"Don't like baby killers," he spat and started whittling a piece of wood.

"Bob?"

"I'm with you, Skippee, hee, hee."

"Jacob?"

"I'd rather swim than ask those murderers for anything. I . . . I think I might be having a little one, too." Several of his mates smiled at the revelation.

"Red Dog?"

"Stand with the Belaurans, been damn good to me, they have."

Brown didn't even wait to be asked. "I'm with my mates, to hell with the Dutch."

"Me as well," threw in Peters.

"Damn right," from Paul.

"Smithers?" Quince said.

Smithers was silent.

"In or out, Smithers?" Quince's voice couldn't help but reveal his growing contempt for the man.

"I don't put much stock in what these blacks do to each other, but them Dutch ain't so stupid they ain't going to figger out what went on soon enough, so there ain't no choice. We're gonna have to fight the only sots that coulda' got us out of this blasted place."

"Cheatum?"

"I think you're all crazy. These natives will sell us to the Dutch for a pittance. But since our junior warlord here and young Jacob decided to take things in their own hands by blastin' those scoundrels away, ain't much else to do."

Quince glowered at the man and most of the others looked away—not one needed to tell them this was an unfair assessment of what had happened.

"Your vote, Cheat."

"To hell with you, Quince, I ain't voting."

Quince said nothing but turned toward Jack.

"Jack?"

"I think we need their ship to get home." The group fell silent. Paul looked hurt and turned away. Then Jack smiled. "I have business a world away that I must settle. I said we need their ship, Paul—I never said we need them to sail it."

Paul turned, wide-eyed.

"You're talking straight out piracy?"

"I'm talkin' defending ourselves and borrowing one of these murdering bastards' ships for a spell . . . one able to make it all the way back to Cuba."

This apparent turnabout on Jack's part seemed to settle the matter. The men cheered, except for Cheatum, who pushed his way out of the gathering. Quince finished the meeting.

"Life changed for all of us when the *Star* went down. I'm not against taking some liberties with a crown ship. Never much liked the Dutch and I've always hated the John Company. Seems we've agreed to find passage home for those as want it."

"Ayes" all around.

As an afterthought, Quince said to Quen-Li, "What think you of all this? You able to understand what we're saying?"

"Quen-Li understand. I with my shipmates. Don't like take slaves. These ships with opium, they go China way?"

"Aye, they do. Ye want to book first-class passage?" Mentor gibed, followed by an uproar. Quen-Li joined his shipmates, laughing at his own expense.

Above the laughter Quince declared, "Then we're all agreed. We take a ship—then sail under the black flag!"

The men cheered in hearty agreement.

Jack felt a profound peace come over him at the council's decision. He had actually come to his conclusion the night before, but acted noncommittal to make sure the men had really thought it through. They were taking a momentous step that would affect the rest of their lives.

The mention of the black flag by Quince had sealed it. The fact that none—save the bully Cheatum, whom Jack thought a coward at heart—had blinked at those words meant there was no room for doubt—all seamen knew the significance of that piece of cloth. So that's how it comes to pass, he thought. He had always wondered if pirates and brigands were cutthroats at heart or driven by circumstance. In this case, at least, he knew.

━≈✿≈━

Quen-Li stirred the pot of seafood gruel, mixed with island pig, which was fast becoming a staple for the shipwrecked mariners. His spoon scraped against the copper, shellfish, and red meat competing for the favors of the olfactory sense. The sun worked its way through the palm frond roof, dancing on the table where Paul's drawings and notes lay in disarray. The two were alone.

"You stand ready to kill, Paul, but you are no killer," Quen-Li said. "And Jack—he kills with great skill and ferocity, but neither is he a killer. He is an angry young man who despises injustice."

Words shaped themselves in the back of Paul's throat. He struggled to restrain them, but they never remained captive for long in his spirit before taking form in the world. "Those are interesting observations, Quen-Li, most astute . . . and well articulated." He sat back in his chair, "Particularly coming from a man who cooks but is no cook . . . n'est-ce pas? Oui ou non?"

Their eyes met for the first time during the conversation. The stirring stopped, then started again. "Why Paul saying such ting, no likee my fish-pig soup?"

Paul placed his quill in his leather pouch, put away his bark papyrus. He folded his arms across his chest and looked silently at the pot for several moments. Without warning he grabbed a mango from the table and threw it hard at Quen-Li's face. Quen-Li's left hand, the one not involved with stirring the pot, seemed to move of its own accord and effortlessly plucked the fruit from the air. The cook's eyes flashed for just a second, then became calm again.

"When you decide to come out from behind your mask, it will be a pleasure to make your acquaintance. But don't mock my friendship or that of Jack with hollow sounds. I believe I know who you are and what you are, but Jack needs to know—from your lips, not mine. Don't lose his trust: it is a thing of great value; much, as to some, is the pulp of the poppy."

⋙⟐⋘

That evening Quen-Li left his self-imposed exile to join Paul and Jack on their frond eating mat. The two friends always laid it where they could watch the sun redden the western night sky. Quen-Li looked about casually to confirm their privacy and then said in a low voice, to no one in particular, "Qu'est-ce qui se passe ici?"

Jack's eyes widened at the perfect French rolling out of Quen-Li's lips; it was as if a savage had recited a line from Shakespeare.

Paul replied without hesitation, "Rien, seulement trois assassins qui regardent le soleil. Two of them amateurs and one professional."

A smile played on the Chinaman's lips. "So you know. It is knowledge that, to persons in other circumstances, would be fatal. But you are my friend, as is Jack, and these are different times." All trace of pidgin had left Quen-Li's speech.

"What in blazing hell is going on?" Jack asked.

Paul shrugged. "Quen-Li, I believe, has some things to tell us."

Jack was never as surprised or fascinated by a man's story as that which emerged from the lips of Quen-Li during the next several hours. Hours in which he and Paul were taken into the confidence of Lord Li Sen Quanjo, a man obviously not used to sharing anything of his inner self; a man who lived an artful lie for many years; a man whose soul seemed lightened by the unfamiliar opportunity for discourse.

Quen-Li told of his struggle with the purveyors of the tarry residue of the opium poppy in Nanking, Canton, and all of East China. Jack learned that the emperor of China had become increasingly impatient watching his people turn into cloudy-eyed cadavers, paying huge sums to support an opium habit fed eagerly by white devils from Britain, Holland, Spain, and America. His proclamations against the massive import of the drug from Turkey and India were blatantly disregarded, and in 1800 he made all possession of the white death a capital crime. But profits were so huge that traffic hardly slowed. Ships of the Honourable East India Company of Gentlemen of Britain, known as the John Company were, along with the Dutch and Spanish, some of the worst offenders. The Dutch Vereenigde Oost-Indische Compagnie, or VOC as it was known, had actually gone bankrupt some ten years earlier, but its ships just reverted to the Dutch government. They now operated with less restraint than ever, since the infrastructure of the venerable company wasn't there to regulate excessive behavior.

Certain Chinese nobles had given up second and third sons to a life of study in secret schools in the western provinces. Here the smartest and toughest were kept in servitude to a single calling. They were taught languages for hours a day by white devils arrested by the emperor's men. They learned the arts of war, particularly the art of assassination, from their own countrymen and specialists from Japan and Korea. Quen-Li was trained from the cradle to take life quickly, dispassionately, and with great skill. Not with the anger of Jack or the idealistic fervor of Paul, but with the precise artistry of a master murderer.

His targets were profiteers in opium. Paul explained

that rumors of the assassin's cult were spreading through the Pacific and into the Caribbean, but few believed such fantastic tales. However, few cooks moved like Quen-Li, even fewer fetched salvaged salt and sugar from unlikely containers that Paul had purposely labeled only in French. "And no one, mon ami," Paul continued, "not even someone with the reflexes of this animal"—indicating Jack—"could have caught that mango."

"Ah, testing me, Paulie, hee, hee."

Jack and Paul's mouths fell open. Quen-Li had sounded for all the world like Hansumbob. If the words had come from behind them, they would have been certain of it.

"Then it appears there may be some convergence of purpose in our lives," Paul said.

"So it appears," the nobleman stated.

Jack spoke softly. "Will you help us?"

Quen-Li was solemn. "Yes."

19

PLANS BORN,
PREPARATIONS MADE

HAVING RETURNED TO Star Islet to work on the ship, the Americans did not see the Dutch pinnace when it entered the harbor back at Belaur. As they were later told by the Belaurans, several men had been on board armed with guns and a Papaloan captive for interpreter. The Dutch leader, a man named De Vries, had asked to speak to Yatoo. The chief delayed his welcome long enough for a fast canoe to reach the islet and inform Quince.

"Jesus, that was quicker than I would have ever guessed."

The men, faces drawn, gathered about Quince to discuss their options.

"Hansumbob says they approached from the east," Quince began. "It's a damn good thing that *Star*'s most sunk or they'd a seen it over the mangroves for sure. Yatoo says he'll hold off on meeting with the blokes until we can come through the swamp and see him first. He thinks he can arrange the meeting in such a way that we can hear what's going on. Course, if the buggers speak in Dutch that don't help much, as none of us know it—" He looked at Paul. "Unless, of course, Lord Le Maire . . . "

Paul shrugged. "I can't speak it but I can pretty much understand it—depending on the speaker and how fast he's talking."

"That's it then. You and I will get behind that bark

curtain in Yatoo's hut and listen to what these gents have to say. Jack, Hansumbob, Coop, and Cheatum will stay hidden with loaded rifles, in case these Dutchmen decide to start talkin' through their gun barrels."

❧❀❧

Heinrich De Vries was ushered with considerable ceremony into Yatoo's hut. He spoke through a dark-skinned man who knew some Papaloan but no Belauran; Yatoo had Graman, his interpreter, who spoke Malay and Papaloan, brought in to sit at his feet. Through the two interpreters the Dutchman and the chief were able to communicate.

Quince and Paul were squeezed into a cramped area behind a bark curtain, where Yatoo's wives weaved baskets while their husband held court. From there Quince could watch the Dutchman through a crack as the exchange took place. After studying him for a moment, "to gain a measure of the man," as the first mate expressed it, he shifted position so Paul could use the slit to observe the man's mouth as he spoke.

Quince had decided at the last moment to squeeze Brown in, too. Since he was dealing with a "damned Tower of Babel," he needed to garner all the linguistic forces he could muster. He moved back so his interpreters could better position themselves, finally pushing back the rear flap of the hut and easing himself out to join his marksmen. The meeting lasted for a little over an hour and seemed to end without incident. The pinnace crew never left the general area of the boat while waiting for their leaders to return. The native children watched from a distance, displaying none of the spontaneity and openness they had shown at the arrival of the Americans.

"They're a surly lot," Coop remarked to the others in hiding.

"Blackbirders ain't known for being a friendly bunch," said Quince.

Jack studied the men's weapons and the manner in which they handled them. One musket was French, the others British, of the so-called India pattern. They were mass-produced copies of the East India Company's traditional shoulder arm, hurriedly made, Jack knew, to meet the crown's perceived arms deficit in the Napoleonic Wars. How his father would have scoffed at their quality! They were quicker loading than a long rifle but had nowhere near the accuracy and fine craftsmanship.

Only one of the three Dutchmen handling the weapons seemed comfortable with firearms. They were just sailors with guns—not trained soldiers, Jack guessed. The man who looked familiar with his piece bothered him a bit, since another, snoozing in the boat, was dressed similarly in some sort of red and green uniform. Were these dragoons? Disciplined soldiers would provide a special challenge in a face-off. At least Jack surmised they would. Sometimes it struck him as outlandish that his judgment was being relied upon to make decisions of such importance. Was he the same Jack O'Reilly, that innocent young man living with his parents in New England less than a year ago?

Even more strange was how comfortable he felt in his new role. That older men increasingly deferred to him in matters of conflict was, in a way, unsettling. Was there something wrong with him that he felt his spirit soar with the anticipation of combat? Was it conflict in general, or was it the struggle against fearsome odds, against people who showed no remorse at killing? People who took advantage of honest, if unsophisticated, men and could kill babies . . . or rip the softness of a mother's throat.

Quince's voice: "Jack! Head down lad, they're leaving . . . you all right? You're pale as a topsail."

~≡✦≡~

The account of Paul and Brown meshed well. De Vries had approached Yatoo with a seemingly reasonable offer. They would forget his indiscretion in harboring murdering brigands who had attacked a peaceful merchant enterprise if Yatoo would aid in their undoing. If, in other words, Yatoo would betray the few whites living under his protection and facilitate their capture by the Dutch, they would not only forgive him but become his ally. In fact, they would help Yatoo subdue the neighboring islands that had long been trouble to him in exchange for their being allowed to keep the captives. He explained that they were indeed not slavers but merchants engaged in the securing of laborers. These laborers would eventually be able to buy their way to freedom after enjoying the many benefits of a rich plantation life. The Dutch had correctly deduced the nationality of the white men from the account of Papaloan warriors involved in the skirmish weeks earlier, plus another Papaloan's description of the flag that the strangers flew over their makeshift camp at Star Islet. However, they didn't seem to have knowledge of the shipwreck or that the islet was in fact a salvage camp for the *Star*; they apparently assumed the Americans were a group of renegades or stragglers let off by some vessel.

All Yatoo had to do was arrange a parley with the Yanks on the open beach near the village. The *Peter Stuyvesant*, the Dutch vessel, would anchor just offshore, a fortnight hence, and a delegation would land, unarmed, to speak with the Americans. The latter could bring their guns, and the Dutch, though without weapons, would have the assurance of safe conduct because of the presence of their armed vessel. They had checked the water depth on the way in to visit Yatoo and had determined that Belaur had an excellent harbor. They could anchor their ship much closer to the beach than at Papalo, allowing them to more easily take on trade goods.

Yatoo need not worry further about the recent unpleasantness. They would see to the American renegades. The chief of Belaur would not only be forgiven his involvement in the murder of two of their men, but be given ten Papaloan slaves as tribute.

The chief made a great show of thinking about the Dutch offer and finally assented—but only if the number of Papaloans was raised to fifteen and he was given two muskets with powder, shot, and anything needed to operate them. Brown later said he felt chills run down his spine when Yatoo so solemnly agreed. "I had to remind myself that we wouldn't be hiding there if he really intended to double-cross us," he told Jack.

It was immediately clear to the Americans what the Dutchman's intent was: capturing them was the driving force of the visit, but with a dose of treachery they could also neutralize Yatoo. He was the only native chieftain that had the temerity and power to offer serious resistance. Crushing him would teach all the islanders in the archipelago a grim lesson.

Clearly, the Dutch were ignorant of the existence of the *Star*'s remains in accessible waters. They also didn't seem to know how many Americans there were, or how well armed. Wisely, Yatoo had been of little help in that regard; he spoke of the Yankees as if they were a handful of survivors with a gun or two, and not much to be concerned about. At this point, Paul couldn't resist an aside. "The distinction between what those blackbirders are doing and slavery must be a subtle one. I can't grasp it at all."

Several of the men murmured agreement, but Cheatum stirred restlessly.

"Might be. But they're operating legal-like and your

smart remarks will get choked off quick by a noose if we ever get in front of a magistrate—even in an American court. And these savages, they'd fare well by selling us out."

"Cheatum." The voice was Quince's. "We've already voted on this and you still have time to back out. Don't be such a damned fool—Yatoo didn't fall for that prattle."

"From what Brown said, Yatoo seemed ready to sell us all in an eye-blink," Cheatum retorted. "Hell, he's as ready to take Papaloan slaves as the pope is to accept Presbyterians."

"Yatoo's no saint, but he's no fool either. Don't you think it unusual he was so ready to betray us with our men listening in?"

"He could still be planning a double-cross: that's an awful strong force to take on out of loyalty to a bunch of stranded white-eyes."

"No. If the thought ever entered his mind, it left during that talk. Yatoo was just confirming how much of a liar the Dutchman was. The chief knew the demands he was making were ridiculous—hell, the Dutch went overboard on their first offer. They're figgerin' him for an ignorant savage and he was wondering how far they'd go." Quince lit his pipe. "Also, didn't it strike you funny that he was having this kind of parley with the Dutch and he didn't even have his warlord there?"

"What of it?" Cheatum was petulant, but from his inflection it was clear he was curious.

"Jawa was meeting with some Papaloan refugees when the Dutch's guard was down and sizing up the prisoner pens—hell, he even got aboard their goddamn ship for a look-see, acting like a Papaloan coolie. I just got back from a meeting with him, and that's what he told me."

Jack smiled. The Dutch had seriously underestimated the shrewdness and boldness of the "savages" of Belaur.

"Anyway, quiet now and just listen, without yammerin', to the whole events of the meeting best as Paul and Brown can remember, all of ye." He looked pointedly at Paul and Cheatum. "Then we can think about it over dinner, and everybody will have their say at council."

Paul finished relating the details of what they had overheard without further interruption.

⊰⊱❋⊰⊱

As the Right Honourable Brotherhood settled back on a full stomach, Quince dispensed a ration of grog and told them all to lay off any further rum or sakau for the evening. Jack admired Quince's instinct about such things. Instead of a babbling free-for-all, he had his men eat, gather their thoughts, and think before embarking on a disciplined discussion.

Mentor spoke first. Jack noted he had an odd way of waving his hands in front of himself before talking, as if making way for the impact of his own observations.

"Those slack-jawed, clay-pipe-smokin' Dutch bastards. If they anchor in that cove off the village, all they need do is release their stern hook and the *Stuyvesant* would swing broadside to the parley. Then, when they was in range they'd snug off to the hook and they'd have a row of iron dogs pointed right at us."

"Aye," from Coop. "They wouldn't need to have their men armed on the beach if they had a dozen cannon full of metal scrap pointed at us."

Quince nodded. "That's what they're about, lads. I don't know how they plan to get their own people out of the way, but they could sure sweep the beach clear of anything living from that range. Besides, they'd kill every native man, woman, and child and make that village look a pile of smoking palm trees. That would take care of us and be a lesson every village and tribe in the whole island chain wouldn't have any trouble understanding."

Jack listened carefully, but a corner of his mind was working feverishly. The Dutch perhaps had forty or fifty Europeans capable of using firearms and a ship that could deliver a withering broadside. The more he thought about it, the key seemed to be in surprise, in capitalizing on the enemy's confidence and arrogance. Something was needed to spur them, make them act rashly, without thinking.

They had to get the Papaloans on their side. Jack remembered the look on that woman's face in the clearing; there were probably many people from Papalo who would be willing to forget their differences with Yatoo. Indeed, that's what Jawa must have had in mind, given the latest intelligence from Quince. He could not have gotten on board that ship without help from the Papaloans. And, damn, they had a fine ship. A three-master, a bit bigger than the *Star*. If only—

"Jack, what say ye? I know yer pot's simmerin' and we best let you vent the steam a'fore you bubble over," Quince said.

"How about we give them a reason to come at us with their emotions instead of their brains? Why not raid that damned pinnace they came to Yatoo's meeting in, and have the Papaloans help us?"

Jack knew the Papaloans already knew of him; his reputation as Dyak, one of Yatoo's foreign warriors, had grown with the retelling. The Papaloans would respect a man who had attacked a boatload of their warriors and fought with skill and ferocity.

Quince eased back against his backrest.

"It's plain to anybody that the Dutchman's purpose is to nail us and Yatoo," Jack continued. "They don't need him to help gather slaves. This isn't Africa—nowheres to run—and they have plenty of native help from other islands anyway. Partly thanks to us, Yatoo's been the first serious threat to their profits, and they're not about to let it go unavenged."

"Go on, lad," from Mentor.

"We need to make sure they don't get a chance to train their guns on the village and—we need to take that damn ship."

"Yer daft," from Smithers. "Once we—"

"Hear me out." Jack's tone was that of a request, but his eyes burned a warning that stilled Smithers in mid-sentence. "We've spoken already of maybe taking a ship. Why not this one now? She's a beauty—fast, well built—"

"We know. But she's also armed," Quince said. "When we spoke of taking some ship before, we were thinking more of borrowing a lamb than attacking a lion."

"True, Skip. But these men have no intention of letting us live—if not for what we did, then, as Paul has been hinting, for what we know. I don't think the Dutch want anyone seeing what they're up to here—it's not going to go down well in Europe. We either run, leaving the Belaurans to the wrath of the Dutch, losing the remains of our ship, and risk being caught anyway—or we turn the tables on them. From all that's been said, I think they've seriously underestimated both us and the Belaurans."

Jack spent the night convincing the council of his plan. It was daring, he agreed, but nothing short of some daring move could get them out of their predicament.

"What if we insist the parley take place in the hook, the sandy spit just south of the village?" Jack asked. "Then the village wouldn't be under their guns."

"They'd cut us to pieces—" Smithers interrupted, but Quince cut him short with a wave of his hand.

"Where you going with this, Jack?"

"We need to sting them. Make them mad, put them in a lather to come after us even if it means meeting at the spit, where it's harder to maneuver their ship and they can't cover the village. We set a trap for them when they position for their broadside and cut their lines, so they run aground. Then their cannon won't do them any good, and more importantly we have a chance of getting their ship."

"How in hell are you gonna cut their stern line?" Smithers asked. "Ya figger they won't have a half dozen muskets and a swivel gun ready to maul any boat or swimmer that gets near to it?"

"What if they can't see us?"

"You gwin' ta make us invisible, Jack?"

"What if we were already positioned underwater, on the path the ship's stern would have to swing to?"

"The bell? But it would stick out like a sore thumb against that white bottom," Paul voiced his concern.

"I'm thinking we could cover it with a blanket that we dunked in something sticky and stuck sand and coral to it somehow."

"Tar'd do it," Coop said. "We got least a barrel of it."

The council went late into the night. The seamen were hardened to a world of risk and had weathered storms and survival by being tough once decisions were made. They were under their greatest threat yet, but once they resolved to follow Jack's plan, no further bickering would be tolerated.

The meeting that followed among Quince, Yatoo, Jawa, and Jack also went well. Jawa's usually impassive face broadened into a brief flicker of pleasure when he understood the crux of the plan. In turn Jawa explained to Yatoo that "the Dutch think we're animals and that we and the Americans have the hearts of women for battle." Yatoo said nothing but his jaw muscles tensed below the skin.

"Also," Jawa continued, "Gan Roba of Papalo lives."

Yatoo seemed surprised at the news that the Papaloan warlord was still alive and uncaptured. "He offers his allegiance to you and vows to fight to the death by our side. He has about thirty men left who can still wage war."

⤐❖⤏

For the next week, twenty men—twelve Americans and eight Belaurans—practiced from sunup until midday shooting the rifles salvaged from the *Star*. They picked an islet south of Belaur where there was no chance of the sound reaching the Dutch. Jack marveled at how quickly the group made progress. Unlike even the best-equipped European armies, the stranded Americans had a virtually unlimited supply of powder and shot with which to acquaint themselves to their weapons, and the only limits on their ability to train was eye fatigue and noise—even with wadding stuck in their ears, the sharp, brisk reports of the long rifles were painful after a while.

Jack taught them to lay the barrels on forked sticks like his father had shown him to do when testing arms. He helped each man sight-in his piece and fire at objects at varying distances, getting the sense of elevation necessary for long shots. By the end of the week the men were consistently hitting man-sized targets from distances as great as three hundred yards. With the day of the parley approaching, Jack shifted the emphasis to moving targets, showing them tricks he had been taught by his young hunter friends back in New England. Native children dragged thatch and wooden targets for the shooters and even pushed canoes by with makeshift targets erected in them.

Each day Jack blindfolded the riflemen and had them practice reloading and firing their weapons. The young American was tireless and his enthusiasm infectious. The Belaurans included some men Jack's age; they treated Jack much as they did their own warlord, with deference and awe. Yanoo and Matoo, stepsons of Yatoo, were particularly dedicated and quick to learn.

Jawa, for his part, treated Jack as an equal, and took his own turn at firing the weapons, though he opted not to be one of the marksmen because of the amount of time it would require to train properly. He needed his spare hours to work with his own men in their reconnaissance of the Dutch camp, and spent long evenings with Jack hunched over a fire with Brown and Graman as interpreter, refining their strategy.

Jack became more at ease. Action was in the offing. The defense of his new family against a despicable enemy calmed him in a strange way. In the evenings Jack and Paul let the Belauran children dunk them in the shallows and sneak up on them, breathing through hollow reeds. Even his time spent with Wyalum had been more enjoyable. They had not made love, but one evening she had come into his hut and had placed his head in her lap; he had fallen into a dreamless sleep with her stroking his hair and cheek. But all these activities were simply a respite from thinking of the work ahead, and ultimately of his main mission—Jack O'Reilly had business half a world away that still consumed him.

20

SHOWDOWN

PAUL, BELIEVING HE had to redeem himself in some way for his comportment during the shooting episode at Papalo, insisted on accompanying the Belauran scouting parties. They were engaged in the risky business of spying on the activities of the Dutch on land and the disposition of the sailboat they used for daily transport. The harassment attack planned by Jack to provoke the enemy could only be successful if they had reliable knowledge of their day-to-day operations.

Jack feared Paul's desire to prove himself might make him a liability; on the day before the planned raid on the Dutch, he was proven right. Two Belaurans that Paul had accompanied on a reconnaissance trip returned without him. The distraught men explained that they were lying in hiding, observing the prisoner pens, when they were surprised by a Dutch party returning from a foray through the swamp behind them. When it was certain they would be discovered, Paul had leapt to his feet and run out in the open. The Belaurans couldn't understand what he was saying, but Paul was acting strangely. The armed men took him prisoner but didn't go searching for others, which seemed odd to the scouts. When the Dutch were out of sight, the Belaurans stayed hidden for some time longer before carefully making their way back.

Jack intently listened to Brown interpreting, trying to comprehend the full meaning of what had happened.

He suppressed his panic for Paul's safety and analyzed the situation. Paul had obviously sacrificed himself to save his native comrades, which Jack could tell greatly moved the men. But like the Belaurans, he was at a loss to explain why the Dutch wouldn't have sounded a general alarm and searched for the other infiltrators—a one-man reconnaissance in this situation would have made no sense.

None in the Brotherhood uttered a word as Jack sat wrapped in his own thoughts for what seemed hours. Suddenly, he stood and with a grim look of determination announced that they would proceed with their plan despite the possibility that Paul would be tortured into telling what he knew. "For one thing," he announced, "I quit telling Paul any details of the raid once I knew he was set on taking part in the scouting." Jack tried to sound businesslike but his heart felt like it was full of lead.

⊸❋⊷

The scruffy party of blackbirders took Paul straight to the man in charge of the camp. They seemed to Paul to be a mixture of Dutch and English with some French thugs thrown in—but the leadership was mainly Dutch.

"This bloke came running out of the bush yelling at us like we was his long-lost cousins, Sergeant. Says he's some kinda Monsieur La Merde—"

Paul fairly screamed in the man's face, "Le Maire, you blessed idiot! Count Le Maire, and I demand to be taken to a gentleman of substance to whom I may express my gratitude. I will not be spoken to—"

"Now shut yer trap, laddy, lest I knock yer royal teeth outta yer head," snapped one of his captors.

The sergeant of dragoons raised his hand for silence. He looked Paul over with a stolid face. "Yo spek Anglisch, American?"

"A little," Paul answered. "I'm French, captured by the Americans and forced to help in their nefarious plots. Parlez-vous français?"

"He's full of shit to his lyin' ears," came a voice from the back of the crowd of dragoons. Paul thought the man sounded British. "He's one of 'em. Let's hang 'im from a yardarm of the *Stuyvesant* so the damn Yanks can see him easy with their scouting parties."

The sergeant addressed himself to the bunch that had brought Paul in. "You check for others?"

"Well, we . . . what others?"

"He may or may not be what he says. Go back and check that area thoroughly where you found him, see if there is sign of others." Then turning to one of his own dragoons, "Take him to Arloon and De Vries."

The sergeant's English is quite good after all, thought Paul. Clever man.

Paul was praying his bluff would hold long enough for his friends to escape. He never thought he would be grateful for the association with nobility that came from his father, but being a prig now might just save his life. The blackbirders were suspicious but he could also tell they were unsure: having a French nobleman leaping out of the brush and grabbing their legs in gratitude was not what they expected from a Belauran war party.

❧❀❧

De Vries sipped from a cup of steaming chocolate, one arm resting on the poop deck rail of the *Stuyvesant*, and studied Paul. The day had started hot and humid, and now the clouds behind him were threatening, heavy with rain. Captain Arloon had a cup of tea in his own hand. The men had been speaking English in Paul's presence. Paul knew this was significant. They were buying at least part of his story, that of being a nobleman, and treating him accordingly: Paul had pompously demanded a stool, and De Vries had a servant provide one. But using English also meant they weren't concerned about how much he knew. Paul hoped that didn't indicate an intent to do him in forthwith.

Captain Arloon did not speak French but could get by well enough in English. De Vries seemed to want Paul to be witness to the conversation; it was almost as if he felt a kinship with Paul, the only other person present of high birth. Paul had thrown his father's name around gratuitously and emulated all the mannerisms of the classes he had learned to despise. He believed that De Vries knew vaguely of his father and was considering what sort of reward or favors might be in order for rescuing such a connected person.

Paul believed that none of the Dutch, including De Vries, was convinced he wasn't in collaboration with the Americans; but it hardly mattered now. Paul's knowledge of their plans posed no threat a pistol ball couldn't eliminate and he might even be of some use. It hardly made sense to torture Paul for information, as they found it almost impossible to shut the young man up. He had regaled any of his captors who would listen with stories of atrocities committed by the Americans, particularly one ruthless Jack O'Reilly.

Paul gathered that Arloon had been reluctant to support De Vries's planned assault; he didn't like the thought of maneuvering his ship so close to the reef, and the prospect of more bloodshed was not attractive. De Vries's type seemed to bother him. This fit with what Paul had gleaned from Quince about the Dutch East India Company. Ruthless men were fast dominating the remnants of the trade since the company had turned its assets over to the government. Many of the old hands found their lack of scruples disturbing.

De Vries suddenly directed his conversation almost exclusively to Paul. He described how the blacks were precious cargo that would fetch decent prices in the

South Pacific and excellent prices in any of the mainland ports on the way back to Europe. They were semi-
legitimate cargo, one could argue, for they were not
slaves but pressed labor. They were cargo that loaded
and unloaded itself without days of docking and handling fees, and it was even unclear that duties need be
paid. Paul nodded and shook his head at what he
thought were appropriate times. Thanks for the lesson
in scurrilous business practices, you incredible ass.

"Best of all," De Vries went on, "a ship carrying
human cargo is too politically awkward a prize, given
the winds of war and politics blowing in Europe."

"Vraiment, vous avez raison," agreed Paul.

With a sly look on his face, De Vries explained further that a ship carrying human cargo in these times
presented enough consternation and distraction to port
officials that they rarely spent much time looking for
opium. Although the Dutch dared not enter inland
waters of China—where there was even a slight chance
of being caught with white death by an emperor's
patrol—there were always Chinese shore-runners who
would take that risk for them.

Jesus, Paul thought, who does he think I am, his goddamn apprentice?

"Boat ho!"

The pinnace, on a scouting mission, must be returning, Paul thought. There was some commotion on the
beach that he couldn't quite make out; then he saw several canoes make their way out from shore. From his
scouting forays, Paul knew a flotilla of canoes would act
as lighters, transferring cargo if the tide was out. If the
tide was in, only one or two were necessary to guide the
pinnace around coral heads.

The tide was in, so it puzzled him why so many canoes
headed out to greet the craft. Arloon seemed also to be
watching with interest. De Vries paid no attention and
went on talking about the state of preparedness for

their imminent departure to Canton and on to Capetown. It strengthened Paul's growing suspicion that there would be opium deep in the ship's hold during the final haul.

Several shots rang out from shore. Glancing back toward the island, the Dutchmen registered alarm at the sight of smoke billowing from Papalo, a village, Paul knew, which the Dutch had in effect turned into a temporary detention center for their "laborers." De Vries yelled for a spyglass, which materialized immediately from the watch officer's kit. Sailors crowded the port rail to see what was happening; one seaman who owned his own telescope was bombarded with questions from his mates.

Paul tried to make himself inconspicuous. He knew what was happening, but only in a general way, since Jack had insisted none of the scouts be apprised of any details of the impending raid.

Before the sailor with the telescope could launch very far into a description of events on shore, shots rang out from behind them . . . from seaward. They could only be from the pinnace. Something was obviously very wrong—even Paul was at a loss. He caught Arloon looking at him, and he was glad that his face was probably registering how nonplussed he was.

De Vries's glass was still trained on the shore, where his precious human cargo was caged; he seemed hardly aware of the actions transpiring with the pinnace. The sailors and Arloon, however, seemed ambivalent which way to look. All the canoes had converged on the pinnace, and there seemed to be some sort of altercation involving shots that had now quieted.

The pinnace was under way again but was now headed toward the *Stuyvesant*, several canoes following in its wake. Arloon seemed anxious to hear what had happened from the men operating the fast-sailing craft.

Many focused their attention toward land where the

fires seemed to be spreading, and they could hear a new outbreak of gunfire. Paul knew this must be Jack's doing, but suspected it was some sort of diversion. A poke at the ship itself would be the most provocative to the Dutch, but how was he planning to do this? Paul couldn't imagine. It was broad daylight—approach with canoes would be suicidal.

Paul suddenly realized that De Vries had been talking to him as if he was a confidant in frustration. De Vries could now see most of what transpired on shore, but it still made no sense. A company of dragoons was visible to the right. They seemed to be pinned down with their backs to the sea. Two other splashes of red and green were prostrate on the beach, apparent casualties. The ship's crew, along with Malay and Chinese handlers, were regrouping their native captives. They seemed to be trying to stay well out of range—of something, but what?

"How can a company of armed soldiers be held down by a group of savages and a few renegade Americans?" De Vries blurted. The only shooting they could discern came from the dragoons firing back into the thick jungle brush.

The Dutchman's own pinnace was now bearing down on them under full sail. It would arrive within moments, and the men on the pinnace were waving at them wildly. One large, heavyset man stood on the bow, waving a piece of dark cloth. De Vries and the men on the *Stuyvesant* were totally puzzled. Paul wasn't. His eyes widened; he knew that bearlike shape.

In the midst of this seeming chaos, the pinnace suddenly jibed. Her boom swept like a pendulum in a wide, sweeping maneuver; the craft's direction had been skillfully turned 90 degrees to starboard. As the stern swung around, Paul could make out a pile of dunnage laying against the transom and two men nestled down amidst the sacks, as if taking cover from small-arms fire. Paul, crouched low, watched De Vries's eyes narrow as it slowly dawned upon the man that he was in danger—too slowly. From the corner of his eye, Paul caught two flashes in quick succession and almost simultaneously heard the Dutchman yelp. A fraction of a second later the sound of the shots reached them. De Vries turned, assuming he had been grazed by a rifle ball or splinter, and began to examine himself for damage.

The dragoons onboard immediately returned fire with a salvo of musket shots, some of which found their mark in the pinnace but not in their assailants. The crew of the sailing craft had hunkered down behind bags of produce and spare canvas and let the boat ride a favorable wind that whipped her seaward at an excellent clip on a starboard tack. Their port heel would take them out of range and out of the harbor. Paul deeply wished he were with his comrades.

The men in De Vries's boat were speechless. Two tended to a dragoon who seemed mortally wounded, and the others kept staring at De Vries with a strange look. He swiped at something that had caught on his brow and barked in exasperation, "Why are you damn fools gaping at me and not running those bastards down? And how the hell did they get our pinnace and . . . Lord save me."

De Vries turned pale, realizing why the men were staring. It was no piece of wet canvas on his forehead—it was a sizable ribbon of his scalp he had been trying to wipe away. Paul almost felt sorry for the man. Most of his right ear was shredded, and there was a clean white streak where the ball had torn his scalp forward like peeling a potato and left the mess hanging over his face; the bone of his skull was miraculously untouched. He fainted momentarily, then raised shakily to his knees to watch the *Stuyvesant* gunners attempt to fire its bow chasers at the receding pinnace. Everyone knew they had little chance of hitting her.

In a worsening state of shock, he leaned forward and threw up over the gunwale before sinking into a second faint. Paul knew, however, that the image that had burned itself into the minds of De Vries and the crew was the piece of dark cloth the fat man had been waving at them as they approached in the small sailboat—a black banner with a smirking white skull embroidered on it and two bones crossed beneath it. As the pinnace sailed away, Paul saw it rise up the mainmast—whipping the air with a fearful vengeance.

⊰❋⊱

The ship's surgeon did as well as he could by De Vries. Most of his scalp was back in place, but the best the doctor could do with the ear was remove some of the dangling flesh—it was an ugly wound that would make the man shop carefully for wigs the rest of his life. Most of the sailors cared little for the foppish, demanding company man, and Paul sensed they rather delighted in his new look. De Vries in no way shared their light view of the matter and retired to his cabin where he brooded in a dark rage. When he finally came back on deck, he called for the ship's captain, and Paul could hear him yelling that no effort be spared in the capturing and executing of the Americans and making an example of all the God-be-damned savages that had in any way colluded with them.

Paul deduced that Arloon, from his manner, agreed in principle but his instincts told him to cut his losses, secure the blacks still in captivity, and depart these waters. It was apparent to Paul that the raid by the Americans, and whichever the hell natives were really on their side, had shaken him and adversely affected his men.

Paul wondered why the Jolly Roger had such an effect on seamen, for as enraged as the Dutch master and officers were, their men were disconcerted. They were quick to point out that the pirate-captured pinnace had actually swept at one point right under the guns of the *Stuyvesant*. The Americans had taken it by having a trio of Belauran canoes paddle out from hiding to greet the pinnace before the Papaloans. Three Americans were lying prone in the canoes with weapons. The one called Dyak simply told the shocked coxswain of the Dutch boat to "swim or die." He swam.

The shooting they had heard was from a Dutchman in one of the pursuing Papaloan canoes. A return shot by the Americans from the deck of the pinnace had struck the lead paddler in the Papaloan craft and it had capsized.

The captured Papaloans had muttered something about "Dyak" and had warned the Dutch that some sort of fearless young warrior led the Americans. It was this Dyak whom they attributed with the shot that had relieved De Vries of his ear. Paul looked at the Dutchman as if to say: "What did I tell you?" then whispered, "Dyak indeed!"

"What did you say?"

"He's Jack—Black Jack O'Reilly. I thought you knew."

"Knew what?"

"He's as wily and foul a pirate as ever prowled the Caribbean and he's come here now. Christ, the man is evil incarnate. He's here with his band, living like a whoremaster king." Paul knew the Dutch were skeptical of what he said but his currency was increasing with many of them. They would also expect him to be truthful if he was anxious to save his neck.

"Tell us more about this Black Jack," barked one of the dragoons.

"What is there to tell? He kills all he can't subjugate and eats his victims' heads just to make a point."

"Do you think we're children needing a bedtime story?" Arloon sounded disgusted.

"Eats them, I tell you," Paul continued. "You know of those men killed weeks past?"

"What of 'em?" from a voice in the crowd.

"Was O'Reilly did them in. I saw him coming back into camp laughing and swinging the head of one of the poor devils. Black Jack threw it to one of his bitches and told her to cook it rare and spare none of the juices." The Dutch sailors were now looking at each other warily; maybe this captive was willing to tell all he knew.

"What of the other man killed? His head wasn't taken."

"I couldn't guess, he always takes . . . unless it had been somehow spoiled or ruined," suggested Paul.

"Aye it's true," one of the Englishmen mumbled to De Vries. "Faroon was found with his jaw and skull smashed to jelly."

"See, I knew it," interjected Paul. "The head was spoiled."

"Dyak, Americans, and all the God-damned Indians be damned to hell," screamed De Vries. "Set sail for that cove."

"Silence!" Arloon shouted. "Gather all the officers, mates, and dragoons."

Paul stepped to the side as Arloon prepared for a meeting of all his principals. None seemed to pay the young captive any heed.

⊰✻⊱

"The men are jittery, and with good cause. The Jolly Roger is their way of saying that they don't give a rat's red ass about us, our dragoons, and our ship with its twelve-gun broadside. It's their way of saying these are their islands, and they consider us the prey and not the hunters," the first officer of the *Stuyvesant* said.

"Are they insane besides being criminals? Do they wish to die?"

"I might point out, Mr. De Vries, sir, that in our dealings with them thus far we have lost five white men and two of our Asian crewmen—to say nothing of what they did to you. We have only this one captive—deserter, whatever he is—to show for our troubles."

"That's because they don't stand and fight. We'll simply corner them where they will have to fight like men. They have no stomach for a face-off."

"Sir, permission to speak." The sergeant of dragoons addressed himself to the captain. He was a grisly man, no ambitions past what he already was, Paul guessed, a man who had the experience of many bloody encounters carved deeply into his face and cared nothing for rich-boy ship managers who prattled when they should be listening.

"Your opinion is always valued, Sergeant," Arloon remarked warmly.

"I have no doubt we can take these men in a disciplined confrontation, soldier to soldier. But it is my duty to apprise you of the situation as I see it."

Arloon nodded for him to continue; Paul had the feeling this man knew his business.

"We have knowledge that they possess at least five shoulder arms and a pistol."

"Aye."

"To our knowledge—and we have discussed this at length among ourselves—they have fired these weapons a total of nine times." He looked at the officers, as if waiting for the thought to sink in. "With those nine shots, they have inflicted nine casualties. These men may be no soldiers but they follow orders—maybe they were part of a ship's crew, and they are well led—and the bastards can shoot."

"Yes, but—" De Vries attempted to interrupt, but the sergeant, who recognized only the captain as his superior, continued speaking.

"They have some sort of strong bond with the savages, particularly those of Belaur. We're positive that at least one of the men, possibly more, who handled a rifle during the armed attack on the prisoner pens was a native."

"What!" De Vries exclaimed in surprise.

"Gentlemen, that savage shot one of my men in the heart from over a hundred yards away."

Paul couldn't make himself any smaller where he had stowed himself next to a deck gun. The information about the Indians being trained to shoot was something he obviously should have shared with them if he was being as forthcoming as he tried to make them think.

Murmurs broke out all around the table until Arloon raised his hand for the man to continue.

"Also, it wasn't any musket; that kaffir bastard was shooting a long rifle. Fine weapon—the Americans use them on their Kentucky frontier, can't imagine why they'd have one here. I don't know what to make of all this, sir, but I didn't get these white whiskers and scars on this ugly mug from underestimating my enemy. Please don't put us in a position where we must depend on trusting the natives, and don't figure these Americans for a few drunken renegades with guns. They seem to think we're fighting on their soil and we're the only foreigners here. And that one"—he pointed to Paul—"I trust him not at all. He's one of them or only recently converted to save his skin. There, I've said my piece and respectfully await your orders, Captain."

De Vries stood straight and looked the captain in the eye. "I've heard enough," he said. "Of course we're dealing with desperate men and possibly pirates, but I didn't think I'd ever see Dutch soldiers flinch in the face of duty." Most were embarrassed at the unfair assessment of the dragoons' courage, but said nothing. "Damn it, we head to Belaur on the morning's tide or there will be hell to pay in Holland."

"They won't meet us at the village now," the sergeant said.

"What!"

"They insist on the spit south of the village. It too has a deep cove we can maneuver into. They say that is where they will discuss terms of surrender."

"Then get us there."

Arloon looked at DeVries and said very quietly, "I will do that, sir, but mark you, man, do not—I say, do not—say one word to my men as an order during the maneuver in that cove." Arloon was as red as the setting sun. "Your council of merchants and royal decree be damned. If you interfere in that action, I'll shoot you myself."

He turned to Paul. "I don't trust you either, but it makes no difference. Listen to me well." Paul stood frozen. "You're no fool. Whatever your allegiances are or were, you know by now that by two days hence we shall own these islands and there will be no place to run. If we release you and find that this chief . . . Yatoo, what's his name?"

"Yes, Yatoo," Paul replied.

"If this Yatoo has been convinced by you to help us and we have no indication you helped them resist, we will not only *not* hang you, we will provide you transportation out of these islands to a civilized port."

"Very gracious of—"

"Shut up. If he joins with the Americans, as I suspect he might, his promises to the contrary, you will die a miserable death. Am I understood?"

Paul couldn't believe his luck.

"Oui, je comp . . . yes, I understand, absolument."

"And I will be assured that you will not even think of pulling a trigger against one of my men if I let you go."

"Of course, I—"

"No, my assurance will come in another form." He turned to a mean-looking second mate. "Carsten, take him to the rail and break his right index finger. Then take him by launch to where he will be found in the morning by Belauran scouts."

Paul froze inside. He never felt so devalued as a human being. The only thing that kept him from dissolving completely in panic was the fact that everything happened so fast.

As predicted, by late morning, he was found and whisked to Belaur by heavily armed scouts, his finger broken, and nearly his spirit.

━═❈═━

"They're coming, all right—we can see the tip of the foremast over the palms on East Key. It's making way around the outer reef." Paul's voice grew tight with excitement as he stepped out of the first of the three Belauran scouting canoes that had just arrived at the spit. Jack studied his friend's expression and manner as he stepped ashore. Even with the prospect of battle so close he could not help contemplate what Paul had been through. Paul cut a pitiful figure. Right hand splinted, he had not stopped shaking since being found and brought in the night before by Belauran scouts, nor to Jack's knowledge had he slept. The brutally cold act of breaking his finger had deeply upset him, even more than the ignominy of being captured. He could not speak of it except to say, "They did it to me without feeling, Jack. No anger, nothing, just like the child they brained in the clearing. I fainted with fear and pain and . . ."

Jack had tried to calm him but he would have none of it. As soon as Hansum had splinted his hand, Paul insisted on going back out with the boats. Before leaving, he ran back and pulled Jack aside where the others couldn't hear and whispered, "I peed myself when they did it—before I fainted—and . . . and they laughed."

Jack wondered if, for the first time in his life, Paul Le Maire really wanted to kill someone. He forced down the rage that sought to possess him when he thought of the physical and spiritual damage done to his friend— he must keep a cool, clear head. He turned his attention to the matter at hand.

Jawa and two dozen of his best warriors stood in a circle with Jack and Quince, going over the details of the plan. Things were moving on schedule, Jack concluded, and Jawa needed no further explanation. Quince asked Jack if the small diving bell was in place. Aye, it was; it blended in well with the bottom when seen from above. And the trees—if one looked carefully, he could probably make out the artful camouflage of fronds and sticks. From behind, it would be easy to discern they had been converted into sniper perches.

Jack and Quince had just completed their inspection of the sand trenches, dug into the far side of the spit in which Jawa and his twenty-four warriors would be secluded. None of these men had firearms, although the six Americans with them carried the pistol and five of the rifles. Eight of Jawa's recently trained marksmen would be in the trees armed with long rifles. In the village itself, Yatoo and every man who could fight—about a hundred and fifty all told, plus thirty Papaloans—had left their weapons concealed in their canoes. When the ambush was sprung, and the Dutch were occupied by the force in front of them, Yatoo would enter the cove from the rear—it would be a day of glory for all the people of the archipelago. Yatoo would die or he would live, but his name would be honored forever.

⊰※⊱

Quince and Jack stood on the beach in the open. About a dozen natives in full ceremonial regalia, including war clubs, surrounded them, but none except the two Americans carried firearms. The *Stuyvesant* dropped its bower hook and let itself be swept broadside to the spit before its crew expertly secured a stern anchor. The gunport covers were already raised, and within moments the ugly muzzles of twelve cannon were played through the open ports.

"Big surprise," muttered Jack. He was amazed how predictable the enemy's behavior was. The Dutch had not discussed details of their plan around Paul before sending him off, but they didn't need to. The Brotherhood had anticipated this move since hearing the substance of De Vries's talk with Yatoo weeks before. Only now the Dutch leaders had been provoked into committing their major asset, the ship, on terms specified by the Americans. Thank God you're not as smart as you are cruel, Jack thought.

"It's what you might call negotiating from a position of strength," yelled De Vries from his perch on the quarterdeck to the figures on the beach. Smug bastard, Jack thought. He hoped their situation seemed hopeless to the Dutch. The American leader and Indian allies were assembled on the beach for the parley, and there would be no chance of escape from the narrow spit of land. They would be chopped to pieces attempting to run back to the main island. The white men on both sides knew that after the ship's initial range-finding volley, the murderous carronades would be loaded with chain and metal detritus that would rake every living thing on the beach.

The village would have seemed peaceful enough when they passed it, Jack reckoned—normal activity, many canoes lined up on the beach. From Paul's descriptions, Jack was sure he could make out the key players. Captain Arloon and the sergeant of dragoons were obvious from their demeanor and uniforms, De Vries from his bandages and big mouth. After they dispensed with the Americans on the spit, they probably planned to let the dragoons move to the village overland while they swept back past the compound and reduced it to shambles with the ship's heavy guns.

The sergeant of dragoons was strangely quiet, however, as was Captain Arloon. De Vries had heeded the warning to yell no orders at any of the sailors or soldiers. They cared little what he screamed to the enemy on the beach—their disposition would, in the final analysis, be his call. But both veterans seemed uneasy to Jack—he knew they felt that something was wrong here, and they carefully scanned the cove for a trap.

De Vries finally scoffed, "What, no tricks from your fat self or young banty rooster? Perhaps we'll be merciful to you if you beg, and just hang your friends. We'll only cut out your tongues, or remove other vital parts, and keep you alive for hanging in Amsterdam—or maybe trade you to the English crown." De Vries's command of English was much better than Jack would have guessed.

When there was no response, he continued, "The terms are simple: unconditional surrender or die like dogs."

"We accept," Quince said calmly.

After a short, surprised silence, De Vries blurted, "Finally, some common sense."

"Yes," echoed Quince, "we accept. Now if you would have your men toss their arms over the side, close the gunports, and raise a white flag, we will go easy on you and spare most of your lives."

The mocking answer was too much for De Vries; he turned to the captain and screamed for him to kill the upstarts.

Jack stood forward.

"We will show you how men die, Dutchman." Jack motioned to his men, spread evenly along the edge of the low surf.

The voice of a Dutch officer carried clearly over the water. "You don't have a prayer, surrender or die."

"We must know if your powder is dry before we surrender," Jack yelled to the captain of the *Stuyvesant*.

"You are quite mad, pirate," came the reply. "Enough foolishness, this is your last chance. If you throw down your weapons now we'll spare all but your leaders, and they'll be given a fair trial."

In answer, Jack swept his rifle to his shoulder in one smooth move and, without seeming to aim, fired at the captain. The shot missed and struck a splinter of wood off the overhead which buried itself into the face of one of the Dutch officers by the captain's side. The response was almost immediate. A broadside rang out, pushing the vessel sideways in recoil. Two of the islanders dropped, wounded, but most of the deadly barrage missed the thin strand of beach, the majority of projectiles falling short or sailing harmlessly over the men's heads. This was expected by the experienced sailors on both sides. Jack knew the gunners now had the range and the next round of fire would be much more lethal. This is where it all gets decided, Jack thought. Maril and the boys in that bell better have done their job.

"Captain, we're adrift and headed into the beach!" the *Stuyvesant*'s first mate screamed.

"But how—did the hook slip?"

"Damn it, no, Skipper. Somehow the bastards cut the line."

"Thank God," Jack said aloud as Quince let his breath out in a long sigh. The men on the ship cast puzzled glances toward shore. They could not fathom why their enemies kept position on the beach, making no move to run or return their fire. Only those next to a fallen man had broken ranks, to minister to their comrades' wounds.

As the ship gradually continued to shift position, the air suddenly filled with lead, raining down from above. A withering fire from concealed rifles somewhere—in those damned palms—started raking the deck, where the officers were clustered. They were totally exposed. There was the thud of lead hitting flesh, the sight of men falling to the deck, some groaning, most silent.

Below, the cannon muzzles were beginning to reappear through the square ports but the ship drifted toward shore and the gun barrels were deflected hopelessly upward. As the vessel ran aground, the port side dipped down, then upward, as the keel scraped over the uneven sea bottom.

"Now!" Jack yelled. "Charge the bastards!"

He watched Arloon's jaw drop and a look of panic sweep his face. Directly in front of him dozens of warriors seemed to be materializing from the thin sandspit, splashing madly through the shallows toward his grounded ship. Some Americans also appeared from the same sandy grave and had dropped to their knees at the water's edge, where they began firing rifles with deadly effect through the open gunports. The captain appeared to abandon the thought of any broadside and called out to "fire at will!"

Jack would never have believed such an explosion possible. It was deafening. The sleek *Stuyvesant* lifted several feet in the air, much of its upper stern vaporizing in a ball of fire and smoke. The captain and most of the men on the stern were blown into the sea from the force of the blast. The Americans and Indians threw themselves on the beach, covering their heads with their hands as pieces of wood, machinery, and body parts flew by.

As the sound of the blast died away, the lagoon grew eerily silent. The flotilla of canoes that had just rounded the spit, led by Yatoo, seemed frozen in place. The men who had been charging the ship stood or knelt, their arms over their faces. Jack, lying next to Quince on the beach, was speechless.

Sweet Jesus! Madre de Dios, what the hell happened? The confusion seemed to affect both sides equally, but the first to recover were the battle-hardened Dutch dragoons, most of whom, positioned forward on the ship, had been spared the main force of the blast. Jack, still stunned at the miraculous disintegration of the ship he had coveted, heard the sergeant order the ship's boats brought up to pick up the officers, most of whom were killed or badly wounded in the blast. He told his men to hold fire as the rescuers picked a few survivors floundering in the light surf. Without commands of any kind, fire had ceased from the American side. The American sailors, along with their Belauran allies, were transformed into uneasy spectators in a strange drama in which, moments before, they had been lead players.

As the officers were pulled into one of the boats, it was soon apparent to Jack that, although wounded, the captain and De Vries were still alive. The boat into which they had been deposited started pulling for the far end of the spit to regroup away from their enemy and their ship. Quince and Jack, decisive and aggressive in battle, were strangely paralyzed in the face of this boggling turn of events. What kept repeating itself in Jack's head was—My ship! My way to Cuba!

From the side of the cove, a Belauran canoe suddenly made way toward the Dutch boat holding the captain and De Vries, which was now engaged in fishing out survivors. Paul sat in the canoe's stern, holding a rifle taken from a fallen Belauran. Two natives were paddling, but the progress seemed to be directed by Quen-Li. This was just one more strange development in what appeared to Jack an altogether surreal scene. He and the others stared in wonder at this new inexplicable turn of events.

The captain stood shakily in the stern of the launch as the Belauran canoe approached; De Vries lay prostrate in its belly, Paul could see, bleeding profusely from his nose and good ear. The canoe caught up to the boat as it rounded the stem of the *Stuyvesant*, out of the protective cover of the dragoons clustered along the rail and some distance from most of the American marksmen.

"Captain Arloon?" The question from Quen-Li came in perfect English, his voice carrying across the quiet waters clearly.

"Aye . . . yes, that's me. What . . . ?"

"I have a message for you from the emperor of China." With that, he drove a Belauran spear through Arloon's throat. A one-armed dragoon in the boat raised his weapon to shoot Quen-Li when a shot rang out from the canoe and the man was blown backward into the water. A wisp of smoke trailed from Paul's weapon.

With the captain sitting in a heap and staring vacantly in front of him, blood streaming from his neck, Jack heard his friend proclaim in a voice that seemed not that of the Paul Le Maire he knew, "Oh Captain, you know something interesting? Something you can think about in hell? I'm left-handed." The canoe back-paddled swiftly with no further engagement between the men in either craft.

Quince dropped to his knees, mouth open, repeating, "What in blazing deep-sea hell is going on? What in . . . ?"

Jack turned to him. "Skipper, uh, there's . . . well, there's a story there you need to know about." Jack actually didn't know the full details himself, but from what he had just seen and heard, he could pretty much guess.

With most of the officers killed or wounded, the sergeant of dragoons took command, and no one on the ship seemed inclined to argue. Jack could overhear a short parley taking place with the dragoon leader speaking from the bow of the *Stuyvesant*. An apparent act of the god of chaos had interfered with the affairs of men. The instrument of divine intervention: a humble Papaloan woman. The sergeant explained the mystery of the explosion in fair, if broken, English, "Dat Papaloan bitch did it. She ran into ship magazine with a torch when we opened it for the powder monkeys to reload."

"Papaloan?" a voice asked.

"Aye, she came aboard several weeks ago. Fair-skinned kaffir to service the officers. Seemed to relish it, cozy with all the men whenever they wished . . . she pretty much got the run of the ship. Her son and her man were killed in that first incident with you Americans that started this mess."

The image of a woman's face sprang into Jack's mind, one that would be there the rest of his life. A beautiful, haunted, brown face of a Papaloan girl clutching a bloody bundle in her arms, rocking back and forth on her knees, grief so deep she had no way of expressing it.

"Quince, the girl in the clearing—"

"I know, lad, I know."

Negotiations went quickly. The dragoons and remaining Dutch sailors could still cause significant bloodshed if forced to a desperate last stand. At this point no one seemed to have the stomach for it. Yatoo had entertained following up on the advantage, but Quince convinced him the spoils of the *Stuyvesant* were a magnificent prize—and two dozen dragoons could inflict terrible losses, ship or no ship. Their captain and most of their leaders were dead and they would be happy to put as much distance between themselves and this archipelago as fast as possible; but if they had to stand and fight, who knew what might happen. The bloodshed wouldn't be worth the gain, Quince argued. If these were British or French, or the Dutch twenty years ago, the chance of reprisals would be great; but in this age the Dutch would be happy to find softer targets, even if news of this battle reached their homeland.

The sergeant never knew for sure what had happened in the boat with Arloon and never asked. He was a practical man. For Quince's part, even when Jack and Paul explained the background of Quen-Li, the first mate couldn't absorb it in the context of everything else that had happened. He decided it was just one more event in a day he would never fully comprehend, and asked about it no more.

As the chiefs and men talked, Paul watched some young native boys pushing stray arms and heads around in the shallows. They were fascinated with the grisly testimony to the power of the white men's magic—a magic which they didn't seem always able to control. Paul had killed his first man and he was numb. It had been so easy: point a muzzle, flick a finger—yes, just like that— and you toss some soul off the planet.

What's that they're saying? Ah, kill the badly wounded they've decided—more finger-flicking. The rest will be given canoes and food, and pointed south. If they make it several hundred miles down chain they'll come to a strait where an occasional white sail is seen and they may find their way home. Their trail will be followed for five days by a Belauran and American war party. If it finds any stragglers, they will be killed. If they aren't all gone by morning, they will be killed. If they ever return, they will be killed. All in all, a straightforward if not very gentle arrangement.

Quen-Li came by and sat with Paul. He did not flinch as Paul did with the sound of each shot; he just looked into Paul's eyes and smiled when it was all over.

"Life is sometimes hard, my young friend, and victories hollow. You have given me my life back for a time and I will make good use of it. Thank you. The air feels good in my chest tonight, I am glad not to be breathing the dirt."

"Quen-Li . . . Arloon was on your list?"

"Yes."

"Anyone else we know? What about De Vries?"

"No, not De Vries."

"But another? Who?"

"Maybe one other."

"Who, damn it, who?"

"Captain Deploy."

"Sweet Jesus."

"Bonne nuit, mon ami."

21

RECLAMATION

JACK STOOD LOOKING at the burning hulk of the Dutch ship, recently standing so proud in the lagoon. She spewed an acrid mixture of gunpowder and burning timbers, and with smoke pouring from her innards, her death was imminent. Jack could not rejoice in its sinking, even though the enemy had been vanquished.

The sun balanced itself on the foreyard, casting a brilliant hue through the haze. Quince broke the silence.

"She were a fine ship, lads. Pity the captain acted like an ass. I've seen them smolder and burn like this for days. She'll be down by her bulwarks by morning." He turned and walked away, the rest of the men following in ones and twos, at once relieved, triumphant, and saddened by the day's events.

Jack crouched against a palm tree, staring at the wooden pyre.

"What are you thinking?" asked Paul.

"Oh, I don't know, really. Just wondering what this is all about. You know, the deaths, destruction. Wondering what it all has to do with me and my need to get back to the Caribbean." The two friends sat silently, watching the sun perform its magic on the cobalt sea. "I was thinking what a shame it is to lose such a magnificent vessel as lies there, the *Peter Stuyvesant*."

"He was a hated man," Paul stated emphatically, gazing out at the calm lagoon. "A man whom the British defeated and—"

"How do you know all this about the captain?" Jack interrupted.

"Not the captain, idiot. I mean Peter Stuyvesant, the man who founded New Amsterdam."

Jack looked at him, puzzled.

"New York to you, O unlearned one," Paul replied. "A controversial leader—but then maybe all leaders, by definition, are controversial."

Jack continued to gaze at the ship, only half listening to Paul's words. He suddenly stood. "Let's find Quince and the others. I've got an idea that may solve our problems—or add to them."

They walked briskly down the beach and found the rest of the *Star*'s crew gathered around a small wood fire.

"I have a proposal I think will work," Jack announced, "but we need to act fast."

"It be late for fireworks, laddy. We've done that once today," said Hansumbob from the edge of the campfire. The tired sailors laughed halfheartedly.

"I propose we douse the fire on the Dutchman and save her."

"Aye, so we can do it all over again tomorrow, Jack?" Red Dog answered back.

Jack continued, ignoring the remark. "We could salvage what's remaining of her and mate it with the *Star*. It seems as if what's missing from the Dutch ship is what's left of ours. We can replace the Dutchman's mizzen with the *Star*'s remaining mast, then fore-and-aft rig all but the foremast. That'd leave us with a barkentine, and rigged that way we have enough men to crew her."

The men were quiet, taking in the words of this young man who had once again acquitted himself well in the recent battle.

"She's startin' to list to starboard even as we speak, lad," Quince stated.

Jack turned to the lagoon, where indeed he could already perceive a tilt.

Quince rose from the beach. "All hands hear this: whether we save the *Stuyvesant* for future use or not, it will certainly be too late if we wait and talk about it tomorrow. So here's what we'll do: we'll board her and attempt to douse the fire. If it seems too risky, we'll abandon ship and let her sink—but we've got to get crackin' if we intend to save her."

The group acted instantly. A small boat was pushed back into the sea by Coop and Mentor. Several other men boarded canoes and began paddling toward the half-sunken vessel.

The Dutch ship was blown apart from the fantail forward to the mainmast. The mizzen had splintered and fallen back across the gaping hole in its deck; the deck beams were destroyed all the way aft, from the entrance to the officer's quarters past the helm. Bits and pieces of the frame ribs pointed grotesquely into the night sky. The fire seemed to be centered in the lower part of the hold, but so far had left the structural floor timbers unharmed.

Quince started the men on a bucket brigade, half of them trying to douse the fire, the other half bailing madly and manning the bilge pumps, trying to keep the ship afloat. Though exhausted from the day's events, the men pitched in mightily and worked through the night.

By dawn the fire was extinguished and the ship seemed to be out of danger. The sailors all lay about in various stages of repose, blackened by the smoke. It had been dangerous work, and Quince stood wearily, his face a scorched mass of dried sweat. "If this idea of yours doesn't work, Sir Jack, it will be your royal arse. Mind what I say." The first mate lowered himself to the sooted deck and fell asleep.

Elated, Jack gazed at the blackened prize. His idea had worked—at least the first stage, and with any luck the rest remained just a matter of hard work. God knows he wasn't afraid of that.

During the next few days the men tried to clean up the ship to see just how much damage had been done. The aft deck was a jungle of splintered masts, line, sail, and charred timbers. Quince started several working parties to salvage as much of the hardware, line, and blocks as possible, as they would be needed later. Jack and Paul had been given the task of assembling the pinnace that lay atop the forward deckhouse. They were pleased to find a gig and jolly boat in good repair.

The Belaurans were diving in the bilge near the mainmast step, trying to retrieve the ballast rocks to keep the ship afloat. Mentor was in charge of the working party who painstakingly hauled rocks up from the hold and heaved them over the side. The strong backs of the men and women of the village were of great help, but it was still difficult work. Quince yelled to a couple of hands to start emptying the remaining gunpowder into a sail remnant and then to seal the empty barrels so that they would be buoyant. There were over fifty barrels of the precious powder, and though some of it was wet, it could be dried later. Although the ship would not be in any immediate danger if the weather changed, any sort of heavy sea would pummel her against the beach in quick order.

⊰❈⊱

Several weeks went by before Quince deemed the *Stuyvesant* safe to move. The natives pitched in heartily to help salvage the ship. In the evenings with the work complete, many of the young people, in high good humor, dove from the rail, carving the crystalline water with their bodies. Some climbed into the rigging, their screams of delight filling the night air.

Quince decided to call a meeting to explain how they would proceed.

"It's to be a difficult task for all hands if we're to get this barge down to the islet hard by the *Star*," he said.

"What's the point?" Smithers piped up from the back. "All I see is hard work and nothin' to be gained. It'll take the better part of six months to get this wreck down to the *Star*, swap poles and gear, and get her right to sail. What's in it for me, I say? What say the rest of ya?"

They said nothing. Whether out of fatigue or disagreement, Jack couldn't be sure. Smithers and Cheatum were sprawled in the sand next to Quince, both looking straight up into the night sky.

"Stuff your grub locker, Smithers," Quince said, "or I'll jam a cro'jack 'tween your pins."

Nervous laughter came from the group.

"Aye, Skipper, don' ya do that—he'll have a grin on his face for days." An anonymous voice had come from the center of the group.

"Who said that?" Smithers jumped to his feet with a shout. "I'll have his tongue on a plate. Who said that?" His voice was a shriek. A blade had suddenly appeared in his hand.

Quince waited a moment to let him cool.

"Smithers, rest your haunches. It won't be six months. It'll be closer on a year and no one meant you any harm. We're all tired—put your blade away and sit."

Quince's delivery came in an even voice. Jack held his breath until Smithers in fact sat, mumbling and unrepentant.

"As I was saying," Quince went on, "we're but a few, and if this work is to proceed and be shipshape, it will take every man to make it so. We'll do the following: in ten days, on the twentieth of the month as best as I can figure, we'll be at high tide about four bells to morning. We'll let the *Stuyvesant* drift out and with luck, the morning winds, which of late have been from the south, will push us out of the lagoon. We daren't put up sails as we're without rudder and mizzenmast, and most of the starboard bumpkin's been burnt away . . . and the backstay, with so little purchase, would surely give way and bring the mainmast down soundly 'round our shoulders. So we'll go out bare poles."

"What's to keep us off those rocks, Captain?" Cheatum asked.

"As you well know, Mr. Cheatum, I'm not the captain—nor even your duly elected standard-bearer—but until someone comes up with a better idea, this is what we'll do: we'll have the pinnace secured hard to the aft starboard rail or what's left of the rail. She'll be strapped with barrels Coop has made buoyant. On the morning we leave, we'll have every available hand and all the Belaurans on the port rail hiked out. As the ship tilts to port with the movement of the sea, we'll continue to cinch up the pinnace to try and make the starboard side come up above a safe waterline. This being successful, I'll be on the bowsprit to help guide the boat and gig to lead us out of the lagoon. Once at sea, we'll continue rounding the eastern edge of the island. With God's wisdom, we'll drift south down to our isle of broken dreams . . . any questions?"

Silence was the only answer as the men contemplated this next adventure. Slowly, they wandered up the beach to their various shelters.

Then Hansumbob began to sing:

Bare poles he said, and said it strong
   'Twas stated loud and true.
Pete lives she does; she sails once more
   With a fine but unruly crew.
Legend has it that they sailed this way
   For forty years and more.
Chins held high, they roamed the seas
   Till their bones did drift to shore.

Hansumbob hummed a few more notes, pulled his blanket around his head, and fell asleep.

━⊰✷⊱━

On the morning of the twentieth, after being up all night, the crew reached the tattered ship. The Belaurans had arrived with baskets of fruit and baked fish, and at midnight a party had broken out. Quince allowed the sailors some leeway these last days, for though most of the crew had great confidence in the first mate, they seemed on edge with the prospect of taking the disabled *Peter Stuyvesant* into the open seas without rudder or sails.

"Mr. Cheatum, I would like you to be in the jolly boat on the port side," Quince ordered. "Take up a station about thirty or forty yards forward of the bow and ten yards further abeam to form the port side of a Y shape. Take five men with you. Mr. Dawkins, you'll be in the gig opposite Cheatum. Form your Y and keep your line taut. On my command, you must pull hard to starboard or port, as this ship will be an ungodly handful. Good luck."

The sailors manned the small boats and lashed lines twenty feet aft of the bow on either side. Then, as close to four bells as they could estimate, they cast off their long shore lines and the huge ship started drifting slowly out of the tiny lagoon. The Belaurans had finished their job earlier, cinching up the pinnace to the aft starboard rail; now they shouted encouragement from shore, mixed with raucous laughter. The sailors, though, kept to the task at hand.

"Cheatum, pull a little stronger to port." Quince spoke with confidence. "We're drifting too far to starboard."

Cheatum's crew turned their boat to the west, the starboard boat allowing their line to drift slack. With just a few course changes, the *Peter Stuyvesant* seemed to be drifting through the inlet in good shape. The coral heads on the port side were just about abeam of the ship, the two small boats astern evenly spaced and pulling hard toward open seas. Cheatum was deep in animated conversation with Smithers, whom he had chosen to be on his crew. The two were engaged in their own private joke when their boat hit a submerged coral head. Cheatum, who should have been standing in the bow watching for just such an occurrence, cursed loudly and grabbed an oar, attempting to extricate his jolly boat from the shape just a foot below the waterline. The *Stuyvesant* and its great mass continued out the inlet; the gig on the starboard side continued to pull hard, bringing the large ship further to the right.

"Back off on the gig, mister! Pull back hard to port!" Quince shouted from the deck of the *Stuyvesant*.

As the ship's fantail spun slowly to port, the line from Cheatum's jolly boat passed under the *Stuyvesant* abeam of the helm, where she stuck hard on the damaged hardware of the rudder. Quince ran to the line that had passed under the ship, shouting orders to both boats simultaneously. As the jolly boat was dragged closer to the *Stuyvesant* by her caught line, Quince grabbed a new line coiled neatly on a belaying pin and tossed it to Cheatum. "Secure this line and I'll cut the old one. And Mr. Cheatum, I'll have a word with you when this be over. Rely on that."

Cheatum secured the line. He ordered his men to take up the slack and pull hard to right the *Stuyvesant*. Jack, seated in the jolly boat, was startled by a loud commotion on board. He noticed that Quince was involved in a confrontation and was unaware of a snagged line on deck that entangled itself around Quince's left foot and came adrift from the rudder post, wrapping around a coral head. With the speed of a musket ball, Quince was swept from the deck into the sea. Cheatum, in his hostile mood, had not seen Quince disappear. But Jack and the men in the gig rowed quickly to where he had disappeared under the water. Jack dove in, bringing him to the surface.

Shaking the seawater from his eyes, Jack found Quince's right hand was a bloody mess.

Jack quickly transferred him to the *Stuyvesant* and wrapped him in blankets. Luckily the ship had cleared the inlet and the balance of the reef, drifting away from the island, for the time apparently out of danger. But that couldn't be said for Quince.

Hansumbob, Jack, Paul, and Quen-Li carried Quince below to a small berth, hard by the companionway ladder. They bundled him up with more blankets and gave him a tot of rum, which he promptly spit up.

"Leave me, lads, mind the ship," he whispered through clenched teeth. "Try to get her at least a half mile offshore, in case the wind backs around." Jack nodded without moving, staring at Quince's mangled forearm and hand.

"Look lively now, up you go. One of you relieve Cheatum from the jolly boat and send him to me."

Dawkins, mouth agape, left willingly. Quince's face was bathed in perspiration, his eyes wide and searching. He swore softly as Jack unwrapped the bloody bandage around his arm. The skin had been ripped from forearm to thumb and lay wrapped around the fingers like a piece of parchment. A small thread of blackened skin, stretched between the elbow and little finger, seemed to be the only thing holding Quince's arm together. The bone and muscle lay exposed, stark in their whiteness, the arm looking like a ripe fruit that had been peeled.

Jack motioned to Paul, and they moved out of earshot of Quince. "I have an awful feeling about the events of the past hour," Paul said. "It doesn't bode well for the start of this short journey down to the *Star*."

"I couldn't agree with you more," Jack said. "But we

have to keep alert so we'll make it. Why don't you go topside?"

Jack could hear Cheatum shouting for Quince on deck.

Mentor, working the port towing line, pointed down the companionway ladder. "He's in a berth below!"

Cheatum came rolling down the steep steps. "Bollocks! It's a helluva time for him to take to his kip if ya was to ask me."

Jack nodded for Paul to leave.

"Who in hell do you think you're orderin' about, you trumped-up captain? If I had—" Cheatum caught sight of Quince's crushed arm. "Holy mother of God. What have you done to yourself, Skip? Jesus."

"Never mind the blood and bones. Listen careful, now." Quince hiked himself up on his left elbow to look squarely at Cheatum's surprised face. "I want us to forget our differences for the time being and try and get this rig safely down to our bay."

Jack watched as the two old sea dogs spoke.

"Yes, of course . . . it's just that I can't take me eyes off that arm of yours. God, man. How did that happen?"

"When my foot got tangled in the line it pulled me overboard but not 'fore my arm got wedged between the bulwark and the chain plates. I became just another link in the line and somethin' had to give. It was my skin that lost the battle." Quince took a quick breath. "If you and your bosom friend Smithers had been watchin', this wouldn't have happened." Cheatum pursed his lips and dropped his head.

"As I said earlier, I'll deal with that later. For now, you are the most experienced seaman aboard and must get this ungainly barge safely to her berth next to the *Star*."

"I've never liked you," Cheatum said, shaking off his distracted manner. "I guess ya know that—and as you say we'll deal with our differences later. But beyond that, I want you to know I never believed in this stupid scheme from the start. Why in hell ya have ta listen to this snivelly faced lubber Jack O'Reilly, I'll not know. I've half a mind to thrash him as we speak."

Jack took a long breath and blew it out, relaxing against a bunk.

"You'll do nothing of the kind, you ass," retorted Quince. "The ship's in danger, can't ya recognize that? Whether we shoulda made this voyage or not is beside the point. We've committed now, and even a dunce like you must see that."

Cheatum seemed to contemplate striking him; he probably would have if not for Jack standing close. Quince gave him a withering glance. Common sense prevailed and Cheatum stood resolute, waiting.

"Think, man. The ship comes first." Quince was near to passing out.

"Right. What would you have me do?" Cheatum stood with his arms locked firmly behind his back, jaw set. He was not unlike a punished schoolboy, Jack thought, waiting for further instructions.

"Keep her pointed easterly as long as possible, giving yourself plenty of sea room off this northern shore." Breathing heavily, Quince dropped back down flat on the berth. "Don't try to cut too close to the cape at the end of the island. Once around the cape, you'll be able to see the islet and the mast of the *Star*. By any means possible, try to make land before nightfall. You'd be in extreme danger if you're caught between this mass of islets if night comes."

"We're making maybe a knot," Cheatum proclaimed. "How would you have me get this whale of a craft 'round this cape and then start beatin' into the souther-ly winds? We'll be goin' fantail to the north with no can-vas up."

"Use your seamanship, lad. Use every bit of knowl-edge you've squirreled away in that blockhead of yours. Think, man. I'm about done in. Think."

"I can't think of a way to move this vessel against the wind without sail. The jolly boat and the gig being rowed and towing this hulk won't do it. We need sail."

Quince again rose up on his left elbow. "When the explosion occurred, it took away the mizzen and the backstay for the main and the foremast. Don't bother to try and brace the main. Concentrate on securing the foremast, run several lines from the foremast just above the fore topsail yard, secure them aft on port and starboard on the chain plates. That should brace the foremast well enough for a working jib. Only use it to swing the bow 'round and in very light air when tacking. It should give you enough headway to maneuver. With the jolly boat and gig pullin', it should be enough."

Jack smiled. Even half unconscious, Quince was a better seaman than Cheatum fully awake.

Cheatum worried his lower lip. "Any first-year apprentice could have told me that. I thought ya had an idea."

"Whatever you do, don't use more than a small jib or you'll have the mast in the water. And splinters up your arse," Quince continued, ignoring Cheatum's attitude.

Jack saw Cheatum gawking at Quince's battered arm and thought the second mate wanted to poke at it with his dirty index finger. Instead, without a word, Cheatum walked slowly out of the ill-lit berthing area.

Jack went aloft, securing lines run up the ratlines by Paul and several sailors. The work on bracing the foremast proceeded slowly. Cheatum was used to giving orders and having men jump to, but with nine men running the small boats, there were few to do the heavy hauling of double and triple lines up the mast and cinching them to the chain plates with block and tackle, as he had commanded. By late afternoon they had a working jib up, and at least directionally they were able to guide the ship without the small boats having to do so much of the work.

It seemed apparent to Jack, though, that the crew would not make the islet this day. They were close enough to shore to set a kedge and secure the small boats. Once back on board the ship, the men, who had been rowing all day, collapsed on deck.

"There has to be a better way of moving this hulk," an exhausted voice rose from the group.

"There is," Cheatum said, staring up at the foremast. "Tomorrow I'll run out a staysail, and if need be, a reefed foresail."

"Will she hold?" Mentor asked. "Those lines ya ran today look pretty flimsy."

"She'll hold, and you just mind your own domain and leave runnin' of the ship to me."

"I don't know who put you in charge. But I for one will be glad to see Mr. Quince back on his feet."

"Listen to me, you poor excuse for a bosun." Cheatum took hold of Mentor and jerked him up quickly. "It don't matter none who put me in charge. I'll beat the living daylights out of any man who wants to argue with me. Quince, from the look of his arm, ain't gonna be back, so quit your bellyachin'." Cheatum dropped him and strolled to the port rail. Smithers joined him and they spoke together quietly.

Jack, sitting against the starboard rail, wondered how long it would be before there was serious trouble on the *Stuyvesant*. Without Quince, it seemed impossible to accomplish all the tasks that needed to be done on the *Star*. But Jack was determined to get the *Peter Stuyvesant* and the *Star* mated, and if he had to put Cheatum and Smithers in their place, so be it.

❄

Quince was in distress. Hansumbob had put himself in charge of trying to make him comfortable but there was very little that could be done. He carefully peeled

Quince's skin back over his arm, cleaning it as well as he could. One of the problems was that the arm was broken, the exposed bone fragments piercing the already battered flesh.

"Hansum, get Peters to sew me up so I'll start to healin'." Quince's lips were parched, his skin cold.

"There be plenty of time to sew ya up, Mr. Quince. The wound needs to clean itself. There be tar and who knows what else in that arm. Just you mind what Ole Bob has to say, there be time."

It had been nearly twenty hours since the accident, and Jack knew the first mate had been in excruciating pain since. He lay back, weak and disconsolate.

By mid-afternoon the following day, the *Stuyvesant* had made it three quarters of the way across the bay toward the small islet. But a contrary breeze picked up and the large ship made little headway. Smithers and Cheatum were at the bow, peering longingly at the islet shore, less than a half mile away. Jack and a few other restless souls stood nearby.

"Cheat, you're going to have to make a decision soon as to what to do; ya can't stay out here tonight," Smithers said. "Who in the hell knows where we'll drift to, with this little setup. We could be on the rocks by mornin'. And we can't anchor probably for another six hours, if then, as we won't be close enough in."

"All right, men, hear this," Cheatum said. "We're going to have to man the boats again. We're not making enough way. And should we be caught out here tonight if weather comes, we'll be lumbered."

The men grumbled but set to in the small boats. By midnight they arrived at the small islet and dropped anchor. Still, they were another half day from getting the ship safely around the southern side to the small protected bay where the *Star* lay fantail to the wind. With no real leadership, the men were tired and angry, taking to arguing and blaming each other for their plight. Little work was done, and Cheatum seemed torn between shouting and threatening. On occasion he would drift off by himself, or complain to Smithers.

Jack began helping Hansum with Quince, who passed in and out of delirium. Someone needed to be with him constantly.

"He be in a bad way," Hansum said. "Yessir. Real bad. Wouldn't surprise me if he was to pass on over. Yessir. Wouldn't surprise at all."

"He seems to be real hot with fever, Hansum. What can we do to stop it?"

"We can jus' keep bathin' him with cool water. That's about all. Yep, that's about it."

Jack went on deck and strolled; most of the sailors were on shore, stretched out in the shade of coconut palms. It was hot and no one seemed to be in the mood to deal with the complicated reclamation of the *Stuyvesant*.

At the other end of the ship, Cheatum and Smithers had just begun a meeting with several of the crew. Cheatum strode to the rail and shouted to the hands on shore, "Ahoy, you lubbers, get your lazy bottoms here on deck in the next ten minutes—we're havin' a meetin'. Shake a leg, do ya hear?"

"What's this about?" Paul said to Jack. "Are we finally going to get started on the work at hand?"

"I'm not sure. . . . Knowing Cheatum, I'd doubt this has to do with work."

"Do you think he called us here so we could see what a manly gait he has?"

Cheatum, overhearing, turned quickly toward Paul.

"I seem to be the most senior and the most experienced sailor here, so this is what I've come up with." His eyes flitted from man to man, alternately challenging and looking for support. "Several of the hands and I have decided we'll not be part of this harebrained scheme of trying to mate this hulk to the *Star*. It's too much work by half, and I have my doubts it could ever be completed." Cheatum paused. "A group of us will take the pinnace. We'll stock her with fresh water and provisions and take our chances on making it south with the trades to the Philippines, where we'll try to find passage back to the States."

The silence slowly thickened; most of the men were at a loss as to how to deal with the news. Jack had been worried that something like this would happen. The fact that it came from Cheatum was no surprise.

"Who will go?" came a weak voice.

"Haven't decided yet, but it definitely will be me, Smithers, and three others, as that's all the pinnace can hold. What with all the food and drink we'll need." Cheatum's gaze stopped on Jack and Paul. "But there are several that I know won't be goin'."

"You'll not be taking the pinnace, the jolly boat, or the gig anywhere until after we've all taken a vote on how we're to proceed in this matter," stated Jack. "There's also Quince to deal with. He's desperately ill. I'd think a sailor of your years would think twice about leaving a shipmate to die."

"Why you pip-squeak. I've half a mind to snap you in two." Cheatum's words began to agitate the men.

"Well, you got the part about having half a mind correct," Jack said, smiling. "We'll take a vote, and the majority will rule. And if you still want to try me after the vote, I'll not be hard to find." Jack faced the men squarely and spoke in an even voice. "All in favor of allowing Cheatum to take the pinnace and four men, raise your hand now." Only two agreed—Smithers and Cheatum. "It looks like you'll be staying here, second mate, with our happy little family."

Jack turned to the others. "Quince is in a bad way, men. Something needs to be done soon if he's to stand a chance." Jack winked as he moved past Cheatum and

Smithers, feeling their eyes on him as he went down the companionway ladder.

Paul sidled up next to Jack and gazed down at Quince. "You are one brave son of a bitch. What in the hell were you thinking, speaking to Cheatum like that?"

"He's a bloody coward—and besides, we had no choice. With the loss of five men, we could never save this ship."

Hansumbob had taken a filthy piece of sailcloth off Quince's arm and was bathing the wound with cool water, trying to get the swelling to go down.

"Jack, there seems to be bubbles a comin' up under the skin. I don't think the skin flap, what I pushed back over his arm, is goin' to take."

The tight quarters were alive with a stench—a brownish pus seeped out from under the skin where Hansum had laid it back against the tattered arm. Quince's eyes were closed, the fever eating at him.

"What's to be done, Jack?" Paul asked.

"I've never seen anything like this," Jack said with trepidation. "Maybe someone in the crew would know what to do. Let's ask."

Jack sprang up the stairs. The men were still standing about, discussing the recent vote. "I want every man to file past Quince and take a look at his arm. Then let's meet back here and see if any of you have any ideas."

The men quickly made their journey then met back on the quarterdeck. Jack waited for an answer. Most of them tried to ignore his presence.

"What is it? Come out with it. Who has an idea? What are we to do?"

The men sat and said nothing.

Quen-Li spoke. "Arm very bad. Must come off quick. Otherwise Quince die soon—tonight I think. Better one arm than no life."

Jack turned to the other men. Red Dog spoke up. "I've seen this before. The bubbles under the skin. The rot come from the wound, the stink . . . the arm's dead, that's what. He soon be dead, too. No doubt about it." The sailor spoke gruffly but with sympathy.

"Why don't we take a vote, Jackson?" Cheatum said. "That seems to be the order of the day. Since it's goin' to be a democratic society, let's all vote on how to save Quince. An aye to snip off the offendin' member, a nay to let him lay and rot." Cheatum heartily enjoyed his labored joke. Some of the men grinned slightly. But Jack, in the absence of any other idea, thought the recalcitrant seaman might have something at that. He had taken it upon himself to institute a vote on the Cheatum sail-away idea; now they would vote on a decision that might take a man's life.

As before, the majority ruled. "All right, we'll take his arm," Jack declared. "Who will do it?"

"You." The shout from Cheatum came bursting through his ugly mouth with a vengeance. "You, Dr. Jack. You lad, you're so confident in your ability to make decisions. You with all your worldly knowledge. You with your fine sense of what is proper. Just you."

Jack looked at the men. No help there. All were frightened at the prospect of one of their mates dying, but none wanted to touch the arm.

"Right. I'll begin at once. Who'll help?" Jack wondered why he expected more from these grown men. The fact that most of them wanted only to follow a leader puzzled him.

"I'll be there," Paul stepped forward.

"We must act quickly," Quen-Li added.

When the men returned to Quince, they found him unconscious, and their efforts to wake him failed. Jack feared he was already dead.

"Quen-Li, get Coop's saw," Jack said. "I'll need it to cut the bone. Paul, I'll need a sharp knife and some heavy string and needle from the sail locker. Also, try to muster up some rum. Hansum, get a long piece of iron and put some men to heating it over the forge—it needs to be red hot, and make it quick." The men all left to get the various items, leaving Jack alone with Quince. "I'm going to do the best I can for you, Skip. I've never done this nor has anyone else aboard ship. I'll do my best and pray."

Quince didn't answer. His breathing was shallow. When the men reassembled, Jack spoke. "I'll cut down through the muscle and leave a piece of skin to fold over the wound; then we'll sew it up. Sounds simple enough, doesn't it?"

No reply.

"Paul, you hold Quince's arm above the elbow. Hansum, get a tot of rum ready and hold his head. If he wakes, give him the rum, and for God's sake, hold him still. Quen-Li, hold his legs. I can't believe he's going to sleep through this. Ready?"

They all nodded. Jack took the sharp knife and made a quick incision completely around the arm, jogging out at a point on the upper forearm for the flap. Blood flowed from the shallow wound and Quince groaned. Jack never stopped but cut quickly through the muscle. While he worked, he heard Hansum softly singing what sounded like a hymn. He became unaware of it when the artery spurted fresh blood up his arm to his elbow. Undeterred, he grabbed the saw. Slipping a number of times in the blood, he cut through the hard bone in three short strokes, provoking a sudden cry from the patient. The offending arm fell heavily on the crimson floor. Quen-Li began to murmur something in his native tongue. Jack called for the needle and string.

The arteries were flowing freely, though not as wildly as Jack had expected. The blood vessels seemed to recoil into the pulsing muscles of the stump, as if the body had its own plan to slow the bleeding. Not really understanding why but knowing instinctively it must be done, Jack folded the arteries over and pinched them.

His hands almost invisible in the gore of the wound, he took three stitches in one artery to stop its bleeding. Another artery deep in the underside of the muscle was not as big as the first but also bleeding. Jack again pinched it off and sewed it neatly. He paused for a moment to think and then took the large piece of muscle on top of the forearm and laid it across the bone. Quince came fully awake, screaming. Through the labored shouts of pain, the young man spoke in his ear. "It's Jack. Your arm has become dead-like. It's full of pestilence. There's nothing for it but to take it off."

Quince's eyes popped open and for a moment he seemed lucid. "You'll not take my arm, lad. I'll have your heart! You'll not take it—please."

"Listen. We've taken it already. It's just a few stitches and it's over. I need for you to lie still and show your grit."

The first mate seemed to calm slightly, but it was all the men could do to hold him still on the berth.

Jack swabbed the area of the wound and asked for the cauterizing iron. Paul handed it to him. In one quick motion, Jack lay the iron on the raw end of the wound, effectively sealing the arm. Quince's screams made the hairs on Jack's arms rise. After the hot iron, Jack again brought the muscle over the bone, lay the flap across it and began sewing. He felt, rather than heard, Paul slump to the floor.

By this time the first mate lay fairly still, shaking slightly. Hansum had given Quince nearly half a liter of rum and it finally took effect. Jack felt barely able to breathe, but knew he had to complete his work. He finished sewing the skin, cut the remaining cord, and looked at the wound. It seemed neat enough. He took a swig from the bottle of rum and passed it around to Quen-Li and Hansum. As an afterthought, he washed the blood from the stitching with the rest of the rum, wrapping the arm in a sailor's undershirt that hung from the upper berth.

Jack dropped the knife, needle, and cord along with the saw. He scooped Paul up from the sticky floor and pulled him up the ladder, propping him against the port rail. A fresh breeze came off the shore, and Jack drew in the clean air. He raised his bloody hand and gazed at it. Surprisingly, it was steady. He wondered how he had accomplished the amputation. A sense of pride swelled in his chest which he quickly tried to squelch.

"Is it over?" Paul was very pale.

"It's either over, or just beginning. We'll soon see."

❈

The next morning the pinnace was gone—along with Cheatum, Smithers, and nearly two hundred pounds of foodstuffs from the galley of the *Stuyvesant*. Furious, the crew gathered on the foredeck.

"The cowardly bastards have taken half the fresh supplies." This from Dawkins as he paced back and forth.

"Well I for one say let's not worry about something that can't be changed. Let's use whatever skills we have to resurrect this craft," said Jack. "Everyone, what do you say?" The whispers from the men were positive. "I see the ayes have it. How shall we start?"

Coop spoke. "The *Star*'s quarterdeck, rails, an' helm need to be stripped off 'er an' stored. Whilst that work's being done, the *Stuyvesant*'s ribs need cleanin' up, waitin' to be mated."

No one spoke after that. There were many skilled fellows on board but no one seemed to want to be in charge. Reluctantly Jack said, "I have a considerable knowledge of metalwork. Especially with the forge." Still, no one spoke. Jack continued. "Coop, where will you be working—on the *Star* or the *Pete*?"

"I'll begin on the *Star*. I'll need two helpers." Again silence.

Jack looked around. "Quince will be down for a few

days, so unless there's an objection, I'll make up a duty roster. Will that be satisfactory with all?"

The crew seemed to perk up. They rose as one and looked to Jack expectantly.

"When Quince returns, I'm sure he'll have a grand plan for all of this, but until then, let's do what we can to get started."

The men set to, seeming pleased at the prospect of having a goal.

Jack went below to see Quince. "How are you feeling, Skipper?"

"Better. Much better." Still pale, but cool to the touch, he had just awakened. "I have what seems to be a giant drinking headache, which I suspect comes from too much rum." He struggled for a weak grin. "What's the news on deck?"

"Well, the men were reluctant to get started. Not unwilling—just without direction. I told them I'd make up a work detail and they seemed pleased at that."

"Yes, they would be. They need leadership. I'm surprised that Cheatum stood for any meddling on your part."

"He's gone."

"Gone? Wha'd ya mean?"

"Him and Smithers took the pinnace and half the foodstuffs and left. Probably at first light."

"That jackass. I'll have his hide, I will. I guess ya have to expect this kind of thing from a damn fool like Cheatum. I told the captain when he first came aboard he was trouble. Where do you think he's off to?"

"Yesterday he said he was going to the Philippines. We all voted him down, but he went anyway."

"If I ever see that fat toad again, I'll have my hands roun' his throat good and proper." Quince became too animated and tried to settle down. "I've irritated my hand again. I'll have to remember to let it heal. There's still considerable pain in my fingers."

Jack dared not speak.

"You have a funny look on your face, lad. What is it?"

"Your hand . . . don't you remember? We had to take it."

"What are you saying?" Quince rose and brought his right arm up to eye level. "Sweet Jesus Mother of God, what have you done, Jack?"

"We had no choice. You were steaming with fever. You had dead skin all about and there was pus running out of your arm like . . . we all felt it was the thing to do." Jack leaned heavily against the far bunk.

"Who did it?" Quince had a dark scowl on his face.

Jack couldn't meet Quince's eyes. "I did."

Quince lay his head back down and stared at the ceiling with a vacant expression. Then, after a few moments, he started to laugh. "You? You did it?" He laughed until he couldn't contain himself. "I'll bet you were scared outa yer wits, weren't you, lad?"

Jack looked at this giant of a man in this filthy bunk. How could Quince, who had just realized his arm was gone, lie there laughing?

"That was only the half of it—I felt I couldn't breathe. Paul fainted, Hansum was singing hymns, Quen-Li was chanting some chink gibberish. It was pure hell." Jack was laughing now, too.

Quince's face was red. "Help me out of this piss hole." He raised himself up on his left elbow and gazed through tears at his stumped right arm. Jack helped him to his feet and held him tight around the waist as the big man wheezed and staggered to the ladder.

"Damnation. I'll have to teach you about playin' with knives, lad. Or keep me eyes peeled sharp or you'll have my leg."

What a strange pair they must appear to be, Jack thought. The giant Quince bent in pain, Jack's right arm firmly around his waist, escorting him to the port rail.

"So it was left to you, Jackson?"

Jack nodded.

"It took guts, that I know—you'll make a good-un someday, lad. You surely will." Jack wondered whether he would have been able to do the operation if he hadn't so dearly wanted to get back to Cuba; or if indeed he had reacted as a man, confident in himself and what he could accomplish.

⊰❋⊱

The weather changed almost hourly during the next fortnight, from heavy winds to threatening clouds and rain and back to wind. But the men seemed to be right with the work, and struggled through the wet conditions.

High up in the rigging of the *Star*, Paul shouted to the men below that war canoes were coming hard and fast from the north. Jack took one of the long rifles and dropped down on the stripped quarterdeck. He could see four natives in each boat, with two bareheaded white men slumped in the forward canoe. Cheatum and Smithers.

The boats slipped into the calm lagoon, dropping the passengers off in waist-deep water. Without a word, the warriors turned and headed back to the island.

Cheatum and Smithers stood with the waves lapping at their backs. All hands on both ships turned toward the men with tropical sunburnt faces and clothes hanging in tatters.

"Give us food and water." Cheatum was the first to speak.

No response.

"For God sakes. Our craft was swamped ten days out, we bailed her, but the foodstuffs were ruined." He rocked back and forth, arms spread in supplication. "We had to turn around and we made it back to the big island but we couldn't survive in the bush so we asked the Belaurans to bring us here. They weren't too hospitable, I'll tell ya."

Still silence. The two men stood shaking in the gentle wash of the lagoon.

"Oh, for Christ's sake, can't ya see the joke to it? Right, well we took the pinnace and the foodstuffs and we broke the boat and ruined the food so what are you going to do about it?"

Nothing.

"You don't own this damn island! I say we deserve another chance!" Cheatum took a couple of tentative steps toward shore. Smithers lagged behind, unsure. "Let's take a vote. What say, Jack?" Cheatum asked. "Are you the big man now?"

"We took our vote already, remember?" Jack smiled.

"Oh, you're a hard one, you are. Give us a smile, a drink of water, a biscuit, and all's forgiven. What say?"

"I say this, you toad: if you and your friend want to stay on this island, you'll sleep in the trees away from the rest of us and do a full day's work, including standing watch like the rest of us—but you'll not get a ration of rum until we take a vote on whether you deserve it. And you'll apologize to every man who stands here before you. And you'll do it now."

Cheatum sputtered for a moment while Smithers spun around to look at the disappearing canoes. "You don't give a man much—"

"That doesn't sound like the beginning of an apology to me," Jack interrupted.

"What could be the consequence if I was to say we're going to start to walkin' to shore and get some of that water in the cask, have a bite of that fish cookin' on that spit, and say to hell with you? What would you say to that, Master Jack?" Cheatum's voice was strong, his defiance resolute.

"I'd say the first one to take a step toward shore will get a musket ball in the back of his head. And it really doesn't matter to me which one it is."

Jack brought the rifle up to his shoulder and pulled

the hammer back on the flintlock. The sound seemed like a thunderclap in the still lagoon. Jack knew they both did not doubt they were a short pace away from death.

Then the apologies came quickly, Cheatum practically begging forgiveness. Smithers was less animated, but forthcoming nevertheless. The two men dropped their heads and waded toward shore.

Quince observed the exchange from across the quarterdeck and winked at Jack. "You've not made any friends there, lad. I guess you know that sooner or later one or both of those blaggards will come for you."

"I'll welcome it."

—=✵=—

The work dragged on for months. Jack seemed to grow stronger both physically and mentally as the two ships slowly mated. The crew melded together well, each man's skills used to the fullest.

Coop took charge of the actual rebuilding of the *Stuyvesant*, dismantling board by board the quarterdeck, wheel housing, cabin under the quarterdeck, all the many frames and as many hold stanchions as could be salvaged. He stored these on shore or in the forward deck of the ship. The most difficult job had been dismantling the mizzenmast on the *Star* and restepping it into the hold of the Dutch ship. Cheatum adjusted the number of lines that ran from the chain wales up into the rigging. He was making an effort to fit in under Jack's jaundiced eye.

Quince spent much of his waking hours wandering about the *Stuyvesant*, coordinating the work on materials that needed attending. Jack worked alongside him, learning about command and the everyday chores of running a ship.

"You'll need to start thinking in terms of the rudder," Quince told him.

"The rudder? What do you mean?" Jack's head was buried in a ledger.

"We do need one—or hadn't you thought it necessary?"

"Well, yes, of course. But I just thought that when the rest of the work was done, Coop would build one from the timbers that were left."

"Not quite that easy, lad. It's a complicated task to fashion one that works well. Also, the hardware. The pintles snapped on the *Stuyvesant*'s rudder, and we'd be hard put to replace them here. We'll need to retrieve the rudder from the *Star*."

"But the *Star*'s rudder was torn off when we were swept into the lagoon," Jack said. "God knows how deep the water is where she lies."

"Nevertheless, we'll need that rudder. See to it, would you, lad?"

Here we go again, thought Jack. They would need to move the *Stuyvesant* out fifty yards closer to the entrance of the lagoon, to use it as a platform over the dive site, and then they'd need a lot of help. It would be a deep dive. Very deep.

Jack figured it would take one set of lines to set the hawser around the pintles, a set of heavy brass pins that fit through the holes in the gudgeon, a bronze fitting secured to the ship's sternpost, something like the hinge on a door. The rudder, controlled by the wheel, was the most critical moving part of a sailing ship—even minor variations in the angle of the water rushing by it could affect the direction of the vessel. Assuming he could get the heavy hawser attached to the rudder, they'd need all the men heaving on a capstan to pull it to the surface.

◄─❖─►

Jack, feeling strangely euphoric, studied Klett in the glow of the candle. The big man, breathing deeply in the confines of the bell, returned his stare, the flame reflecting dully from his eyes. They were both catching their breath after the long swim down. The descent was uneventful—an inverted wine cask rigged by the natives about halfway down allowed them to grab an extra breath or two, and they had no problems this time clearing their ears. In fact, the deeper they went, the less they had to deal with the ear pain.

Maybe it was because Klett was such an imposing figure, a bare chested Scandinavian Thor, that it struck Jack as funny when the man finally started to speak. Klett sounded as if he were quacking his words, like a duck. Jack was momentarily incapacitated, reduced to tears—he was risking his life almost twenty-five fathoms below the surface in the company of a man who quacked.

The minor voice changes they had observed in the bell at shallower depths were now greatly exaggerated. When Jack tried to comment on the matter, he found he could do little better. Klett, hearing Jack, first started to smile then took on a very solemn expression as if he were a schoolboy working on a difficult math problem. Jack felt himself immediately propelled into another round of hysterics. "Crissake, Klett, don't start trying to think, we'll be dead men for sure."

Enough. He had to gather his wits. Jack forced himself to stare at the side of the bell and slow his breathing. Okay, he thought. What we essentially are is drunk. He realized that the light-headedness they had experienced when working at shallower depths was present here without any exertion at all. And the swim down had worsened it, although his head was now clearing some. Physical activity at these depths greatly aggravated the problem they were having with giddiness; the air seemed to be richer—and sustained them longer—but also made them feel like they had chugged several cups of grog.

Jack felt a surge of confidence. This was remarkable, given where they were. Maybe too remarkable. Somewhere in the back of his mind a warning was sounding. This was a hell of a bad place to start getting cocky. Hey friend, you are one small mistake from eternity. Don't get careless. Luckily, the task they had to accomplish was simple; only the environment challenged them. Klett would leave the barrel and carry a light guideline from the bell to the rudder, which they knew was nearby. The rudder had disengaged at a place easily recognizable from surface features, and Matoo, one of the native divers, had seen it far below him only minutes after the surface divers had started looking for it. Once the guideline was in place, Jack was to take the bitter end of a heavier line that extended all the way to the surface, follow the guideline to the rudder, and tie the heavy line to one of the brass pintles with a "wrap and bowline," Quince had said. Simple enough.

Klett quacked that he was going. Jack watched the big man take a lungful of air and drop below to wrap the guideline to a piece of coral below the bottom of the bell. Then Klett resurfaced in the bell, took a series of deep breaths, and headed off to find the rudder and secure the guideline to something nearby. After what seemed to Jack a long time, he returned and squeaked in a nasal twang that he had found the rudder and all was ready. He said that he could stay longer here on one breath than ever before.

Okay, think! Jack fought down his giddiness and ran over the task in his head one last time. I grab the lifting line off where they hooked it on the outside of the barrel. They will give me plenty of slack from above once they feel it move. Then, I swim like hell with the rope to the rudder, following Klett's guideline, which will be tied to something nearby. Tie a bowline knot to the pintle and swim back down the guideline to the bell. Simple.

Jack took several deep breaths and headed out to tie the line that ran back up to the *Stuyvesant* and the lifting mechanism. He found the rudder immediately and made one wrap around the whole frame, then around the pintle, and began to tie a fast bowline. Bowline? Jack realized his brain was incapable of finishing the simple task. On board ship he had learned to do it without thinking. Now, in desperation, he felt himself reverting to the verse they had used in New England to teach schoolkids this most useful of knots. He twisted a loop in the line with his left hand and started to put the end through the loop, but was it under or over? Did the rabbit go down the hole ... around the tree? It occurred to Jack he was out of breath.

He swam back to the barrel and burst into the airspace gasping and laughing like a maniac. "Does the damn rabbit go down the hole and around the tree? Or, maybe around the tree and down the hole?"

Klett's incredulous expression once again paralyzed Jack with laughter. He was vaguely aware that they had been here for over twenty minutes and should return to the surface.

Saying nothing, Klett took an enormous breath, pulled himself under the rim of the bell, and left for what to Jack seemed hours. Jack's head cleared enough for him to begin to worry when the Scandinavian's head suddenly burst back into the air pocket. Klett gave him a very serious look and solemnly declared, "True da damn hole first, Jack."

Thank God, thought Jack; they needed to get out of there, and he was not sure he could make another long swim without disaster. Affectionately, he clapped the giant on the shoulder and pointed to the surface. Klett nodded and began taking breaths in unison with Jack. As usual, going up was easier than going down. They didn't even stop at the wine cask for more air. It wasn't just that the surface crew was pulling them with the up-line, as they called it; the air in their lungs seemed to last forever. It felt like they could exhale more air going up than they had inhaled inside the bell. The two arrived at the surface almost a half hour after beginning their descent. They expected no problems with rheumatism, since they had spent only a fraction of the time they usually had on the bottom.

They shared with Paul their account of the strange drunkenness they had experienced, then helped the others rig and haul the rudder from the depths. Two hours later Klett had severe pains in his right elbow and left knee, but Jack felt fine. There seemed to be more to this problem of plumbing the depths than they could ever fully understand.

After the dive, it was anticlimactic to place the rudder. It took many days of measuring and fitting to get it to link properly with the *Stuyvesant*, but once it was done, it operated quite well.

The pain in Klett's elbow and knee—and pronounced tingling in his lower arm and leg—finally lessened but never completely left. Neither Jack nor Paul could come up with a satisfactory explanation.

—≈✷≈—

Work finally finished on the *Stuyvesant*. The sails were patched, repaired, and strong enough to proceed. The galley had been completely refitted by Quen-Li; the rigging was either replaced from the stores or spliced and repaired. The decks had been scrubbed endlessly, and although they were charred in a few spots, seemed serviceable. After several trial runs into the open ocean and a few adjustments to the rigging and helm, Quince called the men to a meeting at the bow of the ship.

"It's been a long ordeal. You've all pulled your weight, and I, for one, appreciate the effort." Pausing, he looked over the crew. "I've been told one of you will be staying on the big island."

A nod from Dawkins. Jack could see Dawkins's mistress, the native girl Mele, standing on the beach waiting patiently.

"We'll drop you off in the Dutch Bay on the big island. There we'll pick up the three Belauran boys who have chosen to go with us." Quince looked around with a grin. "Although why they would do this, I'll never know."

Laughter erupted from the crew.

"I figger Manila is the closest place we can go to finish off repairs and restock for our voyage home. The boatyard will take the *Pete*'s general cargo and supplies in trade for labor—least as long as the port's open. Hard to guess who might be shootin' at who these days."

There were general nods all around; Manila would be the port of choice. Jack had his own ideas where it would go next; all he need do was convince the crew when the time came.

"We'll spend the next two days provisioning the ship with fresh water, fresh fish, the dried fish that Quen-Li's been preparing, coconuts, and as many vegetables as we can store. We have only the remnants of a chart to get us to the Philippines, but they'll do."

"Excuse me, Skipper." This from Paul. "I wonder if I might interject a piece of business?"

"Yes, of course, Paul, what is it?" Quince seemed to be feeling magnanimous.

"I was wondering about the name of this ship."

"It's the *Peter Stuyvesant*. What else?"

"What, indeed. I was wondering, since it's really two ships combined in one, I think it's only proper to rename her."

"Do you have a name in mind?"

"Yes, sir, indeed I do."

"I'm not surprised. Proceed."

"How about *Étoile Pierre*. You see, it's the combination of *Star* and *Peter*. I think that would work, right?"

Paul waited for approval but heard nothing but stark silence. He looked to Jack for help. His friend just shrugged his shoulders and grinned.

"I've got it—*L'Étoile du Pacifique*, well, it seems obvious—'star of the Pacific.' More silence followed. "Okay, how about *Étoile Brilliante*, 'shining star' . . . well . . ."

Snickering ensued, the crew obviously enjoying the performance.

Paul stopped to think, wishing he were somewhere else. Almost to himself, he mumbled, "*L'Étoile Chercher chez-nous*, 'it takes us home.' I wish I was there now."

Then he had it: "*Étoile Trouvée*." He paused for a moment, looking to the heavens. " 'The star that is found.' " He cupped his hands as if holding a small star. "You see, the *Perdido Star* is lost, consequently the new ship is the star that is found."

Hansumbob, sitting on the deck, unlit pipe hanging from the corner of his mouth. "What do it mean again?"

"As I explained, it means 'the star that is found.' "

"Well, Paul, it 'pears to me that's what we should call her. *Found Star*."

Thus it came to be. The vessel would officially bear the nameplate *Étoile Trouvée*, which would help confound any authorities suspicious of the doings of an American-named ship with *Star* in its name. The crew worried that their reputation preceded them. For all other purposes she was the *Found Star*, or as the men called her, the *Star*.

"One more piece of business." Quince seemed to be relishing this moment. "Another vote. A vote on whether Cheatum and Smithers finally deserve a tot of rum."

The spell was broken. The crew all laughed, slapping Cheatum and Smithers on the back. In high spirits, the men split into small groups to begin their final chores. Cheatum and Smithers both stole quick glances at Jack and hoisted themselves over the side. The looks were not lost on the young man.

BOOK THREE

22

EAST 121° SOUTH 8°

FOUR DAYS AWAY from the islet that had been their home for almost a year and a half, Jack saw the last of the island birds swoop toward the fantail of the ship, gathering the sparse scraps Quen-Li had thrown overboard. For the past week, knowing they were under way again, Jack's resolve in regard to de Silva had strengthened. At last there was a real chance that "compensation," as Quince had called it, might be in the offing. A current of excitement ran through his body as he climbed with Paul to the top of the mainmast to shorten sail. They could see for miles. Not a wisp of cloud obscured their view of a vast blue sea.

"A horse, a horse. My kingdom for a horse," Paul said.

Jack grinned. "What are you blabbering about?"

"Oh, nothing. I was simply wondering if I would ever see the meadows and woods of Virginia again."

"Not if certain members of this crew have anything to say about it."

"Yes. I've taken to sleeping with one eye open."

"Not a bad idea, my learned friend."

Jack looked down and found Cheatum glancing up into the rigging.

The second mate stopped in the waist of the ship and shouted to all within earshot but to no one in particular, "I own part of this scow, and I want privileges!"

The six or seven crew members who could hear ignored him; they continued working, not wanting to make eye contact.

"You hear me, you bunch of lubbers? I want respect!"

"Doesn't one have to earn respect?" whispered Paul. "Or am I just being old-fashioned?"

"The only respect Cheatum understands is a fist in the belly," said Jack.

Jack started down the ratline. By the time he and Paul were down, Quince had come on deck.

"What's this about respect?" Quince asked.

"I did more than my share on this tub, and considerin' my knowledge and the number of years I been to sea, I think I deserve it."

"You deserve no more or less than any other tar aboard this ship. And don't let me hear you talk of it again." Quince turned his back and walked to the rail on the port side.

Cheatum began an animated argument with Smithers and several of the crew members. Quince turned.

"Cheat—what the hell are you doing? It seems you're not content unless you're stirring something up."

"Not at all. I just want what's mine."

Quince adjusted his empty right sleeve and strolled methodically toward him. "And what do you think is yours?"

Cheatum puffed out his chest and spoke not only to Quince but to the rest of the crew. "I want twenty-five percent of this ship."

Jack leaned against the port rail, wondering what it would take to shut this lout's mouth.

"Aye," Cheatum continued, "I think it only fair. Quince, you and me be the most experienced dogs on board. I think we divide it in half and the rest goes to the crew. What say ye?"

"I say you're daft, man. Every man on board has broken his back to put this ship together, so put a stopper in it and lay on some work, sailor."

"Who put you in charge?" The two crusty salts glared at each other, Cheatum with a bully's grin on his face,

Quince with a sense of resignation. Seconds passed like minutes. The entire crew assembled on deck, waiting to see who would emerge victorious in this confrontation that had seemed inevitable since the *Star* piled up on the rocks.

"After Mr. Mancy died, I was the senior person," Quince said. "No one put me in charge. It was just the natural turn of events."

"Well, I don't see it that way. The way I see it, you was in charge as long as the *Star* was a goin' concern. But this ship is different."

"Different how?"

"It's a whole new ship. I say we start from scratch. We choose who we want as skipper. What say ye, lads?" Silence. "All those in favor of choosing a cap'n, raise your right arm." Cheatum smirked at Quince's empty sleeve.

The men were silent.

"Dammit to all. Speak up, you bunch of lubbers. You know you don't want this one-armed gimp as your leader. Speak up."

The men stood frozen, expressionless.

"I'll be in charge, at least until we get to Manila," Quince said evenly.

Jack knew the first mate was in a tough position with his right arm gone, and he itched to say something on his behalf, but he held back, thinking his words would do more harm than good.

"Which reminds me," Cheatum pressed. "Why was it decided to go to Manila in the first place? Who made that decision?"

Quince stared hard at the second mate. "Before my accident, you would never have spoken to me in this manner. . . ." His voice trailed off, and he shrugged. "All right, you son of a whore. Take out your blade. I'll do you with my left hand."

Cheatum's smile split his ugly face; Jack knew this was exactly what he wanted.

The men began clearing the way for the confrontation. They made a large circle, excited by the prospects of seeing a fight to the end. With weapons in hand, Quince and Cheatum began circling each other for several minutes, making ineffectual thrusts.

"I'll slice you fore and aft, you pumped-up pig," Cheatum grunted.

Jack knew he had to act if the ship was to survive. He stepped between them, combative, facing Cheatum.

"Cheat, you're well named. You are, indeed." Jack could hear Quince breathing hard behind him.

"Step away, Jack. I'll deal with you later." Cheatum frowned.

"No. The way I see it, you're taking unfair advantage. You've goaded a weakened man into a fight you know he can't win. I won't allow that to happen."

"Let it be, Jack," Quince said. "It's inevitable. I'll take him. Step aside."

"With all due respect, Mr. Quince," Jack continued, "once he dispatches you, I'll be next. Probably in my sleep, if I know the second mate—and I think I do."

With a grunt, Quince collapsed.

"You see, Cheat, your foe is down with nary a scratch on him. Wouldn't you feel proud to bury your cutter in his helpless hulk?"

With a guttural yell, Cheatum lunged at the younger man. Jack stepped aside with contempt and seized Cheatum's right wrist, twisting it into the air. The demonic look that the crew had seen before came into his eyes. The sharp blade dropped to the deck, where it stuck and quivered. Cheatum's scream of pain was stifled as Jack locked his left arm around his neck and forced the bigger man to his knees.

"I'll kill you with your own knife if you move an inch," he said.

Cheatum gasped assent and relaxed. Jack picked the knife out of the deck and tossed it overboard. His gaze stopped on Smithers, who seemed uncomfortable with Quen-Li, Hansumbob, and Paul surrounding him.

"I'm ashamed of all of you," Jack said, looking around for the first time. He walked in a wide circle, staring the sailors in the eye, standing in front of each until they dropped their gazes. There was a silence on the ship; what wind there was rocked the boat gently. "You're grown men delighting in someone else's scrap. I don't care how long you been to sea or how old you are or how tough you think you are."

Smithers stepped forward and addressed the group. "This young pip-squeak has the balls of a brass monkey, I'll say that for him. But listen here, all of ya. Quince can't lead and that's clear. We're a band of brigands, and we'll be branded such as soon as we touch shore. I say we head for the Sunda straits, sneak into Jakarta, then head for the Cape of Good Hope. What say ya all?"

Mild shouts of ayes and nays; there didn't seem to be a clear-cut margin one way or another. Regaining his strength, Quince stood, clutching his empty right sleeve.

"I may not be up to running this ship with an iron fist, so to speak," he said. There was laughter and Quince grinned at his unintended pun. "But listen up—we can't go directly through the straits. We need provisions. We got to think in the long term, not the short." This seemed to make sense to the disgruntled men. Jack marveled, once again, at Quince's sheer strength of will. He seemed to always be fair and firm, but uppermost in his mind was always the ship. "I propose the following: an equal split of the ship decided by the number of men here, excluding the Belauran boys, who understand they're on salary, what say you?" The men all agreed.

Jack contemplated this. "I'd like to say that I want my share of the ship divided up amongst all of you if after the stop in South Africa, we head for Cuba, where I have a plan to make you all rich. As some of you know, my parents were murdered in Cuba, and I'm sure their plantation has been confiscated. I intend to retrieve it, and I make all of you this promise—you will be wealthy indeed. You have my word."

"It's generous of ya. But we would 'ave gone with ya anyway, ya id'jut," Hansumbob said quietly.

Paul stepped forward. "To make my friend's offer even more attractive, I'll also forfeit my share of this vessel if we head toward Habana after Manila." He bowed grandly at the group, and with a sweep of his arm backed away from the band of sailors, stumbling on a hatch coaming and landing butt first in a pile of coiled line. Jack thought Paul brilliant at finding just the right bit of levity to punctuate a moment of importance.

It was agreed they would indeed stop briefly in Manila for refitting, finishing repairs, reprovisioning, and arranging cargo for the passage to South Africa. Then on to Cuba.

After the meeting, Jack found Paul at the rail, peering at the bottomless ocean. He touched his friend's arm.

"Thank you for the vote of confidence. I think that, coupled with your performance as a grandee-turned-joker, swayed the crew."

"It was nothing, O one without learning. I was simply extending a helping hand to those less fortunate than myself. I believe in the adage—"

"Save it, Le Maire; but thanks anyway."

"Incidentally, Cap'n, just what plan do you have to make all these men wealthy once we've reached Cuba?"

Jack looked to Paul with a certainty given only to youth. "I'm not sure. But I'll do right by these men. Or die trying."

23

MANILA

THE *FOUND STAR* encountered surprisingly little official folderol on its arrival in the port of Manila. Flying an American flag, neutral in the wars wracking Europe, and carrying an innocuous cargo of island trade goods, it attracted little notice. Manila was a racial potpourri and no one seemed to care about the presence of the islanders on the crew. The tattooed men simply returned the curious stares of the Spanish port officials, who eventually signed entry permits for the ship. The customs officers asked only that the several cannons be stowed in the bilge during its stay in port; they particularly wanted the bow chasers removed from open view on the deck. Several pieces of Dutch silver and some intricate wooden carvings from the islands speeded the process.

Jack went with Quince to help him find a prosthetic hook. Every few minutes the first mate would step out of a merchandise shop they'd find on the waterfront and show a new choice to the young man. Jack vetoed them all until Quince appeared with one of solid brass inlaid with ivory, as befitted a man of his stature. It was duly bought, and the two men went off to join their shipmates at the centers of libation.

The men of the *Star* absorbed the revelry about them as they wet their throats at the Boar's Inn. It was their homecoming to European drinking establishments, and they were surprised how much they had missed the aimless, recreational patter of their own world. The talk had been about the battle of Trafalgar, but when Jack and Paul ambled to the edge of the throng of listeners, they attended to a sailor's tale of shipwreck and piracy with great interest, for it seemed to involve islands of the West Pacific not far from where the *Star* had just sailed.

"Aye, the scuppers ran red with blood—I seen it with me own eyes. The Dutchman's head, eyes gouged out, hung from the mainsail lower yard. If ever there was a ship where the devil played a bloody tune, it was the poor *Mary Lee*." Jack had heard of the *Mary Lee*. It was a general cargo packet, under contract to a British missionary society, he believed, but never knew it flew a Dutch flag or had fallen prey to buccaneers.

"And the women were a sorry sight, enough to make a man cry. Tied over the cannon they were, naked, with their nether ends to the sky while the savages had their way with them until nightfall. Then they lit the ship on fire and you could hear their screams as the poor defiled lasses burnt to death."

Jack wondered who could do such a thing.

"I'm telling you lads, Blackbeard was a man of the cloth compared to these blackguards—eat the heads of their victims, too. If you're ever given the chance to kill yourself with a dull knife, take it—take it, I'm tellin' ya, before you let yourself fall into the hands of Black Jack O'Reilly."

Jack almost dropped his mug of ale. He stared open-mouthed at Paul.

Paul smiled. "Blimey, Jack, you never even shared those ladies with the rest of us."

"It's not funny . . . I mean . . . damn, the man's daft."

The bar suddenly quieted; Jack's last comment, louder than he intended, was overheard by the storyteller.

"Daft is it? You numb-butted upstart. I'll show you daft."

The man walked toward Jack, groping clumsily for a

dagger under his jacket. His comrades sized up Jack, Paul, and the table of swarthy men in the corner that had grown ominously quiet. "Easy there, Duncan," a sailor said. "There's no need for that. The lad meant nothing by it."

Jack regained his composure, "Sorry, mate, meant no insult to you—'twas the bloke you were talkin' about I was thinkin' must be daft. Totally daft, and a murderer at that."

Mollified, the storyteller let his comrades guide him back to a table with only a parting remark on the impudence of young sailors these days. Jack apologized again and bought the man and the house a round of drinks, the alcohol quickly dousing all flames of discontent.

Jack returned to his own table and shared the drunk's story with Quince and the others.

"Why in hell would he tell such lies? God's blood, there's enough horror in the world without having to create more. It's those damn survivors from the *Stuyvesant* that have been spreading that slander. Guess they made it back all right."

"Could be," said Paul. "But it might not be all bad to have the reputation of a devil when you're considering doing a raid on hell. And Cuba is the closest thing to hell we'll find in this world."

"Aye. Sometimes the fear of a pirate can accomplish more than the man in his flesh," said Quince. The others nodded but Jack was still disturbed at what his name had become. There was real fear in the eyes of the men who heard the sailor's story.

When the bar emptied somewhat, Jack asked the bartender, a man apparently of English extraction, if he knew any more of this O'Reilly character.

The man told him not to worry. "I hear he's actually in these parts and has cut some deal to get his ship overhauled. He pirated one from the Dutch but they're kinda' close-mouthed about it—they musta' been up to no good when he jumped 'em. That's why he's such a topic of conversation hereabouts—don't get famous pirates in the area too often. But you won't be seeing him around among civilized folk. Anyways, his days are numbered. There's one of his majesty's men-o'-war been alerted and will be cruising the harbor any day now. Yeah, the HMS *Respite*, that's what I think I heard someone say."

"Aye, thanks keeper, I feel safer now. I have a ship myself I'd like to have unloaded in the harbor. No telling what a man like that might do."

"Nah, mate, you're all right. O'Reilly would be crazy to stay in these parts for any time. He's got all the navies in the Pacific lookin' for 'im. Hell, the English is the most worried. They figure he might surface and get a letter of marque from the Americans."

"The Americans?"

The bartender stared at him.

"You have been away, lad. America and the Brits are working themselves up for another scrap."

"Old sod, a lot has transpired in our absence," remarked Paul.

He and Jack had rigged their hammocks topside near the helm, a quiet, breezy place when at anchor. As Jack didn't respond, Paul continued, "Seems like the world has kept on turning while we've been having our adventures. You'd think God would have been so distracted by our doings that he wouldn't have time for the carryings-on of mere nation-states."

"Yeah, I guess. . . ." Then, "Bollocks! I just don't believe it."

"Eh, sir?"

"Eat the heads! Can you believe it? Who could have thought up such rubbish?"

"Oh, fiddle-faddle, what's a few eaten heads amongst pirates?" Paul turned in his hammock and took a more serious tone. "It's the business about the English that interests me."

"That's no big surprise," Jack said. "The British never have gotten over our tussle some years back and have been doing all kinds of provocative things—and, well, the letter of marque, you know . . . they figure the Americans are going to license whatever citizens they can to raise hell with their commerce."

"Citizens, my arse, Jack. They're going to issue letters to the meanest sons of murder and mayhem out there, aargh! The Morgans, the Black Jack—"

There was a loud thump as Jack kicked Paul out of his hammock, onto the deck.

"See! See there, O'Reilly! What civilized person would have done a thing like that?"

"Go to sleep," Jack murmured as Paul crawled back into his netting. "Good night."

"Good night yourself." Pause. "Head-eater."

There was no response from the other hammock.

24

ORCHID

THE CREWS OF MOST ships tended to hang together when they were in strange ports, and this was especially true of the men of the *Star*. They had, after all, shared storms, shipwreck, survival, a life among savages, and a series of violent confrontations that had ended in their being branded pirates. What had been the half-whimsical creation of the Brotherhood of the Shipwrecked Men of the *Star* had taken on a surprising reality.

The Belaurans, dark and barbaric-looking to the European eye, had become blood brothers to this strange group of Americans, and even Cheatum and Smithers bristled at affronts to any of the shipmates, including Jack. They had considered killing Jack themselves, of course, but that was a family dispute, as even Jack knew, and they stood by him when dealing with threats from others.

The men had been enjoying the delights of Manila in groups of three to four, depending on their taste in rum, women, or both. Quince told Jack that he wanted to rein the crew back in so they could start concentrating on the future. Thus it happened that on the end of the first fortnight in Manila he made the entire crew gather for drinks at the Pink Orchid, an elegant inn Paul had selected which catered to wealthy foreign merchants and traders.

Even dressed in their finest clothes, the men of the

Star were clearly not ready for the class distinctions in a place like the Orchid. The establishment housed as much drink and prostitution as the waterfront bars, but its clientele was awash in self-importance and status.

The evening got off to an inauspicious start, for the presence of Quen-Li was immediately challenged. Luckily, the Belaurans had chosen to stay shipboard that night, or their welcome would have been even cooler.

Quince, dressed in his blue officer's cloak stolen from the *Stuyvesant*, was in an expansive mood. He placed his massive left arm in a friendly manner about the neck of the concierge, showed him the bright new hook on his right hand, and explained with utmost sincerity that Quen-Li was his twin brother and a British nobleman. If the proprietor cared to question the issue further, Quince would, he said, insert his shiny new hook into the man's rectum, pull out his intestines, and loop them around his cravat. He and his diminutive brother were able to read innards as some men read tea leaves. They would forecast the concierge's future without charge, since it would be a short one.

A glance at the crew of the *Star* as they mingled in the foyer convinced the man of the correctness of Quince's logic, and for the next two hours things went smoothly enough, though a few of the guests asked to have their tables moved, away from the Brotherhood.

Charlene was actually the source of the real trouble, Jack was to opine later. She was a woman of questionable grace but unquestionable mean-spiritedness, inhabiting one of the more active gaming tables. Klett, the *Star*'s good-natured but slow-witted giant, was immediately taken with her beauty and vivaciousness; she was immediately taken with the target the big man offered for ridicule and abuse. Her green and purple dress with raised bodice bordered on the obscene, as did many of her mannerisms. Her hair was pinned tightly with a gold band except for the loose curls she let bounce off her face in studied carelessness. She had some education and was quick to flaunt it to the delight of several male companions. All of Klett's awkward attempts at conversation were met with barbs that kept her associates laughing.

When Klett's mind wrapped around a clear, useful concept, he guarded it with uncommon loyalty; Jack had seen this many times. The world was a place that held its share of confusion and Klett resented people who said things to unsettle accepted principles. The big Scandinavian had a respect for the intellect of Paul Le Maire that bordered on awe. Although he would quarrel over minor issues with the young man—and though he was the occasional butt of Paul's irony—he took as gospel Paul's pronouncements of a scientific or metaphysical nature. Paul, in turn, had a warm spot for the big man and would come to his aid if he thought someone was victimizing his friend.

The critical point of contention came when one of Charlene's male friends referred to China as the Far East. An innocent enough assertion in most circumstances, but it confused and annoyed Klett. Paul had said on several occasions that they were heading west from the islands, toward China.

Klett turned to the dandy, "Sir, you must be mistaken. I am a sailor these many years and am quite certain China is west of here and should not be referred to as the Far East."

"Charlene," the man said. "Did you hear that? Can you believe this oaf?"

There followed several comments in which Charlene quoted lines from some of the better known works of Shakespeare. Paul caught the last few. Seeing Klett's increasing discomfort and noting for the first time that Jack was standing quietly in a corner throughout the exchange, he thought it time to defuse the disagreement. Jack's face was a barometer for storms best heeded; in the last few moments his easy smile had been replaced with that dark, intense look that too often preceded ominous events.

Paul brushed by several of Charlene's admirers, to a point from which he could place his arm about Klett's shoulder.

"Come hither, my friend, there are gay people in this room more deserving of your company. Fret not over the cruel croaks of these foppish frogs nor the sharp-tongued, dull-witted lass who shares their swamp. Her poor grasp of the bard is equaled only by the poor grasp of her girdle. I fear you may, in future, repeat some of her malapropisms and lose your reputation for repartee."

"Well I never!" gasped one of the powder-wigged prigs. "You ill-mannered young jackanape."

"Perhaps I am a jackanape, but I don't ridicule well-meaning strangers. You've had your fun and may continue entertaining yourselves at someone else's expense. It should not prove too taxing, since boors are usually easily amused by each other."

A large, heavily built man, who had been at the fringe of the group of revelers, stepped forward. "And what if I lay a fist in your impudent mouth?"

As if explaining to a child, Paul said, "What if, indeed? I suspect that a moment after you silenced my impudent mouth, Klett here would pound you into a pile of haughty British dog offal, speckled in red. Or worse, my friend in the corner would lose the battle he has been waging for the past fifteen minutes with his murderous disposition, and carve you and your wigged friend like a Christmas goose."

Both the massive man and the prig looked toward the corner, whereupon their expressions mellowed. Even Paul was somewhat surprised at the dramatic, dampening effect Jack had on the men's rising tempers. It struck him that he had never seen such a dangerous-looking character, and Jack was just nineteen. Indeed, his friend had changed. His sun-bronzed, powerful frame, now grown to a height of six feet two inches, could not be hidden by the delicate clothes. His stance was as relaxed and alert as a cat's and his eyes burned through a potential foe as if observing vermin teetering on the edge of mortality. The men turned and ambled off with a parting comment about "speaking to the management about the lower class of people being let into the establishment."

Few outside the immediate area of the gaming tables had noted the incident, and those who did went back to what they were doing. Paul led Klett to a table where men from the *Star* were heavily into their drinks, entertaining each other merrily. He shoved Klett down at the table and asked Hansum and Coop if they would kindly get him involved in a backgammon game. He, by Jove, wanted his friend to enjoy one of the few opportunities at civilized society without any further chance of mayhem. But when Paul sat at a smaller table with Quince and Mentor, he found he was going to have to deal with an angry Jack.

"Damn you, Le Maire, I'm not murderous," his friend hissed.

"Right, and if I say it again, you'll kill me." Quince and Mentor both chuckled, but Jack was miffed and unsmiling.

"Now look you."

Paul, for his part, was getting increasingly exasperated. He jabbed his fork in Jack's direction. "Old sod, it was just a figure of speech—but it's also based on true observations."

Quince and Mentor listened solemnly to what they figured would be one of Paul's soliloquies. "I love you like a brother, but you must admit, you've developed the habit of thrashing an uncomfortably large percentage of the people you meet."

Jack, agitated and unsure of what to say, looked at the two older sailors for assurance, but they just studied the wood grain in the top of the table.

Paul continued, "Granted, your temper has proved handy in our circumstances. And true, you show a strong sense of righteousness and judgment in how and when you fight. But damn it, Jack, you're carrying around a chip on your shoulder the size of a hatch cover. You come alive when you fight. Oh, you're more able to enjoy yourself than you were before our adventures in Belaur—hell, you're actually fun sometimes. But man, Cuba's buried inside of you like a hot ember."

Paul had obviously been working up to this for some time; there was no stopping him now. "You've got to purge this from your guts. You'd have skewered those two men in an eyeblink. Why? Because they ridiculed Klett and threatened me. With words! You really are becoming Black Jack O'Reilly. People have good reason to be afraid."

Jack stared blankly at the table as Paul spoke. His friend's words were strangely disturbing to him. Paul had overstated the case, but not by much. He wouldn't have skewered the men as nonchalantly as Paul indicated, but Paul was right about having to fight to maintain control. The people bullying Klett, making the fool of his friend, then threatening Paul when he stood up for him, was irrationally provocative to him. He was finding violence too satisfying a solution—it confused and frightened him.

"There's more to live for," Paul went on. "Quen-Li once said you kill but are no killer—I don't know if that's true anymore. There's a lighthearted, happy person in there that used to temper the fighter in you, that gave it balance. Whatever it takes, we have to finish what needs finishing in Habana because that coal is going to eat its way out some day."

Jack got up and started to leave.

Paul followed him. "See that Chamorran serving girl? She's been eyeing you all night. If you were healthy inside, you'd take more pleasure in making her tear the sheets off the bed than you would in running your sword through some buffoon's guts."

Jack bolted outside, but Paul pursued him.

"Look, man. These men are your brothers—they'll even take a chance on some crazy journey to help you set things right on the other side of the world—but you need to get right with yourself—" Paul stopped abruptly, realization dawning, and put his arm around his friend's shoulder.

"That's it, isn't it? Brothers—I mean—you turn into the angel of death when your new family, your shipmates, are threatened, don't you? Afraid you didn't do enough to defend your first family?"

Jack had bitten through his lip; blood was dripping down his chin, onto his white vest. The young man collapsed to a sitting position, his shoulders started shaking. Some people on their way into the Orchid became curious, but there were now two large, formidable looking sailors standing with their backs to Paul and Jack, puffing on their pipes, their demeanor suggesting the onlookers stare somewhere else.

Jack collected himself and started to walk back toward the *Star*.

Quince called, "There's compensation in this world, lad, and I think the time has come to get some of it. And you're not alone, lad, there's a bunch of us ready to pack our bags and head to hell with you, remember that. Even Black Jack O'Reilly, the devil himself, needs help in Habana."

As Paul followed Mentor and Quince back into the Orchid, his thoughts were still with Jack. Green wounds. For some reason the term "green wounds" kept popping into his head. Totally engrossed in his thoughts, he passed a group of men clustered about a table where someone was earnestly holding forth on some subject in low raspy tones. Paul froze in his steps—he recognized that voice.

"That was him I tell you, the one the natives call Dyak. That knave you almost got into a row with is Jack O'Reilly."

"Black Jack O'Reilly! He seems young. Are you sure?" The man nervously asking the question was the one who had threatened Paul.

"Of course I'm sure—I don't forget people who shoot me. If this was a civilized part of the world, I'd have that wretch arrested and hung." Heinrich De Vries looked much the worse for wear since Paul had last dealt with him aboard the *Stuyvesant*. He was just as pompous, but his reddened eyes and a twitch in his upper lip showed the strain of almost having his head blown off, losing a ship he shared responsibility for, and what must have been a grueling journey to some form of rescue in the islands.

De Vries continued, "That big rogue with him is their leader. I didn't recognize him with that hook he's now sporting for a hand." Paul had edged close to the others in the group surrounding De Vries and looked into his face; he felt himself shaking with anger as the feelings of fear and humiliation swept over him from what the Dutch had done to him. De Vries had shrugged his shoulders when Arloon had ordered his finger broken, as if he couldn't be bothered with such minor issues.

"So, Heinrich, who will it be?" The group parted as Paul loudly posed the question to De Vries.

De Vries's look of annoyance turned to astonishment tinged with alarm. "What? It's you! What did you say?"

"I said, who will it be? You know . . . friends, Romans, or countrymen? I mean somebody's just got to lend you an ear—you're looking awfully lopsided, old bean."

The group of men were dumbfounded, but Quince

and Mentor, finding where Paul had disappeared to, were happy to add to the conversation.

"Sweet Jesus," blurted Quince. "It's that ugly maggot of a Dutchman. Come on, Lord Le Maire, we'll have to leave this establishment. A place that caters to black-birders is beneath our standards." He grabbed Paul by the collar and yanked him back to the table occupied by the Brotherhood, leaving De Vries sputtering in his wake.

"Paul, I'm going to wring your neck someday. We don't need to advertise our presence any more than we already have." Then to the rest of the shipmates, "Our banty rooster here is gonna get us kicked out of the foreign sector, or arrested. I don't know what it'll take to get the authorities here provoked, so drink up and it's back to the ship." He glanced back in the direction of De Vries's table. It was vacated; the man must have left by the back door.

25

FIERY
DEPARTURE

LYING HALF ASLEEP on the bunk in Quince's cabin, Jack watched the first mate regard the stump of his right arm, then thrust the tip of his hook through a ring in the bottom of an oil lantern swinging from an overhead beam in his cabin. As the ship swayed, the prosthesis cast a bizarre shadow, a batlike creature circling the room . . . Jack imagined the creature lighting on Quince's head.

The *Found Star* had undergone a remarkable overhaul at the hands of the Philippine craftsmen. Jack had marveled at the skill and speed of the workers. Many of the repairs the Americans had painstakingly made in the islands were efficiently fortified by the artisans in less than a week. Soon the keel, keelsons, and major structural elements of the lower hull were declared sound after inspection. Most of the energy from the explosion of the powder magazine had vented upward—due, they were told, to the damping effect of the water. The reinforcement of the stern superstructure and midships area was completed in less than a month.

A sweet sailer to begin with, the reborn *Found Star* retained her sleek lines where wood met water. Now she was freshly careened, sheathed below the waterline with copper, and trimmed in mahogany. Along with a less pronounced fantail, the changes gave her a dark, trim profile to match her performance. With her new rigging, lignum vitae blocks, and dark hemp cordage, the ship was a thing of beauty.

In a strange way, though, she looked "too damned much like what she is," in Coop's words. She seemed some sort of marine predator, a perception the men didn't want to encourage in civilized ports. Through force of circumstance, the men of the *Star* had become sharks in a perilous sea; as a drunken Paul put it, they had chosen to "take up arms against a sea of troubles rather than bear the slings and arrows of outrageous fortune." To the great relief and cheers of the Brotherhood, he had passed out before getting much further.

Quince clumsily shuffled aside the papers he had been examining earlier in the evening. He told Jack he really could feel his fingers sometimes. It didn't seem fair a man should suffer the loss of a limb and still have to put up with aches and pains in his nonexistent extremities. He rummaged now though bills and receipts for services rendered and paid for. Jack promised to look them over, too.

The last of their spoils from the original Dutch owners had been spent on the repair, refitting, and reprovisioning of the *Star*. Smithers had chosen to take his share and melt into the bustling maritime world of Manila. He bore a gullet of ill will for his shipmates, and none were sorry to see him go, except perhaps Cheatum. What surprised Jack more than Smithers going was Cheatum staying.

The possibility of riches in Cuba was chancy, as all the men knew. A decision to stay with the *Star* was more an act of allegiance to their mates and the new way of life thrust upon them. The seafaring world of the Western Pacific was a place of high risk and uncertainty. News traveled slowly, and no one seemed to know who was fighting whom from month to month, what flag might be that of an enemy. Seamen were used like chattel; but the men of the *Star* had tasted something else. For better or worse, they were now all part owners of a ship, in theory more rich than they ever could have dreamed of becoming.

They had no legal status, but most of the successful merchant enterprises in the Pacific broke the law routinely. No one in Manila had challenged them for their act of piracy and, in fact, they sensed a measure of respect in their interactions with others once it was known they were men of the *Star*. Jack's name was spoken with awe, but it seemed to make other seamen wary rather than hostile.

Now that the ship was almost ready for sea and obviously carried no cargo, the officials were becoming a little more tense. Twice in the last week they had asked Quince about his departure plans. He mused to Jack that in the twilight of his career as an honest seaman he was suddenly a figure prudent businessmen feared, a principal in an enterprise that caused foreign patrol sloops to be warily alert and nearby merchant vessels to double their night watches. And in a port as tough as Manila.

Well, they would be leaving soon enough. They would give no warning of their departure, he reckoned, but he knew that any flag vessel, not just Dutch, would be watching closely and might interfere before they could clear the area for open ocean. A well-armed, fast barkentine shipping out in ballast was suspicious enough; East India Company packets sometimes sailed long distances without cargo. But the *Star* was no company ship, and she was reputed to be under the command of Black Jack O'Reilly. Quince said there would be no fanfare; Manila would just wake one moment and the *Star* would be gone.

Although they had reoccupied their ship since the overhaul, the Brotherhood voted to spend a last night on the town. Jack hadn't quite bounced back from his depression after the incident in the Orchid, and declined to join the festivities. Quince, Jack, and Hansumbob would stay aboard while the rest of the men went ashore in two longboats.

Earlier, Jack had walked to the port side while his shipmates were boisterously boarding a launch to starboard. A small boat carrying several Chinese gentlemen had quietly pulled alongside the *Star*. He had motioned for Quince to come watch.

The Chinese crew of the skiff was quiet, well dressed, and formal. An older man took to the ladder to come on board and embrace Quen-Li. Then, in turn, the four men who had been rowing stood in the boat and bowed to the *Star*'s mysterious cook. He returned the bows to each one, much like an admiral acknowledging the salutes of inferior officers.

It appeared that the closer to China they sailed, the more evident was the emperor's network. Jack guessed Quen-Li was checking in with his countrymen. He wondered if there were any new names on Quen-Li's list.

Quince turned to the men leaving for the night's revelry and yelled to Mentor, "Keep those grog-sloppin', whorin' ship's hounds to the lee of any trouble they can't handle."

"Aye, Skip," he answered back, already on his way down the rope ladder.

Jack, who had joined Quince at the rail, yelled after the men that perhaps they should gag Paul now—it would increase their chances of coming back alive. The men hooted and pounded Paul on the back while he made obscene gestures at Jack as they rowed into the night.

⇥❈⇤

Jack must have drifted off momentarily when a thump awakened him. Quince was still in his chair, moving his head to the swing of the shadow bat in his cabin, his eyelids drooping. For the second time Jack heard the thump to the starboard side of the ship and now what sounded like muffled imprecations. This time he could tell Quince heard it, too. Quen-Li, he figured, was in the galley, and Hansum up forward. So what the hell was it? Too early for the lads to return.

"Bob, that you?" Quince grabbed his swinging false limb and started to strap it in place, expecting a knock at the door from the ship's poet. Instead, the door flew open, crashing against the edge of the closet.

Two brutes in striped shirts stepped in, one addressing Quince in a thick, cockney accent. "Ya comin' peacefully, guvner?"

"What in blazes? You pressing me on my own damn ship? Are you daft? I'm a ship's master!"

They had not yet seen Jack, who'd rolled out of the bunk and under the table just as the door flew open. "Just doin' our jobs, guvner, now don' ye be givin' us a 'ard time and we'll go easy on ye." Outside Jack heard a commotion which must have involved Hansumbob.

"You limey, harbor scum, whoresons. You hurt one of my men and—" Quince spit the words from between gritted teeth.

But the two had Quince before he had his arm full on, so he could only manage an ineffectual left to the snout of the second man. He stopped resisting, but shook free so he could leave with dignity. The big men were brutal but not stupid; if they could get a man Quince's size topside without having to drag him, they were happy to lead him through the companionway unfettered. They were also used to responding to authority and were uneasy about manhandling what, to all appearances, was a ship's officer. As the last man turned to leave, Jack grabbed both of his feet and pulled for all he was worth. The man crashed to the floor, his fall softened by stumbling against the back of his partner on his way down. "What the hell?" his partner yelled.

The first man turned to Jack, trying to focus in the gloom under the table. By the time he could see, Jack's fist smashed into his eye. But Jack was frustrated that the man hadn't fallen to the floor harder. Summoning all his might, he dove out from under the table and hit the thug, who now had his hands over his injured eye, a short hammerlike punch to the jaw. He turned quickly to where the other man should have been but saw only Quince, who was in the process of yelling to his mate to watch his back. Too late—something thudded across Jack's head, and he was thrust immediately into unconsciousness.

When he recovered, Jack felt himself being dragged up the companionway and tossed in a heap next to the binnacle. He watched Hansumbob try his best to resist but the two thugs were too much for him. Not a violent or especially strong man by nature, it surprised Jack how hard Hansumbob punched the man holding the sap, a sock full of lead shot, which fell from the man's hand and through a scupper into the harbor. Having already felt the effect of the sap himself, Jack was relieved that it couldn't now be used on Bob. Helplessly, he watched Hansum being dragged toward the starboard rail, the powerful arm of one of the burly men wrapped around his neck.

"All right, Yank, ya going down the ladder under yer own will or you want te wake up with yer noggin busted?"

"I'm going," muttered Hansum, but he worried over Quince. "Say, fellas, ye don' need to be botherin' with the skipper. The poor skip's only got one—" The fist that hit him in the cheek came from another man Jack hadn't seen before; the blow seemed to surprise even the brute holding him.

"You fookin' simpleton, shut up."

Smithers's voice. These men seemed to be a press-gang, but to board a ship in a foreign harbor and to press a ship's captain was preposterous—it had to be Smithers's doing. Hansum's eyes bulged in righteous indignation.

"Smithers, you're a traitor and coward sure."

But Smithers was not to be distracted now. Quince was being escorted to the rail, his hook half on and his face dark and resigned. A twisted smile widened across Smithers's face when he saw Quince recognize him.

"Yeah, it's me, you one-winged gimp."

Quince said nothing but regarded him briefly, as one would a child who had deeply disappointed him.

Jack noticed something in his stunned, half-conscious state that made him unsure he was really awake: a cat-like figure perched in the shadows behind Smithers. The apparition was only a couple feet behind him, but no one seemed to notice as they tended Quince over the side, to the ladder.

"Let's get our bleedin' asses out of here," came a shout from the launch. "There's a damned boat headed this way from shore."

The gang leader sounded anxious, uncomfortable. They'd obviously never been asked to raid a ship like this before, and even if someone, Jack would wager a one-eared Dutchman, had paid them well, and a traitor from the crew agreed it was a stolen ship—well, he just didn't like it. "What's keeping you idiots up there?"

Hansumbob, dragged to the rail, blurted once more at Smithers, "Ye'll be sorry ye bald-headed bastard, when Jack and the boys get a holt a ye."

The intruders, except for Smithers and the man that held Hansum, were over the side with Quince. Smithers turned to Hansum, raising a heavy wood batten. " 'Fore I turn your lights out I'll let you know that they won't catch us, you buffoon, 'cause we ain't goin' for shore but for His Majesty's fourth rate," jutting his chin in the direction of the *Respite*, a British man-o'-war. The batten went higher, "Hold 'im where I can crack his thick skull."

Smithers broke off when he noted who was lying next to the binnacle. "Hey, you blessed morons, that's him, that's O'Reilly!"

But the cat—a kind of Chinese-looking cat, Jack thought, but hard to see, like in a dream—suddenly laid a paw from out of the dark over Smithers's shoulder and gently stroked up his chest, like a woman's caress.

Smithers stared down quizzically at his chest. He hardly had a chance to form an expression of surprise before the hand suddenly snapped up violently, like a striking snake, and his Adam's apple was crushed into the back of his throat. His head, grabbed by two hands, twisted until he was staring backward over his shoulder. Jack heard his neck break. There was the face of Quen-Li looking into his own. No expression. My God, thought Jack. He almost felt sorry for the remaining thug. He didn't stand a chance.

The man holding Hansum hadn't seen Quen-Li. He was trying to assure his leader over the side that he was coming fast as he could, but he turned at the sound of Smithers's neck cracking, and watched him fall to the deck, spasming. "Good God—" He caught a movement of what seemed like black cloth swishing behind him and he unconsciously released his grip on Hansum, at which point his captive kicked his heel up and slammed the man solidly in the groin. His groan was stifled by a hand clamped over his mouth from behind, followed by a deadly strike from a dagger to his side.

"Come, Bob," Quen-Li said to Hansum, motioning for him to help him lift the big man's body. Jack willed himself to stand. He couldn't be of any help, but he staggered over to the rail to see what was happening as Quen-Li and Bob edged the man over the side.

The leader in the boat, seeing his man's head appear

at the rail, yelled frantically, "Johnson, damn you, hurry!" He started up the ladder when Johnson came down on him as deadweight, taking them both into the harbor.

"Jesus," the leader spluttered, regaining the surface. The men in the boat quickly pulled him back aboard. "What the hell is the matter with Johnson?"

"Christ, boss, he's dead. Skewered like a pig."

Before the shock of that realization could fully hit home, another body crashed to the center of their launch from above. "What the hell—"

"It's that damn Smithers!"

The men in the launch panicked. They cast fearful glances at the gunwale of the *Star*, and pushed off with their oars, rowing wildly. The leader, regaining his wits, screamed at them to head for the *Respite*. "Those long-boats are picking up speed!"

The men from the *Star*, who had been lazily returning, had finally realized something was wrong and had galvanized into action. They had seen the strange boat and knew something was amiss.

The men in the press-boat with the *Star*'s leader in tow, pulled with everything they had for the British ship. The last Jack could see, they were casting glances down at Smithers, whose purple face and protruding eyes were staring up at them from his twisted form.

Even when they were out of sight, Quince's voice carried back over the still water. Jack heard him say, "You boys ever read the Bible?"

"What?"

"Yer about to inherit the wind. Why don't you save yourselves the grief. Do you really think Black Jack O'Reilly will let you keep breathing after you raided his ship?"

"Shut up, you old fool," screeched the leader.

"Aye, I'm a fool all right . . . for speaking to dead men."

Jack felt Quen-Li and Hansumbob lift him under the arms; they had heard, too. They walked Jack back to one of the pallets on deck and set him down. He was still woozy from the blow to the head, but his desperation at Quince's capture was bringing him around.

~=੩ ❊ ੪=~

Jack stood on the deck of the *Star* with a grim look on his face, listening quietly to Hansumbob and Quen-Li as they recounted Quince's kidnapping. The men were outraged. How could they possibly retrieve their shipmate and leader from the clutches of a British man-o'-war?

They directed their comments to Jack, looking to him for a solution. Not yet twenty years old, and the seasoned men of the *Star* treated him as their undisputed leader. Even Cheatum, strangely silent, perhaps because he had been so closely associated with the traitor, offered no challenge to Jack's authority. Mentor, closest in age to Quince, seemed the most shaken.

"Jack, what are we gonna do? We've got to get him back."

"And send that damn De Vries to his maker," added Jacob, "so's he can rot in hell right next to Smithers."

"First things first," Jack spoke calmly.

Coop, staring at the man-o'-war, remarked, "Even with most of her regulars on leave, her complement is five times our number. And there's no way of gettin' a raiding party anywhere's near that ship with them maintaining a naval watch."

Jack gazed at the warship, impregnable, bristling with guns. Wood flotsam floated against it, as it did all vessels in the harbor. He saw watchmen in several small picket boats, lanterns mounted on them, ensuring that no intruders could get near the vessel.

"I think I know a way to board her, but I don't know how to handle the crew. They outnumber us by too much." He watched another log join the rest of the garbage collected against the *Respite*'s hull with the outgoing tide. The ship was a formidable sight; the flotsam appeared like leaves and branches blown by the wind against a great citadel.

Paul said, "Well I don't know how you plan to get on board an English man-o'-war, but if you got to the captain fast enough, you might not have to fight the crew." The men waited in silence for Jack's response.

"Maybe that's the answer." The effect of the blow on Jack's head had almost completely worn off. As he stared at the imposing warship, a plan was forming.

"Yeah, but there's still the little matter of the British navy maybe not wanting us to come aboard and attack their captain," Jacob said.

"Then we shouldn't ask them," answered Jack. "While we've been standing here jabbering, plenty of man-sized objects have approached that ship without causing alarm."

Coop interjected, "That muck in the water?"

Paul, catching Jack's meaning, remarked, "If you're thinking of holding on to some of those logs and floating up to her, I don't think it'll work. They'd see your arms or head sticking out, particularly when you get near those light boats, and they'd lift you out by the neck with a rope—right on up to the yardarm—and leave you swinging."

"Aye," responded Mentor. "They'd see us sure, Jack."

"Wait," Jack continued, eyes afire. "Remember when we fooled around in the shallows in Belaur, with the kids? Remember those reeds they taught us to use, the ones we'd breathe through a foot underwater."

Some of the men reached for their tobacco pipes, rubbing their chins and necks, a mannerism they often adopted when on the way to being convinced of one of Jack's schemes.

"Coop, think you can auger some holes through a

couple of old spars after we find out how they lay in the water?" Jack asked.

Coop nodded.

"And Paul, can you find some of those bamboo shoots the workmen left in the hold?" Paul, knowing there was no stopping it now, headed below to get the reeds.

Soon there were two spars floating in the water, looking like any flotsam. The reeds were cut flush with the surface of the wood at the top and extended several inches below the bottom. Coop added a set of cabinet handles on the undersides, near each of the protruding reeds. A man could swim under the spar, hold on to the handles, and breathe through the bamboo tubes. They had selected reeds of sufficient diameter that enough air would reach the men's lungs without their having to breathe too hard.

Before departing with Quen-Li, Matoo, and Yanoo—the three others who would carry out the raid—Jack looked at the remaining men intently. "Make the *Star* ready for sail and get axes ready to cut her mooring lines. When we go I suspect we're not going to have time to windlass in the anchors."

"Bless ya, lads," Mentor said. "You get Quince back from those bastards and take care. We'll be there when you need us."

Paul, clearly agitated, hugged each man, Jack last. "I think this might be the most harebrained stunt you've talked us into yet," he said, his eyes full of dread.

─┄✳┄─

Breathing was easy enough—maintaining direction was the problem. They couldn't keep on course without popping their heads out of the water for a peek to correct for drift and lack of reference. Ironically, it was the lights on the protective perimeter boats that provided the necessary points of orientation. Jack finally turned all his attention to steering and Quen-Li provided the propulsion.

With a quickening of his pulse, Jack became aware of something else now visible in the dimly lit water: sea snakes, which seemed drawn to the light and began poking at his hands occupied with holding the bottom of the spar. He knew from his experience in the islands that the animals were too slow to be dangerous if you paid attention and pushed them away. But there were other things on his mind at this moment, and if one of the snakes was able to gnaw through his skin, it could deliver a dangerous, probably fatal, bite. Great, just great! His impulse was to hurry, but that might draw attention from the boats—also fatal.

They knew they would be noticed if they moved too fast, so once they were certain they were on course, they progressed slowly. Eventually they were past the light boats, and the HMS *Respite* was a large glow directly above them. Jack edged them toward the stern until he detected a new, orange light. He knew this was the color of the stained glass in the ship's aftercastle; seeing it meant they had passed below the fantail, where they could not be spied from the ship. When he banged his foot on the top of the *Respite*'s rudder, he stopped.

Raising his head, Jack scanned the water's surface and judged they were safe from detection. The men in the watch boats were half asleep and paid no attention to anything inside their perimeter. He inched along the log to tap Quen-Li on the head but the Chinaman had already surfaced. The two men were naked aside from the leather belts around their waist and shoulders to hold weapons, including a pistol tightly wrapped in oiled canvas. Their faces covered with lamp black, it occurred to Jack that they must appear fantastic creatures. A slight bump and a second log joined them. The two Belauran warriors emerged from under their camouflage. Fantastic, indeed.

As suspected, the ship's stern had built-in handholds above the waterline to facilitate maintaining the wood and servicing the rudder. Jack grabbed the first iron brace and hauled himself up the curved underside of the fantail. Jack had picked the Belaurans for their strength and agility. They knew enough English now to follow orders, but mainly they simply followed Dyak, so no words were needed. Their eyes burned with the fierce hunger of young warriors bound for glory in the execution of a daring deed. Jack knew the risk of death was a small consequence for men of their upbringing.

For once, their luck was good. Apparently, though Britannia ruled the ocean, the one attack her famed warships were not prepared for was from naked madmen crawling up her hull in a peaceful harbor. The watch was disciplined and alert, but confined to the main deck, crow's nest, and pickets. And they were watching for vessels, not swimmers.

The party found the ship easier to scale once they rounded the chine; in a matter of moments they were at the captain's walk, only one bored guard, standing at ease, in their path. Late though it was, Jack could hear voices and laughter coming from the captain's cabin. He motioned to one of the Belaurans and pointed to the guard. Seconds later the Englishman was sprawled in a corner, unconscious from a blow with a Belauran war club.

Things had gone so easily that Jack was unprepared to be in this position so soon. Thinking of nothing better to do, he politely knocked on the door of the captain's cabin.

There was a rustling and a murmured, "Who the hell would that be, Leftenant?"

"Couldn't imagine, sir, unless the watch wants to report something."

The door opened and an officer in a blue coat stood,

ooking questioningly into Jack's face, then down the
ength of his naked body, then at his companions. His
aw dropped open. He made a half effort to close it
again when Jack punched him full on the chin. The man
staggered back into the cabin and fell in a sitting posi-
:ion in a red-upholstered chair.

The captain, a man of considerable stature, stood
before Jack without fear. Jack pointed the flintlock pis-
:ol at the captain's chest. "Pardon me, sir, but we have
:ome to retrieve our skipper who was falsely imprison-
oned and brought aboard this ship against his will—an
llegal act, one, uh, well of, uh, piracy—yes, piracy, no
matter who does it—even a sovereign—"

"And who in the red, green, bloody blazes of hell are
you?" The man's composure was admirable given the
:ircumstance.

"I, sir, am Jack O'Reilly, warlord—uh, first mate—of
Étoile Trouvée—the *Found Star*—and have come for my
skipper."

"*Étoile Trouvée*? A French ship? But you're an
American, fully apparent from your poor command of the
tongue—even the French speak English better than you
colonials."

Jack was unnerved. Didn't the man realize he was a
finger pull from death? Then again, he realized, so were
they all. He saw the man whom he had struck recover
enough from the blow to rise to his feet and draw his
sword. One of the Belaurans stepped toward him, but
Quen-Li restrained the native by kicking his foot out,
and striking the flat of the blade, sending the sword clat-
tering to the floor.

Jack swung his gaze back to the captain and said with
resolve, his own temper flaring, "You may remember we
are no damn colonials to you anymore since we kicked
your damn limey asses out of our country. I demand you
arrange for our skipper to be . . . what in hell are you
smiling about?"

"Balls, bollards, huevos to the dons, I love it. You crazy bastards crawled your naked Yankee, Chinese, and black asses up onto a British fourth rate to retrieve your skipper, who I take it we've somehow mistakenly pressed."

"Well—yes—no mistake though—"

"Christ, Sebastian, do find this fellow, what's his name?"

"Quince, he—"

"Yes, Sebastian. Quince. Get this Quince up here." He waved the man toward the door.

"By George, what a tale," the captain said. "Wouldn't believe it if I hadn't seen it with my own eyes." Pounding the table, he relapsed into fits of laughter. "Look at ye! Dicks swinging in the tropical breeze, and where'd you get the savages and the chink?"

"These are my shipmates and associates," retorted Jack.

"Assoc—" The captain was disabled by his own laughter. Suddenly there was a commotion behind them and the companionway filled with armed men.

Jack held his pistol up. "Captain, you'll give us our skipper or even though we lose our own lives you'll never live to tell this funny tale."

At that, the officer drew himself up to his full height. "Son, you address me as Captain Nesmith, mind your manners, and you might get off this ship with your skipper, your associates, and your brass balls intact." He stuck his finger into the barrel of Jack's pistol. "Put that away, lad, before I stick it up your arse." It was time for Jack's mouth to hang open.

Nesmith turned to the crowd outside the cabin. "Sebastian, you back with that Quince fellow?"

"Yes, sir."

"Well, send him in here and get all those armed men off the deck. If I was depending on them for my life, I'd be a fond memory by now. Then come in here with my chiefs of staff."

Totally unprepared for the turn of events, Jack returned his pistol to his belt and moved to the side, motioning his men to do so, too.

There was now room for the British officers and Quince to enter. Jack felt a surge of relief on seeing Quince, angry but otherwise without a scratch. It took seeing the big man in fine fettle for Jack to fully realize how worried he had been.

The captain was smiling. "Mr. Quince, I understand that some fools operating under my authority pressed you unwillingly into His Majesty's Service right from your own boat."

"That's correct, sir."

"I was not aware of that and assure you the guilty will be apprised of my disapproval. I apologize—I believe this has something to do with that whiny Dutch merchant who shaved too close over one ear—aha! So you're the pirates he's so perturbed about."

Quince began to protest but Nesmith cut him short.

"Makes no nevermind; he's a scurrilous dog. However, these naked lunatics of yours did attack a Royal Navy vessel, entered the captain's cabin—" Here the man's battle with the absurdity of the situation started to succumb to laughter again. But he turned suddenly serious. "You will all leave here unharmed in the next hour if none of my men were killed or seriously injured."

Sebastian interrupted to say that a guard had been struck, but had regained consciousness, not seriously hurt.

Nesmith stretched, grinned, and winked at Jack. "You'll all be free to go; but I insist that first you tell me your story. Methinks we will never hear one like this again."

◄═ ✹ ═►

At noon the next day, the Christian Sabbath, the *Star* suddenly pulled anchor and sailed out of Manila harbor. Customs, port officials, and a number of merchants must have cheered in relief. Jack saw De Vries watching from the port side of the country ship *Bauxter*, along with the local leader of the auxiliary thugs who worked with the British press-gangs.

Fourteen hours later, at 2:30 A.M. Monday, the *Star* reentered Manila's outer harbor with no running lights, all lanterns doused, and a black flag flying from its main topgallant. It passed silently by the *Bauxter* and several other ships to the inner harbor.

At 4:30 A.M. the *Star*'s sails filled with the usual outgoing morning breeze. She passed the merchants of the inner harbor slowly, with reduced sail, and then came alongside the *Bauxter* with all sails reefed. "Yo, watch of the *Bauxter*," hailed Quince from the quarterdeck, Jack standing beside him.

"State your intentions," came the startled response.

"A message from the Brotherhood, for Heinrich De Vries." The *Bauxter* watch summoned his captain and De Vries. The latter came onto the deck rubbing sleep from this eyes and cursing the damn Spanish customs officials who had no doubt roused him.

"Says they have a message for you, sir."

De Vries cupped his hand over his good ear and turned it towards the ship, a mere fifty yards from him. His eyes shot to the mainmast and the black flag when simultaneously he heard the report of a Kentucky long rifle. He stared at his hand in disbelief. The middle finger was missing and a significant part of his left ear was intermeshed in his remaining fingers.

"Couldn't bear to leave a man in such a state," Quince called. "Smaller wig and hat size and they should fit evenly, though now you'll kind of look like a walking prick wearing a merkin. Bon voyage."

The *Star* emptied six guns of its broadside at the

waterline of the *Bauxter*, dropped all sails, and headed full tilt out of the harbor. At 6:30 A.M. the captain of the *Bauxter* ordered all hands to abandon ship. The *Bauxter* sank at 6:55 A.M. with no loss of life.

Jack would take to his grave the memory of their breakneck sortie from the Philippine harbor, every soul in the port wakened by the blast. Quince, on the quarterdeck, never looked happier or prouder. In deference to the HMS *Respite*, they lowered their black flag and raised the Stars and Stripes as they made their way past it. The British sailors crowded the rails, marveling at the cheeky Yanks that had bearded the Dutch merchants.

Quince ordered a salute fired for the British ship. It was returned from one of the thirty-six cannons on its port side. Hansumbob, in the crow's nest, swore later he could hear the sound of laughter; it seemed to be coming from the area of the *Respite*'s quarterdeck. Although the Americans might soon be going at it again with the English, they had been fairly treated by this captain and wished him well.

It would take many days at sea before the men all calmed down; the Brotherhood was definitely frisky. As Mentor said, "I reckon we're on a fool's errand, but damn if we ain't a magnificent bunch of fools."

26

CARIBBEAN BOUND

WHERE DOES THE time go at sea? Paul pondered, serving his shift on the starboard watch. The ocean spread in every direction. Huge, blue-gray rollers lifted the ship and surged it forward, assisting the wind in its work. Paul felt himself grow heavy as the deck rose under his feet, then light as the swell passed. The effect was hypnotic, memories of land and his family evoked by the endless sliding of wood over water.

A week at sea from their triumphant departure, the Brotherhood seemed content, welcoming the sense of security that came with returning to familiar routines. Away from ports and harbors, the sea was a place of refuge. In these far reaches of the Southern Pacific, a vessel might cruise for months without ever seeing another sail. No crowds, no press-gangs, no Dutchmen bearing blood grudges; just the pulse of wind and wave. Even the coming and going of the sun lost meaning in the seaman's world of four-hour watches. Night and day merged in motion.

Heading due south, looking for the trade winds that would carry them past Ceylon and on to the Cape of Good Hope, they were between lives, Manila already a dream in their wake and Cuba far ahead of them. The men did their chores and sank into their own private rhythm with the sea—much to absorb, much to antici-pate. The drills were their main distraction. Jack had the men practice endlessly with the rifles and cannon, occasionally even tracking back over their own seaway, blasting at jettisoned crates and other makeshift targets. They made a game of it but Paul knew Jack had serious intentions and wanted the small group's marksmanship highly honed.

He marveled at how Jack brought the men out. Perhaps all men have some of the warrior in them, and Jack made sure that over the weeks the group shared their martial skills. The Belaurans demonstrated the art of wrestling and wielding clubs. Quince and Mentor were a surprising source of knowledge on the use of cutlasses. Only Quen-Li kept his distance from the training. It was clear from his rare smiles that he approved of the drills; it was just that the Chinese cook was a man apart, one for whom, Paul knew, taking life was already a way of life.

Weeks rolled into months as the *Star* sliced its way south. A brief, uneventful stopover in Cape Town preceded the five-week haul to Cuba.

Paul expected Jack to be intense, agitated, morose, on this last leg of the trip. In fact, he was strangely calm, relaxed. He spoke of his childhood and his family's fateful decision to move, even the incidents in Cuba, but he was more reflective than passionate. Paul realized that with the mission under way, his friend was already feeling some release. Relief from the nagging need to take action.

Paul watched the crew of the *Star* complete the metamorphosis that began from the time they went aground in the South Seas; a "sea change into something rich and strange. There's a black star rising in the east," he mused.

—※—

Inside Jack there was a quiet turmoil. His surface nervousness and agitation had disappeared—there would be no more waiting, no more indecision, the prow of the *Star* sailing toward his destiny, whatever it might be. He was heading for the birthplace of his nightmares. That line that Paul often quoted from Shakespeare—something about the "taking up arms against a sea of troubles"—yes, that was it, "and by opposing, end them."

The face of his mother; sometimes he couldn't see it anymore. Her eyes, but not her face. But he always saw the face of de Silva. Asleep, he sometimes saw his mother's neck, pulsing blood, though not when he was awake. But de Silva, he could see his face, in the brightness of day. He could see Sergeant Matros's face, his father's hands—yes, he could see those. He could see that dagger, could feel his hatred, running cold and deep.

27

NINETY MILES
FROM CUBA

"WHAT THE HELL is this place?" Ole Bob barked at Paul.

"The Dry Tortugas. Discovered by Ponce de León in 1513. He called it Las Tortugas, the turtles, 'cause a lot of turtles used to hang out here and made good eating."

"Seems mighty wet to me."

"Well, he's not the one that called it 'dry.' That's a warning for mariners on the map that there's no fresh water here."

One anchor was set, and as the ship swung into the wind, another was about to be released by Mentor, standing next to the cathead on the port side, on Quince's signal. As standard precaution, he held an axe in his hand, to cut the retaining lines if the pin didn't work.

"There ain't nothin' here but sandy sand and more sand and a few acres of bushy sand with squawkin' birds," Hansumbob complained.

"But it's quiet water," Paul said. "Good anchorage where we can spend a couple nights, collect eggs from the birds, and approach Habana from the north. It's ninety miles that way, and it'll look to the Spaniards as if we're merchantmen coming in from the United States. Running in ballast from a few hundred miles away to pick up cargo makes sense, Bob. They'd be like flies on us if they knew we ran without cargo all the way from the damn Philippines. At least that's what Quince's and Jack's reckoning is."

"Well, Paulie, that's good enough for me, hee, hee."

Hansumbob made his way over to the cathead to help with the ground tackle, muttering, "Yeah, the plan's good enough for most of us, but Cheatum will probably have something to complain about."

As it turned out, even Cheatum was silent, as if he had come to some inner resolve that allowed him to bide his time. But Paul was watchful of him always.

There were eggers from Habana squatting on one of the keys; mainly poor folk from Cuba or the Floridas who lived there part of the year, when birds migrating from the mainland were plentiful. They had fresh water from a rain catchment they had rigged; for a not-too-inflated price they sold it to the *Star*, along with fresh eggs. They even sold some of their own store of fruits when they realized the sailors from the barkentine would pay handily for them.

On the third morning of their restover in the Tortugas, Coop, who had been on watch, shouted a warning from his perch. "Two sails, ship-rigged. Yeah it's a brig, and it looks military, headed for the harbor."

Quince had the *Star* prepared for action. He wasn't expecting this. This sprinkle of keys and shallows should rarely receive a visit from larger ships—they tended to avoid it. According to the Spanish, Florida was still a part of their dominion in the Americas, although the United States was claiming it was really an implicit part of the Louisiana Purchase—there was tension over the issue. Quince ordered the U.S. flag run up and all men to the battle stations, as they had rehearsed so well in recent months. Men stationed in the rigging could either shoot from a good vantage point or set sails, depending on whether Quince chose fight or flight.

The brig picked its way tortuously through the coral reefs, preparing to enter the lagoon. Quince knew there was only one safe direction for it to take, given the prevailing winds, so he simply held the *Star* at anchor, ready to chop lines if necessary. The *Star*'s crew watched silently as what they could see now was an American brig-of-war made its entry. The brig was well handled; she was definitely intending to come within hailing range. As it dropped anchor, the vessel swung sharply around so her port side was exposed to the *Star*.

Jack, standing beside Quince, could see the faces of the officers on the poop.

"I'll bet they're curious," Jack said. "Think about it; a ship with a French name flying the Stars and Stripes and rigged for battle."

A first mate with a horn and good hailing voice transmitted the orders of the skipper: "Sailors of vessel *Étoile Trouvée*: you are being detained for inspection by the United States brig-of-war *Adams*."

"Detained?!" Quince needed no bullhorn. "We ain't going anyplace, so how you going to detain us?!"

A moment's hesitation on the brig and the big voice of the man again rang out. "How about retracting those gun muzzles and lowering your gunport covers . . . real gentle-like."

"How 'bout kissing my round red arse . . . real tender-like."

There were several more moments of hesitation on the brig while the skipper reviewed his options. Jack imagined himself on the deck of the *Adams*—something he found himself doing more and more in confrontations—trying to see himself through his antagonist's eyes.

The *Star*, though slightly larger in overall length than the *Adams*, had a much smaller complement of men, but Jack knew it would bother the naval officers that the men on the dark sleek ship were so well deployed. Those not manning cannon were dispersed through the rigging and along the gunwale . . . each with a musket. Muskets, hell. On closer inspection it would occur to a seasoned soldier that those shoulder weapons were long rifles, Kentucky style.

"They're figgerin' they could probably win a scrap with us but it would be costly," Quince said to Jack. "And hell, the American navy is so damn small they ain't likely to be bothering their own citizens—they maybe figger we're a French buccaneer flying false colors."

Jack fervently hoped the brig would leave them be— the last thing they needed now was a fight with an American warship when he was so close to his goal.

Again, the voice boomed back from the brig, "If that's the way you want it, you'll soon be putting out fires and kicking your dead overboard. Be reasonable, mate, or you'll be tasting hot lead soon enough."

"Might be," Quince shouted, "but I didn't spend my youth fighting against the British to be harassed by some puffed-up uniforms in a ship from my own country. And you may address me as 'Captain' or nothing at all, young man."

There was a commotion on the *Adams* and a man stepped from the shadows. Hansum, who was watching through a spyglass, remarked excitedly, "Looks like some right important fella is taking over the talkin'."

Mentor, who knew naval uniforms, took the glass from Bob and gave a low whistle. "Mr. Quince, that there is a full captain in the American navy walking up to the rail. I think the lieutenant is going to defer to him—don't usually see a cap'n like that on a brig!"

The man they were referring to stepped to the rail and spoke in a voice that, unaided with the horn, carried well over the water.

"Look here, Captain. Before we go reducing each other to splinters over some prideful misunderstanding, it might pay to make sure we have ample reason."

"Aye, that's probably so," from Quince.

"If you come to us via ship's boat, I give you my word we will not harm you. And if it occurs that we must fight, we will let you return to your vessel and resume command before engagement."

It was now time for hesitation on the *Star*. Quince looked at Jack, who shrugged, then nodded affirmatively. Quince cupped his hands over his mouth. "That's on your word as a gentleman and officer in the United States Navy?"

"Indeed it is."

"We're coming over, one oarsman, my war—uh, executive officer and myself."

A boat was quickly lowered on the far side of the *Star*.

Quince and Jack disembarked in a manner that ensured they didn't obstruct their own ship's gun muzzles—a fact Jack was sure wasn't lost on the officers of the brig.

They know we're battle-hardened veterans of some sort or damn well-disciplined buccaneers, Jack thought. He smiled at Quince calling him an executive officer. They had been thinking like warriors and not merchants for too long—merchant ships did not have executive officers, to say nothing of warlords.

They reached the other ship. A ladder was extended and Quince and Jack were helped over the gunwale by sailors, who then stood back in deference to their officers.

"Captain," the distinguished-looking man spoke courteously to Quince, "allow me to introduce myself. I'm Captain Bowdoin and this is Lieutenant Feller, who is the commanding officer of this vessel. He has permitted me to conduct this parley in his stead. Sir, you should understand that we have a duty to ensure the safety of vessels of our new nation and the legitimacy of their actions on the high seas. Why return our lawful queries with belligerence?"

Quince, somewhat relieved by the officer's civil tone, responded with equal politesse. "Sir, we have been on a long journey where we suffered shipwreck and witnessed many horrific acts by lawful authority—some committed against us. We've come to respect authority only when we are sure it is not born of tyranny."

Good Lord, thought Jack. Quince had been paying more attention to the philosophical ravings of Paul than he had imagined. The American captain and the lieutenant seemed impressed with this response.

"Perhaps so, Captain. But still, we must ask if you're carrying proper ownership papers for this vessel. Your transom shows no sign of home port."

"That's because this ship is born of the sea. It is a combination of the *Perdido Star* out of Salem, which was wrecked with us aboard in the South Seas, and the hulk of a Dutch blackbirder."

"Most interesting. But do you have ownership papers from the Dutch master. It seems a most intact, and if I may say, elegantly appointed vessel."

"No papers, sir. The captain of the *Peter Stuyvesant* died from a sudden onset of lead poisoning. He was a blackguard from a nest of blackguards and serves the world much better as crab food."

The lieutenant stiffened at this allusion to what could only have been an act of piracy, but said nothing in the presence of his superior officer. Jack, silent with a dagger in his belt, stood a pace behind Quince with his hands clasped behind his back. He glanced about, taking in what he knew the lieutenant realized, somewhat nervously, was the armament and deployment of men on the *Adams*.

Captain Bowdoin suddenly turned his attention to Jack, as if something had just fallen in place in his memory. "You wouldn't happen to be Jack O'Reilly?"

Though surprised and taken off guard, Jack responded matter of factly, "Aye, sir, that would be me."

Bowdoin placed his hands on his hips. "Black Jack O'Reilly, scourge of the Western Pacific?"

Jack looked in the man's eyes unwaveringly. "Sir, I'm

probably the person behind that silly myth, but I'm far from a scourge, except to those who attack my shipmates."

Bowdoin turned to Quince. "No discourtesy intended to you, Captain, for continuing to address your, uh, executive officer. May I continue?"

"Of course."

"Granted, Mr. O'Reilly, there are many unfounded stories that come from those parts," Bowdoin said. "And granted, you may have had some reason to sink a Dutchman, and to travel all the way to the Straits of Florida from the Pacific in ballast." He pointed to the waterline of the *Star*, which definitely was too high for a ship carrying cargo. "But I wager you have no papers of ownership for this ship and are probably considered a pirate by several sovereign nations."

Jack's heart dropped. He was strangely sad that he would be seen as a criminal in his own land. He realized for the first time that, despite the family's problems in Hamden, he considered himself a loyal American.

"You're right about the papers but I can't say what other nations think, if anything at all."

Damn it, he thought, glancing at the Stars and Stripes fluttering from the mainmast. My father fought for that flag. It's where I grew up. It's my home.

"Well, I can tell you what they think. The Admiralty has received written complaints from the Dutch and British about your doings."

Jack and Quince stiffened. It appeared the conversation was in a downward spiral.

"Well, sir," answered Quince. "If you take the complaints of Dutch blackbirders more to heart than the interests of your own countrymen wronged in foreign lands, I'm afraid there might not be much more to talk about."

"Ah, but there is, Captain." Bowdoin looked both in the eye. "I happen to hate the goddamn Dutch and could not care less what you and Black Jack have been up to with them, though I expect it's just as you say." He began to pace. "I must tell you also that we're damn sick and tired of being bullied by the British and French and every other son of a sea cook who enters our waters—even the Spanish are giving us fits off and on."

Jack couldn't see where this was leading, but he felt a faint glimmer of hope; something a barkeep had told him in Manila had popped back into his head. Something about problems between the British and the Americans.

"What say you to a letter of safe passage signed by me?"

The surprise must have been evident in Jack's eyes; he could certainly see it in the faces of Quince and Lieutenant Feller.

"Our navy is pitifully small, gentlemen. We are months, or short years, from another conflict with the British and maybe the French. We cannot possibly face them ship to ship, but we can damn well use good patriotic seamen who will man privateers." He looked at them both again appraisingly. "I judge myself good at taking measure of a man, and it's clear to me that the both of you, pirates, saints, or whatever you might be, are men of your word."

"That we are, sir," stated Quince.

"Gentlemen, if you'll sign a statement swearing that you and your crew will accept a letter of marque or commission by the United States Navy if hostilities were to resume with our enemies, I will sign the aforementioned letter of safe passage."

Quince stared at the deck for almost a full minute. "Sir, we are men of humble roots; we have our loyalty to each other, but we despaired of having a home to return to." His voice almost breaking, he continued, "You have given us back our country. We have scores to settle, though not with anyone you are sworn to protect—then we will be at your service if you call us."

Jack felt Captain Bowdoin's eyes on him. The surrounding officers and sailors were frozen in silence, the only sound the creaking of the ship timbers in the gentle swells. He could not fathom why Quince's words had made him feel so moved, but something told him they had a similar effect on Bowdoin and even the ship's crew.

Jack held his hand out to Captain Bowdoin. The captain accepted it.

"I add my word to that of Mr. Quince. Should we be called upon by our country, there will be a fast ship with a crew that fights like hell preying on its enemies."

"I don't doubt it, Mr. O'Reilly." He heard Bowdoin instruct Lieutenant Feller, "Please see to the letter of passage, Lieutenant, and I will sign it."

A table was erected on the quarterdeck, and when the lieutenant had written a simple declaration of inspection and safe passage to any port in the New Republic, it was signed by Bowdoin and accepted by Quince.

As the sailors helped them over the rail, Jack felt a firm hand on his shoulder. He looked up to see Captain Bowdoin studying him. In a voice only Jack could hear, he earnestly whispered, "Son, do what you have to in that rat's nest, then leave whatever it is that consumes you—leave it go! Bring your friends home and live a life."

⊰ ❊ ⊱

Jack reflected back on the incident, still not believing. They were now scant miles off Cuba, carrying an official letter signed by a senior officer in the American navy which basically ensured that when they had finished their business in Habana, they actually had a country they could return to without fear of hanging. The stop in the Tortugas had been a tremendous stroke of fortune.

It was hard to think of good luck now, though, as the morning mist cleared and he found himself approaching Habana from almost the exact direction he had not so many years ago. The lighting on the hills, the smell in the air; he had come full circle in more ways than one. He stared in the direction of Matanzas Province and felt the deep stirring in his vitals, a sense of loss and fury. Perhaps Bowdoin was right: he must go home and live, but first some must die.

COMPENSATION

JACK STOOD COLD and wet, staring at Count de Silva's villa.

He had been unable to sleep and paced the ship's deck for hours. On impulse, he had slipped off his tunic and shoes, jammed a knife in his belt, and dove over the side, swimming the one hundred yards to shore.

The *Star* had been anchored for three days, waiting for the quarantine to lift. The men had been impatient. "What's the plan, Jack?" "What's it goin' to be, matey?"

At Quince's instigation, the council had met and confirmed Jack as the new skipper of the *Star*. Quince would remain first mate. If the sale of the finca or booty obtained from the raid on de Silva's villa was rich enough, Jack would pay off the others' shares and become the ship's owner and master.

So here he stood in the middle of the night, shivering half naked across from his enemy's house. Jack had many schemes, none clearly thought out. He realized that each time he started to devise an idea, his thoughts turned to rage and he was unable to think clearly. He had dreamed of approaching the count in a public place and confronting him with his crimes. Humiliating him in front of his peers and then killing him in a duel, or slipping quietly into his bedroom at night and slitting his throat. Or better yet, hanging him from the yardarm of the *Star* as it sailed slowly and majestically out of Habana harbor. He knew secretly, however, that none of these plans would come to pass. His unabated anger was leading him around by his nose, and he must take things slowly.

First, he must find out about his property; the deed to his mother's land would have to be sorted out. There was also the matter of Quen-Li's disappearance the first night they had anchored. Only when he had settled this matter would he deal with the count, for no one had seen the slim Chinaman leave the ship. He had simply disappeared. Jack cared a great deal for Quen-Li and it troubled him that twice when he swam to shore to look for the mysterious Oriental gentleman, he found no trace of him.

The swim to the wharf from the *Star* now seemed to him a little silly, but having seen the villa, the years of fantasizing about the count seemed to dissolve into a cold sense of the course he would take. He started back to the ship. "One step at a time, Jack boy," he mumbled. "One step at a time."

The quarantine was lifted the next morning, and after tying up, Jack swiftly made his way off the ship, arriving quickly at the main street of Habana. He asked locals where the American consul resided and was repaid with a wave of the hand toward Calle Juan Carlos.

When Jack entered the consul's outer office, he found a clerk, a self-important young man, who glanced up from his newspaper. "Yes, what is it?"

From his accent, Jack thought he came from the American South. The fellow dropped his eyes back to a month-old newspaper.

"I would like to speak to someone about property that belongs to me."

Without looking up, the young man said, "And just exactly what would you like to speak to them about?"

Jack raised his index finger to the top edge of the paper and slowly brought it down until he could see over it. "I'll explain that to him when I see him, won't

I?" There was something in Jack's voice that persuaded the young man not to delay any further.

"I'll see if the associate consul can see you. Have a seat."

After nearly half an hour, an effete, older man beckoned Jack to a small office which contained only a desk and one chair. Jack stood with hat in hand before the man. In no hurry to initiate conversation but finally wondering about office protocol, Jack introduced himself. "My name is Jackson Alexander O'Reilly. I have been—" Jack stopped, wondering how much to say. "Well, to put it bluntly, I've been traveling the past three years and haven't had time to consummate the transfer of my mother's property in Matanzas into my name. I—"

"Have you kept up the taxes on said property, Mr. Jackson?" The man's eyes and voice were expressionless.

"O'Reilly, sir. And no, I haven't. It was my understanding that until the deed had been properly transferred, that wouldn't be a problem."

"Well, O'Reilly, or whatever your name is, you're wrong. Your place most likely has been sold for taxes. In any case, you don't seem to be of the landed gentry, a latifundista, as they say here."

Jack glared at this puffed-up politico. "Excuse me, whatever your name happens to be. I'd like to speak to someone who can help me. You obviously aren't interested, and my time's just as valuable as yours."

"Oh, well I see." The man looked at Jack for the first time, sneering. "You should have told me you had limited time. It's the consulate general that you want. May I make an appointment for you, Mr. Jackson?" Jack gazed at the fool and nodded, not trusting himself to speak. "How would four o'clock this afternoon be, Mr. Jackson O'Reilly, sir?" Jack left the office after providing the details on the property, and walked out into the avenida. He took in the fresh air in deep gulps, trying to calm himself.

He wandered back to the ship. They had been in Habana three days and they had not been pleasant ones. What had happened to Quen-Li? The Chinaman's personal effects were still on board, yet no one had seen him. Cheatum was missing also, but he had taken his things—along with various items that were not his—and slipped off the ship in the middle of the night.

Jack made his way up the gangplank to speak to Quince. "Any sign of Quen-Li?"

The one-armed first mate shook his head. "Nary a sign. But Hansumbob said he saw Cheatum speaking to some of the crew on that large galleon tied tandem with that Spanish bark."

Jack looked across the small harbor to the ship. He could just make out the name—*Agresor*. "Well, if he's looking for a job, that ship is well named for him." They shared a laugh.

"Jack, if you're planning something along the lines of revenge, make sure we have a way out of this harbor. It's small and not very maneuverable."

Jack looked toward the open Caribbean Sea. "I have to go back to the American consul. I'll see you tonight."

"Any luck with the land?"

"Not yet."

Jack stepped off the gangplank. Quince's question about a plan got him thinking. As he walked toward the consulate, he found himself passing the count's hacienda. Was it fate that had brought him this way? He gazed at the house that seemed the source of all his misery. On impulse, he borrowed a pen and paper from a shop owner and scrawled a message to the count—one that he felt would not be ignored. He stuffed the note under the clapper and retraced his steps to the American consulate.

The consul himself sat behind a large desk in an elaborate office, American and Cuban flags bordering a painting of Thomas Jefferson. Jack sat before him.

"Your claim of ownership of this property at milepost twenty-seven in Matanzas Province seems completely unfounded," the consul said. "I am frankly baffled that you would come in here and demand—nay, threaten— my clerk and the associate consul with what seems a spurious claim."

Jack bit his lip, trying to maintain control. "I felt, sir, and maybe wrongfully, that I was being dodged, or that no one was interested in my problem."

"Your problem, young man, is that your respect for the proper way to proceed in these matters is complete- ly lacking." The consul shuffled some papers in front of him. "Now I'll leave you with the following. The prop- erty that you speak of, Hacienda de la Roja, or finca milepost twenty-seven, was bought for back taxes by one Alfonso de Silva on the fifth day of December 1805." The consul looked up with a smile. "So you see, young man, you are just about three years too late. And as for your behavior, you should be ashamed of your- self, conducting this business in a manner that would reflect badly on the worthy citizens of our country."

The small office seemed to close in on Jack. De Silva had the land. He felt a chill spread up his spine and he started to shake. His knees felt watery, and he wondered how much the consul could see.

"I've instructed my clerk to have a member of the guardia escort you back to your accommodations." The consul paused solemnly. "Let this be a lesson, Mr. O'Reilly." The official leaned back in his chair. "You're dismissed."

Jack was beyond rage. He glared at the politician and forced a smile. Rising slowly, he left the office, to be met in the outer office by three members of the guardia civil.

Once outside, Jack headed for the wharf, even though he realized he could not lead his escorts there. He avoided looking at them, determined to lose these fools long before they found out where he was going. The guardia seemed content to just walk behind him, chatting away. Jack was startled to hear one of the guards address another as Sargento Matros. He turned around, looking quickly at Matros. It had been three years and the man obviously did not recognize Jack. After all, thought Jack, the sergeant had been much more intent on murdering his mother and father than taking notice of a seventeen-year-old.

Jack turned right on Calle Juan Carlos, away from the ship. At a small inn he turned abruptly and darted up the stairs, standing in an alcove on the third floor. He watched through the open atrium as the guardia wandered around looking for him. Soon losing interest, they left.

Jack bounded down the stairs, following the soldiers. They stopped at a tavern filled with what seemed to be half of the guardia in Habana. He watched from across the avenida as Matros imitated Jack's flight up the stairs. The sergeant had changed little in three years. Jack had not forgotten his pig eyes and flowing mustache.

Now that he knew where Matros could be found each evening, Jack allowed himself to ease away, fighting the urge to bound across the avenida and plunge a dagger into the beating black heart of his enemy. Feeling light-headed, Jack steadied himself against a lamppost, looking to the world like just another drunk. He began the walk back to the *Star*, his soul filled with violence.

⊰ �֎ ⊱

The next morning Paul and Jack left the ship, their destination Matanzas. Jack had asked Paul to go with him; they would try to find where Jack's parents were buried. They jumped on the tailgate of an empty lumber wagon, blending back into the dark interior. The driver of the four-horse team saw them, however, and rubbed his thumb and forefinger together in the universal symbol of money. Jack smiled, tossed the driver a coin, and they drove on.

Before long, Jack and Paul stood on a small rise, staring out at miles and miles of stripped fields. They were at milepost 27. Nothing looked the same. The cane had been vibrant and full when Jack had last seen this spot; now it had been cut. Short stalks sprouted in rows, like grave sites. They found nothing that would indicate a massacre. Paul watched Jack pace the red earth. Eventually, with the realization that his parents were not there, Jack gazed at his friend, then started down the road back to Habana, Paul following.

After several miles they stopped for tea in the village of Soñar. As they were leaving, Paul spoke to the proprietor while Jack waited in the street. Then they once again started west, Paul guiding them up a winding trail a half mile above the village. There, covering an acre of ground, was a small cemetery. It took them only moments to find the modest marker with the inscription: "Two unknown souls resting in peace. Heaven help them. December 1805." Apparently the townspeople had taken this man and woman, when found, and buried them. Jack slipped to his knees in silent prayer.

After several minutes, he rose and looked around at the well-kept graves. His voice was thick.

"Let's go back. I have business in Habana."

—≅ ❈ ⊱—

Jack leaned against the stone building, watching the guardia celebrate the end of another working day. Matros and several other soldiers had arrived early and were heavily into their liquor. When Jack gauged them amply drunk, he crossed the street, entered the tavern, and ordered a glass of beer. He had never acquired a taste for it, but felt less conspicuous with the drink in front of him. A guitar's strident tone rang above the noise of the soldiers. A small fight had broken out between a uniformed civil guard and a woman with too much make-up and too little common sense. She cursed the soldiers, only to be rewarded with a clout to her left ear. She retreated, sobbing, into a back room. The atmosphere was rife with malice. Jack bided his time. He felt sooner or later Matros would recognize him.

Around midnight, as the soldiers were starting to drift back toward their barracks, Matros himself stopped next to Jack at the bar. He stared at the American bleary-eyed. "¿Cómo se llama usted?"

Jack was relieved; his patience had waned. His thoughts momentarily returned to his mother, face down in the road, eyes glazed, lips moving soundlessly. "No habla español, señor."

The sergeant got closer and breathed into his face.

Jack smiled at him. "Do you speak English?"

The sergeant seemed to understand the word "English." "¡Inglés, no! Español solamente."

Jack stepped away. "I'll have that hank of hair spouting from your face clutched in my fist before the night is out, you son of a whore," he said. Jack's smile was so broad it would have taken a cynical man indeed to discern the anger behind his words.

The sergeant did not seem to understand, nor, Jack felt, could he remember his face. Matros ordered another drink and signaled for the bartender to refill Jack's glass.

Jack didn't touch the gifted beer, but dropping his smile he looked straight ahead, watching the sergeant in the broad mirror behind the bar.

The man tried to get Jack's eye. "¿Su nombre, su nombre?"

"El hijo de Pilar."

Jack grabbed his ale and slowly let the amber liquid

spill onto the bar, never taking his eyes off the sergeant. He dropped the glass at the soldier's feet and walked toward the door. The sergeant stood dumbfounded. The tavern became deathly still. There wasn't a chance this insult could be ignored. There was a wonderful sense of well-being that surged through Jack as he walked slowly out of the tavern. It was almost like a dream.

"¡Cabrón!" the sergeant bellowed, rushing into the street. He caught up with Jack halfway down the block and spun him around with a hand as big as a breadfruit. Jack looked over his shoulder at the half dozen guardia who had followed. He deemed there were too many to fight, so he turned, knowing the sergeant would follow. The sergeant towered over Jack, pleading with him to show himself as a man and defend his honor. Jack continued walking, glancing behind him. Finally, there were only the two of them. The rest had started back.

Jack turned. "¿Me recuerda? Remember? You followed me from the American consulate the other day."

The sergeant tried to focus. "Your español good, cabrón." He exploded in Spanish: "Why do you insult me for doing my duty? You foreign son of a bitch."

"Was it also your duty to murder my mother, Sergeant Matros?" Jack asked in Spanish. The man blinked in disbelief, then, in recognition, uttered, "You should have been dead, like your whore mother. But no matter, you will be, soon." A dagger appeared in the sergeant's hand. He made a slow clumsy lunge but Jack stepped aside easily and drove his foot into the man's knee.

Matros went down but was still full of fight. Jack grabbed at the hand holding the blade. The sergeant was strong but no match for Jack's speed and determination. With both hands, Jack bent the sergeant's wrist back until it cracked. Matros's scream swept the night. He tried to roll away but Jack relentlessly pounded his fists into him. Breathless, the American sat atop him, grabbing his thick mustache with his left hand. Then he stretched Matros's head back, exposing his fat neck, and the dagger made a ripping sound as it sliced through the soft skin. Matros's pin eyes became as big as doubloons, the life pouring from his throat onto the cobblestone street.

⊰ ❈ ⊱

It took Jack only minutes to get back to the ship and to quickly recruit Paul and five others, all with weapons, to follow. Without a word they made their way up the deserted streets to Count de Silva's hacienda, where Jack ordered the door stove in. No one seemed to be home. They ransacked the villa, ripping down heavy drapes, breaking dishes and glassware. Two frightened servants huddled in a corner of the great hall. Jack yelled to them, "¡Vámanos!" and they scuttled out the broken front door. The men of the *Star* took heavy silver goblets, gold plates, and anything that seemed of value, tossing them into makeshift bags. Jack stopped at a small table near the front entrance. The note he had sent to the count earlier in the day was on the table. It had been opened and presumably read.

Jack stood at the front entry and screamed for his men to torch and burn everything to the ground. They began setting fires everywhere.

Paul stood watching. "I don't think we'll be invited back."

With a savage glint in his eye, Jack grabbed an andiron from the fireplace and drove it through the face of a beautiful grandfather clock.

"I think you've lost your sense of humor, Jackson," Paul said.

"Let's make our way back to the ship, lads," Jack called out. "We've got a fireworks display to start."

⊰ ❈ ⊱

The *Star* eased her bulk away from the quayside, the eerie silence markedly different from the usual roar of orders; on this night everyone knew his job. The only sound came from the creak of timbers, waking from their two-week rest, and the occasional snap of sails dropped by the crew aloft.

At the helm, Quince whispered to Jack that they were lucky to have a shore breeze. "It'll carry us midstream and we can begin to tack. I'll tell you, I have a real knot in my craw, shipping out without that little chink on board. I'll miss that Chinaman. What's the plan, Jackson?"

For a moment, Jack thought also of Quen-Li. He hated starting the action in earnest without knowing the cook's whereabouts, but he could delay no longer. "The plan is to provide Count de Silva enough light to be able to see his warehouses burn to the ground. I've promised him a fireworks display, and by the name of God, I'm going to live up to my word."

"What took place at the embassy?"

Jack spat out an oath and sprang to the rail, calling to Mentor, swinging gracefully in the mizzen, "Ahoy up there! Look alive! Secure that bloody sheet 'fore it wakes the bleedin' town!" Mentor scrambled for the loose line. Jack returned to Quince.

"The consulate was unsympathetic. You'd think I was a criminal by the way they treated me.... I've given up the idea of trying to recoup the fields. They've been sold for taxes." He paused and a wicked smile broke his face. "I intend to harvest a different sort of goods."

"Jack, you'll do your best work if you remain calm. A cool head begets warm results."

Jack looked at Quince and winked. "Are you good to man the helm?"

"Aye, aye, Skipper," Quince answered.

Jack leapt from the quarterdeck to the waist of the ship, whistling softly to the men aloft to come down.

"Load the port and starboard guns. Stay starboard-to for now. We'll fire one round on each pass for range, then finish with a full broadside. Incendiary rounds, Paul, wrap them with oil rags. Scamper topside with the eyepiece and give us the range after the first round. The rest of you listen up. Once we've salvoed, we'll start our tack and try to come about a full one hundred and eighty degrees. So we'll have to look lively. Now turn to, get those pieces loaded."

Jack returned to the quarterdeck and Quince.

"I hope the wind holds. We'll be in hell's path if we find ourselves in irons at the end of the bay."

"I'll lay off as much as I dare, to keep up our way. But she'll be close."

Paul and Jack had talked earlier about the targets, two warehouses and an open long shed overflowing with dry goods. The fire from de Silva's hacienda kept the buildings along the waterfront in stark relief.

From high in the crow's nest, Paul called out for the helmsman to come five points to their port. Quince responded with a deft spin of the wheel. Another call from Paul confirmed the target.

Jack cupped his hands to his mouth. "Where away, Paul?"

"Coming up on three hundred yards off our bow."

"What range when we're squared up?"

"Two hundred yards."

Jack looked at Hansumbob, bouncing from one foot to the next, waiting for orders. "Bob, what's your cannon set at?"

"Two hunnert yards. Just like the man said. Yes, just like the man said. He said 'two hunnert,' so that's what I set her at, sure did, yes sir. Just right smack on a hunnert an' a hunnert. Cranked her up there myself. She was already set on zero, Jack, so I took four full turns and it came up on two hunnert, is that what ye wanted?"

"That's it," Jack said with a grin.

It was Jack's plan to fire a round to get the range just before reaching parallel with the warehouses. It would give them just moments to readjust the rest of the cannon for their salvo. Jack sprinted back to the quarterdeck, staring intently into the night. He called back to Hansum in a low voice, "Stand by, Bob . . . ready now . . . steady . . . fire!"

Hansumbob placed the wick with the reddened coal on the touch hole at the end of the barrel. A slight flash balanced by a tremendous boom filled the Habana night as the shot tore across the water. Jack heard Paul shout from high in the masthead that they were short fifty yards.

Jack turned to Mentor and told him to crank up half a turn and fire, starting with the number one gun. The gunner lit off his cannon, followed immediately by the next four. Paul reported at least one direct hit on the warehouse to the west. It appeared to be on fire.

Jack sprang back down to the gun deck. "Reload! Reload! We've two minutes before we come about!"

The men were already hauling the heavy cannon out of their ports and swabbing the hot barrels. Jamming the powder package into the long cylinders, they rolled the heavy iron balls wrapped in oily rags into the barrels and tamped them with the blunt end of the swab. Hansumbob reloaded first, as he had fired first. "Fire at will!" Almost in unison the starboard guns sent another flaming salvo into the western warehouse.

Jack yelled to Hansum to have the gunners stand to on the port side. He heard them securing the pieces just fired and scurrying across the ship to the port guns as he ran back to Quince at the helm. "If we come about hard now, where will we end up?"

"We'd be better to wait a minute, Jack, so our guns will be perpendicular to the shore."

"Aye, give me the word." Jack watched the fire from the hacienda, too anxious to stay in one place. The smoke rolled skyward, blackening the early morning sky. There were people scurrying about in a vain attempt to squelch the building's flames. Jack's concern for Quen-Li distracted him even now. They must try to find him; their triumph would seem incomplete with him gone.

The port guns had been loaded and the crew had released the port sheets. They were holding the starboard lines, waiting for their orders, grinning as they watched the fires blaze freely in the warehouse to the west. Quince shouted, "Stand by to come about!" There was wild anticipation on board as the whole crew realized that if they weren't fast enough in this next operation, they would be caught dead in the water at the end of the bay, extremely vulnerable because of the light air.

Quince commanded the men to look lively. He spun the heavy wheel to his right. The *Star* seemed to shudder for a moment, then her bow swept across the view of the burning warehouses. The crew coordinated with Quince beautifully, bringing the ship back along the path they had just sailed, albeit fifty yards closer to shore.

"Good job, lad. You'll make a seaman yet!" Jack bellowed to Quince. The older man laughed.

"Mind your guns, nipper, and let me guide the ship."

Jack looked at Hansumbob. "How far inshore do you think we've come?"

"I figure forty to sixty yards closer, Jack. Yep, that's what I figure. I figure forty—"

"Right."

Paul shouted they were coming up on parallel, and Jack had his men crank down a half turn. Hansum fired his cannon, and Jack could see the shot explode in the center of the dry goods. The rest of the cannon followed suit, and the warehouses were all alight.

Jack turned to the first mate. "Mr. Quince, sir, I think it's time we found our way into open water."

"Aye, Skipper. Open water she is."

Quince turned the wheel 20 degrees to the north and made for the mouth of the harbor. Jack stood in the fantail, leaning against the rail, transfixed by the blazes. The warehouse fire had blocked his view of Count de Silva's hacienda. Jack wished he could have stayed and watched the count's home burn to the ground.

Quince turned the wheel over to Mentor, easing his bulk next to Jack.

"I should like a word with you."

Jack nodded.

"You handled yourself well this past several hours, but let me tell you, lad: don't indulge yourself in anger."

Jack said nothing.

"This last five minutes you've been standing here, talking to yourself, spewing venom at a city ablaze. You have a crew to tend to, guns to reload. Let's turn to."

Jack glanced back at the bay. "The burning wasn't enough. I thought it would be, but it's not. I want him desperately, Quince."

"All in good time, lad. If he has a way to retaliate, he will. If not, we'll lay off for a bit, then beat our way north for cooler climes."

Jack turned to help the crew reload as the ship carved her path through the lightening red sky.

⊰ ✳ ⊱

The *Star* hove to, riding the gentle swells of Habana's outer harbor, the sun just beginning to peek over the horizon. No active flames remained on the wharf as far as Jack could tell, but smoke hung as a thick cloud over the entire town. Most of the damage had been confined to de Silva's holdings, but merchants and town dignitaries mingled with the waterfront riffraff, obviously trying to make sense of it all. There had been no concerted attack on the town, just one ship on a rampage against certain properties—Jack knew that Spaniards understood blood grudges.

Crowds had gathered in the heights and on an unpopulated spit of land wide enough for traffic at low tide. Carriages were drawn up to the water's edge, their occupants staring at the sleek dark ship that had caused so much havoc.

Jack leaned on the rail of the quarterdeck with Quince, Mentor, and Paul. "They don't know what to think," Paul said. "They realize somebody in their midst just heard a whisper from hell, but they're not sure if maybe he didn't deserve it."

"Aye," from Quince. "The buggers don't know if we're the instrument of the Lord or the devil."

His comment was punctuated by report of a cannon from the castillo, then another. The fort would periodically let fly with shells from their longest distance ordnance, all falling far short of the *Star*.

"Guess they feel like they ought to be doing something," Jack said.

Some of the merchant vessels were pulling anchor and edging away from the *Star*, closer to the protection of the town's guns. They flew white flags to emphasize that they were neutral regarding whatever the hell mayhem had torn the night asunder. The presence of the merchantmen played well into the plans of the Brotherhood; Quince and Jack had judged correctly that the castillo would prove ineffective against a single rogue ship plying its way quickly through a harborful of merchant ships, particularly at night.

When they had passed within range of the castillo's cannon, they made sure to keep the lawful merchant vessels—laden with goods from Spain and valuable human cargo from Africa—between them and the fort. Not one of the few desultory shots taken at them so much as nicked their ship's wood or canvas.

Jack felt it dreamlike, that tense but silent exit from the inner harbor. The *Star* passed one ship after another, their officers and crews commanding their men to keep clear of their deck guns and show no hostile intentions as the dark ship with an even darker flag swept by.

"Quite a few of those ships could have outgunned us," Quince offered reflectively. "Only they had more to lose, to their way of thinking, and it wasn't their fight."

"It was more than that," said Paul, emerging from his self-absorption and casting a glance at the dark piece of cloth fluttering at the *Star*'s mainmast. "It never ceases to amaze me that once you identify yourself as a wolf, the sheep and cows back off, no matter how big they are."

"What? What are you blatherin' about, Paul?" Quince had that look of stolid forbearance he assumed when Le Maire was priming himself for one of his soliloquies.

"Just that, you know—I mean, here Jack goes, asking all the proper officials for justice, and they smirk at him. Now that we've defied their laws, burnt their butts, and spit in their collective eyes, hell, they treat us with a measure of respect. I mean, look at them. They're not so haughty now."

"Still surprises me they haven't come for us," said Quince. "I thought the dons was keeping at least two pickets around the harbor . . . seemed like a fifth rate and a brig. They'd play hell catching us but could sure outgun us if they did."

"Been wondering that myself," remarked Jack. "Maybe they figured enough blood has been spilt over that murdering de Silva. Long as they can keep their damn slaves and make their damn money to keep their women in fancies, these righteous businessmen could care less for his poor fortune."

The entire crew of the *Star* had left their posts and

were gathered at various points along the starboard rail, savoring the moment.

"Ya aren't having second thoughts about going back after de Silva, are ya, Jack?" Mentor spoke in his usual measured tones.

"No. We can't go back in there without ending up dancing from a gibbet. . . . We've burnt his home to the ground and destroyed his business—we'll have to let things settle down before we show our faces again."

"I believe we've done worse than kill him, tied as he is to everything he owns," added Paul.

"But I do worry for Quen-Li. That concerns me even more right now than not having de Silva's head in a bag. I thought we'd rouse him with all the havoc we caused. I'm really worried something's happened—I know he would have come back once the ruckus started—if he was able."

Others ayed to that, especially Hansumbob, particularly distraught that his "Chinee friend what had saved his life" was missing.

Paul took a deep breath. "I sure wish—" he started, when suddenly the bulwark on the port side of the *Star* seemed to explode into a thousand pieces.

"What in hell!"

The report of the cannon followed instantly, slightly behind the ball itself. Jack turned in time to see another puff of smoke from a ship bearing down on them from the east. With the sun at its back, the Spanish brig-of-war came out of the bright glare at full sail.

"All hands to quarters," Quince bellowed instantly. Then to Jack, "Caught us napping he did, right out o' the sun. That Spaniard's a clever one."

Jack grimaced. He couldn't remember the last time he had let down his guard but vowed it would be an even longer time before it happened again. Then his instincts took over.

Seeing they were at a distinct positional disadvantage—and outgunned—Jack yelled to Red Dog, "Hard to port! All sails to the wind!"

Quince gave him a quizzical look. "That'll take us right under her guns."

"That's what I'm counting on."

A second shot from the picket's bow chaser hissed harmlessly through a low piece of sail and on over the side, where it splashed and skipped in the bay several times before sinking.

The *Star*'s sails caught wind as soon as they unfurled, and the vessel was transformed from a floating hulk into a sleek sea wolf. Even caught off guard by a larger vessel, she had the lines of a predator, not a victim. And by God she would act like one.

"Head for the Spaniard!" Jack shouted. "Collision course!"

All eyes fixed on the fast-approaching brig. With a smile, Jack yelled to Quince, "Are you thinking I'm daft?"

"Aye, like a fox."

Jack knew Quince now understood that his daring move had taken the advantage from the attacking ship by putting both at equal risk. With one gut-level order, the young skipper had evened the odds.

With a sense of satisfaction, Jack watched the Spanish captain hesitate. The unexpected maneuver seemed to have totally thrown him. The brig heeled to starboard to avoid collision, which allowed it only an ineffectual broadside at the *Star* on the turn. Though the *Star* had no time to return fire, no projectile from the brig found its mark.

"They've dropped the wind from their sails," yelled Jack. "Lay it on, every strip of canvas."

"Great bollocks of the papist prince, 'at was friggin' beautiful!" Coop couldn't contain himself.

The *Star* fairly leapt through the water as the Spaniard was forced to come about and resume pursuit after losing all her momentum.

"Remember that cove to the west?" Jack said.

"Aye," Quince replied.

"Let's make for it. It's out of view of the harbor and we'll settle with the Spaniard on our own terms."

"She outguns us!" yelled Paul. "Even if we win, we'll suffer heavy losses. Why not make for open sea?"

"The cove. Make for it!" Jack turned Paul aside and said in a low voice, "I've no intention of engaging her. She has four times our complement and I don't fancy dying in a death grip with some poor bastards just doing their duty. But I don't fancy chasing around the ocean trying to get away from her, either." Then to Coop, "Get Jacob and the Belaurans and start making fast our biggest length of chain to any barrels you have big enough to float one end of it."

The brig entered the cove under reduced sail. The skipper had obviously developed a new respect for his adversary and was wary of approaching too close to a lee shore. Jack, placing himself in the man's head, knew the Spaniard wondered why the sleek raider had allowed itself to be cornered so easily. The *Star* was facing out of the cove from the windward side, but had reefed sail and to all appearances seemed to have dropped an anchor from the stern. Jack knew the men on the brig could, through a spyglass, see the heavy hawser trailing into water aft of the *Star* and trace it up to where it played through an aft fairlead and was secured to heavy mooring bitts. The drag of the line did serve somewhat as an anchor, with the *Star* stationary.

"I'd pay a king's ransom to see the look on that captain's face if he knew that anchor line we're trailin' runs all the way across the cove to them barrels his men are pointing to off his lee side," said Quince.

True, the pirate ship now had an angle on the wind that would allow it to clear the cove on one sharp tack, but it would have to pass within easy range of the brig's broadside, which was being cleared for action.

"He knows, he just bloody knows something's wrong," said Peters.

Jack had all the cannon on the port side prepared for firing but then pulled everyone except Mentor off the guns to handle lines and man the crow's nests with long rifles. Between them, Yanoo and Matoo carried two blankets soaked with seawater into the rigging. They draped it over the perches, set for marksmen in the nests. Between the lead sheathing patches and the wet blankets, the crow's nests had become impregnable perches for expert riflemen.

With Red Dog at the helm, two marksmen in the nests, and Mentor under cover with a match for the six loaded cannon, Jack devoted the rest of the crew to quick, efficient handling of lines and canvas under Quince's direction. He waited until the brig was two-thirds the way into the cove, past the barrels bobbing on her far side. Then he yelled "Now!"

The *Star* suddenly came alive. Reefed sails dropped, sheets tightened, the canvas bulged with air. The Spanish brig swung about and raised its starboard ports, ready to trade running broadsides out of the cove. Within two minutes the *Star* was within range, but it suddenly bore full to starboard as if it would break for sea without engaging. As it turned, and each cannon came to bear briefly on the enemy ship, the *Star* fired in succession. Mentor simply moved from one loaded piece to the next. A wide swath of scrap metal and nail flew at the brig with an elevation such that the metal careened about the weather deck and forced the men to seek cover. Simultaneously, the men in the *Star*'s rigging fired their rifles but aimed only at the poop, forcing the captain and the officers to drop to the deck.

Jack recognized the confusion the *Star* had caused aboard the brig, but none of the *Star*'s tactics would seriously damage the enemy vessel. As the captain gave the order for the first broadside, he must have rejoiced in the prospect of his ship-killing projectiles tearing into the fabric of the American pirate. But his joy was to be short-lived. Jack heard the captain stifle his order to reload. The brig lurched. Knowing he couldn't have possibly run aground, the captain would be questioning the helmsman. The man's panicked voice carried across the water, "Madre de Dios, Capitán—"

Jack heard the shriek and rattle of chains tearing across the brig's rudder bearings. Almost the entire length of line from the *Star* cleared the water as the hawser tightened and pulled the floating barrels into the far side of the brig's rudder like a cannon shot. Jack motioned to Hansum, who, standing ready with an axe, chopped through the taut line before it ripped open the stern of the *Star*.

As the Spanish ship swerved crazily to port, clearly out of control, a cheer went up from the crew of the *Star*. Klett and the others on the forward deck lowered their trousers and waved their bare derrieres at the officialdom of the Spanish colony, while Quince broke into a brass-arm-above-his-head jig.

"Take her north," yelled Jack, as they cleared the cove and gathered speed. He turned to examine the damage from the enemy's broadside, which had "torn up the furniture but done no real harm" in Mentor's view, when his sideways glance spotted the sail of a larger ship that had just beat its way out of Habana harbor. It was a large Spanish merchant that Quince surmised had been converted from a fifth rate, allowing it to carry a good array of guns while using the main gun deck for stowage of goods.

The ship was clearly not heading for them but seemed to be making for the Gulf Stream, the standard route for a return trip to Europe. The Stream would give it a boost on the northerly portion of its trip back to the Old World. Jack's first inclination was to pass it without incident, which would certainly suit the merchant. Home-bound for Spain, it would have "plenty to lose," in Quince's parlance. Most likely silver from the Potosí mint, porcelain, and silks that had made their way to Acapulco from the Manila trade, then over land to—

"Sweet Christ, Jacob, what the hell is that pennant she's flying?"

Jacob, looking through his glass from the crow's nest, yelled back down, "It's that same damned design we saw at de Silva's hacienda. . . . Blimey, Jack, that's the damn *Cubano Agresor*, de Silva's ship!"

No one needed orders from Jack. Red Dog locked the helm with the holding lines after setting an interception course for the ship. He had both hands free to inspect the two pistols in his jerkin, ensuring the powder was dry and the lucky chicken foot he had purchased in a strange dark shop in Habana was secure around his neck. Without question, the Brotherhood was in for another scrap.

The *Agresor* reduced sail and turned to meet the fast-approaching smaller three-master. Quince, who had been staring intently at the water separating the two vessels, turned to Jack. "Act like you're going to cross the T."

"What? I don't—"

"Just do it, Jack. Please."

Knowing Quince would never insist on something without good reason, Jack complied and began the classic naval maneuver of heading directly across the bow of the enemy, so he could fire his broadside in sequence at the ship, which would then only have bow chasers to bring to bear on the *Star*. In this situation, however, the move could be easily countered by the enemy turning to starboard and bringing about her own much larger broadside. Then Jack too caught sight of the streak of light green. "Lord, Quince, there's a reef there. . . . I had no idea."

"Neither does he, lad."

Though most eyes on the larger ship were distracted by the *Star*'s maneuver, the lookout on the *Agresor* must have spotted the danger. Jack could hear him screaming to his captain. Seconds later there was a scraping sound—audible even on the *Star*—and a crunch. The Spaniard was on the rocks and probably had her hull holed beneath the waterline. Yelling carried over the water—some of it seemed to be in English. The *Star* jibed and headed toward her stern quarter, avoiding the fixed position of most of the other ship's cannon, and let go with a broadside.

The larger ship returned fire from the ordnance she could still bring to bear, then suddenly stopped. Jack saw a white flag raised on her mainmast. "What in hell," he said aloud. "They must have more fight in them than that."

Then the full extent of damage from the collision with the reef became apparent. The *Agresor*'s port side fell slowly to her bulwarks. The men on the *Star* were transfixed by the sight; all firing had ceased as the result of Quince's tactical genius. Men were already climbing into lifeboats or jumping ship. Jack heard the captain of the *Agresor* order his officers to shoot the deserters, but they seemed reluctant to do so.

When it seemed the drama could be no greater, the great ship suddenly groaned again and began to turn port down into the waves.

"Jesus, she's sinking," muttered Red Dog. There was another screeching sound, and the men of the *Star* could hear the ballast shifting in the hull. Much of it crashed out of the lowered port side, along with wares and goods. The ship's cannon tore loose and plunged into the sea. Five minutes later the *Agresor* seemed to tilt bow down and settle on the long, sloping reef, her stern partially out of the water at a crazy angle.

The surface was eerily still. Full lifeboats were being rowed toward the Cuban shoreline—perhaps a dozen miles away—and several heads bobbed on flotsam in the water between the downed ship and the *Star*.

"Pick up the survivors!" yelled Jack.

As he turned to consult with Quince, he heard a commotion from the lifeboats.

"Hey, Jack, you won't believe what kinda human trash we found here."

Jack's heart went to his throat, praying it was de Silva. But as he ran to the port side, he could see it wasn't. The ugly blob of humanity dragged into the *Star*'s launch was Cheatum. Minutes later he was on deck, mumbling words of pure terror, then defiant curses.

Jack stood over him. "Men, cut off one of his fingers," he said, "every minute he doesn't tell us something we want to know about that ship. Then throw his balls to the sharks."

Cheatum turned white.

"No, wait, change that order, don't throw his sacks to the sharks. I forgot our friends Yanoo and Matoo love the nuts of their enemies for dessert."

"You—you wouldn't—"

Jack exploded. He kicked Cheatum full in the face and motioned to the Belauran natives to hold him down spread-eagled on the deck.

"You traitorous bastard, you think I'm playing games?"

Jack took a thick, sharp-bladed skinning knife from its sheath and drove it into the deck between Cheatum's legs, inches from his crotch. The man screamed although the blade hadn't touched him. Jack worked the blade free and pushed it edgewise—hard—into Cheatum's groin, beginning a sawing motion which soon parted the canvas trousers. Paul leaned back against the rail, almost as pale as Cheatum, and murmured in a low voice, "Jack, uh—" He went silent as he caught Quince's glare. The first mate told Paul to hurry over the side and help Hansum gather survivors in one of the launches.

With the first feel of the cold blade, Cheatum lost all defiance; he started whimpering and screaming and told everything he knew. Jack pulled the blade slowly upward, making a shallow incision. "Faster, you pig, I want to know everything." Cheatum gagged and choked and begged for forgiveness. Jack released the pressure slightly. "Your greatest gift from us will be a quick death after we carve you."

Doing anything he could think to appease Jack, Cheatum told of the count's riches on the ship, how he had taken the job as ship's master from the count, and how de Silva himself was down in the ladyhole. Jack's eyes went wide. Seeing a chance for some mercy, Cheatum quickly described how the count had been on the ship the whole time and gone down to check his dearest treasure box when the ship turned.

"And not only that, Jack—I beg ya don't cut me—the Chinaman, Quen-Li, he's down there, too."

This news shocked all of them. The men froze in place, listening hard.

"Could he have escaped?" Most of the men glanced unconsciously toward the lifeboats heading for shore.

"No—Jack—he couldn't. Don't kill me, please."

"He couldn't what?"

Cheatum was at the limit of terror; all were aware that he was defecating on the deck and ready to pass out.

Jack eased the blade away from Cheatum's groin. "Ten seconds, everything you know and you may live without having to join a choir."

"The Chinaman was chained in the hold aft. Just above the ladyhole where de Silva had his personal strongbox. When he found out who Quen-Li was, de Silva had him beat bad and was takin' him back to Spain as a prisoner for the crown."

"I'll bet you tried to save him, didn't you, Cheats? Any chance either one could still be alive?"

"No—no—I don't . . . I don't think so."

Knowing he had heard all that Cheatum knew, Jack let the man go. He turned, sheathing his knife. Cheatum curled into a fetal position, retching.

Jack riveted his gaze on the Spanish wreck with the others, praying for anything that would allow him to save Quen-Li's life. "Where the hell is the ladyhole?" he asked Quince. He was familiar with the term for a secluded area in the bowels of a ship, where women and valuables were sometimes hidden, but he had never seen one.

Quince was ahead of him, answering before he was through. "There!" He pointed to the part of the ship that hadn't slipped under yet. "Christ, Jack, the ladyhole's deep in the stern and the way it's upended, Quen-Li might not be drowned!"

Jack raced for the rail, but the boats had pulled away. Seeing Paul and Hansum as the only ones in hailing distance, he screamed for them to stop. He wanted to tell them to return for him but knew that might take a moment too long. The Spanish ship was balanced precariously in her present position and might slide down the reef face at any time.

"Paul, for God sakes! Quen-Li might be in yon stern section!"

Paul and Hansum quickly waved to Jack then turned and headed for the ship's stern. Jack was going to yell to them to send back the other launch for him, but Hansum and Paul were already rowing like madmen and couldn't hear him.

"Christ, Quince, I need a boat!" Jack shouted. "Paul and Hansum are going to risk their lives to find Quen, I know it—damn, they're gonna get caught in that hulk if it goes under."

"Yer right, the two of 'em's got more heart than common sense, and they love that Chinaman. . . . There, the billyboat under those tarps; let's get it over the side.

Brown! Red Dog! Matoo! C'mere and help us get this thing in the water."

Jack yelled back to the sailors as he dropped into the billyboat. "When you get enough men back here from the other launch, see if you can maneuver the *Star* and anchor where her stern will swing parallel to the wreck site."

As Jack and Quince and Matoo pulled for the *Agresor*, they could see and hear it move again. "Hurry, Matoo," Jack yelled. The Indian, though he could make a canoe paddle sing, had little experience with oars. As powerful as he was, he could not keep up with Jack's frenzied pace.

Their boat soon banged unceremoniously into the launch Bob and Paul had rowed over and tied to the ship's port rail. It was empty. Jack, beside himself, yelled down one of the aft companionways, "Paul, Bob, where in hell are you?"

Hansumbob's voice carried back from somewhere inside.

"We're in here, Jack. We've found the strongbox but can't find Quen-Li. Paulie's gonna try dropping through the next hole into the bilge."

Just then the *Agresor* shifted.

"Goddamn it, get the hell out of there, both of you. It's going down!"

Jack felt he was coming apart at the seams. He was about to lose three good friends including the young man who had almost become a part of him. Quince motioned Matoo to untie the other launch and their own from the *Agresor*; in case it went under, it wouldn't drag the boats down. There was only silence from below.

"Sweet Jesus." Jack jumped onto the ship and started to pull himself down the stairs, yelling, "Paul! Bob! Damn you both!" He made it down one deck below before he could see Bob trying to reach below him in rising water. "Bob!"

"Oh, Jackie, Paul's not back up the hole." Hansum was gasping and soaking wet. Jack realized he hadn't returned his call because he had been holding his head under to reach for Paul.

"God, no, no, no." The ship shifted again. Jack yelled for Hansum to grab his hand. Hansum tried twice and slipped, then without warning, the movement of the ship dramatically changed and Hansum was thrown on top of him, and both flew crazily back up the companionway. The ship was inverting. Suddenly Jack was choking on seawater, but he kept a firm hold on Bob, and within seconds they were washed out of the vessel and floating on the surface. The *Agresor* was gone.

Now both launches and the billyboat were drifting over a slick of flotsam from the ship. They crawled into the boats with Matoo's help. Jack, speechless, held his head in his hands. He couldn't believe it—if only he had ordered them back to get him. If only he had never said anything. Now it wasn't just Quen-Li, he had lost Paul. "God, it's my fault."

Hansumbob, equally shaken, sitting in the other launch a few feet away, just said, "No, Jackie, ye can't be blamin' yesself. God knows ye tried."

By this time there was very little distance between the *Agresor* and the *Star*. The crew had managed to anchor, and the stern was swinging from two bow hooks only a couple dozen yards from where the Spaniard had sunk.

How hollow his victory was, Jack thought. He had just drowned the man he had sailed half a world to kill, but he could only think of Paul, sacrificed in a futile effort to save Quen-Li. "Damn you, Paul. Damn you for a fool," he yelled at the surface of the water.

Quince looked sadly up to the rail of the *Star* and asked Coop, who, from his higher vantage point, could see through the surface glare better, "How far down is she? Any chance of recovering the bodies?"

"Don't know," Coop replied solemnly. "Her stern is broke off and still standing upended on the bottom. She's shifting like she's still got some buoyancy."

Jack stood and peered down into the green gloom. "What did you say? Buoyancy?"

"Yeah, Jack." Coop started to repeat his description of what he could see from the rail.

"For God sakes, man. Give me a length of iron bar!"

"What?"

"Bar, Coop, and be quick about it." Seconds later he caught the bar, lowered to him by a line from the deck of the *Star*, and leapt into the water.

"Toss me a line," he called back to his shocked associate, "then get Yanoo and Matoo in here each with a piece of pipe quick and have them go down and bang on the hull of the Spaniard, toward the stern."

"An air pocket!" Quince yelled to the others. "Jack's figured there must be an air pocket in the ship, or it would slide on down the reef."

Jack gulped in air and made for the hull. Reaching it, he started banging furiously, then listened until his bursting lungs forced him to the surface. On the way up he saw the Belaurans heading down to follow his orders. As long as he held onto the rope, his head out of the water, there was no sound. Curiously, if he dipped his ears even an inch below the surface, he could clearly hear the Belaurans banging on the hull.

He took longer, deeper breaths this time and started to descend. Again he could hear the Belaurans banging as soon as immersed. Suddenly his heart began racing. It wasn't the Belaurans. Out of the corner of his eye, he could see the natives' legs were kicking at the surface. The banging came from the wreck. He swam to where he thought the sound came from and began pounding like a madman. The returning sound seemed to emanate from all around him . . . he couldn't tell exactly where it was coming from but, by God, somebody was alive in there . . . it had to be Paul or Quen-Li. God, let it be them.

When Jack hit the surface and started gasping his discovery, the Brotherhood went into a frenzy of activity, talking, yelling, offering ideas.

"Let's make another bell," yelled Red Dog.

"I'm gonna dive for 'em," Klett said. "Let me in there, me or Jack could make it down that far; gimme an axe."

"Yeah, get some for the Belaurans, too," yelled Coop.

In an even voice, Quince ordered silence. "Okay, lads, I know you're excited but let's put our brains together, not our mouths."

Jack, still gasping in the water with the line in his hand, added, "We can't just chop our way through the hull. If we hit the air pocket, we'll let the air out and kill them sure. We have to approach by diving under. It looks to be about ten fathom to get beneath her."

"I kin make a bell again, real quick," Coop said.

"Not quick enough," Quince said.

"How about something already made," offered Mentor. "What's the biggest barrel you got, Coop?"

"That brandy cask, I guess." He pointed to a barrel that was roughly six feet in height and four and a half feet in diameter.

"That'll do!" yelled Jack, as his shipmates helped him onto the deck. "We've got to act fast. Get Yanoo to run a line down to the lip of the upside-down bulwark and secure it, then invert that cask and weight it until she slides down the rope and stops at the tie-off spot. I can make it one way to the barrel as long as there is air in it when I get there."

"I'll find some thin line to put in the barrel, to use as a guide." Klett chimed in.

"Right."

Within minutes Jack had regained some composure by lying on his back and taking deep, easy lungfuls of air while his shipmates frantically went about their preparations. He tried to relax and heard the cheer when Yanoo reached the surface and said the line was now secure to the ship. The crew got the weighted barrel in place, then there was sudden silence after they let it go. It wouldn't quite sink, and Jack heard Quince prevail in his opinion that they should just get the Belaurans and Klett to force it down for the first several feet if they could. When the air in the barrel began to compress from the weight of the seawater, it would start falling on its own. Quince was right; a cheer soon followed.

"Okay, Jack, we're ready. Think ya can do it, lad?" Quince's worry was reflected in the faces of the others around him.

"Got to," was all Jack could think to say. "Hell, through no choice of our own, we're probably the most knowledgeable people at diving in the whole damn Caribbean. We may as well use it to save our brothers."

He couldn't believe he was diving again. Things had happened so quickly in the last two days that they seemed unreal. Years of waiting and now, suddenly, he felt he had been given no time to prepare. Time meant nothing; he had no idea when he had slept last. He felt that his soul, following the calm of his long trip home, was now riding out the swells of a great storm, first dipping into the depths of loss and despair, then soaring with triumph and revenge, then back again. Now Paul, the person he felt closest to in the world, and Quen-Li, a part of his strange new family, might still be alive in the wooden tomb below.

Jack accepted the ballast rock Klett handed him to aid his descent. He took several deep breaths and dived beneath the surface, knowing from his experience in the Pacific not to rush. With one hand on the line, he slid down, letting the weight of the ballast stone do the work. He pushed any desire to breathe out of his mind, acting as if there was no limit to how long he could exist

on a single lungful of air. It came back to him at once—
that squeezing sensation in the air pockets in his head,
especially his ears.

He must keep clearing his ears before they hurt too
badly. He grabbed his nose and blew. Success—a popping noise followed by relief. Then again, and now easier, again. In what seemed less than half a minute he was
at the inverted wine cask.

Amazingly, he felt hardly out of breath. In one smooth
move he grabbed the rim of the cask and pulled himself
inside. As expected, it was less than half full of water, and
he greedily sucked at the pocket of life-giving ether from
the world above. Klett had tied the end of the coil of thin
guide line to an eyebolt, and all Jack needed to do was
grab the coil and head out on his search.

The upended ship was not as dark as Jack supposed it
would be. Light poured in from rents in the hull, but he
suffered from distorted vision. It was the question of the
same damn blurriness they had never been able to solve
in the South Seas. Still, he felt strong, and as he had
noted before, breaths taken from this depth seemed to
last longer. Now out of the barrel, he played the line
behind him and swam up toward where the air pocket
must be. At one point he banged into an inert form and
recoiled when he realized it was the dead body of one
of the Spanish sailors.

After ascending what felt like the right distance, Jack
found himself in what seemed a hopeless tangle of
wreckage. He felt an urge to release some of the precious air in his lungs—it had been dribbling out of his
mouth and nose on the way up—and he wondered if
that was because he had headed to shallower water
after gulping "thick air," as Paul called it, from the barrel. He secured the line to a timber and retraced his way
to the makeshift bell. There would be no luxury this
time for making mistakes or experimenting; he had to
find the survivors fast.

Refilling his lungs, Jack reviewed what he had seen at the highest point in the hull. The dark area to the right was probably the best bet for an air pocket. If there was a cavity that held air, it would have no holes letting in light. He would try that.

As he made ready to depart again, Yanoo and Matoo arrived at the barrel. At considerable risk to themselves, they had already rigged two small containers for air and struggled down with them to freshen the pocket in Jack's bell. Jack was overcome with a depth of gratitude that surprised him. Jack O'Reilly might be living a dangerous and obsessed life, but he wasn't doing it without friends. He felt strengthened, encouraged. It mattered that there were men up there who would stand by him.

By following the line, then grabbing the remaining coils and pushing for the darkness above him, he found his way quickly back to the point he had reached on the first dive. Suddenly his head burst into air, striking a hard obstacle. He gasped, cursed, and took some deep breaths.

As if in a dream, a familiar voice came out of the dark. "Bonjour, mon ami. Kindly breathe a bit more softly, it is becoming close in here."

"Quen-Li! Damn you for a Chinese madman, it's you!" Jack was ecstatic.

"Yes, my excitable young friend. It's me—you expected Confucius?"

"Christ, I can't get to you. Timbers are blocking my way. Are you all right?"

"He's a bit the worse for wear, Jack, as am I," Paul answered.

"Paul!" Jack couldn't believe his ears. Even in the pressurized air, Paul's voice was easily recognizable. "You son of a bitch, I thought you drowned." The resentment in his own voice surprised Jack. Along with a flood of relief came the realization of how angry he had been at his friend.

"Glad to see you, too," croaked Paul, sounding a bit like a man who had already drowned.

Quen-Li spoke again, his voice sounding strained even if his composure was unchanged. "We have a complicated situation here, Jack."

"Complicated! Blazing balls of the pope. We're under a goddamn ship and . . . you'd be a memory if I didn't hear you tapping, and—"

"Jack, calm down and listen."

"Okay, my friend, speak. You're right, time's not on our side."

"My right arm is chained at the wrist and the chain extends back under the water level to where it is secured to an iron ring."

Jack exhaled loudly but said nothing.

"My left arm is broken—a—uh—a measure taken by the count to ensure I could be brought back to Spain without further attrition to the count's men. . . . A story for another time."

"Broke your—damn it all! If I could get my claws into that slimy bastard's throat—"

"Jack!"

"All right, go ahead."

"Another complication . . . with one arm broken and the other chained below me, it should have occurred to you that it would have been hard for me to return your taps to the hull."

Jack, totally perplexed, stared toward the dim outline of his friend. "What?" After several more seconds, "But Paul—"

"No, at the time he was quite unconscious."

"There's someone else in here?"

"Not exactly in here, but on the other side of that broken bulkhead—he's a bit shy. Didn't know I was here at all until you arrived and we started talking." Quen-Li spoke conversationally. "Come talk to us, my companion in this tiny world. I heard you whimpering and yelling as you pounded for rescue . . . your salvation is here . . . speak."

"I . . . I can pay a fortune. Please save me from this tomb," a voice with a Spanish accent stammered back.

Jack felt paralyzed. The distorted voice was one he would never forget. He replied with no emotion, "So, it's you, de Silva."

"Listen to me, O'Reilly. I have riches you've never dreamed of. I—"

"All you have that I want is your neck. I would hate to see you drown before I could caress your throat with a sharp blade." Jack followed his words with a furious lunge, but all his strength could not force his large frame through the constriction formed by the timbers.

"Jack," Quen-Li said firmly. "You must calm yourself as never before and make some decisions that you will live with always."

Jack listened quietly.

"Even without you in here breathing like a furnace I doubt we could last another hour, more like half that time." He took a moment to catch his breath. "De Silva's strongbox with the better part of his wealth— since you've torched everything else he owns—is in that compartment with him. He kept it and me safe in this ladyhole beneath the ship's waterline."

"But—"

"Don't interrupt. If you have the crew beat through the hull above us, before this ship slips further down the slope I believe we're on, you can grab his riches and remove his head when he splutters to the surface."

"No!" Jack wailed.

"Listen, Jack."

"No, damn it, you listen, you smooth-talking Chinese lizard. I'm the captain of the *Star* and I make the decisions. That plan would leave you and Paul in here drowning like rats, and that's not going to happen."

"Jack, Paul should be able to make it through the hole our men chop through the hull."

"Don't Jack me. You've already wasted a passel of my time. The Brotherhood does not give up its own. Here's the plan—we cut through the hull from the outside below the air pocket and pry your chain ring off. Once you're free and we get you and Paul to the surface, then I'll deal with the count and his riches. If the ship slides off the reef before that, so be it."

"O'Reilly, wait!"

"Shut up, de Silva! I'm bringing an iron bar down. I believe I can force it past this mess of timbers. Then Paul can bang on the hull from inside while we axe our way in from above—Paul, you up to that?"

"Aye, Jack." His voice seemed a bit stronger. "But wait."

"What is it? Time's wasting."

"Bring a bottle of wine."

Jack stared into the darkness. "Are you mad? What do you think this is, a bleeding birthday party?"

"Jack, I'm serious, get me a wine bottle with a cork and pop it, turn it upside down, and hold your thumb over the lip on the way back—I have an idea." Nutty as the request seemed, Jack knew better than to argue with Paul.

He took a moderate breath and headed back down to the barrel. The water level was slightly lower—only possible if the Belaurans had been hard at resupplying it. From there he made his way quickly, hand over hand, to the surface.

The crew was astonished. Hansumbob clapped his hands and hooted like a banshee with the others when he heard that both Paul and Quen-Li were alive. Many of the crew's eyes narrowed when hearing of de Silva's survival.

"Broke the Chinaman's arm?" asked Hansum with a sickened look.

At this point, Cheatum, still in mortal fear of his life, decided to share his knowledge. "Fellas, when the count's men found out that Quen-Li was a . . . you know—"

"What of it?" snapped Jack.

"Well, they, all seven of them, jumped him. They mighta well as tied into a mountain lion. The reason you didn't have much opposition when you raided de Silva's hacienda was that four of the guards was attending funeral services for the other three."

The men broke into smiles. Quince slapped Bob on the back. "Guess brother Quen hasn't lost his touch."

"I knowed he'd be all right," said Bob with a proud gleam in his eye. "But Paul and—how we gonna get them out?"

"We don't have much time," interrupted Jack. "Here's the plan. With Paul in there steadily pounding, it's still going to be a trick to find exactly where to cut in from the outside. Too low and we're on the other side of the frame from Quen-Li's iron link. Too high and we let the air out and we'll drown him for sure—and Paul if we're not careful. No more jabbering from anybody unless they got something important to say. Red Dog, Jacob, Mentor, get another bar lowered down to the bell. Klett, you and the Belaurans make ready for some heavy work axing and picking down there once you know exactly where the sound is coming from. You others tie ropes to the divers' waists and pull them up when they get tired so they don't have to waste energy swimming."

"Don't worry about this end, Jack," yelled Quince. "You just get a fix on a spot we need to break through and pull Paul and our Chinaman the hell out of there."

"Oh, I almost forgot," added Jack. "I need a wine bottle with the cork removed—don't even ask why, one of Le Maire's ideas."

Quince rolled his eyes at Jack as Coop dashed off for the bottle.

With the uncorked and inverted bottle in hand, Jack slid down the rope once again. On hitting bottom, he squeezed himself into the big barrel, still clutching the wine bottle, and made his way without incident to the air pocket.

The level of the water had risen a good three to four inches since he departed. Saying only, "no time to waste," Jack forced the bar through the constriction, then handed up the wine bottle.

"How's Quen-Li doing, Paul?" Jack had surfaced again in the pocket, still beneath the constriction.

"Fair, just fair, Jack. The water's getting close to his chest and he's pretty beat-up and fatigued."

"O'Reilly, I tell you I have something you want." It was de Silva again.

"I know, just try to make it to the surface so I can enjoy it."

"O'Reilly, I have the key to the Chinese man's irons."

The only sounds in the dark enclosure was heavy breathing through the mouths of four desperate men.

"Really, I have it and I could make it through the bulkhead and pass the key to your friend," the count said. "The only thing I ask in return is your word. Your word that you and your men don't kill me when we reach the surface."

Jack's insides twisted into a knot. He couldn't bring himself to say anything.

"Jack, damn it. If he has the damn keys it's going to be our only chance. I think Quen-Li's getting weaker," Paul urged.

Again silence.

At last, Jack spoke. "De Silva, you may have the one thing on this earth that can save you from me. Listen carefully: hand those keys to my friend, then with his help you enter through the bulkhead. When the men chop through from the outside there will be confusion. Paul's not a strong swimmer. If you help him bring

Quen-Li to the surface—if they both arrive at the ship alive and well—I—I swear not to kill you."

"And none of your men—"

"Shut your face, don't dare trifle or bargain with me!" Jack's scream echoed in the hollow chamber. "You heard the terms. Now bring the key or what happens from here on won't matter for you."

Jack listened in the darkness as Paul and de Silva scrabbled through wooden beams and wreckage he could only catch vague glimpses of. After several minutes, Paul was near Jack and lifting Quen-Li's good arm. The clinking of iron keys was bell-like in the underwater tomb. Suddenly, de Silva's voice broke the silence; he was now in the compartment with the others. "Wait, wait . . . the Chinaman, he must promise, too."

Quen-Li responded in almost a whisper with a tone as cold as a rapier, "The emperor of China does not make bargains."

"There, I knew it. Treachery! This one is an animal. He killed my men like they were—"

"Shut up, de Silva, if you want to live," Jack said. "I won't tell you again." Then to Quen-Li, "Damn it all, listen to me. It's not just your life now, it's Paul's. Let's get this over. Promise the bastard!"

After a seemingly endless silence, Quen-Li spoke. "De Silva, in deference to my friends—and my young captain who has to make an even greater sacrifice than I in not snuffing your miserable life, I—I agree not to kill you—for a while."

"A while?"

"If you help us to the surface I will give you thirty moons of life. My final offer."

"Done, done." The count handed Paul the keys. "Go ahead and unlock him."

There was a clanking of steel and a jangle as links fell loose into the water below. "He's free, Jack!" blurted Paul.

"Thank God, but you've got to start pounding quick. I think this ship is shifting—the water's raised another three inches while we've been talking. Pound, damn it. It's critical they come in at just the right point or they might still let the air out and not free you."

Paul lifted Quen-Li higher, to a more comfortable position. "Now for the wine," he told Jack.

"You're daft," said Jack.

Paul retrieved the bottle from its perch and poured off the top quarter of the liquid. "Probably seawater," he said by way of explanation. He raised the bottle and drank deeply, turned quickly, and offered some to Quen-Li. The Chinese man had learned not to question Paul's odd behavior and he too took a draught.

"Paul, for the sake of Christ!"

Paul offered the bottle to the count. "De Silva?" The count waved off the young lunatic. He next proferred it to Jack. "Jack?"

"What the hell," he said, grabbing the bottle and taking a deep swig. "Are you happy now?"

"Getting there. Now listen." Paul poured the rest of the wine onto the surface of the water, like a priest making a benediction. "This wine bottle may be our salvation."

Paul thrust the empty bottle upside down into the water next to Jack. "There's a name written down the blown glass, Jack. I think it's Sobrett—tell me exactly where the water's stopped that forced its way into the bottle when I pushed it down."

A glimmer of comprehension formed in Jack's mind. He let his eyes adjust and, reemerging said, "It hits the bottom of the R. Yeah, a bubble starts right at the bottom of the R."

"I can't be sure of this, old friend, but the way I reckon is, if you head back down, never inverting this bottle, and then ascend back up the hull, never going to the surface . . . you'll find a place on the hull where the bubble goes back exactly to the bottom of the R. That, my friend, should be precisely the same depth as in here. Once you know that, there's only one thin line along the hull that can be the right place. You run your ear along the line till the pounding is loudest—that's where you need to break through."

Jack absorbed his friend's words with amazement. He didn't know the physics involved but somehow it made sense.

"And listen," Paul added. "If you're off a couple of feet this way or that, it won't matter much as long as the hole is correct relative to the depth of the air pocket—once you're sure of that from watching the bottle, go for it."

A moment later Jack was swimming for all he was worth back to the barrel. He carefully held the bottle upside down and away from the air he breathed from the bell. Then he streaked off again for the surface, bubbles streaming out of his nose.

Halfway to the surface, Jack could see and hear Klett and the Belaurans off to his side slamming axes and picks into the hull of the Spanish ship with frantic movements. He broke from the up-line and swam toward them.

He saw that by the time he reached the rescue party, although he could clearly hear the banging, the bubble in the bottle had pushed past the R. They were at the right frame but the wrong depth by a good five vertical feet. Placing the bottle directly on the hull, he traced it back down until the bubble matched where it had been inside the base of the air pocket.

His lungs bursting, he smashed the bottle into the hull at the exact point. It broke, simultaneously making a distinct white scar in the fouling that covered the wood. By now the others had seen him; when he lunged for the surface with the last of his air, they followed.

"Did you see where I smashed that bottle?" Jack

asked, gasping. "Put all your efforts there." Klett, without replying, headed back down with the Belaurans. Jack was at the end of his physical limit; he lay on the deck of one of the ship's launches, saving his final energy to help get the survivors to the surface when they emerged.

It was probably only ten minutes before a shout went up and there was a roiling of air bubbles under the boats. "They're through," yelled Quince. Jack rolled back over the side, swimming like crazy to the wreck.

Klett was just ripping out a plank when he arrived. The hole was perfectly placed. Some air had escaped but Jack could easily make his way through to the inside and emerged once again in the air pocket, this time above the constriction. The water level was considerably higher and the occupants now had to swim. De Silva had his hand under Quen-Li's good shoulder and used his other to hold onto a piece of bulkhead above him. The hole made by the rescue party was now just below the water level in the pocket. In addition to providing an escape, it also allowed in light, making it possible to see.

Jack grabbed Paul first and, dropping two feet below the water level, he shoved his friend through the broken planking into the waiting hands of Matoo, who took him to the surface. Jack returned and stared into the eyes of de Silva, still holding Quen-Li. The pocket was now bathed in a flickering, eerie light. The Spaniard returned his look warily.

"You go through the hole first and wait. I'll help Quen-Li get through from the inside. Take him through the hole gently, Count, and pray he makes it to the surface alive," Jack said quietly.

"I . . . I am not a very good swimmer."

"Learn quick, you bastard."

De Silva was not lying this time; he struggled to swim, careful not to drop Quen-Li. Jack caught up, grabbed his enemy and his friend, and with a powerful stroke began dragging both of them to the world above.

━≋ ✸ ≋━

That evening the entire crew of the *Star*, de Silva, and Cheatum sat on the midship deck of the ship. The count's chest of coins had been opened but lay undisturbed in a corner. The council of the Right Honourable Brotherhood of the Shipwrecked Men of the *Star* had met and made their decisions.

Cheatum and the count were led to one of the ship's dinghies, helped over the rail, and told to sit side by side, opposite to where Jack was sitting, wearing a cold expression. Jack tied one of each man's hands to the oarlocks so they could row but not move them past the center of the boat. When all was complete, Jack knelt in front of them. Cheatum was pale, Count de Silva's eyes darted wildly.

Jack held the count's dagger, turning it over in his hands again and again. He drew it from the sheath slowly and replaced it a dozen times. The men of the *Star* had gathered at the rail and watched the scene below silently—it was apparent that their young leader was journeying in his mind's eye through space and time.

Jack emerged from somewhere deep within and spoke in a deliberate voice, eerily soft. "Cheatum, lay your hand on the seat between you and de Silva. Count, please put your hand on top of Cheatum's." De Silva immediately did so, as if being compliant would help convince Jack to keep his word—the count obviously still couldn't believe he was going to have his life spared.

Jack looked to the sky and said matter of factly, "Mamacita, look—the man who made you sick with fear, your murderer—see how pitiful he looks now? I notice his eye's slow where you gouged it to save me."

De Silva turned pale. "O'Reilly, you promised. You gave your word."

"So I did. Father, what do you think?" Jack yelled to the sky. "Should I keep my word to this man? Did he keep his word with you and Mamá?" In one swift move he pulled the count's dagger from its sheath and drove it through both men's hands deep into the wood of the seat. Ignoring the agonized screams, Jack leaned over and said in the count's ear, "My father said, 'Yes, keep your word even with him. Let the pig go.' You are lucky he was such an honorable man. No?"

He rose to the wale of the *Star*, put one foot on the ladder and with the other pushed the dinghy adrift. Soon, the two castaways seemed to get enough control to be able to row in unison toward the distant glow of the night lights of Habana.

Jack and the others watched the two disappear into the darkness. Quen-Li, his arm reasonably well set by Red Dog and Quince, sat wrapped in blankets, in a chair devised for him by Hansumbob.

"I bet I know what you're thinking, my single-minded friend," Paul said.

"What would that be?"

He gestured to the full moon in the heavens. "Twenty-nine. You're thinking, counting that one up there, this man has twenty-nine moons left to live."

"Perhaps. But life has many mysteries. For all I know I myself may not live twenty-nine moons. Certainly the count has taken home with him much to think about."

"Indeed," Paul replied. "But once he makes it back to Habana and tries to pick up the pieces of his burnt and ransacked life, he's going to start thinking about time in a very special way—and I believe it will involve an obsession with counting backward from thirty."

Looking to Jack, Paul said, "And you, compadre. I know my rash act meant you couldn't rid yourself of the curse that has plagued you for three years—but you did save our lives when you made your decision down there. I hope you never regret it."

Jack leaned against the rail and considered Paul's words for a moment.

"I will never regret it. In a strange way you and Quen-Li have saved me from myself. Watching that miserable wretch paddle away in the moonlight has somehow freed me from the poison in my vitals. Killing that man would have been a poor trade for the lives of my mother and father, and somehow—I don't know. Somehow, it might have set me on a course for the rest of my life that I really don't want to sail."

"Jack," Quen-Li began in a low, soothing tone.

"Yes?"

"Your wisdom is beginning to catch up with your strength and courage—remarkable for one so young. My young friend, you are a warrior, not a murderer. You have killed all about that man that needed killing. You honor your parents' memory by choosing the lives of your friends over the satisfaction of revenge. Breathe deeply, Jack, and think of life; you have no further business here, it is time for you to go home."

Quince placed his hand on Jack's shoulder. "For what it's worth, lad, I think brother Li is right; it's time to hold your head up, a rich man, a life ahead of you and your duty done. Let's go home."

"Yep, he has raisins, Jackie." All turned to Hansum questioningly, except for Klett, who was nodding solemnly with him.

"What did you say, Bob?" Jack asked, one eyebrow raised.

"You know, I heard Paul and you say 'em words, like the Frenchees." Hansum had a way of bringing sensible discourse to an abrupt halt.

"Saints preserve us," muttered Paul. "The ship bard was telling Quince that he's right. Il a raison, non? And who else understands him but Klett, the ship's philosopher of fewest words."

Jack placed his arm playfully around Hansum's

shoulder. "Yeah, Quince has got raisins all right, and so have you and Klett." He turned around and looked each of the crew in the eye. "And the rest of you men, the council has met and you've all decided to sail with me to Salem. Your equal share of this money is yours to do with as you wish when you arrive there, but I want you all to know that I would be honored to keep your company for as long after that as you wish."

Quince stood and shook hands with his comrades. "I say three cheers for Black Jack O'Reilly and the devil take the hindmost." The deck echoed with the men's cheers.

Jack yelled back over his shoulder, "Douse the running lights till we clear the coast." Then, his voice cracking, unable to hide his tears, "Lower the black flag and raise the Stars and Stripes, first mate. Set a course for Salem."

EPILOGUE

THE TWO FIGURES coming off Summer Street turned left onto North. A bell struck twelve, signaling that the service at First Church had finished, and they headed up the short block and stood in front of the church as the congregation proceeded down the steps.

"We've been at this almost a week," Paul said. "When are you going to give it up?"

"Not until I find her. When you see her, you'll understand."

"God, man! You're twenty years old. The owner and master of your own vessel, a rich man by anyone's standards. You could have half the women in Salem with a smile and snap of the fingers. What's this in lieu of?"

"Don't disturb me while I'm concentrating."

Jack peered at the dwindling number of people leaving the church. A few of them lingered on the sidewalk, conferring with the pastor. One last group came down the steep steps, the preacher among them. There she was.

Jack gasped when he saw her. His dream took on shape and substance. She was talking with her group and animatedly describing to the old preacher something that delighted all of them. As they said their goodbyes, Jack nudged Paul.

"Let's go—we'll follow back a ways."

"If that is your long lost love, O naive one, she sure doesn't seem to be pining for you."

"Shut your grub locker. I'm trying to figure out what to do."

At the corner of Front and Market the group split, four going one way, Colleen and another girl going up Market.

Jack watched her walk. She was different. Somehow fuller, more womanly. She seemed to glide down the street. Jack's heart was tripping over itself. He remembered how the sun had caught her hair and burnished it. God help me, he thought, she seems to be shimmering now.

He took a deep breath and pulled Paul's arm. "It's now or never, Paulie." Now or never. He followed her up Market Street. "Stay close. I may need your help."

He drew within five feet of Colleen and her friend.

"Excuse, me, miss. Could you please give me directions to India Wharf?"

The two girls stopped and turned. The red-haired one in the green taffeta smiled brilliantly. "Pardon?" she said.

Jack, shaking, said, "India Wharf. We're lost and need to find India."

The girl's smile vanished. She examined Jack for what seemed a minute. A full minute. "Yes, of course. From here it's a bit of a trick."

She never looked around or pointed the way one would normally do, but simply stared straight into Jack's eyes.

"You'll be looking for Fish—the street, that is. It swims around and becomes Wharf." Her green skirt fluttered as she spoke. Jack could smell apple blossoms. He wanted desperately to reach out and touch her freckled skin. There was no sound, it was as if his ears were plugged, the world beating in his chest.

The longer she spoke, the slower her speech became. Jack's face was expressionless.

"Norris Wharf," she went on. "Hodge's, and it becomes Derby—"

"Toward the end," he said, "it becomes Becket's ship yard, and that would be India."

The girl finally just quit speaking, and paused for a long while.

"You've grown a bit of hair around your lip and chin, and you stand a bit straighter, but you still haven't been able to find India after three years. Jack, is it?"

"Colleen, is it?"

"Yes, it's Colleen, indeed. And it's actually been three years, four months, and sixteen days. If you're counting."

Jack started to speak. Then he laughed hopelessly. "Counting is all I've done, and it seems nearer to ten years."

The Ballad of the Star

They sailed 'round the world
With topsails unfurled
Those courageous men of the Star
Battered and torn
They rounded the Horn
To visit lands strange and far

They swum 'neath the seas
As slick as you please
To fix their ship what was broken
They found shoes, guns, and knives
While riskin' their lives
The stuff all worked but was soakin'

When the Star's in their dreams
The Spanish don screams
The fat English lords
Fall on their swords
And even the bandit Chinese
Crawl away on their knees

But none fears them as much
As the damn bloody Dutch
Who thinks they're so smart and wily
They pray in their pews
And soil their fine wooden shoes
When they cross young Jack O'Reilly

Now their journey is done
Their battles are won
But their story is far from over
'Cause a promise was made
To fight the British blockade
From Maine to the White Cliffs of Dover

The preceding being a poetic account of the remarkable adventures during circumnavigation of the world by the men of the good ship *Star*. From the recollections of Hansumbob Burton, able-bodied seaman and official poet of the journey. This composed in the twilight of the year of our Lord 1810 and scribed for the author who hath not the gift of the pen, by his friend and shipmate, Lord Paul Le Maire, member of the Right Honourable Brotherhood of the Shipwrecked Men of the *Star*.

ACKNOWLEDGMENTS

The authors were helped and encouraged by many through the three years it took for this book to take form and substance. In order to recognize some we will risk inadvertant omission of others.

We thank our agent Noah Lukeman for believing in our book in its earliest and roughest stage of development and for guiding us skillfully through the publishing process. Thanks also go to Esther Margolis for gambling on authors new to fiction and devoting her energies and that of her staff at Newmarket Press to bringing our creation to completion.

Our editors included Dick Marek, who convinced us that "point of view" was more than an opinion. He along with John Cook at Newmarket Press helped us bring discipline to our storytelling that makes a rousing good tale into a marketable novel.

In no particular order, we want to name a few individuals who supported us along the way: Larry Murphy, Patricia Lenihan, Kit Duane.

We thank our wives, Betsy and Barbara, for much advice, counsel, and guidance in the obsession with Jack, Quince, and the lads.

Finally, both authors would like to offer special thanks to Betsy for the pivotal role she played beyond that just mentioned above in the execution of this work.

Betsy served as facilitator and chief of operations in our joint writing effort, spending countless hours organizing clean drafts from Gene's scrawl and Dan's PC disks that used software dating back to the Manhattan Project. She was truly essential in making it happen.

ABOUT THE AUTHORS

GENE HACKMAN's acting career has spanned forty years in theater and film. After a four-and-a-half-year stint in the Marines, he began his stage career in New York and on tour, then went on to star in such film hits as *Bonnie and Clyde*, *The French Connection*, *The Conversation*, *Crimson Tide*, and *Unforgiven*. He has received numerous honors for his work, including two Academy Awards®. His yearning to write started as a small boy, when he spent much of his free time in his grandfather's small newspaper office in Danville, Illinois, and accompanied his uncle, a reporter, on assignments. Like his coauthor, he is an avid reader and shares a passion for the sea and diving.

DANIEL LENIHAN has been diving for the U.S. National Park Service as a park ranger and archaeologist since 1972. In 1976, he created the only underwater archaeological team in the federal government, and in 1980 was appointed the first chief of the Submerged Cultural Resources Unit (SCRU) of the National Park Service. He has taught diving for research, law enforcement, and rescue purposes. His work has been featured in documentaries on CBS, ABC, BBC, PBS, the Discovery channel, and *National Geographic*, and his writings have appeared in numerous publications, including *Natural History*, *American History*, *Naval Proceedings*, *Ship-*

wreck Anthropology, and the *NSS Cave Diving Manual*. He is coauthor of the Fodor's guide *Underwater Wonders of the National Parks*, and served on the editorial board for the *Encyclopedia of Underwater Archaeology* published by the British Maritime Museum.

The two men have been friends and neighbors for almost a decade, and live with their families in Santa Fe, New Mexico. This is their first novel.